Peyton

and

Isabelle

Peyton and Isabelle

Avery Yearwood

Prologue

Boston, 1984

Peyton lounged on the fire escape, his tan arms roped around the rail, swigging from a bottle of beer. He was starting college in two months, and he was standing near the edge of a cliff.

Once he leapt, his fingers wrapped around the smooth bar of a hand glider, anything was possible: he might fly through the clouds, the wind at his back, or shoot straight down, like a bullet, and bury himself in the earth.

He reveled in this feeling, laughing through the easy days of summer, where nothing much mattered. There were no late nights at the library, his eyes blurry, his head pounding, his fingers ink-stained and raw. There were no hard choices to make.

He tipped his head back for the last drop of beer, and climbed in through the window.

His mother was curled up on the couch, her fraying camisole exposing her thighs. Her mouth closed around a Marlboro cigarette. She pointed at the door with a slender finger, where Joseph stood, wearing black slacks and a dress shirt.

Joseph lowered his eyelids, and his hands fidgeted nervously against each other.

"We're late."

Joseph—Peyton's brilliant and rabidly insecure classmate—lived in an apartment downstairs, and he followed Peyton around like an abused dog.

Peyton was often annoyed with his tremulous nature, his general fear of the world.

Peyton kissed his mother on the cheek, inhaling the smoke on her breath, wanting to pull down the camisole and cover up her thighs.

Joseph asked Peyton's mother if she was going to the fireworks, and she shook her head, her eyes amused. "I have to work."

Joseph nodded, as if he knew all about working. No one knew about working around here, Peyton thought. Not like the suffocating darkness of the coal mines, the possibility of death lingering in the stale underground air, your back and arms always sore.

Peyton lobbed his beer bottle into the kitchen trash and it clanked in. He grinned, and walked over to Joseph, hitting him on the shoulder.

"Okay, buddy," he said, guiding Joseph's boney back out the door.

"Bye-bye," his mother sang, and walking down the hall, he pictured her half-smiling, smoke drifting out of the corner of her mouth.

He wished, for a moment, she would wear normal clothes, be a normal mother. Then he remembered her canary laughter, her delicate beauty, her determined, tipped-up chin–and he smiled softly, shrugging

Normal is overrated, he decided.

Jogging down the building's wide stairs, they could hear the car honking repeatedly, and Joseph scrunched his pale eyebrows in annoyance.

"Can't he wait?"

Peyton laughed. "William doesn't wait for anyone."

William's father was incredibly wealthy—the owner of a publishing empire, selling books, newspapers, magazines—and their classmates and teachers treated William like a celebrity, following him at a respectable distance, content with whatever friendly gesture he tossed their way.

Girls had sex with him and stole his worn clothing, giggling as they hoarded his shirts and boxers in their lockers.

Peyton occasionally acknowledged William's extravagance—his twenty-thousand-dollar Patek Phillipe watch, his hand-made European clothes, his vacations in Argentina—and hated him for it. He was a self-indulgent bastard. But he was also charming, quick with his smile, and free of any insecurity or fear.

Peyton swung open the building's metal door, and saw the evening sky was dark blue, eroding to gray. The silver Porsche 928 waited by the curb, and William's hand laid open on the horn. It was a sleek, beautiful car and Peyton wanted to pull William out, toss him aside, and drive away, slamming the gas pedal until the speed pinned his body to the leather seat, and the air ripped past his windows.

William grinned, and revved the engine. Peyton held the passenger door open, letting Joseph scramble in the backseat.

"About time, ladies," William said. He smile was half-cocked as he gazed out the front window.

"Shut up," Peyton said, sliding in the seat and slamming the door. He reached into the long pocket of his khakis and pulled out another bottle of beer, popping the cap off with his keychain.

Joseph's head pushed between the seats. "You shouldn't drink that in here."

William and Peyton smiled at each other.

"It's illegal," Joseph protested.

They laughed, and Peyton turned on the radio, flipping it to his favorite rock station.

Happy Independence Day, people. Get where you're going. The streets are hopping and the fireworks are coming soon. Meanwhile, here's Springsteen with Dancing in the Dark...

William sped down the Cambridge streets, ignoring the stop signs and weaving brazenly around pedestrians and cars. The cold beer, his sixth tonight, slid Peyton into a warm haze. The world was covered in a gentle fog.

"You guys ready?" William said as he took a sharp right, toward Somerville.

"Hell, yeah," Peyton said, grinning.

Springsteen's deep, throaty voice called out, *hey there baby, I could use just a little help* and Peyton thought of Isabelle. He wished she were already in the car, her long, slender body on his lap. He felt a surge of excitement for her, for what they were about to do. He imagined himself in the locker room before a football game, the anticipation rising thickly in his throat.

Some of the streets were closed, and they drove in circles on their way to Isabelle's house. As William swerved in and out of traffic, cars honked, and Peyton leaned out the window.

"Fuck you!" he shouted, laughing, and flipping them off. William smiled at an aggrieved driver, a middle-aged man in a beaten-down Toyota Carina.

Joseph tapped the consol between the two front seats, checking his Velcro wristwatch. The neighborhoods were noisy, filled with people pouring out of their houses.

When they finally pulled up to Isabelle's blue duplex, they could hear the city fireworks exploding over the Charles River. William honked his horn, and after a few minutes, Isabelle came running out, her long white skirt swirling around her legs.

She climbed into Peyton's lap, and he wrapped his arms around her, feeling her pale blue t-shirt, rubbing the sides of her arms, smelling her neck. It was smudged with paint. She whispered she loved him, her clean breath warm against his ear.

He traced the equilateral triangle of freckles on her bicep with his finger, whispering he loved her too. He loved her more than anyone, except maybe his mother, and resting his hands on her thighs, a shroud of contentment fell over his beer-soaked mind.

William accelerated into the street, heading for Boston. He turned up the radio, and tapped his fingers on the steering wheel in time with the music. The four of them were a motley crew, the sole members of their high school's philosophy club, and after three years of regular meetings, they had formed a friendship they all knew wouldn't survive the demise of the club.

During their last month of meetings, they'd built fireworks in William's basement, only idly discussing philosophy.

The fireworks, the shape of large cantaloupes, were with their launch tubes in the backseat of the car. Peyton pulled Isabelle closer to his chest, feeling the dips between her ribs with his fingers, thinking this was the last time the four of them would be together. He would miss this, their strange little world. Isabelle's white-blonde hair was in a thick bun, and he undid it, running his fingers through it, stretching it to her lower back.

Joseph pushed his face farther between the front seats, straining to raise his nasal voice above the rock music as he asked Isabelle about her painting. As she turned, Peyton smelled the fresh peach in her hair, and he inhaled it, satiated.

"It's good," she breathed slowly, biting her lower lip. She looked out the back window, over Joseph's head, and Peyton could see her attention flitter into the night sky.

Peyton lowered his window, and hot air blew into the car.

"Hey, look," Isabelle exclaimed.

Peyton held her waist tighter and leaned out the window, following her gaze. They were crossing the Charles River. The fireworks exploded high in the dark sky, and then arced down like suicidal stars.

Coooool, he thought.

"Ours will be just as good," Joseph shouted, leaning up against the seat, trying to see out the window.

Yeah, right, Peyton thought, laughing.

"Hey," he whispered in Isabelle's ear. He bit the lobe gently. She turned her head slightly. Her angled green-oval eyes reflected the light of the fireworks. They were feline eyes.

He squeezed her hand, lacing their fingers together. Over the bridge, they entered a neighborhood of apartment buildings. The breezes blowing by the car smelled of barbeque, and as they drove deeper into the city, the crowds thinned out. Their rock music blared over the vacant streets.

Joseph's breath warmed Peyton's neck. He was talking, but no one could hear him over the music. The car lurched to the right and Isabelle's head smacked the top.

Peyton punched William's right shoulder.

"Sorry, man," he said, laughing.

The car came to a stop and the loud music shut off.

The night seemed preternaturally silent. Peyton could hear a wasp buzzing. Isabelle opened the passenger door and climbed out of the car, and Peyton stumbled behind her, laughing. The thought crossed his mind, like a boy sprinting over a shallow creek: he had drunk too much. He always drank too much.

An old car frame, overrun with weeds, occupied the far corner of the abandoned lot. Faint voices and laughter floated by, barely audible before vanishing. Peyton kicked an empty beer can and it bounced a couple times before rolling to a stop in a thick clump of wild grass.

"Okay," William said, taking one of the bags from Joseph. "Screw Guy Fawkes!"

Isabelle grabbed Peyton's hand. Her fingers were bony and warm. As they walked to the concrete slab in the middle of the lot, Joseph lagged behind.

"Joseph," William said.

Joseph stepped backwards, the strap of the duffle bag cutting across his narrow chest. "You know," he said nervously. "What if somebody sees us?"

William laughed. "Nobody is around," he said, waving his hand in the air, as if to show Joseph what he'd won: an empty, trash-filled lot.

The back of an apartment building stood on one side of the lot, but it was far away, maybe half a football field. Otherwise, there were a few trees, and a slope behind that, which led down to a busy road. They could hear only the lightest rumble from the cars driving past.

"Joseph," Isabelle said, dropping Peyton's hand and gliding over to Joseph. Even in her flat sandals, she was a few inches taller than him. She put her hand gently on his forearm. Peyton wanted to scream. Sometimes he hated Joseph.

Peyton shook his head, and studied the green firework William had put on the concrete slab. With its blue fuse, it looked like a plump round fruit with a rat's tail. Peyton wished he had another drink. He could feel his edges coming back to life.

Isabelle gently relieved Joseph of the bag, hoisting it over her shoulder, and pulling Joseph's arm with her free hand. Joseph was such a pansy, always trying to ruin their fun, Peyton thought, and he muttered, "Stupid," as he pulled a tall weed out of the ground and ripped it apart.

"Alright," Isabelle announced loudly, as she laid the other firework on the concrete and stepped back.

"Okay," William said, rolling his eyes at Peyton, a grin on his face. William pulled out a box of matches and hunched over. "Ready?"

"Yeah," Peyton said, crouching over next to the other firework, unraveling its long fuse. Isabelle and Joseph walked fifteen feet back, their laughter chased with excitement.

William held a match and the box in the air. His clear brown eyes, deep-set by his prominent forehead, were calm, reflecting a lifetime of privilege: for him, nothing could ever go wrong.

And he was here, with them, Peyton thought.

"Okay," Peyton said, smiling gamely, the knowledge that they were doing something illegal electrifying his buzz.

William handed him a solitary wood match with a red head. The red head trembled in Peyton's fingers. William pulled off another match and lit it. The matchbox was in Peyton's hand, and he clumsily struck it. It didn't light.

He struck it again.

"Go," William said, holding his lit match to his fuse. Peyton lit his blue fuse and the flame started eating it.

Shit, Peyton thought, and scrambled up, sprinting as fast as he could.

He pulled to a stop behind Isabelle and Joseph, breathing heavy, and as he turned, he saw a bright white light, like the blinding flash of a camera inches from his face. Loud bangs blasted his eardrums.

Peyton flinched as the fireworks soared up into the dark sky, the heavy noises echoing in his ears, beating their drums. The fireworks, hundreds of feet in the air, burst into a green and white shower of light.

Peyton smiled, thinking, wow, we did it. It was beautiful. More beautiful than anything he'd ever created. The strands erupted and dissolved into the black sky.

He turned to Isabelle, reaching his hand out for hers. Her face was tilted to the sky. Her round mouth parted in fear and confusion, like an augur who was struggling to interpret an omen in some favorable way.

"There's supposed to be more colors," she said frantically, her eyes falling down to meet his.

"What do you mean?" he asked. He glanced at the concrete. The launching tubes were empty, their insides streaked with black residue.

"Fucking hell," William said, and his voice had an uncertain edge to it. William was never uncertain. He pointed across the field. A small orange fire danced inside the upper floor of the building. The window was shattered.

"What?" Peyton said. For the first time in his life, he felt like what he was seeing did not exist. Because it could not exist. He rubbed his eyes, and when he opened them, he was disappointed to see the same image. The fire gathered quickly inside the apartment, and its arm licked out the window, reaching for the night's air. Peyton surveyed the building's walls, and the old, crumbly wood stripped his drunkenness away, like clothes ripped from his skin.

Isabelle took off running.

William sprinted after her, quickly gaining on her sandal-hobbled strides. He tackled her in the weeds and their bodies slammed to the ground.

"Stop it!" she screamed, withering and kicking. "We have to get them all out!"

William picked her up and threw her over his shoulder. Peyton was furious and wanted to punch William, tell him to get his privileged hands off Isabelle, but the feeling lodged in his toes, and he couldn't move. One of her sandals fell to the ground and Peyton stared at its delicate white straps among the dirty green weeds, dumbfounded.

She was sobbing and beating William's back with her fists, screeching, and Peyton found this horrifying, but still, he could not make his feet move.

"We have to leave!" William shouted at Peyton as he ran past, Isabelle thrashing over his shoulder.

Peyton shook his head—no, that's wrong, he thought. There were people inside. He could see them in the lower floors of the building, in their apartments—watching television, a man at his refrigerator, a woman reading. Their ordinary lives were unfolding, while a fire, their fire, burned above. Sweat rose on Peyton's flushed forehead, and his ears rang out, and he was suffocating.

"Peyton!" William shouted, struggling with Isabelle's long limbs—her feet kicking his chest, her fists hitting his back.

Peyton shook his head no, but he grabbed Isabelle's legs firmly, his unsteady mind propelled forward by William's certainty. He thought of his mother, with her hope-filled, bright eyes, her gentle mouth. He had to save her, from the men she never loved, from the constant grind of poverty. He needed to stop time so he could think—he had to think—but he knew the flames were marching on, growing large, gorging themselves on the dry wood.

An image of his mother in bed, her blue eyes electrified with salty tears, her heart exhausted by another worthless man appeared before him, and he held on to it. He would be locked up. He'd lose his scholarship. What good could he do for her then?

They had to leave. His heart settled on this. So, he thought, it must be made of ice.

Isabelle flailed like a live wire, flinging her knee in his stomach, and he held her closer, avoiding her face, knowing his resolve, no matter how cold, was fragile.

She screamed his name desperately, her voice hoarse and punctured with sobs, and still, he kept his thoughts on saving his mother. He didn't want to think maybe he was running for himself, maybe he was the one that didn't want to live a life of grinding poverty anymore.

William pushed Isabelle against Peyton and instructed him to lock her in the car. Peyton opened the car door and sat in the passenger seat, pulling Isabelle, holding on to her wrists. She took big gulps of air, crying. William slammed the door and ran back through the field.

Peyton stared out the front window, taking solace in William's quick strides, trying to ignore Isabelle's cries, and think only of his despondent mother. Joseph stood in the field like a plastic toy soldier, watching as the fire covered the whole upper floor and climbed to the roof.

It seemed, from inside the car, like a movie—the red-orange flames dancing and the black smoke thick and dark against the gray sky. It would have been a lovely image. But of course it was ugly, hideous even, and for a moment, Peyton thought he might cry.

In the field, William shouted something to Joseph, and grabbed him by the back of the shirt. Isabelle leaned over, scrambling for the door, and Peyton held her back.

She bit his wrist.

He cursed under his breath. His skin burned and he pulled two of her fingers. He pulled harder, waiting for her to let go. There was no doubt he was stronger than her. He went right up to the point of breaking them before she opened her mouth, her teeth leaving his skin. His wrist was wet, and he peered over her. It was covered in blood.

"Isabelle?" he asked, inhaling sharply.

She was sobbing and leaned back, shifting around gently. She rested her head on his chest, abruptly quiet. He lightened his grip on her wrists.

"Isabelle?" he said, his voice almost cracking this time, feeling somehow that if he lost her now, he would lose her forever. We don't have a choice, he thought urgently, as if she might hear him. We have no choice. It won't help. It won't do any good.

"Leave me alone!" she screamed, hysterical, and he leaned back.

He sucked in air, and looked outside the car, wishing William would hurry. He needed William's certainty. Thoughts, doubts swirled beneath him, and he struggled to stay above them, not see them. They must smell the fire by now anyway, right?

William walked with Joseph thrown over his shoulder, Joseph's arms and legs stuck stiffly in the air, like plastic limbs. In the distance, the black smoke trailed higher in the sky, gathering in circles.

A scream echoed across the night, and this—a real person's cries—called Peyton back, or down, he wasn't sure which, and he tumbled into the sticky fingers of his doubts.

A figure stood in an upper floor window, to the right of where the fire had started, its fleshy arms naked, leaning out.

"Where is the fire escape?" Peyton yelled. "Where is the fire escape?"

The figure crawled up onto the windowsill. It was a hefty woman, wearing a billowy nightgown.

"No, don't do that," he muttered, pushing Isabelle's limp body aside and getting out of the car, shutting the door. The woman straddled the windowsill, one hand inside the apartment and one hand on the wood siding.

"Peyton! What are you doing?" William shouted as he jogged to the car, Joseph's body bouncing on his shoulder.

"Look at that woman!" Peyton shouted back, pointing to the building. The woman pulled out her other leg, and crouched on top of the sill, her knees at her chin, her head twisting around. Her face was a blur.

Peyton ran to the woman, trying not to think about what he was doing, ignoring the voice inside his head screaming for him to leave.

He heard William drop Joseph and his feet pound the ground and his breath grow louder. Peyton's legs were wobbly and unsure, and he tried to speed up, but his body wasn't going. He was running on wood planks, and he wondered where Isabelle was. Why wasn't she here now? Isn't this what she wanted?

William's hand fixed on Peyton's bicep and he whipped around.

"You can't help her, Peyton," William said calmly, catching his breath. "She's too high up."

Peyton turned to the woman. She was on the fourth floor, and now he could see she weighed nearly as much as him. Her leg slipped down the side. She hung awkwardly, her slip caught on the window, scrunching at her waist. She teetered unsteadily, and screamed, her one leg bent on the sill, her arms clinging to the side of the window.

"Where is the fire department?" Peyton shouted, running his fingers through his hair. He kicked a rock, cursing.

"Peyton, we have to get out of here," William pleaded, and for once he did not sound like a man. He sounded like a frightened boy. "I'm sure someone called already."

The woman's leg slipped farther, and then her body fell, her head slamming against the building, her arms futilely chopping the air.

Peyton covered his ears and sprinted to the car, mumbling loudly to block out the shrill screams and the impending THUD. Yet he still heard it, the sickening crunch of a human body slammed against the ground. If someone jumped off the Empire State building, how long would it take their body to reach the ground? His physics exam, last week.

It made him nauseous. What noise occurs when the body hits the ground? Can the person survive? How many bones must be crushed?

He screamed at the voice in his head, telling it to shut up. Isabelle was curled in the seat, her long limbs rolled up in a ball, her hands covering her face. He lifted her up and wedged himself underneath her, slamming the door. He closed his eyes. He couldn't breathe or think or see. He felt only the weightless arms of dread wrap around his chest.

He heard William jerk the seat forward and shove Joseph in. Joseph's head thumped against the side of the car.

"We have to go," Peyton said. Even from here, with his eyes squeezed shut, the flames lit up the sky.

"No shit!" William said. The door slammed and the engine started. Rock music blasted out of the stereo, and William cursed, flicking it off.

Isabelle was limp in Peyton's arms. He couldn't feel her body rise and fall. The car accelerated and dumped over the curve.

"What happened to that woman?" Peyton asked.

"What woman?"

"The woman who fell off the windowsill," he said, opening his eyes.

"She fell," William said, his voice dry.

"She's dead?"

"I don't know! It's a long fucking way down, Peyton. What do you think?"

"Pull over!" Peyton shouted.

"What? Why?"

"That payphone! Pull over to the fucking payphone."

William pulled the car over to the curb. "Don't give your name," he said.

Peyton gently moved Isabelle and ran to the phone. He was about to pick it up, and then he thought of his fingerprints. He pulled off his polo shirt and used it to pick up the phone and dial 911.

"911 Emergency," a woman said.

"At the corner of Lindley and Chestnut, there is an apartment building on fire. People are already dead," he said, hanging up.

Back in the car, William took off. "You didn't have to do that. People were already outside."

"Shut up," Peyton said, his head pounding. He couldn't think. It had moved too fast.

"I don't understand how the hell that happened..." William muttered.

The hum of the engine filled the car. As they merged onto a major road and joined the traffic, Peyton felt, for a moment, like it hadn't occurred, like life was as he'd always known it. Cars were speeding by, filled with people on their way home from parties, shows, friends, the fireworks. Two girls in the back of a station wagon laughed.

It was just another night, ending.

A siren wailed obnoxiously, and Peyton lurched, as if a gun had gone off in the street. A siren rose up from another direction, and then another. The high-pitched ringing came closer. Peyton covered his ears.

"Peyton," William said firmly.

"What?"

"You're bleeding."

Peyton remembered his wrist. He leaned his head to the side and held his arm out. He kept his eyes pegged on his arm. Flashing lights he didn't wish to

11

see passed by. He used his shirt to wipe up the blood, and then tied it tightly around his wrist.

William's face settled into a purposeful, resolute expression. He drove in the right lane, staying behind a blue Honda. The Charles River seemed black and idle, like a dead snake. Two cop cars, sirens blaring, sped by in the other direction and traffic parted seamlessly, opening and closing. That effortless power, Peyton thought, would soon close down on them.

Peyton rested his head against the seat and closed his eyes. "What are we going to do?" he asked, staring in despair at Isabelle, who still lay comatose in his lap. She was his best friend but she seemed so far away. He gently rubbed her arm, but it felt like a foreign object, as if it were the arm of a faceless mannequin. The peach smell of her hair was sickening, and he moved his head.

Joseph readjusted himself, and his shoulder rubbed against Peyton's as he leaned forward, between the two seats.

Peyton's head pounded from the liquor, the loud blasts. The fire. He reminded himself he wasn't alone. William would save them. Or, he thought bitterly, he would somehow save himself and the rest of them would be screwed.

"Okay," William said. William peered thoughtfully into the night sky, his square jaw tipped slightly to the side, his brown eyebrows lightly raised. "I'll drop everybody off." He shifted gears as he turned into Isabelle's neighborhood. "We'll talk this over tomorrow night, rationally."

"What's there to talk about?" Isabelle said loudly. She sat up straight and scowled at William, who glanced over at her. "People might be dead."

"You don't know that," he said. "Anyway, there was nothing you could have done."

"YES THERE WAS!"

The noise was shocking. Peyton covered his ears; William flinched; Joseph recoiled into the backseat. Peyton was furious; he wanted to shove her outside. His head hurt. She didn't stand to lose so much.

"Stop it!" he said.

A dried ring of blood circled her mouth. She stared at him desperately, her lips trembling, and she cried out, her face breaking like a plate slammed to the ground.

Peyton looked out the side window, at the ordinary houses, wishing he was inside one of them. Ordinary, for once, seemed good enough, even something to be grateful for.

William blew out a long breath of air. "Peyton," he said. Peyton ignored him, recognizing the familiar streets near Isabelle's house. He wanted to hold Isabelle, but he didn't. He kept his hands by his side.

"Shut up, William," Isabelle sobbed, her body shaking erratically, like wind chimes before a hurricane. "I'll wait, okay? It doesn't matter now."

"Joseph?" William asked, unflustered, the adult calm in his voice fully restored.

"Yes," Joseph breathed softly.

"Good," William said, his tone perfunctory, as if he had tallied the necessary votes at a club meeting.

William pulled up to Isabelle's house and she leapt out of the car as it was still rolling, slamming the door in Peyton's face. Her house was dark and her white skirt floated across the lawn like a ghost. She fidgeted with the lock, pounding the door with her fist. She rested her cheek on the wood.

Peyton knew he should go with her—she was his, after all. But he didn't move as she struggled. He couldn't face her. He couldn't do what was right. After she opened the door, she shut it violently, and Peyton's chest was heavy, and constricted.

William drove slowly through the residential neighborhoods. Peyton closed his eyes again, feeling Isabelle's absence, as if part of him were running up her stairs and throwing himself on her bed, sobbing, asking for forgiveness, promising to come clean.

The car was claustrophobic and hot, like an oven. Peyton's head was at once lightheaded and pounding, as if someone had pumped it with air and tightened a vise around it.

The car came to a stop.

"Peyton," William said. William was staring straight ahead, at the empty street. "Tomorrow, right?"

"Right," Peyton said. "Come on, Joseph."

Joseph nodded slightly, his eyes vacant. He stepped out of the car and his normally impeccable dress shirt was half-untucked and rumpled. This, of all things, struck Peyton as particularly portentous, as if it signaled that none of them would ever be okay.

"Tomorrow," William said, not glancing over.

Peyton wanted to punch him. How could he act so fucking calm? Peyton threw the car door shut. He put his hand on Joseph's back, leading him to their apartment building. People were out on their porches, drinking. Peyton struggled with the key, inserting it the wrong way in the lock.

They climbed up the empty stairs. The muffled sounds of television, music, and laughter reached them through the thin walls. He was suddenly grateful his mother was at work.

Peyton stopped in front of Joseph's floor.

"Joseph," Peyton called. Joseph turned around. He looked confused, like he wasn't sure where he was.

"What?"

Peyton pointed to his door. Joseph nodded slightly and came down the steps.

"Will you be okay?" Peyton asked.

"Yeah," Joseph said, nodding his narrow face up and down. "I think I'll just sleep. Right?"

"Yeah. You know where to find me. Otherwise…" Peyton said. Seeing his bloodied polo shirt wrapped around his wrist, Peyton squeezed Joseph's shoulder and nodded.

He rushed up the stairs, taking them two at a time, climbing up, up, up, out of breath, running down his hall, clumsily unlocking his apartment.

Inside, he was relieved, and safe, and he locked the door and closed the chain, as if he could keep the night outside. He leaned up against the door and closed his eyes. He really needed a drink. He would get drunk. But for a second, he stood there, exhausted. He didn't want to think about what had happened. He didn't want to think about what was going to happen.

He slammed his fist against the door, and it stung intensely.

"Fuck," he said, almost crying in frustration. He crouched against the door and put his hands on his cheeks, pulling his skin toward his ears, trying to stretch out the anxiety crawling all over him.

"Fuck," he whispered.

Part I

CHAPTER ONE

Peyton's mother gave birth to him shortly after her sixteenth birthday, and she coddled him with the squealing delight of a teenage girl. She donated the last of her dolls to the church, and made room for him on her childhood bed. The bed was nestled in the corner of the living room, and she slept beside him, her hand draped protectively over his belly.

She slept intensely, and he cried for a long time before she woke up and fed him on her breast. Eventually, he learned to take it without waking her, his tiny hands groping her chest and pulling her nipple to his mouth.

She was consumed with clothes and makeup and gossiping with her girlfriends, and he learned to live with dirty diapers, erratic feedings, and afternoons sprawled out on strangers' couches.

His grandmother, though she knew better, watched this silently.

His mother styled him for church, brushing his few tufts of hair, and scrubbing his hands and face. She held him proudly on her hip. She ignored the mass of people whispering about her in delightfully outraged tones, speculating on who had laid her up.

They lived in a one-street coal town, and the older folk didn't care for his mother, how she pranced around the pub and the church bazaar without shame, thinking she was better than the rest of them even with her unspoken-for child. Men pined after her, and this gave her whole life a nice, easy glow: toothy grins welcomed her; doors opened; pub and restaurant tabs were paid for; convenience store lines were cut short, and rides were offered.

She knew she was beautiful—one of most beautiful women in the county, in fact—and because she had never been particularly good at anything else, her beauty was her sole source of pride. She vigilantly tended to her appearance, scouring magazines for tips and spending hours in front of the mirror. She stroked her long black hair until it shined in waves. She applied makeup and lotions from her baskets of supplies. When she walked, she carried her body regally, her slim back arched in high heels.

She wouldn't have had any trouble finding a husband. Even when she was nine months pregnant, visibly marked by a man, carrying his child in her body, men kept fighting over her, often coming to drunken blows. She played along, indiscriminately flirting, and soaking up men's affections like a plant root soaks up the rain. But it was all for fun. She considered herself on the way out of town, and the men of Lamar County—coal miners—didn't fit in her plans.

This desire to leave her birthplace had sprung up entirely within her, like an invasive species that can survive in only one kind of soil. Neither her friends nor her parents had any intention of ever leaving Lamar County, and they found her notions about this comical and callow.

Her parents had built their two-room cabin in the 1920s and, like their parents, planned to stay in Lamar County until they died. It never occurred to them that they might move someplace else. The sturdy wood beams contained their entire adult lives, and the structure had accumulated thick layers of meaning—Peyton's mother, when she was a squealing four-year old, cut her forehead wide open on the northwest corner; his grandmother's miscarriage left a faded streak on the bedroom floor; his grandfather's fist put a dent on a south-facing beam after a 1959 lay-off; a raise celebrated with red wine stained the kitchen floor.

This living history was comforting to Peyton. He toddled around the cabin, asking his grandmother to tell him stories. He liked to touch the rough curve of a wood beam and imagine his mother resting her hand on the same spot when she was his age, their small palms pressing against one another in space.

His mother was not impressed with this way of thinking. Itching to leave town, she found their lives tedious. Despite having never lived anywhere else, his mother constantly complained about the cabin, how it was sparsely furnished with a hodgepodge of mismatched pieces. A stiff and formal red couch from the thirties sat in front of a modern coffee table from the seventies.

The wood dining table was streaked with decades of spilled drinks. Worst of all, in his mother's view, was the lack of indoor plumbing. A bespectacled government worker had offered to install the piping, but his grandfather had only laughed, closing the door on the eager young man's face.

Peyton's mother had cried out, her eyes beseeching her father, begging him to reconsider. When that didn't work, she became furious. She wanted that instant hot water.

"You want it, you buy it," his grandfather said firmly. "We don't rely on charity."

His mother didn't have the money to buy it, of course. If she had, she wouldn't have been living in Lamar County. As soon as he could walk, Peyton schlepped water from the spring in a metal pail. When he was young, he stopped to rest every few feet, catching his breath and wiping the sweat off his forehead to keep it from burning his eyes.

Once his legs grew long, the distance became negligible, and he covered it in a few minutes by running, the two pails suspended carefully to his side. He imagined he was a carnival act—The Incredible Balancing Boy: "Not one drop of water lost!"

His grandparents owned an entire ridge of land, nearly four-hundred-and-eighty-seven acres. His mother hated this because it took so long to make it to town, but Peyton loved the endless expanse of woods. An only child, he played by himself, pensively tugging on tree branches and digging holes in the soil.

Their ridges were lush and green in the warm seasons, but they were bad for growing crops. People said God must have cursed their land. Their hens often keeled over unexpectedly. Peyton was happy when they did because it meant meat. The fact that it also meant fewer eggs was something he knew, but forgot at the time, his understanding overshadowed by his burning desire for food.

Before he had any words to describe it, Peyton apprehended his Hunger as his constant companion, a separate entity which took up residence inside him. Its presence ebbed and flowed, depending on how much food he could get, but it never really departed.

When he was satiated, he knew the Hunger was merely asleep, biding its time before it sprung up again, more powerful than ever. The Hunger made him feverish, spoiling the clarity of his thoughts, and seducing him to take things that weren't his.

Every morning, his stomach rumbled like rocks in a drum, waking him up. He staggered over to the kitchen, staring at his grandmother's cornbread, reaching his hands out. He could feel nothing but his Hunger, a longing for food in his mouth so intense he imagined eating everything—the cornbread, the uncooked grits, the thick milk—like a dog.

He grabbed at the cornbread, shoveling it in his mouth rabidly, licking the pan. Then he clutched at the milk, and downed it in one series of swallows, his mother staring at him, horrified. He glared at her. She didn't have to deal with the Hunger.

When he was four, he learned to exercise self-control, and he stared at the food patiently, counting to ten in his head, waiting for his serving. The moment the bowl landed in his hands, he ran outside and sat on the porch so he could scarf it down in peace.

By then, because his mother expected him to rise up in the world, he saw himself as a small-limbed adult with a slew of responsibilities. He had to study his books, retrieve and dump the water, tend to the crops, and feed the hens. Only after he finished his chores could he run into the woods and pretend he was a Vietnam soldier, seeing the shorter trees as his fellow troops, and the animals as his Communist enemies.

Hunting was a right of passage in Lamar County. No boy could reach the age of ten without knowing how to shoot. Even Peyton's mother, who preferred business suits and briefcases to camouflage, didn't try to stop him from hunting.

Peyton shot his grandfather's gun for the first time on his seventh birthday. For a year, he had carried the unloaded gun everywhere he went, pulling the trigger when animals came into view. This time, he loaded it up. He killed a white-tailed deer with his first shot. Her graceful trot abruptly ended, and for a moment, she seemed suspended in the air, confused at the turn of events. Then she toppled over.

It was hard for him to believe a single bullet caused the death of such a large animal.

As he proudly ran his hand over the warm body, and the perfect hole in her head, he was angry no one was there to see it. He wanted someone to congratulate him—he had done it on his first shot, slaughtered an animal four times bigger than him. That was no small task. He skinned the carcass, slashing violently, and his hands were soon soaked in her blood.

Excited by the amount of meat, anticipating the taste of it in his mouth, he forgot he was alone. His grandfather would be pleased. He wouldn't say anything, but he would glance at Peyton and nod, approval plastered to his face.

Meat was an expensive item at the grocers, and they were perpetually short on money. His grandfather was a coal miner—he'd been down there since right after the Great Depression—and the pay was good as it got in

Lamar County. But that wasn't saying much, especially since some years, the work dwindled, the bulk of it shipped off to other counties or overseas.

His mother worked, too, as a mine executive's personal assistant. It was a job over two hundred women had applied for. On the day the position was listed, a long line curled out of the mine offices and around the cafeteria, young children running barefoot in the road, the coal miners whistling as they walked past.

Many of these women were significantly more qualified than his mother, who was a slow reader, and had never touched a typewriter. But as she had expected, her beauty was all the qualification she needed. The executive had strolled by and picked her out of the line, and she glowed with excitement as the worn out women surrounding her fumed.

The women waited in line for three more hours. Neither the clerk processing the line nor they knew that, over a long lunch, the smitten executive had offered his mother the position, and would not be persuaded to change his mind by any amount of the clerk's foolproof logic.

This occurred before Peyton was born, but he heard the story from his mother dozens of times. She lit up gleefully every time she described it. The events conformed perfectly to the image she had of herself—the successful executive surveys all Lamar County has to offer, and immediately concludes his mother does not belong; no, she needs to be plucked out from the stack of mediocrity, and given a better life.

His mother didn't bother, even after she landed the position, to learn to read or write very well. She didn't care for "book learning," except as it applied to Peyton. She had seen all the framed diplomas in the executives' offices, and decided education was the way out of West Virginia.

Before Peyton could walk, she put picture books she acquired from the church in his lap. She forced him to look at them for hours, slapping his hand when he tried to crawl away, saying he damn well better study his books.

His mother and grandfather fought about the time Peyton read, as his grandfather didn't see the point, saying he was going to end up in the mines like every other boy in Lamar County. Peyton's grandfather had impenetrable opinions on a lot of matters. He thought Peyton's mother was a disgrace for not marrying.

His mother's face fluttered with cagey fury when her father raised his voice, her eyebrows rising up and down. "Don't worry about me," she said, poorly feigning indifference. Her lower lip trembled like it did when the thunder boomed and the cabin seemed to shake.

21

Peyton hated these fights. It was like he was trapped in the woods, with a dark storm brewing, threatening to let all hell lose. His grandmother remained calm during their altercations, seeing it as puppies play-fighting. She stroked Peyton's hair with her strong hands, whispering in his ear that things were going to be alright.

One of them would give up and leave the cabin, his grandfather stumbling with his bottle of shine in his hand, or his mother, her eye makeup streaked across her cheeks, her body fidgeting like she was trying to get herself clean of a giant spider web.

Peyton didn't know where either of them went, and when he was younger, he didn't really understand what they were fighting about. He only knew he couldn't stand two of the three people he loved in this world butting heads. It created a civil war inside his chest, and this made him sick, like his insides were being torn apart.

As he grew older, he began to understand their words, how they were fighting over what his mother should do with her life. He found himself agreeing with his grandfather. His mother seemed to be living in some kind of a fantasy world. Her clothes were impractical, and she couldn't carry a pail of water to save her life. She spoke of east coast cities like they were Heaven on earth, and though Peyton didn't know anything about those cities, he doubted that was true.

Even so, he defended her. She was his mother, and whether she was right or wrong, he would take up for her. One of the few things in life he knew for sure was, when lines were drawn, he and his mother always had to be on the same side.

When his mother was gone at night, he stayed awake in his half-empty bed. He pictured her walking through the woods alone, without a coat. Or at the pub, an inebriated man leaning over her, a dirty hand clutching her shoulder. Or her twisting her ankle near the river, and limping back to the cabin, leaning on trees as she hobbled along.

Late in the night, after hours of turbulent and intermittent sleep, he heard the rickety clank of the cabin door and his mother's clumsy steps. She fell into the bed, and his side bounced up. She giggled like the teenage girls in the company store.

He was relieved, feeling whole again.

"Peyton," she whispered loudly. "Peyton? Are you awake?"

"Don't wake Pawpaw," he said, reaching out for her hand. The last thing he wanted was a fight.

"Peyton," she said, still whispering loudly, her voice sloppy like spilled soup. "Peyton… I love you."

"I know, Ma."

She hugged him so tight he could barely breathe.

"Promise me you'll take us out of here," she said, her face on his naked belly, wet with tears. He petted her hair. "I'm sick of the men around here. Ain't one of them any good."

"Okay," he said, trying to make his voice confident. He didn't understand what she wanted from him, or where they would go. He was only a boy.

She hugged him tighter, and he choked, unable to get air.

"Good. You're so good." Her grip loosened and she wiped her nose on his belly. She let out a long sigh. "You're the only one who loves me."

Even though he knew it wasn't true, those words bore down on him like a large stone on his chest. A stone he would have to carry.

He kept petting her hair, waiting for her to fall asleep. Outside, no matter how many stars were shining, it seemed like the blackest of nights.

Once his mother's body went soft and her breathing steadied, he put his hand on the mattress, and closed his eyes, his heart aching under the weight of a responsibility he wasn't sure it could bear.

CHAPTER TWO

Peyton's mother stepped daintily into the driver's seat of their 1962 Ford truck. She smiled at Peyton as she turned the keys.

The truck, an old man waking up, coughed a few times before starting. It rolled down the dirt path, tree branches scraping its side with gnarled fingers.

Peyton held his gun upright and the metal was cold against his fingers.

His mother glanced over at him. "Don't you be getting too close to them school kids, Pey. There's people who work for other people and there's people who run the show. You remember?"

"Yes, ma'm," Peyton said, saluting out the window, having only the foggiest sense of what she meant, but wanting to please her. He didn't care for the school kids anyway.

"Good," she said, smiling at him gently, patting his thigh. He looked at her round nails, painted pink. The top of her hand was smooth as a boiled egg, but the palms were rough like his. She rubbed lotion from a glass bottle on her hands and feet every night.

She spread it on his hands too. "All successful men have smooth hands," she whispered. Men with soft hands struck him as silly, but he didn't stop her because it felt so good and as it turned out, the lotion didn't do a damn thing. His hands were calloused as ever.

"Mr. Ramsey is taking us to lunch Friday," she said, tapping his thigh with her fingers.

The truck lurched as they rolled over a bump. Peyton's gun hit the cab's ceiling. His mother glanced over at his feet, which hung in the air.

"You have to wear shoes."

25

He hated dressing up. His shoes were hand-me-downs from a third cousin and a few sizes too big. He had to slide the shoes across the ground like boats on water. But going to the restaurant was well worth it. Last time he got the steak and fried potatoes, with a side order of bacon, a big glass of milk, and finished with an ice cream sundae. His mother's boss had grinned as Peyton had downed his food without stopping to breathe.

"That's a good appetite, you got there, boy," he'd said. He laughed loudly, as if emitting the laughter from deep in his stomach, propelled forth by a bout of gas. Peyton nodded briefly, without raising his eyes from his mountain of food.

Sitting in the truck, with his half empty belly, Peyton's mouth slid open.

"I'll get the steak," he announced.

"Good," his mother said, offering a proud smile as she turned the truck onto the paved road and sped up. "You get whatever you want, baby."

Peyton watched the woods race by the window. The truck trotted along and from this angle, it all blurred together, like patches of colorful cloth strewn together across the sky.

"Don't tell Pawpaw, though. You hear?"

"I won't," Peyton said, although, distracted, he forgot what he wasn't supposed to tell. They kept driving down the mountainside, following the switchbacks right and left.

Reaching town at the base of the hollow, his mother pulled over in front of the one-room schoolhouse. His mother's cherubic eyes sparkled in the full light of day like the blue stripes on a longear sunfish. He leaned over to kiss her on the cheek but she shook her head.

"You'll mess my makeup." She rubbed his mouth with her finger. "Don't you get into any trouble, you hear?"

"I won't," he said, climbing out of the truck with his gun. She didn't seem to notice he didn't have his school pack. She'd been preoccupied lately.

His mother drove off, waving her slender fingers outside the driver's side window. The truck rode through the rest of the one-street town, took a right, and disappeared down the steep road that led to the mine.

Gold and red leaves congregated abundantly on old trees, shimmering in the sun, growing around every building, dwelling in every patch of soil and catching every ray of sun. It made the street seem like a poorly constructed dam, about to succumb to the wilderness rushing down the mountainside.

The town had the schoolhouse, five or six shops, a restaurant and a pub. Walking past Styles, the store for mine executives' wives, Peyton saw a petite woman folding sweaters on a table. She wore a short sleeved blouse and a necklace of shiny white balls.

He figured she lived far up the mountain in the houses with so many parts the people living inside probably never saw each other. He knocked on her window and she jumped, her mouth forming a little O. He stuck out his tongue and sprinted off, laughing, and waving his gun. He didn't feel like going to school, with all the dumb crackers.

* * *

Peyton's grandfather did not have to work on Sundays. During morning mass, his chin fell down on his chest and then popped back up again. Occasionally, Peyton could convince him to come out to the woods after church.

It was a hot and humid October day—his grandfather called it summer's tail—and the naked sun caused pools of sweat to gather on their skin. His grandfather's fingers tied a green string into a noose.

The string acquired a smudge of blackness and Peyton wished his fingers marked everything they touched with that subtle shadow. It seemed like the sign of someone important.

Peyton watched his grandfather's motions solemnly.

"Thar," his grandfather said. His grandfather walked a good thirty feet away and sat down in the tangling, green understory. Peyton ran to keep up.

Bugs moved over them in a fog, and Peyton slapped at his skin, trying to fend them off.

His grandfather closed his eyes and sipped from his silver flask, the one he'd acquired in the War, and Peyton studied the gentle rise of his chest, the square line of his jaw, and the grayish muscles of his shoulder.

His grandfather drank eagerly, his eyes rising and falling from half mast. Peyton wondered if his skin, accustomed to the darkness inside the earth, would burn.

Peyton fidgeted and wandered away to practice. To his disappointment, his snares were lopsided. He wanted his grandfather to demonstrate again, but he knew better than to ask.

He ran back to his grandfather and sat down, leaning against him. His grandfather's muscles were solid, and Peyton decided he would be just like him when he was older. He would work in the mines, and he would chuck coal as if it were hay. He would be the strongest man in all of West Virginia.

The afternoon sun baked his skin, and Peyton closed his eyes, burrowing against his grandfather. He tumbled to sleep, imagining himself behind his grandfather, crawling on a path to the center of the earth with an ax in his hand and a rope around his waist, his life lit by rattling lamps.

Peyton opened his eyes.

His grandfather took a pull of his flask. "Time to head in."

His grandfather moved quickly, and Peyton scrambled to his feet, jogging after him.

"Check that snare, boy," his grandfather said gruffly.

Peyton looked at him expectantly, wishing his grandfather would stay out with him. His grandfather averted his eyes, and grunted.

Peyton reached out for his grandfather's hand, but then, halfway there, he remembered it would be unmanly, and he stuffed his hand in his pocket.

"Tell me a story from the War, Pawpaw," he said. He loved his grandfather's War stories.

His grandfather tilted his chin, staring at the bright rays of sun cutting through the tangled tree branches. Their feet crunched loudly on fallen leaves.

"Thar was this one time," his grandfather began, his eyes back on the forest floor. "My friend Eddie came down with the runs on the march. Eddie had to keep walkin' even though his pants was gittin' covered."

"Eddie was losin' his water and we didn't have no water to lose. He git the runs in the first place from drinkin' mud on the street. I drank from the same puddle but for reason only the Lord knows, didn't git the runs."

"Eddie's turning white so I take his arm and drag him along. This works for a while, but soon enough, a Jap shouts at us. Ya weren't allowed to help nobody. Every man for hisself."

"The Jap keeps on us, and Eddie losin' it, and he about to give up when one of them lil Filipinos comes runnin' through the fields carrying a canteen."

"The Jap lets him git real close, and we thinkin' maybe he's gone let us have that canteen. Then when he about five feet away, the Jap shoots him dead. The Jap picks up the canteen and drinks the water."

"I dunno what the lil Filipino man was thinkin'. But turns out he saves Eddie anyway. Eddie watches the whole thing and he git this look in his eyes, real crazy like. He's still weak but he able to carry on the rest of the way, that madness carrying him."

"So he lived?"

"For then. BUt the sad thing was Eddie ended up dying in the prison anyway. Never could git enough water."

His grandpa took a long swig of his flask, and Peyton smiled at him. "You made it, though, Pawpaw."

"Sure did, and that's the Lord jus as much as me. I coulda died a thousand times in the War if not for God."

Peyton smiled, not quite believing it.

"Ya remember that, boy."

"I will, Pawpaw."

Peyton tried to believe it, telling himself his grandfather would know. But this thought was quickly pushed aside by a ballooning admiration for his grandfather. He drifted unconsciously to what pleased him the most: a grandfather so strong he could survive anything.

They reached the cabin and his grandfather bounded up the steps of the porch, nodding slightly at Peyton before he went inside.

Peyton sat down on the porch and started cleaning his gun. He imagined his grandfather as a young soldier, on the march. It sounded so exciting. He couldn't wait until he was old enough to join the Army.

A couple years into school, Peyton took a good look around the one one-room school house and saw one large family after another. They came in packs of five or six. His own family then rolled in front of him like a chipped marble, and he saw the big crack in its glass.

He recalled all the church masses and the visits to his mother's friends, and he saw more of the same: large families, dozens of them. There were none like his. The composition of his family was suddenly something needing an explanation.

When the other children asked him who his father was, he stared at them blankly. He didn't know. He'd never even asked.

They laughed at his silence. The laughter bothered him, but he didn't alter his expression. The crackers weren't worth reacting to.

"Your father is a foreigner!" they shouted.

"What do you mean?" he asked, his curiosity getting the better of him.

They laughed again. This time he couldn't help it—he scowled at them, wanting to tell them to get lost.

One of the boys, in a voice low and mocking, called his mother a whore.

Peyton charged forward, a coiled spring released by the word. Nobody could attack his mother. He swung his fist upward, and felt the satisfying crunch of the boy's teeth underneath his soft lips.

The boy fell to the ground like a cut tree, his mouth gushing blood.

Peyton kneeled over and punched him again, and again, until he was pulled back by sticky, eager hands. He struggled against the net of fingers, lashing his arms and kicking his legs, but the hands seemed to multiply and grow more eager. He made no ground.

His chest rose and fell furiously, and he hated the boy and the boy's brothers holding him. He hated them for insulting his mother. He hated them for laughing at him. The hate was like a caged animal beating against his ribs.

The punched boy sat up, his bright orange hair falling over his freckled forehead.

"You jerk!" he screamed, and his blood splattered on the dirt.

"Don't ever talk about my mother!"

Peyton could hear his heart pumping, and he laid his palm against his chest.

The teacher glided over in her lavender straw hat and white gloves. She descended on the boy, whose face morphed from anger to hurt.

Peyton would never do that, pretend he was hurt to garner sympathy. He wanted to spit on the boy, the baby, and he charged forward, breaking free.

The boy's brothers lunged, their limbs tangling around Peyton's body.

The boys' hands on his chest disgusted him, as if their dirty, clinging fingers, protecting their own, showed him all he had never had. There were no grubby fingers to defend him. He had no brothers.

He was alone.

He kicked and thrashed, hitting one boy's eye, and another boy's stomach. His boot connected with a shin. Someone punched him in the eye. He scratched someone's arm, and heeled someone's foot. He spit in a boy's face.

When he was finally contained, he took quick, shallow breaths.

The other kids peered at him strangely, smirking, and they seemed like caricatures, chalk figures in the road. He imagined swiping a giant eraser over all of them.

The teacher touched the boy's cheek and brushed back his hair. She helped him stand, grabbing his torso gently, and the boy put his hand around her shoulder.

"I punched you in the mouth!"

The teacher looked over her shoulder, her eyes shaded by her wide brim.

"Go home, Peyton?" she said. Her mouth was tipped down with disappointment. "We'll talk tomorrow."

Peyton curled up his fingers and dug his nails into his palms.

The teacher didn't get it—the boy had insulted his mother. They had all laughed at him.

The boy smiled back at him smugly, his paw resting on the shoulder of the teacher's cotton dress. His blood soaked through the soft white fabric, touching the teacher's skin. Peyton knew she would never wear the dress again. She would wash it and donate it to the church.

Peyton dug his nails deeper into his palms, breaking skin.

The boys' brothers reluctantly let him go, shooting him angry looks, which said this wasn't over. He had roughed some of them up. He gave them back a look daring them to try it. He would take them all on.

As everyone else drifted back into the classroom, Peyton kicked the dirt so it leapt in the air. He cursed and ran into the woods. He'd only given the boy his due.

The world wasn't fair, he decided.

* * *

Long after the sun had fallen beneath the horizon, lying in bed with his mother, Peyton could no longer breathe with the nagging desire tied tightly around his chest.

He whispered, "Ma, who is my father?"

She sighed. A breath of mint-filled air crossed his face.

"He's a great…"

She stopped, as if she had turned down a road and, then, realized it was not the one she wanted to take after all.

"It doesn't matter, baby," she said stridently, rubbing his stomach. "We sure as hell don't need anyone else."

He nodded enthusiastically in the darkness. "I know. But who is he?"

"Just let it be!" she cried and her voice faltered, a crack line starting to appear, threatening to break.

She turned away from him, and rolled up in the fetal position. He studied her long, silky black hair, and the shape of her body.

She seemed more like his sister than his mother.

The gentle slope of her back, its generous curve, prevented him from throwing a tantrum, from demanding to know who his father was. He curled in behind her, pushing his face into her hair, deciding he'd rather go on not knowing than hurt her. She reached over and rubbed his hip.

"That's my good boy," she whispered, and now her voice was syrupy, dripping with love.

He was relieved and warm, turning his head up to the sloped ceiling. He told himself he didn't need a father.

He had a mother—that would have to be enough.

His words to himself eventually wore off, like a snake's skin, and when they did, he found his grandmother in the garden, tending to her rows of late fall crops.

Sweat drenched her leathery face. With her strong jaw, deep set eyes, and prominent nose, she had a sturdy bearing. Peyton could see his mother in his grandmother, but only in the way he could see daughters in their fathers. They seemed like very different types of people, as if something fundamental had shifted from one generation to the next, a nature, long buried, had been brought to life.

In many ways, his grandmother was his father. She was stoic and capable, and expected him to be the same. She was the one who had taught him to use a gun, and skin an animal. She was the one who stared at him sternly when, as a toddler, he had started to cry.

"Mawmaw," he said, standing in the middle of the crops. "Who is my father?"

She paused her digging. "What'd ya her?"

"The children said he's a foreigner."

"Humph," she said, her mouth pursed in thought.

"Peyton," she said finally, squinting at him through the afternoon sun. "Sump things a-betta left unsaid."

He crossed his arms over his chest, seeing black.

Why wouldn't anybody tell him who his father was?

He was about to yell, wildly, but then a particular sense crept up on him. Maybe his father was worthless—a drunken loser, a wife-beater, a lying criminal—and no one wanted to speak his name. Maybe, he thought, some fathers were worse than zero.

"My dad was a soldier, just like Pawpaw," he declared, trying it out, seeing how it sounded.

His grandmother looked at him hard, but she didn't say a word. She crouched over and examined the crops, picking up a clump of weeds.

"He was a hero," he continued. With that, he ran back to the cabin. He grabbed his gun from the porch and pounded down the steps. He was hungry.

CHAPTER THREE

When Peyton turned eleven, he was on the cusp of becoming a man. Everyone in the house treated him that way. His body had grown larger than his mother's, and, standing up straight, he could look his grandmother in the eye.

His grandmother had gradually let him take charge of the house. He patched the roof, painted the walls, and replaced the windows. His grandfather had once handled these things, but the work in the mines hadn't slowed down with his body, and by the time he got off his shift, he was exhausted and his back was sore.

The weather that winter was terrible, six months of clammy hands. They must have caught a dozen colds; their little cabin rattled with hacking coughs, passing from one person to the next in a seemingly infinite loop.

Cold rain poured constantly from a gray sky, and Peyton grew hot living inside his coat. The whole world was dark and wet. Trekking to the outhouse at night meant bundling up and shivering. The frigid water had a way of finding his skin no matter how many layers of protection he piled on.

During the week, Peyton and his mother had to leave the cabin before the sun rose. Their truck had taken to abruptly shutting down, and when it did, they had to walk the rest of the way. His mother shivered in her flimsy tan jacket, pulling the hood over her face to protect her makeup, her neck arched high. She stepped carefully over the bumpy dirt road in her high heels.

After a mile or so, with Peyton running into the woods and back to the road, like a rubber band attached to a slow-moving stick, she'd give up and go barefoot. By the time they reached town, her pantyhose were ripped and muddy and her feet cold as ice. Peyton took to carrying a pair of her thick socks and her boots in his school sack.

That morning, the truck's old windshield wipers made little headway against the relentless rain and his mother drove slowly, squinting through the clouded window, screeching whenever they hit a bump in the road.

"Jesus Christ," she breathed. "That scared the living shit out of me."

"It's just the road," Peyton assured her.

They couldn't see anything through the blue sheets of rain. Peyton fought to go back to sleep. He was tired and hungry. His body ached, like an old car running on fumes, and he imagined himself drowning in gasoline, until all his parts became slick and smooth.

He stretched his legs uncomfortably, his eyes sealed shut, and saw his body growing fat and round, his cheeks pudgy, his limp hands resting on his satiated belly.

The rain's whipping eventually turned into a patter, and then, it was silent. Birds chirped clearly, their sounds no longer covered by the slapping water.

"Well, albee," his mother said. "Look at that."

Peyton opened his eyes. A weak sun rose over the mountain. The skies were still filled with roaming dark clouds. But there was no rain. Peyton rolled down his window and stuck his hand into the cold air. Dry. He couldn't believe it.

Just then, the truck choked, coughing, and after one last bout, it fell silent, the engine shutting down.

"Damn it!" she cursed. "This stupid truck!"

She gently stopped the truck and pulled out the keys. If Peyton reached out the window, he could touch the smoky gray branch of a white oak with its freshly sprouted leaves. Life was coming. She turned the key on and off in the ignition, but the engine did not respond. It was dead. Again.

"Oh, I'm so mad I could spit," she said. "Aaron has to fix this!" She banged her fist on the steering wheel, shaking in anger.

"Least it's not raining," he said. For now, he thought.

His mother opened the truck door and stepped down, slamming the door. Peyton grabbed his lunch pail and tossed it in his school sack. They started walking down the road, his mother with her head held high.

He ran through the woods, pouncing in mud puddles, picking up giant sticks, which he used to thrash newly formed plants and trees. He released a holler, and shadowed his mother from deep inside the woods. "Chh-chhh-chhhh," he emitted, pretending he was shooting his mother with a gun, and then he was killing bad guys, which were coming after his mother from every direction. "Chhh-chhh-chhh-chhhhh."

Soon, he was warm and sticky underneath his coat and sweater and he walked with his mother, reaching out for her hand. The wind blew and water stored in tree-leaf cups fell to the ground. The woods seemed to rattle with animals erupting from the earth.

"I can't wait to get out of here," his mother said, sighing. She held her purse close to her chest and peered at the ground warily.

"Where will we go?" Peyton asked skeptically, dragging a stick through the dirt, leaving a line in the road.

"Oh, I dun know exactly," she said. "Some city. Somewhere we can take long baths with nice hot water. Where I can drive a nice car, and have clean things."

She shook some of the water off her coat. "We'll have a nice couch, and magazines, and pretty pictures in our house. With curtains and good china. Lots of nice clothes and jewelry."

She glanced over at him, and he saw a religious zeal on her face, like the young priest with his fiery eyes when he spoke of the almighty Lord and Heaven.

Peyton twitched with anger. Why did an imaginary life make her so ecstatic? Why wasn't this enough?

It seemed like she was only truly happy in her fantasies.

He tugged her hand closer to his body. He would pull her back to reality. Ma, he wanted to say, be here with me. Love this.

She swung his hand back in her direction, and squeezed it, her eyelids lowering gently. Her mouth parted slightly.

"Ma."

She gulped a breath of air, turning away.

"I'm sorry," she said. "I'm really sorry." She took her hand from him and ran it through her hair, closing her eyes for a moment.

She tilted to him. She smiled softly and winked. "You'd have all the steak and potatoes you can eat."

He smiled tentatively, admitting that sounded good. He pictured a giant platter of steak, potatoes, and bacon, resting in front of him on a wood table, a solid knife and fork in his hands.

"I'm mad at Aaron. That truck's a piece of shit! He has a lot of nerve."

Peyton laughed. "Could we have guns too?"

"Hmm?"

"In our new place—could we have guns?"

"Oh," she said, distracted again. "I don't think so. Guns aren't very civilized."

Peyton frowned, moving a few steps ahead of his mother.

Civilized was his mother's favorite word. It was everything she wanted to be. He still couldn't figure out what the hell it meant. And a life without guns sounded boring. He kicked a twig and it went flying.

His mother walked to the edge of the road and leaned against a maple. Peyton sighed, following her over. She stepped out of her heels, and her feet were blanched and swollen.

He opened his sack and handed her the socks and laid out the boots. Her boots were made of old, faded leather, and crusted with mud. She shoved them on, and seeing them next to her soft, white pantyhose, she made a pained noise, like a crying dog.

She raised her face, and her large blue eyes shined with salty tears. He reached a hand to her cheek.

"Ma…"

She brushed his hand away, turning to the road and smoothing down her dress. "It's okay," she said, her voice full with empty bravado. "It's really okay.'

She sniffled and moved a lot faster, her mouth drawn in a line.

"Are we going to get a TV?" he asked.

"Hmmm? Oh, yes, when we move. But not now. Pawpaw thinks they rot your brain."

"He does?"

"Yes. It's not true, of course."

"Okay," he said, trying to imagine what his brain looked like rotting inside his head. He didn't see anything. He had no idea what a brain looked like. He wished, not for the first time, that his mother knew more than she did. He'd given up asking her about the world.

"Pawpaw's stuck in his ways," she added.

He nodded and they walked forward in silence, enjoying the dryness on their fingers, the sense that they were the only two people in the whole world.

They eventually reached the town. It was quiet, as if it had been deserted before an impending battle. The sky was still dark and gray even though the sun had risen.

She rubbed his cheek with the back of her smooth hand, "Be good, baby. Don't let those crackers get to you."

"Alright," he said, handing her the dress shoes. She leaned on his shoulder—he was half a head taller than her now—and pulled off the boots and the socks, slipping elegantly into her dress shoes. She smiled and stood up straight, pulling the hem of her dress.

"Much better," she whispered.

He kissed her on the cheek, before she could protest about her makeup.

He watched her go with an intensity of feeling. He missed her already, but he was angry with her wanderlust. She needed to stop pining over silly fantasies. She was a grown woman.

He put the boots in his sack, and threw it over his shoulder, pounding up the schoolhouse steps.

The room was empty.

He put his raincoat and sack in his cubby, and wandered to his desk, putting his head down. He was exhausted.

Not long after, footsteps and laughter pounded up the steps, and the Lamberts rushed in, pushing and shoving each other. They peeled off their raincoats and stashed them in their cubbies.

Peyton flipped through the pages in his American history book, searching for his place, trying to remember how far he had read into the Civil War. The others poured in. The little girls came in last, their long hair plastered to their round faces.

The boys near Peyton's age congregated in the first row, hovering around Jon and Raymond arm wrestling. Peyton thought they were stupid. They threw balls of mud, hit each other with sticks and lobbed stones at birds and squirrels.

Peyton ignored them during recess, running to the two teenage girls. He laid his head in their laps, and they stroked his hair as they gossiped about their families and boys in the mine. They smelled of flowers and spoke with chipper voices. It reminded him of his younger years, the long hours splayed out on floors and slender laps as teenage girls had giggled and shrieked above him.

The teacher arrived last, as she always did, with a steaming thermos of coffee. She smiled at the class timidly, stealing herself for another day, and hung her raincoat on the hook next to the door.

Through the streaked glass windows, Peyton stared longingly at her bright red 1968 Ford Falcon Sports Coupe. She had let Peyton sit in it after school. It was the nicest car he had ever been in, and he bet it never broke down like their lousy truck.

Everything inside was red—the seats, the steering wheel, the long consol. Peyton had buckled up in the driver's seat and imagined he was zooming up the mountain, "Vrrrrromm, vrrrrrrrrom," seeing himself take the tight turns, climbing faster and faster to the sky. The teacher, sitting in the passenger seat, her purse in her lap, laughed.

The students quieted down and returned to their seats. The youngest kids shuffled to the roundtable in the back. After lunch, Peyton went to the roundtable for his lesson, taking "his" seat next to the teacher's. One of the boys had taken it a few months back, and Peyton had made him get up. He could feel the teacher's warm breath on his neck.

The teacher was telling them how to multiply fractions in her soft, questioning voice. Peyton drifted in and out of sleep as she talked. Math was instinctive to him and any operation on fractions—adding, multiplying, dividing, squaring—was obvious. He could see what his mother meant about crackers because the rest of the kids struggled with the most basic addition.

Occasionally, when he couldn't sleep anymore, his frustration would bubble up violently in his throat, and he would open his eyes, and yell out, "Can we move on? When am I going to learn anything?"

The teacher's slender hand floated over her mouth, and her eyes opened widely, spooked by his outburst. The other students peered at him strangely, their narrowed eyes and shared giggles suggesting they thought he was crazy as Lou, the old man who lived near the rails.

Then, seeing all their faces, he would realize he was alone. No one knew what he was capable of. He didn't even know.

Sometimes, he would mumble an apology, and the teacher would go on with her lesson, glancing at him apprehensively. Other times, he would stand up from the table, and slam his chair to the ground, and run out of the room, down the steps, and out of the town. He ran into the woods, as fast as he could, letting his arms and legs get scratched and bloodied by the thorns and the vines and the heavy branches, until he was exhausted and out of breath, his legs like dead wood.

He would stop at the highest peak, and stare over the mountain ranges, their great slopes covered with thick green trees, running to every horizon. He would stand there alone, against nature, against everyone he knew, and shout at God, "Why am I so alone?"

His words were always caught and swallowed by the infinite expanse of space. No one spoke back to him.

He was all alone. And he hated God for refusing to answer him.

But now, starving and tired, he remained in his seat. He did not hear the teacher's words; he only absorbed the softness of her voice, floating in and out of consciousness.

Peyton felt like a pebble as he streamed out of the class with everybody else, caught up in their current of plans and jokes. He didn't have any friends, not really. The two teenage girls rustled his hair, and one of the smarter boys smiled at him ruefully. That was it.

He swung his sack over his shoulder and stood in the middle of the sidewalk. He watched them meander down the road. Every single one of them lived in company housing, and he figured if he lived in company housing, he'd have some friends too.

They had a whole social world constructed up there: they watched television; they ran down their narrow streets and into their woods; they built forts and swam in the river; and the older ones slept together and got drunk on stolen shine. It was a world he had no way of entering, and they brought it to school, tossing around references and stories and names he didn't understand.

He longed to catch up and dissolve into the crowd.

This desire flittered on, like a feather stroked across his face in a gust of wind, because he knew it wasn't only living apart. There was something greater, something inside him, separating him from everyone else.

He was infected with his mother's fantasies, and no matter how hard he tried, he couldn't quell her voice in his head, insisting Lamar County and its hillbilly people were a way station on the road to a better life. He didn't understand what this better life would be, but the voice blathered on, like a dogged huckster, hawking utopian dreams, insisting this place, here, was dirt beneath his feet.

The crowd faded into the woods, and he waited for them to reappear on the other side, high on the mountainside. He imagined them talking and laughing and playing games. They emerged from a dense patch of trees, and soon they were only white flecks drifting to the sky.

Peyton turned away, feeling like he was the only person left in the world. A dense fog glided down the empty road, and the rolling gray sky blocked out the sun's light.

It was a ghost town.

He headed in the opposite direction. He climbed into the woods, deciding to take the shortest route back to the cabin. The ground was soft beneath his feet, saturated with weeks of rainfall and untouched by the spring sun. Peyton cursed not having his gun.

He picked up a large stick, finding it soft to the touch. He threw it to the ground and it lost its shape limply, bending in a curve.

"Stupid stick," he cursed.

He kept his eye out for another piece of wood, a crisp one that might break in two.

Near the cabin, someone had parked a black Ford truck. The truck perched on top of its huge wheels like a spider, and it had a chrome front bumper. Peyton imagined it had blasted down the narrow road, knocking thick branches from its path like flies.

Peyton had never seen anything like it, and he ran his fingers over the shiny siding. He remembered his relatives, strangers he had never met, would be inside, and he ran up the path as fast as he could, pounding up the steps.

He threw open the door.

A teenage girl stood in front of the counter, filling the strainer with ground coffee. After she put the water on to boil, she turned around.

Seeing Peyton, she sat down and took a deep breath.

"Hi," Peyton said, sliding into the chair across from her, tossing his sack on the floor.

"Hi," she replied, her voice husky. "I'm Greta. Your fourth cousin in law or something." Her brown eyes were small as peanuts, and they seemed even smaller in her wide, square face. She plucked a piece of skin from next to her fingernail, and then laced her fingers and laid them on the table. Her hands were big and muscular, like a man's.

He smiled. "Do you hunt?"

"No. Do you?"

"Yes," he said, proudly.

"Daddy buys meat." She looked out the window. "You could teach me."

"To hunt?"

She nodded.

"Sure," he said, grinning at his good luck. Girl or not, he would love to teach someone else to hunt.

She smiled. She had square teeth, and her upper lip vanished. Her hand floated up instinctively, over her mouth.

CHAPTER FOUR

Mine accidents happen every few years in Lamar County. Even though everybody knows this, people were always caught off guard, as if secretly they had started believing something about the world had changed, that they no longer lived in the type of place that suffered regular calamities.

The news of an accident passed from miner to miner and then spread like a virus through the streets and the stores and the school and the church and the houses.

The town responded like an injured porcupine—it bristled, its quills drawn and alert.

The miners nervously went back to work the next day, exercising a greater degree of caution, paying closer attention to the gas monitors, making sure every movement was up to protocol. Women and children kissed their husbands and brothers and fathers a bit longer, packed their lunches with extra slices of meat, and told them they were loved.

People disparaged the Piston Coal Company, the workers grumbled loudly, the townspeople roughly used their script in the Piston Company Store. If looks could kill, any mine executive caught in town died a dozen times over.

The fear and the anger pushed the town's people closer together, huddling them against the behemoth Piston Coal Company, and death itself. Church was standing room only. Drinking, philandering and gambling, the ordinary vices of Lamar County, were forgiven. In the face of death, they didn't seem so important.

And then, as the accident receded in people's memory, life imperceptibly slid back to its normal shape. The town didn't have the energy for timorousness, or for enmity of the hand that fed it, or even for vigilance. The people of Lamar County had enough work simply living.

So the miners fell back to their old patterns, and the town's people reverted to seeing the coal company as the quotidian structure underlying their lives, like the four seasons. Only those directly affected by the accident remained altered, forever defined by the loss of a husband, a father, a best friend, or the ability to breathe without a machine, or stand up out of a chair.

Peyton remembered the last two mine accidents. His fellow students had suffered losses and come back to school dumbfounded. He watched them reappear in new forms. A formerly sweet girl reemerged bitter and sarcastic; a plain, ordinary boy became reckless, throwing rocks at moving cars and drinking shine; a daredevil started carrying a Bible close to his chest, preaching the word of the Lord to anyone who would listen.

The day his relatives arrived in town turned out to be Lamar County's worst mine accident since 1969. A gas explosion caused a roof to collapse, and four men trapped in the tunnel died. Eleven men, able to crawl out of the rubble, were injured. They left the hospital with amputated limbs, lost brain function, and charred skin.

One of Peyton's grandfather's close friends had died.

"He was gonna retire," his grandfather kept mumbling, rubbing his fist on a hard surface. "He was about to retire."

His grandfather's mood, already subdued by a life of hard labor, metamorphosed from a solid rock to a dark fog. His face crumpled into a grimace, and he picked at his food like a bird and constantly drank his shine. The smallest incident—a misplaced napkin, the short cut of Peyton's mother's dress, a dropped glass—would illicit his condemnation, and he would glance at the person reproachfully before drifting from the room, leaving black acidic air in his wake.

He shut his bedroom door gently and its rusty hinges rattled and echoed in the cabin. Nobody knew what he did in there. Peyton put his palm on the door, and leaned his cheek against the rough wood, imagining his grandfather would feel his warmth.

But he never did.

"I shoulda been there," he kept whispering. "I shoulda been there."

At church, when the minister tried to explain the mine accident as part of God's plan, saying the miners were now in Heaven, waiting for the rest of Lamar County, Peyton's grandfather stood up, his back hunched, and pushed his way out of the pew.

He quickly made his way down the aisle, ignoring the curious faces. When he opened the doors, the sun lit up the aisle and the shape of his body, and it was almost as if he were walking through the doors of Heaven.

After the mass, they found him on a bench under a great oak, staring out over the valleys.

Peyton wished his grandfather would get angry. It wasn't an act of God, they all knew that. It was the Piston Coal Company installing cheap equipment, more worried about making money than the welfare of their workers. But his grandfather's face wasn't angry. It was resigned to a world he had lost.

His grandmother touched his grandfather's back softly, and he turned his shoulder, his face titled to the ground. He rose up slowly. He followed them back to the truck, his eyes pinned forward, like barren streams reflecting nothing.

The relatives were obtuse about his grandfather's state, as they had not known him before the accident. They assumed he had always lurked like stale air. Margaret was Peyton's grandmother's sister's great-niece, and she had brought her husband Hershel and their three children to stay until construction finished on their new house.

The eldest boy Tyler and his father swaggered into a room, and they were strapping, with shocks of brown hair lightened by the sun. Peyton immediately wanted to hang out with them, figuring they did lots of cool, manly things. The youngest boy cowered behind his mother. He seemed sleek and dark and bitter, like a baby rat.

They all slept on cots in the open room, by Peyton and his mother's bed, and Hershel's raucous snoring kept Peyton up at night. Restless, he would peer over at the family, studying them in their sleep. Hershel's thick, muscular arm was thrown over Margaret's frail neck, and she seemed trapped, as if she had been buried alive, her scared eyes roving around the room. Greta slept soundly, her square chest rising and falling. Adam rolled over, his worn blanket falling to the floor, exposing twiggy arms and legs.

Peyton loved having more people in the cabin, and he pretended Hershel was his father, and Tyler was his older brother. But he also resented the family, feeling like they were responsible for his grandfather's turn. Seeing the relatives as the shadow of his dead friend, his grandfather avoided them, merely grunting as he drifted past.

Peyton thought if the family departed, it might free his grandfather to move on from the accident, as if the family was a stick stuck in his grandfather's wheel. But his grandmother, who must have considered this too, said nothing.

God did not allow her to deny family, no matter how distant, a place to stay. And the family, oblivious, seemed intent on staying for quite some time.

The family lounged on the cots and unpacked their clothes and their kitchen utensils and their shoes, cluttering the cabin. They filled a large styrofoam cooler with meats and sauces and breads. Peyton stole from this cooler in the middle of the night, taking the lunch meat and cheese and bread to the outhouse and gorging.

He knew this was wrong, but the Hunger overpowered him. He was ashamed afterwards. There were crumbs on his coat, the night air was cold on his bare fingers, and the outhouse reaked of burnt wood and excrement.

For a few weeks, Peyton struggled to stay angry on his grandfather's behalf. He banished himself to the corner while the family talked and laughed with his mother and grandmother. Their good mood and his full stomach chipped away at his resolve, though, and he finally convinced himself his anger wouldn't make a difference to his barely-there grandfather.

He started laughing at Hershel and Tyler's jokes, and thanking them for the food, feeling like part of their family. He tagged along with them on the weekends, when they did business. They owned a company called "Hershel and Son's, Making Cabinets Since 1853." Hershel insisted that his family could have been making cabinets since 1853, and in fact, he said with a laugh, maybe they had been. He sure as hell didn't know.

He confidently told this story to mine executives' wives, claiming his family had been living in West Virginia since the early eighteen hundreds, back when it was Virginia, making cabinets for luminaries such as Francis Harrison Pierpont, the "Father of West Virginia," and Ephraim Bee.

Peyton was surprised how easily the women swallowed this tale—their eyes brightened and their mouths opened and their noses rose in the air as they contemplated it, running their fingers over the smooth wood with delicate little sighs.

Peyton was dumbfounded they were willing to pay tidy sums, at least twenty times their cost, for one cabinet. He and Tyler and Hershel grinned at each other, mocking these women who could afford to so carelessly throw their money down the river.

Occasionally, when they delivered a pitch or a cabinet, the woman would give Tyler and Peyton cookies or sugared biscuits and sit them outside on their sprawling, wrap-around porches, asking Hershel to come inside to do some men's work.

"Much obliged," Hershel always said, a smile Peyton couldn't read plastered on his face.

Hershel and the lady disappeared into the deep recessives of the house. Their voices echoed and then vanished. Peyton thought the women were awkward—their hair and faces artificially stiff, their bodies either boney or matronly, their words stilted.

Tyler and Peyton eagerly ate the cookies and gulped the milk. It tasted much richer than the milk at home. After the milk and cookies were gone, Peyton wiped off his lap and asked Tyler if they should go inside.

Tyler laughed, shaking his head. He made a circle with his thumb and finger, and rammed another finger through the hole.

"Yeah right," Peyton said, incredulous. He couldn't imagine Hershel wanting to climb in bed with such a woman. Not to mention the woman's husband would kill Hershel if he found out. "She's married."

Tyler laughed even harder. "Don't be dumb."

Peyton punched him in the arm and soon they were wrestling on the porch.

At one of their deliveries, they heard the woman screaming inside the house. Peyton ran in, ready to help.

Standing in the open foyer, he realized the screams were not out of pain or fear.

He walked back out and Tyler was curled over, laughing.

"Dumbass," he said, pointing at Peyton.

Out of embarrassment more than anything else, Peyton tackled him and they both went flying off the porch, landing with a hard thump on the lawn.

With a whoosh, Peyton was on his back, Tyler on top of him, laughing.

Peyton kicked him between the legs, and pushed him sideways. They rolled over a few times, and then were both lying in the grass, disentangled and laughing.

This is what it would be like, Peyton thought, to have a brother.

He smiled at the bright sun, stretching his arms above his head. When he glanced over at Tyler, they broke into laughter again, a laughter that felt endless. They both knew the whole thing was ridiculous—Hershel, with his rough edges, inside the bedroom of an uptight wealthy woman, probably knocking over a vase and dirtying her white sheets—while Peyton and Tyler lounged on a porch the size of their house, eating fancy cookies and big glasses of milk.

If Hershel or Tyler took notice of Adam, they mocked him, deriding him for his frailty, his cowardice. Peyton joined in this, laughing at Adam's word-garbling stutter, and his quick tears. What a baby, he thought.

After a while, though, he had the distinct feeling he was kicking a bird with one-wing. He pitied Adam's frailty. When Hershel and Tyler weren't around, he tried to be friendly, swallowing his natural distaste.

Adam peered at him warily, as if life had taught him human contact could lead to nothing good. He offered one word answers to Peyton's questions—one drawn-out, stuttered word.

Peyton was frustrated, and about to quit, when he asked Adam what he was reading. Adam abruptly ran at the mouth, his stutter coming and going as he plowed forward. Peyton couldn't follow him—he was talking too fast—but he smiled.

Adam darted over to his cot and pulled out his bag, his movements surprisingly nimble. He came back, and pushed a book into Peyton's hand. Peyton glanced at it—A Separate Peace—and nodded.

"Thanks."

Adam stared at him with such delight, he was compelled to egg him on.

"I'll read it," he said, patting the book reassuringly.

Adam's smile expanded, revealing perfectly straight teeth.

Peyton laughed to himself as he put on his shoes. Such a peculiar little boy, he thought. The weather was warm and he took the book and ran to an open spot on the Redroot River, stretching out on top of a boulder, letting his feet rest in the water.

He liked reading, but he rarely had time for it. There were too many things for him to do. The family's presence had alleviated this, of course. He didn't need to hunt anymore, if he didn't want to; and when something broke down in the cabin, Hershel and Tyler quickly fixed it. For once, Peyton felt like a child, with a father to feed him and patch up their cabin, and an older brother to teach him how to build things.

It was nice to be taken care of. Yet he forced himself to monitor the cabin for problems, and tend to the crops, because he didn't want to become too accustomed to relying on others. Hershel wasn't his father and Tyler wasn't his brother, he kept reminding himself.

They would soon leave him here, alone.

The river was quick from recent rains and the water rushed past, swirling against rocks, creating slushy white rapids. Bugs crawled on him as he turned the crisp pages of the book. The story occurred in a private boarding school, strangely devoid of women. Peyton liked the school, with its clever inhabitants, and its insular, self-sustaining life.

He finished the book before twilight. As he walked back to the cabin, the Hunger groused in his stomach. He picked up a few shagbark hickory nuts on the ground and put them in the pockets of his shorts. He split one open, separating it at the base, and tossed it in his mouth.

He walked and ate, and he thought about Finny, one of the boys from the book. Finny was meant to come across as an admirable figure, but Peyton had found him incredibly weak and cloying. Only a pathetic boy would forgive his best friend for breaking his leg.

Peyton knew he would never forgive something like that. "A man's honor's all he's got, son," his grandfather had told him. "Never trust a man who don't know that." Anyone who broke his leg would be dead.

And why, Peyton wondered, did a loser like Finny end up at an extravagant private school? A vague image of the school, its walls glistening in splendor, buzzed around Peyton tauntingly, and he wished he could swat it away.

He didn't want to know he could be anywhere other than where he was: with the slow crackers, the out-of-date books, the constant pandemonium.

It occurred to him, then, that the school for the mine executives' children, right here in Lamar Country, was likely as nice as the school in the book. He had seen the children in the town restaurant, dressed in plaid skirts, ironed pants, and button-up shirts. Even the five-year-olds wore bowties and jackets. They had plump and rosy cheeks, straight haircuts, and their shoes shined brightly, reflecting the afternoon sun.

Their teachers probably knew everything. Peyton's teachers were like prey animals, disoriented by the packs of students who could barely read picture books. Whatever they knew, they didn't have time to share it with him.

Peyton kicked a tree, telling himself to relax.

He remembered how dumb the mine executives' wives were. And the children might be clean and well-fed, but he bet they were incapable of taking care of themselves. Drop them in the woods and they wouldn't last one night, he thought.

He laughed at that. Their little bowties wouldn't get them very far in the woods. They would be like freshly born infants, their pink skin devoured by the cold winds, their tender bodies rendered useless by the Hunger.

Then he would win.

When he reached the cabin, the sun and its light was falling like a curtain behind him. Hershel and Tyler were sitting on the porch, drinking. The vein on Hershel's forehead was engorged. Peyton had seen the vein before. It meant Hershel was drunk as a wildcat.

Shit, Peyton thought.

All his life he had seen drunk men acting like fools—wandering in the street, crashing their cars into storefronts, breaking each other's noses. Years ago, his drunk grandfather had thrown dishes at this mother, and slapped Peyton so hard he fell to the ground.

Peyton bounded up the porch, keeping his eyes on the door.

"Woah, boy, where do you think you're going?" Hershel said, laughing.

Hershel smelled like beer and shine, and his face lunged forward, scraping against Peyton's left shoulder like sandpaper. Peyton clenched. His old anger toward the family rose in his stomach, forming into a tight ball.

"Have a beer, boy," Hershel said. He leaned over to the cooler and pulled a can out.

Peyton reluctantly took hold of it. He didn't trust drinking, and he lingered with it in his hand, feeling its weight, as if that would tell him the damage. It was cold on his fingers. Hershel stared at him expectantly, and he was thirsty, so he opened it. It tasted sweet enough and he guzzled it down.

It made him feel light headed.

"Our house is coming through, boy. Soon we'll be off."

"Congratulations," Peyton said, staring past the field into the woods.

The trees formed a dark silhouette against the vividly pink sky. Patches of leaves sprouted on their branches, ushering in the bold birth of spring. It amazed him how that worked—year in and year out, so much life and so much death. It never ended.

"Thanks," Peyton said, tossing the empty can in the trash. Hershel nodded, holding his can up in salute.

Peyton smiled and walked inside, relieved he had gotten off so easy. Greta was at the stove, her back to him. His grandmother sat in the rocking chair near the empty fireplace, sleeping. He walked over to her and kissed her gently on the forehead.

The wrinkles on her face reminded him of deep spider webs, one on top of the other. It was strange to think she had slept in this same cabin when her face was completely smooth. Her whole life had unfolded here; each new decade, a web was etched, one after the other.

He had a photograph of her in her early twenties, sitting on a crate in the unfurnished living room, holding his grandfather's hand. They made a handsome couple, vibrant with youth, their fingers intertwined. He doubted his grandmother had attracted many suitors, though. Underneath her wide smile and bright eyes, his young grandmother had a severity to her, a harshness that would strangle the difficulty in life.

Peyton knew this was a trait men wanted for themselves, not for their women. They wanted their women to need them. Like his mother. She had a helpless air about her.

His grandmother breathed heavily now, her breaths stuffed with the grumble of congestion. Peyton wished he could make her well. He hated seeing her and his grandfather enfeebled. It reminded him they weren't unstoppable; that they wouldn't be around forever. And then it would be him and his mother. He would have to take care of her by himself. No one else would rein her in.

He glanced across the room, and Greta smiled at him shyly on her way out, waving her fingers. When she returned, Margaret, tiny and hunched over, like an emaciated sparrow, leaned on her sturdy arm. Margaret rarely spoke to anyone, and most of the time, she perched near the edge of the woods, staring at the sky.

"You're useless, woman!" Hershel shouted, coming in behind Greta and her mother.

Margaret seemed startled by the commotion, but oblivious to her role in it, as if she were watching a strange man yell at birds on the street.

"Never should have married you," Hershel muttered. He pushed them out of the way, knocking Margaret over. Greta lunged for her mother, barely keeping her up. Peyton frowned. Hershel took another pull of his beer and pounded the kitchen table with his fist.

"Where's this dinner already?" he shouted, burping loudly. His eyes roamed for something to do and settled on Peyton's grandmother, whose mouth was parted by her crumpled breaths. He walked over and tried to close her mouth.

"Leave her alone," Peyton said firmly. The words came out before he could consider whether they were a good idea.

Hershel swung around. "Or what?"

The vein on his forehead was a pulsating blue river, and Peyton swallowed, refusing to back down.

"Pa," Greta called. "The food is ready." Half a chicken and mashed potatoes waited on his plate. Hershel staggered over to his chair, chuckling about something only a drunk could find funny.

Greta made her way around the table quickly, filling the rest of the plates. Adam had snuck over from the corner and he sat fastidiously in his seat. His eyes lowered to the table, and he reached out carefully for his fork.

Chicken grease oiled Hershel's mouth and chin. He ate his half-chicken with his hands, voraciously, ripping off large bites. He paused to take more chugs from his beer.

Peyton suddenly wished he could hit Hershel. He imagined dragging Hershel outside and punching his obnoxious smiling face, until his nose was broken and his blood was splattered on the grass.

Except he couldn't—Hershel towered almost a foot over him, and his body was strong and healthy from years of cutting trees and sanding wood and building cabinets. He would break Peyton with one punch.

Hershel banged his beer can on the table, interrupting the quiet sound of forks scraping plates and chewing. "Greta, get me another beer."

Greta rose, wiping her hands on her apron.

"No!" Hershel said abruptly, waving his hands in the air. "I change my mind," he slurred. "Um, Adam, you do it."

"They're on the porch," Greta said softly, sitting back down.

Adam walked outside, slinking into the darkness, and came back holding a can. Peyton wished he would have kept going, into the woods, and returned late at night, long after Hershel had gone to bed. Peyton held his fork in the air, nervously waiting.

Adam handed the can to Hershel, and Hershel jerked it away, cursing loudly.

Adam's fingers, suspended open in the air, trembled. A small dark pool appeared on the front of his tan shorts, and the pool expanded outwards, flooding the fabric on his crotch and his thighs.

They were all dumbfounded. Peyton would have laughed, but he felt too much tension. Hershel was like a loaded gun.

Adam swiveled his head like a trapped rabbit. He stopped at his father, his expression blank, as if he were waiting for his father to tell him what this meant. Hershel's face was hard and unforgiving, like a brick wall.

Adam squalled and ran outside. The redness on Hershel's face flared brighter, and his eyebrows scrunched together in a bitter mystification, wondering how Adam was his child.

He laughed wildly, and stood up, knocking his chair to the floor. It clanked against the wood.

He moved steadily to the door, and swung it open. He kicked the screen with his boot. Then he was gone, enveloped in darkness.

Peyton leapt out of his seat, and scrambled to catch up.

Hershel had run off the porch and downed Adam at the edge of the field. It was dark outside, almost black, and covered by the canopy of tall trees, Peyton could only see the vague form of their bodies, wrapped together in a heap.

He pulled to a stop above them. Hershel strangled Adam's neck, muttering profanities.

"You little fucking pussy," Hershel said, shaking Adam's whole body, like a willow fluttering in the wind.

Peyton leaned over, putting his mouth near Hershel's ear. "Stop it!" he shouted. He could smell the sour piss growing stronger. "He can't breathe!"

Hershel didn't seem to hear him. "You little fucking pussy!" he grumbled, shaking Adam harder.

Peyton cursed to himself—he loved Hershel, his imaginary father, but he knew he had no choice. Where was Tyler? Margaret? He scrambled on Hershel's back, clasping his arms around Hershel's neck, wrapping his legs around Hershel's waist. Hershel laughed boisterously, his hands still choking Adam. Peyton threw his body back as hard as he could, but he had no leverage. He didn't weigh nearly enough.

Adam's mouth and eyes were sealed shut; the back of his head rose and fell loosely against the wild grass.

Peyton panicked. What if he had stopped breathing? Peyton heard the sounds of footsteps running across the field, and he prayed it was Tyler coming to help.

"Let him go!" Greta called, her tone unusually frantic. "Let him go!"

Enabled by Greta's presence, her need for him to do something, to solve the problem, Peyton stuck his finger in Hershel's eye.

"Fuck," Hershel called, standing up and stumbling backward.

He peeled Peyton's arms off his neck and swatted Peyton's legs loose from his waist, shrugging him off.

Peyton was falling. Time seemed to slow as he waited for the ground. He reached out for Hershel's back, but knew it was of no use. Hershel was too far away. As he fell, he hated Hershel's muscular back, his blue flannel shirt, his light brown hair. He wanted to kill him, and if he had a gun, he would have shot him.

The ground slammed against his body. His back and his legs and his arms. He'd managed to keep his head up, and he gingerly lowered his neck.

His whole body ached.

"You little prick," Hershel said, kicking Peyton's thigh with his steel-toed boots.

Peyton groaned—the pain was sharp and pointed, and his muscles contracted. Peyton wanted to scream, but refused to give Hershel the satisfaction. He clutched his leg and grimaced.

Hershel stared at him rabidly, his hand over his eye, and stormed away, cursing. Peyton's thigh seemed to throb in pain, as if it had acquired a heart of its own. It was excruciating, and for a moment, he couldn't move. All he could process was the pain.

He opened his eyes slowly. The tree branches loomed forty feet above, obscuring the yellow moon, letting in only a faint halo of light. He stared at the glowing halo, and it seemed nice and warm. He waited for the pain to stop. He heard Hershel yell something. The light could take it away, he thought. The light could take it away. He repeated this to himself over and over. He couldn't breathe. He couldn't think. It was just pain. The whole world was pain.

Greta's warm hands were on his shoulder and his forehead, but her touches seemed far away, as if they were merely the memory of sensations.

Why had he done this? Why hadn't he just let it go? Who cared about Adam? What if his leg were crushed and useless? And he lost his only father?

He gripped his thigh tighter, reassured it was solid, but that didn't stop the pain. Fucking Hershel, he thought. He imagined getting his gun and blowing his smug face off.

And finally, inexplicably, the pain subsided.

"Shit," he said, feeling a ditzy, wild relief.

"Thank God," he shouted, sitting up. What luck! He was okay. "That fucking hurt," he said, laughing, suddenly finding the whole world humorous.

Greta smiled at him, kissing him on the cheek. He smiled back at her, and he squeezed her hand.

Adam quietly cried, gasping for air, his slender chest rising and falling in an unnatural and awkward rhythm.

"You shh-sh-shouldn't have done that!" Adam squealed.

"What? Why?"

"You should have let him do it. I don't want to live anyway. I hate my life. I hate everything."

Peyton groaned. "Don't say that. You'll be fine."

Hearing his own words aloud, they struck him as untrue. He had a strong sense that Adam's life would not be fine. That it would be composed of one disappointment after another. Because he was weak, and the world, their world at least, did not tolerate weakness.

Adam kept sobbing, and his sobs were more grating than the pain in Peyton's back and thigh. Peyton realized he hadn't stuttered, not once, when he had made his suicidal declaration. Was that the only thing he could say clearly?

Peyton leaned forward, his head spinning. Greta held Adam's delicate hand between both of hers, letting him sob.

"Adam," Peyton said softly. "Come on, let's finish dinner. You'll be okay."

"I ca-ca-can't," he blubbered. He curled up, taking his hand from Greta and grasping his knees, his eyes on a tree stump.

"Okay," Peyton said, resting his hand on Adam's slender back, feeling his ribs. He and Greta stared at each other over his body, their drawn faces acknowledging it as a dark mass of futility.

Peyton was annoyed he was taking everything lying down. He wasn't even trying.

"Adam…" he said, rubbing his back more vigorously. "You should try…"

Adam did not respond. The Hunger lurched in Peyton's stomach. "I'm going to eat dinner, okay?"

Adam nodded sullenly, his head moving slightly. He mumbled something, but it was lost in his stutter, the words garbled beyond recognition.

Peyton patted his back, and then scratched it like he might scratch a dog's, waiting for Adam's breaths to slow down.

When his breathing seemed normal enough, his thumb in his mouth, Peyton stood up, and wiped himself off. Greta kissed Adam on the cheek, and whispered something in his ear. She stood up and tilted her head to the cabin, a rueful smile on her lips. Peyton limped back to the cabin, dragging his dead weight thigh. He was grateful Greta was by his side, and reached out for her hand.

For once, he hoped his mother would come home late, long after Hershel had gone to bed. Looking at the night sky, its particular shade of black, he figured his grandfather would be home fairly soon. He worried about that too. His grandfather would probably be drunk.

That could be deadly. There would be nothing Peyton could do. A boy couldn't stop two trucks from colliding, no matter how much he wanted to. He hated this about himself. He wished he could will his body to metamorphose into a man's.

On the porch, Peyton and Greta stopped, their fingers still intertwined. He rubbed her hand, and she glanced over at him. They took solace in each other, and for a moment they created their own world. It was a world without mean drunks, or boys made of glass.

Peyton was tempted to stay there, where it was easy, a fire of love and understanding crackling at their feet. But he knew the porch was no place for this, with Hershel not ten feet away, and he withdrew his hand, one finger at a time. As he pushed open the door, he could feel their warmth radiating in his bones.

Hershel was telling a joke about a dumb blonde. After he finished, he laughed loudly, oblivious to the room's cold silence. It didn't really matter what the rest of them thought.

His eyes found Peyton's. His expression was inscrutable. "Where's your little boyfriend?" he said.

Peyton bit his lip, refusing to give in. His whole body ached, and he needed food.

Hershel laughed. Greta glanced at Peyton, her eyes warning him to be careful, telling him he was in the right. He kept her gaze. She seemed to be the only one around here with any sense. She dissolved the hate stiffening in his belly.

Peyton climbed back in his chair, gingerly finishing his food. His back was painfully rigid and he shifted uncomfortably.

The food energized his body; he could feel it healing his muscles.

Margaret smiled at Peyton across the table. "Hi," she said, running her finger over the edge of the table.

"Hi," Peyton returned, glancing at Greta for an explanation. Greta shrugged.

Peyton wondered if Margaret was crazy. She seemed to lack affection for everyone except Greta, who took care of her, leading her everywhere she needed to go.

"When will we have a new house?" she asked, beaming. This was directed at no one in particular.

"Mind your own business, Margaret," Hershel responded, rolling his eyes.

Despite himself, Peyton laughed. He wondered how Margaret could leave Adam outside like that, all alone. Her own son, for goodness sakes.

Hershel pulled out a pack of cigarettes. He took one out and lit it with a match.

"Here you go," he said, handing it to Tyler. Tyler nodded and took a drag. Hershel lit himself another one and sucked on it for a long time. They dipped their ashes on Hershel's empty plate.

"You want one, boy?" he asked Peyton. He stared at Peyton with a grudging respect.

Peyton had inhaled a few times before and it made him nauseous. He shook his head.

"Man, you are such a pussy," Hershel said, smiling and shaking his head. This was said in jest, as if Peyton were his buddy.

Tyler stuck his tongue out at Peyton, and jealousy skated across his eyes.

"Fine," Peyton said, sighing. "Give me one."

Hershel handed him the one he was smoking, inordinately pleased. It tasted like beer and chicken as Peyton inhaled it. It gave him a rush of adrenaline, and his heart beat rapidly, like the wings of a hummingbird.

He hoped his grandfather would come home and kick them out for smoking in the cabin, consequences be damned. He never let Peyton's mother smoke inside. It was the only time his grandfather had whipped her with his belt. Peyton had thrown himself in front of the belt, demanding to take her place. His grandfather let him do it, too. He had the faded back scars to prove it.

They smoked silently, Hershel nursing his beer. Peyton pretended to inhale his cigarette, waiting for it to turn into a stub.

"So Peyton," Hershel said, a petty smile forming on his lips. "Where's your father?"

"He died in Vietnam." He almost added "asshole" but managed to shut his mouth.

"Really?" Hershel said, taken aback.

Tyler's dull eyes lit up. "He was a soldier?"

"Yup," Peyton said, stubbing out the last of his cigarette. "Died in battle."

"Abigail never mentioned that," Hershel said. The pettiness on his face was wiped away by admiration.

"She doesn't like to talk about it," Peyton said. He vaguely sensed, like he might sense a stew cooking in the other room, what he was saying was not true. But because he felt so strongly that it should be true, and because he wanted to screw Hershel's vindictive questions, he ignored this, and plowed ahead. "He died saving his fellow men."

Hershel and Tyler were impressed, their mouths slightly open. "Now that's a real man," Hershel said, putting his cigarette out on the plate. Peyton noticed Hershel's right eye was hemorrhaging red, and he grinned, proud of himself.

"None of these hippy flower boys you hear about. Overeducated pussies, if you ask me."

Tyler nodded, his eyes glistening with condescension.

"Women thinking they can be like men. I'll tell you what. Margaret may be a lazy-good-for-nothing, but she sure knows her place." He laid his palm on the table and Tyler's hand moved to do the same. Margaret glanced over at her name, but her expression of empty satisfaction didn't change. It wasn't clear if she hadn't heard or simply didn't care.

"Well, boys," Hershel said, yawning. "Time for your old man to go to bed."

Startled that Hershel had so casually used the phrase "your old man," Peyton's itch to be somewhere else cooled. Hershel's weathered face transformed from gnarly to that of a rugged cowboy.

This is what it would be like to have a father, he thought.

He shivered slightly. His own pleasure discomfited him.

He leapt at affection like a dog, and it disgusted him—how could he be happy to belong to Hershel? Hershel was a small time bully.

Hershel casually slapped Greta's butt as he walked past her, and this infuriated Peyton. His anger at Hershel and his anger at himself blended together, a bubbling poison in his veins.

Greta didn't alter her efficient motions. Peyton, about to scream, couldn't comprehend her tranquility. But he supposed she had years of training.

Hershel opened his mouth widely and stretched, and then stumbled outside to the outhouse. The cabin seemed to expand, the tension unwinding in every direction like unraveling strings.

Peyton pulled himself out of the chair, his body aching. He was determined to get his grandmother out of the way.

He opened the door to the bedroom and pulled back their scrap quilt. Returning to the living room, he shook his grandmother forcefully.

Her eyelids rose halfway, as if that were all the effort they could muster. She smiled at him gently and let him guide her from her chair. Her knee bones cracked loudly and she leaned against him heavily. She marshaled slow steps and his injured back and lame thigh hurt under the weight. He took shallow breaths and glanced away, refusing to let her know he was in pain.

He helped her in bed, and then slid off her shoes, arranging them neatly next to the dresser. He laid the faded quilt over her body, tucking it under her chin and tugging her two silver braids out from underneath her back. He noticed, then, that the hair on the top of her head had thinned, and the slight glow of baldness saddened him.

For a while, he sat near her on the edge of the bed, quietly singing church hymns and stroking her hand. He didn't know if she could feel any of it, but he found it comforting. He needed a break, and he curled up next to her, laying his head on her stomach, feeling the warmth of her body, wishing he could sleep here. Her stomach had grown soft in the last couple years. Once it had been hard as the head of a hammer.

His grandmother had such a strong heart that simply laying beside her, he felt stronger. It was as if her strength was more contagious than the common cold. She never needled his mother for wearing foolish clothes or for longing to leave West Virginia. She only told her to be honest and make something of herself, her eyes reproaching but never interfering. That was something he could understand—every person had to make their own way.

He remembered when he was younger, long days with his grandmother, weeding and harvesting their crops, sweat drenching their skin, the sun baking his neck. They had rarely spoken but they had moved as one body in cadent harmony.

He kissed her on her soft, wrinkly cheek. "I love you, Mawmaw," he whispered.

When he walked out, Greta had almost finished cleaning the kitchen, and he stood next to her, picking up the dish rag.

"You don't have to do that," she said, moving her hands in quick circles over the wet dishes. The discarded ashes sat on top of the trash.

"I want to," he said, taking a dish from her and drying it. Adam was curled in his cot, the blanket covering his face. "Is Adam okay?"

"He's okay. I took him to the bathroom."

"Good," he said, taking another dish. He tried to imagine what would happen to Greta. She wasn't particularly attractive or smart, but she was plain and hardy, like an ox. She'd make someone a good wife.

"Greta," he said. "You'd make someone a good wife, you know."

She dropped her plate, and it clanked loudly on the counter. "Oh," she said, fluttering her fingers through her hair and then picking the plate back up. A pool of red spilled across her face, and he realized she probably never received compliments from anyone.

"Thank you," she whispered.

He wanted to kiss her, on the cheek or the mouth, he was not sure which.

She handed him the last dish, smiling, and started wiping down the table. He dried the dish and put it back in the stack. He wanted to ask her what she planned to do with herself, but he doubted she thought that far ahead.

She hung up her apron and pointed to the plate on the counter filled with food. "That's Pawpaw's."

He briefly held her hand, clasping it gently and then letting it go.

"Goodnight," she whispered.

She left to the outhouse, and once she was outside, he climbed into his bed. He heard Hershel stumble back in the cabin, banging the door. He knocked into a chair and laughed. He fell in his cot, his boots presumably still on, and started to snore loudly. Peyton was annoyed—the grating snore would keep him trapped in a fitful sleep.

Peyton wished his mother would come home now. She would make everything better. He would tell her what a fool Hershel was and they would laugh and she would stroke his hair.

The bed was too big with only him in. He hated sleeping alone. In January, she was gone for a whole week. She brought back a few pictures of herself in New York City, and he had studied them, searching for the elusive explanation behind her dreams. She was standing near the water, her hands on her hips, the Statue of Liberty in the background; she was on a Ferris wheel, laughing; she was outside the theater, an elaborate red dress draped on her body, a cigarette in her hand. The city was gray and dark, with concrete sidewalks and paved streets. It seemed like a steel cage, devoid of life.

He'd been mad at her for leaving, but she was so bubbling over with pleasure as she told him all she'd done, his anger had washed away.

He peered over at his relatives. Margaret and Greta had crawled in one cot, and Greta's hands were wrapped securely around her mother's waist. Adam curled up like a baby, his hands on his neck. He wheezed lightly. Tyler's body was stiff like a soldier's.

Peyton felt smothered, as if his relatives were pushing him into a shape he didn't want to be. And yet he couldn't wish them away. With all their bumptious deficiencies, they still made him feel like he was a part of something larger than himself, a whole better than the sum of its individual parts.

Later, after he had fallen into a sporadic sleep, the creak of the floorboards woke him up. He opened his eyes, squinting. The outline of his grandfather's body was visible in the glow of a small kitchen lamp. His motions were exaggerated, like a pantomime to God.

This meant he was drunk.

He rummaged around in the cabinet and sat down at the kitchen table. He drank straight from the bottle, taking a long chug and then resting his head in his hands, rubbing his face.

Peyton closed his eyes. His grandfather had gotten no better. He was afraid he never would. He was afraid his friend's death would push his grandfather to an early end.

He was impotent to change this, and he clenched his fists and the sore muscles in his body. There was nothing he could do. He hated God. He hated Him for making his life so difficult.

He scolded himself for this thought. It was wrong to question God, and, anyway, wasn't his lot better than most? He remembered a story his grandmother had told him about her life, long before he or his mother were born. For seventeen years, she had wanted a child, and one morning, she was praying on her knees in front of her bed, asking for a conception, when it came to her as clear as spring water: she was making a mistake.

She had scraped her worn knees on the splintered wood, and her whole heart had fought against God's intentions. Nauseous with envy, she lusted after sweet-smelling babies, and cried every month when she bled.

Gazing straight at her decades of woe, she let go of the baleful desire, untying the elephantine noose around her neck.

From then on, she was free.

"Ya see?" she asked.

"Don't lust after what you can't have?" he offered tentatively.

She nodded, patting him on the back with her sturdy hand. He had believed her story but found it hard to imagine. As long as he'd known her, she had been stoic and steadfast, never complaining or pining after a life not her own.

He reminded himself God had a plan. That he shouldn't long for what God didn't want him to have. God would put him in the right place.

This gave him the strength to open his eyes. His grandfather's head was down on the table, an empty bottle next to his arm. Peyton rose out of his bed and walked over to him.

"Pawpaw," he whispered, shaking his arm. "It's time for bed."

His grandfather jerked, and lifted his head. He hadn't touched his food. His pale blue eyes glanced at Peyton dully. There was no sign of recognition.

Peyton stepped backwards. "Pawpaw?"

His grandfather raised his eyebrows, and tilted his head, trying to place Peyton. He seemed only marginally interested in this task, and he gave up, yawning.

Indignation at his grandfather's indifference rose in Peyton's chest, but it was quickly supplanted by a billowing sorrow. To quell it, he told himself it was only the liquor.

"Time for bed, Pawpaw," he said firmly, his voice sounding stronger than he felt.

His grandfather nodded slightly, still showing no sign of knowing his own grandson. It was only a lack of resistance. He stood up, out of the chair, and Peyton led him to the bedroom, swallowing his fear and focusing on the practical business of getting his grandfather to sleep.

His grandfather paused in front of the bed, cradling the bottle, as if he had never seen his wife, or this room. Peyton waited patiently, sure his exhaustion would win out. After a few minutes, his grandfather climbed into bed, and the bottle rolled to the floor. The dirt from his overalls and shoes spread out over the quilt.

He stared at his grandparents, finding comfort in their faces. His grandfather seemed almost content, and his grandmother's mouth crinkled at the corners, as if she were laughing in her dreams. Peyton wished this wasn't an illusion. He wished they were healthy and happy.

Peyton closed the bedroom door and walked past the sleeping bodies to his bed. He tried to brush off his grandfather's behavior as the liquor's work. He had a feeling his mother wouldn't be coming home tonight. She'd been gone more and more. He pulled the blanket tightly around his body and looked out the window.

Gray clouds covered the thousands of stars, preventing them from lighting up the whole world. Peyton shut his eyes and blew out a long breath of air, imagining he could create a wind so powerful it would dissipate the clouds.

He opened his eyes, and the small, optimistic part of him expected to see an infinite expanse of starlight.

But only endless darkness greeted him.

God has a plan for us all, he thought. He must.

CHAPTER FIVE

Peyton often came home from school, and found a goodbye note on his bed, a yellow piece of paper covered with his mother's sloped letters, misspelled words and lopsided hearts. He curled the note up in a ball and tossed it in the trash.

He didn't trust the cities she visited, with their soaring steel buildings, steam-blowing grates, and armies of beggars. They were giant human mazes, their tight corridors lined with sharp and jagged edges.

Occasionally she left on a weekend, when he was home. Seeing her roll her black bag down the hill one Saturday, he ran to catch up with her, aiming to keep her here.

He asked her to stay.

"Baby," she said softly. "I need to work."

Her blue eyes were like glass, and little pools gathered in their corners.

His need to protect her from unhappiness burned his other feelings up. He hugged her, muttering, "okay," and pressed his cheek against hers.

"That's my boy," she said, running her slender fingers through his hair.

He grabbed the handle of her suitcase and wheeled it for her. They walked down the path, to the road.

A blissful smile settled on her face as she picked a red wildflower and twirled it in her hand. She babbled about them moving to a city soon. It had been "soon" for more years than he could remember. Reality never seemed to interfere with her optimism.

He didn't say anything in response. He was suddenly annoyed at her, and himself, feeling like, for the thousandth time, she had conjured up phony tears to get what she wanted.

Near the big oak, they stopped and waited for her boss. She stood on the edge of the road, wanting to keep her dress and makeup pristine. He sat on a tree stump, and decided to let his annoyance go. There didn't seem to be any point in holding on to it. He told her what he'd been learning in school.

She nodded, encouraging him. He knew she wasn't interested in the information—he used to test his sense she wasn't listening by making contradictory statements, and she had never altered her encouraging smile or registered any confusion. He told her because it pleased her that he knew. When he finished his summary, she ruffled his hair, smiling.

"Keep at it, baby," she said. "You're the one who will get us out of here."

The silver Cadillac stormed up the road, and his mother's face opened up like a flower, basking in sunlight. The car's brakes screeched as it came to a stop, throwing dirt on Peyton's t-shirt.

Her boss, large and boisterous in a blue and white seersucker suit, leaned his head out of the car window. "Hey there kiddo, pile in! We have a flight to catch!"

Peyton rolled the suitcase to the trunk, and Mr. Ramsey handed him the keys.

"That's a good boy," her boss said, reaching over and patting his mother on the thigh. "Just like your mother here. Always on task."

Peyton rolled his eyes as he put the suitcase in the trunk. Mr. Ramsey was full of it, he thought. He slammed the trunk loudly and walked to the passenger side, tossing the keys in through the window. He leaned over and kissed his mother on the head, and her hair was crinkly and hard. She had started using some kind of spray in a can.

"Bye, baby," she cooed.

"Bye."

"You be a good boy, you hear?" Mr. Ramsey said loudly. He reached into his wallet and pulled out a twenty.

"Here you go, son," he said, holding it out to Peyton with a toothy grin.

He was a handsome man, but Peyton thought he looked like clown. Peyton hesitated so briefly no one could have noticed. He didn't want to take Mr. Ramsey's money; but he needed the money. It was simple as that.

He slipped the twenty in his pocket. His mother puffed, smiling proudly. It was a large gift by any measure.

The engine roared on. "You study those books!" Mr. Ramsey guffawed, his hand patting his mother's thigh. "Study 'em good!"

Peyton nodded slightly, his face nettled, but Mr. Ramsey did not bother to register his reaction. Mr. Ramsey was looking in the rearview mirror, his arm around his mother's shoulder.

The car sped down the road in reverse, and his mother waved as her face became smaller and smaller.

When the car dropped down a hill and out of his sight, Peyton sighed. He had cut his palms with his fingernails.

He didn't like Mr. Ramsey. He worried he was losing his mother to a shallow buffoon. She was off working in a foreign, bustling city, and he was here in the woods. He wished she could work at home, for someone better than Mr. Ramsey. Someone with a good head on his shoulders.

Each time she came back from a trip, smiling coyly as she walked up the dirt path in her heels, he ran to her in relief, the frantic part of him that feared losing her soothed. The warmth of her body at night, curled up next to his, made him feel like she would never leave him, especially for someone as foolish as Mr. Ramsey.

But now, when she was departing, her face enraptured and excited, he doubted this. He thought he might lose her after all.

And that would be the worst thing in the world.

* * *

At school, Peyton, Greta and Adam formed a group of three. They pushed their desks into a triangle during study time, and ate their lunches behind the company store. Snide expressions occasionally lit up Adam's face, making it clear he thought the teacher and the other students were incredibly dim. The only time he spoke was when Peyton asked him about school work. Adam's knowledge was extensive, and Peyton peppered him with questions instead of the frazzled teacher. Once he understood Adam's stutter, learning from him was effortless.

Peyton's feelings for Adam altered, as he admired his knowledge and was grateful for it. Learning had never been easier. But he still loathed Adam's insecurity and bitterness, the way he hunched down inside himself, not even raising a defensive hand to a world that sought to beat him.

The other students had shown no interest in them, but at recess one afternoon, four older boys wandered near where they were eating their lunch.

The boys stood about ten feet away, snickering. Adam leaned his head deeper in his book. Peyton continued to listen to Greta, who was talking about their new house, but he stared at the boys in disgust. He didn't care for them, how they thought they were in charge of everyone else. And he wanted them to get lost.

One of them smirked, "What a butch. She looks like a boy!"

The other boys laughed uproariously.

Greta didn't even pause in her sentence. Adam fidgeted nervously, a small peep emitted from his lips.

Peyton stood up and went toward the boy, who cussed, "oh, shit" and sprinted across the street.

Who were they to insult his family? They were dumber than a box of screws.

He chased the boy, tackling his scrawny body against the dirt-packed street. Dirt filled his mouth and he spit it out. He held the boy's neck down with his left hand, and the boy squirmed against him, kicking his ankle.

With his right hand, he punched the boy in the face.

The bone in the boy's nose cracked. Peyton's knuckles hurt and he shook his hand out, standing up. The boy's hands went to his nose, covering it, and he pulled up his knees, moving them back and forth in the air while he moaned.

Blood flowed over the boy's mouth and his pale neck. People yelled and rushed over. The three other boys laughed and pointed.

Peyton stood back, satisfied at the damage.

The teacher squirreled past Peyton and knelt by the boy, aghast. She tilted her head and moaned. She yelled at Peyton sharply, "You go home!"

Peyton glared at the other boys and then ran into the woods, annoyed. He watched the teacher clean off the boy's face with her white handkerchief, pressing it firmly against his nose.

The rest of the kids lingered in the street, whispering to one another. He imagined they were talking shit about him, trying to please the boy. The boy and his three friends were vicious to anyone who refused to go along with their games.

Well, who cares about them anyway, Peyton thought.

He could see Adam sitting underneath the oak tree, hunched over, reading his book. Or pretending to at least.

Peyton turned his head toward the crunch of steady footsteps. Greta walked steadily, holding both their packs. Her face was calm.

"You didn't have to do that," Greta said, offering him his pack. He took both of the packs, and strapped one over each shoulder.

"I know. But he deserved it."

Greta nodded mildly, neither agreeing nor disagreeing. A small smile appeared on her lips. "Let's go home," she said.

He smiled, and they started the long walk back to the cabin. Peyton kept his eye out for small animals and patted the slingshot in his pocket. He was going to get it now. His mother would kill him. Fighting was "uncivilized." For some reason, he thought about the children of his mother's boss, how they'd never be in this mess.

At one of their lunches, Mr. Ramsey had pulled his family's photograph out of his wallet, handing it to Peyton. Mr. Ramsey's hand rested on the shoulder of his doll-like wife, and in front of them stood two girls and two boys, all blonde and blue eyed.

Peyton shared their fair coloring, but in every other way they looked like completely different types of people. Their skin was smooth as a baby's, the boys' collars starched and crisp, the girls' dresses tailored. Their six faces resembled each other's, sharing this feature or that—a long, straight nose, rounded cheeks, almond-shaped blue eyes, generous lips—and with those fine features, they all beamed vaingloriously.

Staring at the photograph, with its near radiation of light, Peyton felt like a dark, shabby mongrel. He would never have this wholeness. His life was fractured and unstable, like a pyramid of mismatched playing cards. Their family photo, if they could ever afford one, would show a wisp of a mother with dark hair and ivory skin, a tall, gangly boy with cropped blonde hair, and a wizened, gray couple, long past their prime. What kind of a family would that be?

One where the mother chased after wild fantasies and the grandparents grew weaker by the day, everyone threatening to leave the boy alone.

He glanced at his mother across the restaurant table, and the corners of her painted-red mouth tugged down and her eyebrows furrowed, as if she too could see the photograph, and knew Mr. Ramsey's family condemned their life.

Peyton tossed the photograph across the table and it landed on his mother's salmon. Mr. Ramsey and his mother both said, "Peyton," their voices reproachful.

His mother picked up the photograph with two fingers and the beautiful faces were smudged with pink juice. Her ivory skin flushed, something Peyton had never seen before. His mother was not a blusher. As she wiped the photograph off with her napkin, her fingers trembled.

Mr. Ramsey's face went hard, and he snapped the photograph out of his mother's hand and slid it back into his wallet.

"You need to learn to respect your elders, boy," he said, throwing down two rumpled twenty-dollar bills. He stalked off, the clean lines of his suit cutting through the air. His motions made it clear he didn't need either one of them.

His mother let out one sob, like an infant's cry, and stood up. She rushed from the table, wiping her eyes as she went. Other patrons glanced over.

Peyton wanted to bark at them, Leave us alone! He was furious—at Mr. Ramsey, at his little family, at his mother.

The whole world.

He grabbed the rest of his steak and a roll, and walked out of the restaurant, avoiding the rich diners' supercilious stares, and as soon as he pushed open the door and felt the sun on his face, he had run to the woods, away from Mr. Ramsey stepping into his silver Cadillac.

Deep in the woods and out of breath, the fury in his body had subsided. He'd been engulfed in the colorful trees with their winding branches and sturdy trunks. The life of the forest—the birds chirping, the squirrels scrambling, a stick crashing to the ground—coursed through his blood. He took a bite of his delicious steak. And Mr. Ramsey and his little family then seemed irrelevant, peculiar people from a make-believe world.

And here he was again, escaping in the woods. He tugged at a branch as he walked. It was strange how the farther he climbed in the forest, the less he cared about Mr. Ramsey's children, and acting "civilized." For a moment, he could see it both ways with a simple tilt of his mind—the children's lives were glowing, envious, comfortable, and then, the children's lives were strange and contrived, wrapped up with pretty shackles.

Only when he was completely enveloped by the trees, the town and the road obstructed from his view, did the children and the stupid boy come to mean nothing to him. He didn't need anything—not that boy, not more food, not nice clothes.

"Let's go swimming!" he called to Greta, over his shoulder.

She stared at him skeptically.

"It'll be fun!"

"Alright…"

"Follow me," he said, running through the woods, to the swimming hole.

66

He jumped over bushes and vines and dodged trees, snapping weak branches and stepping over fallen trunks as the packs swung from his back to his chest. He ignored the lingering pain in his thigh. Greta's breath was heavy and her steps broke the leaves loudly.

When he burst out of the woods, he could no longer hear her—he had left her far behind.

He tossed the packs, ripped off his clothes and jumped in the water, hollering. The cold water chilled his skin and he swam to the center of the large body of water, warming his body through quick strokes. He did a somersault, closing his eyes to keep out the dirt and the insects.

Greta smiled from the shore, her feet bare.

"Come in!" he cried.

"It's too cold."

"You don't even feel it." He waved his arms around and kicked up his feet. "It feels great."

"Close your eyes so I can take off my clothes."

He faced the other direction. "Why can't I see?"

"I don't know. It's not appropriate."

Appropriate, he thought. He hated that word. It was his mother's second favorite word, after civilized. They seemed to mean the same thing. He heard Greta's clothes hit the ground and he thought of turning around so he could see her body. He was curious. He hadn't seen his mother naked in a long time.

When she reached him in the water, he threw his hands against the water's hard surface, sending a wave up to her face.

"Hey," she said, smiling and splashing him back.

The water burst up from their pounding fists, like fireworks, until he swam behind her and put his arms around her neck, feeling her body against his own. He pushed her down.

She wriggled underneath the water and swam forward, kicking him in the stomach.

He smiled, thinking, good one, as he propelled himself backwards and floated to the shore.

When his hand hit the ground, he climbed out of the water. He scrambled up the oak tree, unhooked the fraying rope and walked a few steps forward on its long arm. Greta was treading, the rise of her breasts barely visible in the murky brown water.

"Here I come!" he called. She paddled away from the center as he ran a few steps and leapt into the air, his hands clinging to the rope.

Letting go, he fell fast, his stomach flipping in exhilaration. When he smacked the water, it rushed up to greet him and pull him down.

Everything was dark and murky. He reached his hand out, and thought about the fish and the crabs and the insects and the slime, how they had a whole world down here, where they lived and died. A world he couldn't breathe in.

He popped up, spitting out the dirty water. Greta smiled at him.

"You should do it," he said, grinning back at her deviously. He didn't think she would. It wasn't in her nature.

She looked up at the thick rope. "I don't know."

"You'd love it," he cajoled, seeing an opening. "It's great, Greta."

To Peyton's surprise, she nodded and walked out of the water, taking the rope with her. Her pale bottom was wide and rectangular. As she turned and touched the tree, he saw her breasts were large, but also close to her body, as if God had flattened her between his hands. He suddenly desired her, a complicated urge that ran the gamut of wanting to protect her, slap her on the back, and push her body violently close to his own.

She stood on the branch, and a pelt of black hair spread out beneath her tummy. He swam out of the way.

She was like a statue, unmoving, her face locked in a thoughtful gaze. He didn't call out to her. He wanted to know what she would do.

She took a step backwards, and rested her hand on the trunk. He thought she would come back down, but she didn't move. She just stood there. He liked looking at her, seeing the gentle round of her belly, the wideness of her thighs, the broadness of her chest. Her weight shifted, then, and she ran forward, her feet calmly crossing the branch and leaping into the sky.

She flew through open air, her body wrapped around the rope.

He smiled as her eyes looked down in fear, and her mouth opened. She shrieked, but she still let go of the rope. Her shriek was only silenced by the water.

Waves rippled out from where she landed.

Her head rose up, and she gasped for water. "I didn't think I would do it," she said, laughing, her words spilling out eagerly. "I thought I'd chicken out."

He smiled at her, paddling over and wishing he could keep her this way, almost euphoric.

"Come on," he said, pointing to the rocks on the other side of the hole. "Let's rest."

They reached the rocks at the same time, and Greta smiled and took a deep breath. The expression on her face was still incredulous and pleased. They climbed out of the water and spread their limbs out luxuriously.

"That felt good," she said, stretching her arms and legs.

"Yeah," he said. "It feels like a million years ago I punched that boy."

She laughed. "Nobody's ever done that for me. It was pretty neat."

He smiled. He felt good and strong. His feelings for her were brotherly, but they were lined, in a confusing way, with his budding sexual desires. "I'll always protect you," he boasted.

He laid his hand on top of hers and closed his eyes. They let the afternoon sun dry out their bodies, like a warm blanket. Her hand was soft beneath his and he drifted to sleep, content.

When he opened his eyes, the sun had dipped lower in the sky, and he stretched, feeling full of energy. Greta was still sleeping. Her face had eased from its guarded pose and it appeared open, innocent almost. Her large breasts drooped lazily to the side.

The pelt between her legs contained a mountain of curly hairs and he patted it gently, finding the texture abrasive, like a brillo pad. He leaned in to smell it—it was yeasty, like uncooked bread.

A bird squawked and he startled. He laughed quietly, backing away from her.

He scrambled off the rock and pulled his clothes back on. He found a couple of good stones near the water, and putting them in his pocket, ventured into the woods.

When he came back, Greta was in the same place. He hunched over near the edge of the water, tossing pebbles to the center, and watched her naked body, its expansive whiteness contrasting with the gray stone and dirty brown water. He imagined tying her up and inspecting her parts.

She sat up, and he smiled, wondering if his fantasy had somehow caused her to rise. She yawned.

"Hey," he said, striding over.

She smiled shyly, covering her chest with her forearms as she walked around the edge of the swimming hole to her clothes. She put them on, eyes down.

"How long was I sleeping?"

"I don't know. A couple hours."

"Oh…" She frowned as she pulled on her practical shoes. "We should probably get home."

He nodded. As they moved silently through the woods, Greta's sturdiness returned, her eyebrows and lips straight, her motions marking sharp lines. He'd never tell her, but it was how he imagined the Nazis walked. This didn't deter his affection for her, though. He thought her austerity was endearing: it was competent and functional.

Peyton wondered if his mother would come home from work already knowing about his punch. She would cry, How can you do this to me? How will we get out of here if you are acting so uncivilized? She'd tremble and shake her slender fists, and he'd grow hard and distant, wanting to yell, Leave me alone! You don't understand anything!

Peyton thought about camping for a few days. When he came back the whole thing would have blown over, his mother distracted by her own affairs. Yes, he decided, that's what he'd do.

* * *

Hershel took Peyton and Tyler in the truck and showed them their new house. It had four bedrooms and a wrap-around porch, electricity, and three toilets.

"It's a beauty, don't you boys think?" Hershel asked as they idled in the truck, about to leave.

"Yes, sir," Peyton said, his head leaning out the window, his hand knocking the side of the truck. He'd miss the truck's speed and power; he hated the idea of going back to his mother's clunker.

Driving back the twenty miles, over the ridges, Peyton hoped the house wouldn't ever be finished. He was suddenly moody and lonely.

He fantasized about enrolling in the Army, like he imagined his own father had done. He'd heard if you were big you could join up when you were sixteen, as long as you lied about your age. Even though his mother wouldn't like it, he wanted to do it. "Chh-chh-chhh." He'd shoot up the commies, just like his grandfather had shot up the Nazis.

Peyton liked having plans with his relatives stretching out, as if it would keep them here. Greta agreed to pick raspberries from their thorny brambles, and Adam promised to teach him the rest of his algebra book. Even Margaret nodded when he suggested they take a trip to the river when it was hot. He clung to all these plans, the irrational part of him believing if he could only arrange enough of them, the family would be tied down here.

The rational part of him, however, knew they were leaving soon. Hershel and Tyler took more trips to their house, gone for days at a time, fixing up the final details—the light fixtures, the paint, paving the driveway.

Peyton grew quieter, and more withdrawn, exhuming his old anger, and using it to harden himself against the family. He wasn't mean, exactly, but he pulled away. He got back to hunting and trapping. He might as well get used to, he figured, since all the meat would be gone soon, too.

It wasn't really a surprise when, a few weeks later, Hershel and Tyler pounded up the steps early Saturday morning, laughing and talking boisterously.

"Moving day!" Hershel shouted.

Despite all his work steeling himself against this, Peyton wanted to scream out, No! Please, don't leave!

They were abandoning him: that was all he could think.

He frowned as his mother climbed out of bed, sliding her feet into her cotton slippers. She put on the kettle.

"You guys are finally heading out?" she asked Hershel, smiling. "I thought you'd about moved in."

Hershel grinned, lugging a bag of clothes over his shoulder. "Well, it's hard to leave when we have such beautiful women around."

His mother laughed, and the morning light played off her blue eyes.

Greta climbed out of her cot and quickly dressed, facing the wall. Peyton stared at her white back, one horizontal crease in the middle, realizing it might be the last time he would see it. She reached under her cot and pulled out her bag. She smiled at him tenderly; her adoration had not been deterred by his recent distance.

He glanced away, embarrassed, not wanting her to see how much he wanted her to stay.

Peyton decided to go hunting, and changed his clothes, and put bullets in his pocket. On the porch, Peyton jammed his feet in his tight hiking boots. Greta walked past carrying her and her mother's bags, and he watched her go, her frame growing smaller until the woods swallowed her whole.

"Peyton," his mother called, standing near the door. "You need to stay here."

"Why?"

"It's civilized to see people off when they're leaving. Now, take your shoes off and come back inside."

He sighed and stepped out of his boots, stomping over to his bed. He pulled out his Hardy Boys book.

71

His mother was sitting at the table, flipping through one of her weird glossy magazines, with large photographs of skeletal women wearing nonfunctional clothes. Margaret hadn't moved from her cot. Peyton tried to read, but he found it hard to concentrate, and he went over the same sentence many times. He felt like he had been dumped in an oily pit of despair, and if he didn't keep pumping and kicking furiously to stay afloat, he would drown. The Hardy Boys were of little relevance to this endeavor.

Hershel yelled loudly outside. His mother made an O with her mouth, and swung open the door. Peyton scrambled after her, hoping Hershel's screams would somehow change the course of events.

"I don't fucking care!" Hershel shouted.

Adam sat on the ground, his eyes on his lap.

"Hershel," his mother said sweetly. "What's the problem here?"

"Adam is wasting my time."

Adam looked up at Peyton's mother, his eyes desperate, and his face seemed sticky. "I wwww-ant to st-st-tay here," he explained weakly.

Peyton's mother stared at Adam for a while, trying to figure something out. She put her hand on her chin. "Hershel," she said. "You could let the boy stay. It would be good for Peyton."

Peyton didn't see how it would be. Adam was the last person he needed to stay. He was annoyed Adam was the only one who had tried.

Hershel considered this. "If you want to send Peyton with me for a couple months, then I'll switch you."

Adam sobbed.

"Peyton has to finish school here," his mother said. "But Adam would be moving to a new school anyway."

"I'm not leaving him here," Hershel said, waving his hand dismissively. "Adam, if you don't pack your things right now… One, two—"

Adam rose up slowly and walked to the cabin, dragging his feet. They followed him in. He reached underneath his cot for his suitcase. He shoved his clothes and books in it.

His mother walked over and ruffled his hair.

"Here," she said softly. "Let me help you with that." She started folding his shirts and pants. Peyton walked to his bed, not wanting to witness his mother baby Adam.

He didn't want to say goodbye. It was too hard. This was the only real family he'd ever had.

He snuck out on the porch, while his mother wasn't minding him, and pulled on his shoes, and grabbed his gun and more bullets.

Once he was in the woods, he ran as fast he could down the mountain. He found a thick, fallen tree about forty feet from the trail, and slid in the dirt and peered over the trunk. He loaded his gun and pointed it at the trail. When Tyler ran past, he pretended to shoot him, "Ch-chhh-chhh." He smeared mud under his eyes and on his forehead for camouflage.

Greta walked by, her sturdy arms clipping through the air, and he shot a tree ten feet up the trail. His ears rang. She jumped, holding her chest, surveying the woods, her face in its rigid lines. Her eyes passed right over his shock of blond hair.

She resumed walking up the trail, efficient as ever. Damn it, he thought, that was a mild reaction. He sat up against the tree, and once he made sure the path was clear, he ran deeper into the woods.

"Goodbye, family," he whispered.

He returned to the cabin late that night, when the fort he'd built during the day had grown too cold. The cabin was dark. He opened the door slowly, half-expecting to see the cots filled with sleeping bodies.

The room was empty except for his mother, curled up in bed and facing the wall. Only the cots and two boxes of Adam's books remained. Peyton flipped through the books, reading their titles by the light of the full moon. Some of them were splattered with red splotches, and he wondered if Adam had made a feeble attempt to keep them, or if they were just old and stained.

Peyton plopped down on the cot, and stared at the wood ceiling he had repaired so many times.

The whole universe felt empty.

Somehow he knew this cot was his new bed. The era of his childhood was over. He would be in charge now, and a man couldn't very well sleep with his mother. He closed his eyes, and imagined himself running through the woods, up and down mountainsides, never getting tired.

CHAPTER SIX

A few years later, Peyton remembered the family fondly. Their flaws had grown soft as he no longer encountered their sharp edges, and the period in which they lived in the cabin came to seem idyllic. He was fiercely loyal to them, conceiving them as an essential part of his family. This was true even though he had never seen them again.

Right when Peyton and his mother were about to leave West Virginia in her boyfriend Cliff's Dodge, they received a wedding invitation for Greta's wedding. His mother decided they would drive to the wedding on their way out.

Their "soon" had finally come.

Peyton was glad to be leaving even if he revolted at the thought of their destination, a city with industrial air and concrete streets. His mother couldn't wait. Peyton was sure his mother had started dating Cliff solely because he had talked about moving back to Boston, near his family.

Two years before, the coal company had drastically cut jobs, and there had been a mass exodus out of Lamar County. His mother was gutted by her boss' departure, as if he were somehow packing her life in his moving truck, and leaving her body behind, in Lamar County, to suffer without it.

Mr. Ramsey had come to the cabin one night, when his grandfather was working his last shift, and his mother sent Peyton away so she could talk to him privately. Peyton glared at Mr. Ramsey as he walked outside. He stood on the porch and pressed his ear up against the door.

His mother yelled, sobbing, "How can you leave me here in this hellhole? You told me you'd leave Sarah!"

Mr. Ramsey apologized over and over, repeating the same explanation. "I can't, Abigail. I have four kids. I can't do that to them. I'm sorry."

As they carried on, Peyton wanted to charge in and punch Mr. Ramsey. But he knew it would only turn his mother against him and so he waited, furious. He couldn't believe his mother had been sleeping with Mr. Ramsey. Of all the men in Lamar County, why him? He might have been wealthy, but he was a fool. And a married one, at that.

The argument suddenly stopped, and the cabin was quiet. He heard the light sound of shoes coming off and clothes hitting the wood floor, and then, their bodies falling heavily to her bed. Peyton ran into the woods as fast as he could, disgusted they were making love on the bed he'd slept on for eleven years. That was his and his mother's bed, for goodness sakes.

In the woods, Peyton scoured his memories of Mr. Ramsey and his mother. They now had brown and mushy insides. It was foul. The way Mr. Ramsey rolled in and out at his convenience, smiling at her like she was his good, eager puppy, giving her a broken down truck and cheap nylon dresses and a thin gold necklace. That was all pocket change to him. He'd given his mother the scraps of his life: scraps of his time, scraps of his money, and scraps of his love.

Peyton decided he would kill Mr. Ramsey if he ever laid eyes on him.

When he returned, hours later, she was sleeping alone, naked underneath the sheets, her makeup smeared across her face.

She looked beautiful and broken, like a shattered piece of china. He wondered if his mother had believed, pathetically, sex would change Mr. Ramsey's mind. And he had only wanted one last fuck before he returned to his old, prissy wife. This made Peyton so sick he indulged a fantasy of getting his gun and running into the hills and blowing Mr. Ramsey's face off.

Instead, he climbed into bed, trying to ignore the smells Mr. Ramsey had left behind, and nestled against his mother's body. They hadn't slept in the same bed in years, but he fell asleep quickly, her body as natural to him as his own.

His mother was listless for months, complaining about Mr. Ramsey half-heartedly, and sobbing every night into Peyton's shirt. "You're all I have, baby, all I have," she hiccuped between sobs, and he stroked her hair, feeling at once special and pissed off. He was angry with her for having an affair with Mr. Ramsey; he was angry at Mr. Ramsey for not leaving his wife.

But Peyton knew part of him, the selfish part, liked having his mother away from Mr. Ramsey and the stupid life he offered. He didn't want to live in a colossal mausoleum, with a lonely wing to himself; he didn't want four haughty step-siblings who would close ranks against him.

The coal company's scaling back to a skeletal structure forced his grandfather into an early retirement, and the four of them had to live on his meager pension and his grandmother's erratic quilt sales. Rather than refresh his grandfather's old body, the lack of work seemed to depress him further, allowing him to stay in bed for days at a time.

His grandfather hacked up large coughs and urinated constantly. The field in front of their house was covered with lines of dead grass, as his grandfather could no longer reach the outhouse.

His rapid decline did not stop his grandfather from yelling at his mother for her sins, and his rants took on a more desperate edge, as if he felt any words he spoke might be his last. He wagged his bent finger at her, saying she was too old for carousing and demanding to know when she was going to settle down.

His mother softened to her father as he became more fragile, and more often than not, she nodded, kissing his finger and assuring him she would.

But no one believed that. After six months of crying over Mr. Ramsey, she had woken up one morning, put on her finest dress, and announced she was going out. His mother was like that—everything in her life had to be the best, or the worst. Either she was dying of a broken heart, or on her way to the luxury of a big city.

"I can't believe I fawned over him. Why would I want someone that old?" she exclaimed. "And at night, he'd spray these nasty farts over the room." She shook her head. "He thought he was so civilized."

She spilled vivid depictions of Mr. Ramsey's foibles, and Peyton laughed, not really caring if she was exaggerating. The pompous man in his memory grew larger, picking up flaws like a man running through a field of brambles, and eventually he formed into a pathetic, bumbling moron. His image became so hapless, Peyton almost felt sorry for him.

His mother stayed out late at night, and worried, he would run to the pub, his grandfather's headlamp illuminating the woods. Like the rest of the town, the pub was largely empty. He would find her in the corner, smoking a cigarette with a man, or dancing in front of the bar, a couple men pressed up against her, while a few others watched.

She was drunk and she laughed when she saw him, squealing his name delightfully. The men, young mineworkers and the occasional old man in a suit, grunted, knowing he would end their fun. They all, Peyton noted, wore wedding rings.

Back in the cabin, after one of the men had driven them home, he asked her why she hadn't learned her lesson. What was the point of seeing married men? She giggled and said it was only for fun, until they could leave this place.

He had groaned in frustration—her whole life seemed to swirl around a misapprehension. It was as if she had seen a flickering will-o'-the-wisp in the distance, and stood idly on the shore, transfixed by its warm glow. She was convinced she would inevitably join in it, despite no means to navigate the cold waters, or any real understanding of what it was.

Peyton couldn't imagine living in any other place. The rise and fall of the mountains and the whole world that thrived on their surfaces was as much a part of him as his blood. But he too longed for other people. The one-room school had dwindled to eleven students, and the teachers, now sent by the federal government, never stayed longer than a year. They were miserable, staring at the clock, waiting for the day, and the year, to end. The students ran around them wildly, squealing and playing games.

As the teachers tutored those struggling to read, and nervously stared out the window, as if they were waiting for a car to drive up and take them away, Peyton took charge of his own studies. He convinced the teachers to order more books, updating the school's pitiful library, and he pummeled through them. He liked the straightforwardness of education; it came so easy to him, and as he accumulated more knowledge, the world expanded.

What he saw with his eyes was only a fraction of what existed. Everything around him had a story longer than time. He liked knowing why trees died, why the sun rose and fell on different horizons, why water froze, and the history of the land he walked on, from the empty universe, to the glaciers shifting before human time, to the Indians running free, and, finally, to the battle over the soul of young Virginia.

Yet, the more he knew, the stupider and more tedious the people around him seemed, and he developed an acute sense of resentment, which he blew off by fighting and chasing girls.

His childhood desire to have girls dote on him had grown into an adolescent desire to devour them. They remained a curiosity, and he forgave them their flaws at least until he'd gone through them. Every time he had a girl, he felt like he was getting away with something. It didn't matter to him, so much, whether the girl was pretty or not.

Almost every girl had something worth looking at, and advice Tyler had once given him turned out to be true: the plainer the girl, the easier she was. The prettiest ones were a hassle. The prettiest girl he had been with—an elegant redhead with milky white skin and green eyes—had slapped him and sent her brothers to beat him up. Her brothers had given him a black eye and two scars on his knuckles. He'd given them more back, and they'd left saying he was fucking crazy.

The night before they were leaving West Virginia, it was hot and humid. Their few things were packed up in cardboard boxes. His grandfather had refused to talk to his mother at dinner, except to ask why she wasn't marrying this fellow she was running off with. "God damn it, Abigail," he muttered. His mother promised she'd get married when they got to Boston, but his grandfather only nodded gruffly, doubting her words. Peyton didn't believe her either. She didn't like Cliff very much, let alone love him. She made faces when Cliff talked and when he wasn't around, she mocked his Boston accent, disdain lighting up her eyes.

His mother had gone to sleep early, telling Cliff she needed to rest for the wedding, and Peyton wandered in the woods alone as the sun set. Incredulous he was leaving the mountains, the summer woods, full of growth and life, took on a particularly clear air as he saw it with deprived eyes. Surrounded by the leaves, branches and vines, which reached across his face as he walked through the woods, he was calm.

At the same time most of the coal people had left town, a few vacation homes sprung up on the mountainside. Peyton initially hated them, seeing them as interlopers, but then he realized the homes were rarely occupied. He'd taken over the houses, climbing in through the unlocked windows. He had sex in their beds, enjoyed their soft sheets; he read their books, drank their wine, and slid across their shiny wood floors in his socks; he played their stereos and, when he was drunk, stared mystically at their abstract paintings.

He walked over a ridge and saw an architectural monstrosity with green plastic siding and floor-to-ceiling windows. The interior lights were bright, and the house was a glowing cube in the darkness of night.

A group of teenagers lounged in the living room. Wine bottles and glasses covered the surfaces. Their motions were loose and their clothes were stiff. They were like the teenagers he had seen in magazine advertisements, the ones gleefully drinking Coke on the beach. Their hair was in place, the girls' makeup was perfectly drawn. He couldn't identify exactly what it was: they just looked clean. He imagined himself inside, scrubbed and coifed; he wondered if they would have anything to say to each other, or if their differences ran much deeper than the dirt on his skin.

Walking to the other side of the house, he found two convertibles, with their tops down, parked haphazardly. He wished the keys were in the car so he could take one for a spin. The backdoor opened and the teenagers spilled out onto the deck, laughing loudly. Peyton scrambled against the side of the house.

"Cindy, you better be careful. Hicks are hiding in the woods," one of the boys said, laughing.

"Shut up," the girl squeaked jovially.

"No, really, last year a prep school girl was found dead in these woods."

"That's not funny," she said, with an edge to her voice. "Anyway, you'll protect me, won't you?"

"These hicks have guns to catch their dinners. There's nothing I can do about that."

"John," the other girl reprimanded. "Cindy, this place is completely safe."

Peyton peered around the edge to see the other girl. She was smoking a cigarette, and she leaned over the rail, her butt wagging gently in the air, an upside-down heart in tight white slacks. The other boy put his hand on her butt.

"Cut it out, Tom," she snapped.

"You're sticking it out, what do you think is going to happen?"

She snorted. "Hey, let's go swimming in the lake," she said.

"But it's dark," Cindy whined.

"Don't be a baby," Tom said.

Peyton imagined Tom was hoping to see the girls naked. After more protests by Cindy, the four of them grabbed towels and walked into the woods, their two giant flashlights marking their path. Peyton knew the swimming hole they were going to. It wasn't that far. Once they'd cleared the ridge, Peyton walked inside their house. He picked up an open bottle of red wine—Chateau Montrose—and took a long drink. It tasted weak and left his mouth feeling dry.

In the bedroom, he ruffled through a boy's leather duffel bag. The leather itself was beautiful—deep brown and soft to the touch. He found a silver flask, inscribed with the letters T.S.H, III, and put it in his pocket. He snickered when he imagined the boy demanding to know what happened to it, accusing the girl of taking it.

Underneath the boy's plaid underwear, he felt a thick wallet. Peyton couldn't believe his good luck. Rifling through it, he studied the boy's driver's license—Thomas Stewart Harrison, III, a big nose, a flash of light blond hair, and an arrogant smile. It was as if he were saying, "Yeah, that's right. I am the shit."

What a prick, Peyton thought. He took out three twenties, leaving Thomas Stewart The Third a five and a one.

That would go a long way, he said to himself, pleased.

He drank more of the wine, and looked in the girl's suitcase, a hard, green box. Her clothes were folded neatly, in bright colors, and he rifled through them. Inside another, smaller box were rows of makeup, and tangled piles of jewelry. He unthreaded a gold necklace with a dangling heart.

It seemed expensive. He debated taking it for his mother. With another long swig of wine, he dropped it in his front pocket. The girl had plenty more. He put the wine bottle down and carefully repacked her suitcase.

In the living room, he finished off the bottle and left it on the counter, puckering his mouth in disgust. In the bright lights, he suddenly felt exposed. Maybe they had come back and were watching him from the woods.

He hustled outside, and was relieved he couldn't hear anybody. He was light-headed from the wine and walked in the direction of the swimming hole. It was stupid to risk running into them, but he found himself drawn there, wanting to know what they were doing. As he approached the swimming hole, he softened his step and quieted his breathing.

They were splashing, the girls letting out high-pitched screams. He felt a rush of envy—he still had no real friends of his own, only a boy he got drunk with, and the girls he fucked.

Peering from behind a thick oak, he saw they were all in their underwear. He watched Cindy's white breasts bounce in the water. She kept squealing and laughing as the boy doused her; her blonde curls flattening. The flashlights were pointed upward, sitting on dry ground, illuminating the hanging tree branches.

Peyton saw their clothes in a pile, wanting to steal them and run off, forcing them to traipse through the woods in their underwear. He wondered how close he could get without them noticing. They seemed oblivious, consumed wholly with themselves. He walked swiftly around the swimming hole, making a large loop, and stood at the edge of the wood.

Tom demanded the girls climb on their shoulders so they could have a water fight. Peyton stepped back into the woods as they moved to shallower waters. Cindy squeaked as she got up on the boy's shoulder, and the other girl climbed up easily, slapping Tom's hand when he grabbed her butt.

"Relax, babe."

They teetered into deeper water, and Cindy and the girl tried to knock each other over, as the boys moved back and forth. Cindy was still squealing, and Peyton knew he could grab the clothes, but he was mesmerized by the two girls in their wet underwear. It made him jealous, but it also satiated him, especially Cindy, with her voluptuous hips and breasts.

The girl toppled Cindy, who slapped the water, back first, screaming. Peyton smiled. Cindy came back up spurting, while the rest of them laughed. The other girl climbed down.

"Ewww," Cindy said. "This water is dirty!"

"Of course it is," the boy said. "It's a lake, not a pool."

"It isn't a lake, idiot," Peyton muttered, moving farther back into the woods.

"Will you get me my towel?" she asked, pouting, her lower lip sticking out.

"Why don't you get it?" the boy smirked, paddling to the center of the swimming hole.

"Oh, I'll get it, Cindy," the other girl said, exasperated, walking out of the water. Peyton could see her ribs. Her bra seemed decorative, rather than supportive. She leaned down and picked up the towel, and on her way back up, her eyes met Peyton's.

She stopped mid-motion.

He smiled, feeling guilty, and her lip twitched left, and then she smiled too. She wiped herself off with her towel, still smiling at him. Then she turned away, and handed a towel to Cindy, who waited in the water.

"Thanks," Cindy giggled, sticking her tongue out at the boy, who stuck his out back.

The brown-haired girl turned to Peyton, and cocked her head, smiling at him curiously. He smiled, almost laughing, feeling foolish for being caught. He backed up a few steps, and then took off running.

Once he cleared a few ridges, he stopped, and laughed. He pulled out the gold necklace, dangling it in the moonlight. He decided to give it to Greta. It would be too small around her sturdy neck, but she'd love it. Knowing Hershel, it would be the nicest thing she owned.

After he walked for a bit, anger and jealousy leapt upon him, and he was suddenly sure the girl had been mocking him. Hick. He imagined running back and setting their house on fire. They'd come out, covered in smoke, screaming, and watch impotently as it burned to the ground.

Peyton cursed at God, telling him He'd created a twisted society, giving riches to buffoons like Tom the Third, and peas to good people like his grandparents. And for what? So Tom the Third could drive a shiny red convertible, and his grandparents could die an early death.

Peyton wished he had his gun. He wanted to kill something, stop it in its tracks.

"You suck!" he shouted, imagining a large body floating indifferently in the sky.

He's indifferent because he doesn't exist, Peyton chided himself.

Peyton's belief in God was one long string of empty lights. When he was young, the bulbs had emanated a strong glow, illuminating his path forward. Then the bulbs had exploded under the weight of his life, and his anger and fury, and patches of darkness appeared, the string gradually growing dimmer. Until one day, without him even noticing, it went dark.

He no longer believed in anything. He still carried the string, wishing he could relight the bulbs. He wished he could believe in a master plan, where justice would ultimately prevail, and people's flagrant and selfish wrongs would disintegrate in the brutal fires of Hell. But he didn't.

Peyton picked up a stick, and thrashed it against tree branches and shrubs. He could barely see. The trees created a dense canopy and moonlight only occasionally peeked through. An owl hooted loudly. After endless hacking, Peyton found himself in front of the Harrison cabin. The lights were out, and their chickens rustled noisily in the coop.

Heidi slept in a lean-to behind the house. She moved out after the birth of her sixth sibling. She was five years older than Peyton and the first girl he'd been with. From here, at the edge of their cleared land, he could see the shape of her body in her bed. Heidi was chubby, with rounded cheeks and the gentle start of a second chin, and she blushed whenever someone paid her any attention. As far as Peyton could tell, she was stupid, having left school at fourteen, but he couldn't be sure since she hardly spoke. He walked up to her bed, and gently shook her shoulder.

"Heidi," he whispered.

She opened her eyes, confused. When she woke up, he could see her face turning red, and he watched the color spread over her neck and ears like spilled water.

"Come with me," he said.

She smiled and nodded. Hunched over, she put on her tennis shoes. She was wearing cloth pants and a t-shirt and as she walked, her breasts flapped loosely, like sacks of oats. He was still angry, and he kept walking until they were far into the woods. She hugged herself, looking at him nervously, waiting for him to tell her what to do.

"Hey…" she said.

He smiled at her, but he knew it was a sinister smile because he was pissed off—his head was pounding and he wanted to hit somebody. She smiled back dumbly, tucking one strand of her straggly hair behind her ear.

He had a great urge to be violent—to slam her body to the ground, and pound her until he was empty—and as he touched her, he didn't trust his own hands. He was so furious, he felt as if the slightest wind would cause his grip to turn tighter until she was on the ground, grasping for air.

It was as if she had caused all of the injustice in the world, and if he could just smother her, the world would be set right. His fingers played around her neck, and he moved them down to her waist, where he'd do less damage.

She let him kiss her, but that wasn't what he wanted. He pushed her to the ground and she fell with a loud thump.

"Hey," she said, sitting up and rubbing her backside.

She looked like such a dumb cow, sitting their blankly, her face about to cry. He straddled her and pushed her back to the ground and kissed her. She kissed back in her sloppy way—sucking his lips—and her hands and legs wrapped around his back.

Caught in her sloppy, foolish grip, he was suddenly disgusted. He pulled away, and rolled over onto the ground.

"What's wrong?" she asked.

"I don't know," he said, feeling confused and still angry. "I'm sorry," he added, without much feeling.

"Oh," she said.

He stood up, and offered her a hand. She came up slowly, and he pressed her pudgy body against his.

"Don't you want to lay together?" she asked shyly.

"Heidi, go to bed, okay?" he said, feeling a strong urge to protect her against himself.

Go, go, he wanted to shout, get out of here.

"Okay," she said, her blush coming back quickly, spreading over her face, her features contorted in shame.

She frowned and walked toward her house. Watching her chubby figure move down the path, he was tempted to run after her, and throw her to the ground, this time holding nothing back. He clenched his fists until his palms bled; he concentrated on the fact that Heidi was helpless, and that she was not the source of his barely controllable anger, which was rising up in his throat, demanding to be let out. He didn't care if it was her fault; he wanted to pummel her; he wanted to pummel something to death.

He willed himself to leave, and took off running. He ran as fast as he could, his face and arms scratching against branches and vines. He smacked into a trunk, twice, and stumbled away, his forehead bleeding and bruised.

When he got back to the cabin, he was soaked in sweat. Out of breath, he laid down in the wild grass, wanting to scream. The moon was almost full and out from the woods, he could see it clearly—the old man's calm face. He was exhausted and his head ached, but his anger hadn't disappeared, and his descent into darkness was interrupted by images of the brown-haired girl laughing at him, saying matter-of-factly, "Hick." In his mind, he slapped her, throwing her to the ground, but she just laughed at him, finding him more pathetic each time he hit her. With a final punch, she fell silent, the life beaten out of her.

Only then did he fall asleep.

* * *

He woke up to his mother calling his name. The sun was bright and his skin was hot. He was amazed he had not woken up earlier.

Stretching and standing up, he smiled. His mother's hair was up in a bun and her body was covered in a silky emerald dress with a bow front and center. It struck him as ridiculous, yet beautiful in a strange way.

"We have to go, baby," she said. "What in the world happened to your forehead?"

His fingers felt dried blood. And then, as if she had no time for crusty foreheads, she cooed, "Help me move these boxes."

"I'm hungry," he said.

"Don't worry about it. There will be plenty of food to eat at the wedding."

He yawned and walked over and grabbed the biggest box. She carried the smallest one and he was back from the end of the road by the time she'd made it a quarter of the way down, walking daintily in her heels.

He went back to the cabin and drank a large glass of milk. He had a light headache and remembering the wine, he reached in his pocket. He found the crisp twenties and the delicate, gold necklace. It made him giddy. He hadn't had so much money in a long time.

The bedroom door was closed, and he could hear his grandfather's snores. Peyton put his hand against their door gently, wishing them well. He had a feeling he'd never see them again, and last night, when he'd said goodbye, he'd found himself embarrassingly fighting off tears. He put his cheek against the wood, remembering his grandfather teaching him to make snares and clean a gun in his firm, taciturn way, and sitting in his grandmother's broad, sturdy lap, as she told him everything was going to be okay.

Peyton took a washcloth out of the sink, and cleaned off his forehead. He tossed the cloth in the hamper. He picked up the final two boxes and carried them down the trail. His mother was sitting on the large box, her legs crossed, facing the road.

"How sad is it that we only have four boxes of stuff?" she said, laughing.

"I'm worried about Mawmaw and Pawpaw," he said.

"They'll be fine. They're stronger than horses."

"Yeah, but they're getting old. How are they going to get enough to eat?"

She rolled her eyes. "Don't be silly. They're people of the earth. They'll be fine," she said. She smiled at him broadly and clapped her hands. "We're finally getting out of here, baby. I've been waiting for this all my life."

He nodded, more reserved in his mood. He was glad they were leaving, but he didn't think it would be that much better in Boston. Far as he could tell, life was going to be hard no matter where they went. The envy surged in him again, and he went into the woods and picked up a stick, which he yielded against a trunk, breaking it in two. His mother had made him leave his guns. All he'd have in Boston was his knives.

"Come on, silly," she called. "Here's Cliff. Be nice. I don't want anything going wrong."

Peyton sighed as Cliff pulled up in his old Dodge truck. It was pale blue and covered in dirt.

"Hey, there," he called, stepping out of the car. He was a stocky man, with a pregnant belly hanging over his jeans. He sauntered over to Peyton's mother and kissed her aggressively.

"Careful," his mother said. "You don't want to mess my makeup, do you?"

"I sure do," he said, grinning, winking at Peyton. Peyton raised his eyebrows and frowned, wishing he could punch Cliff.

"This is it?" Cliff said, pointing to the boxes.

His mother nodded. Cliff and Peyton threw the boxes in the back and Peyton climbed in after them.

"There's room up front, boy," Cliff said.

"That's alright," Peyton said.

"Suit yourself."

His mother smiled ecstatically at Peyton, squeezing his hand, and Cliff helped her into the passenger seat, patting her butt as he did. Peyton shivered. Cliff, with his bulbous nose, crooked mouth, and curly black stubble disgusted him. The thought of Cliff and his mother together made him nauseous, and he pushed the thought away.

The truck started with a rumble and moved down the bumpy dirt road. Peyton stared at the trees, the rises and falls, and the road disappearing beneath the truck, disbelieving this was the last time he'd see it. He drunk it up like a dehydrated man, trying to hold on to it, having a strong desire to yell, "Stop!" and jump out of the truck and run back to the cabin. He could, he knew, live with his grandparents and finish school here.

The truck slowed at the turn, and he debated making a run for it. He imagined himself hunting, the mountains, his grandparents, the cabin, and he leaned close to the edge. Then he pictured his mother in Boston, alone, and the large black hole he'd have in his life.

Who was he kidding? Leaving his mother was impossible.

Cliff accelerated, and the warm sun and harsh wind beat down on Peyton's face. Loneliness draped over him, and already, he longed for the woods. When they merged on a major road, Peyton slid down to avoid the screaming wind. He pulled the blanket underneath his head, and with the gentle heat and the bump of the car, he fell asleep.

He woke back up when they hit bumpy road. He yawned and raised his head. They were in the woods, heading up a ridge. At the top, old cars were parked randomly in Hershel's yard. As Cliff parked, Peyton riffled through his box, finding his one button-up shirt, the one he wore to church. He stretched it out, trying to remove the wrinkles.

He put it on over his t-shirt and hopped down, hoping that everybody else wasn't dressed like his mother. They walked up the driveway, which was smooth and paved, finding more cars in front of the house. A fairly new red Chevrolet truck was right near the house, and Peyton wondered if it belonged to Hershel, if his business was doing that well.

Laughter and noise floated out to greet them. The house was as he remembered it—towering, pale yellow, with a spacious, wrap-around porch. Upstairs, on one of the balconies, a lone rocking chair moved back and forth.

Dense gray clouds forecasted rain, and the howl of the wind suggested a real storm was coming. They walked along a concrete path to the back of the house. A glossed wood deck had plastic tables on it, and in the yard, white chairs were lined up around an aisle. It looked nice.

Hershel waved from a crowd of men on the deck. They walked up the deck stairs, and he met them at the edge, beer in hand. He hugged Peyton's mother against his wide chest. His white dress shirt was stained with sweat.

"Welcome to our humble abode. Peyton, you've turned into a man, I can't believe it. How old are you now?"

"Fourteen."

Hershel slapped him on the back, grinning. "I'll bet you rack up the ladies."

Peyton laughed. "I do alright."

"Abigail, who's this?"

Peyton's mother smiled tightly, her eyes warning him. "This is Cliff. Cliff, this is my distant cousin-in-law, Hershel."

Cliff and Hershel shook hands.

"Drinks are over there, guys, help yourselves," Hershel said, pointing to a table with coolers on top. He slapped Peyton on the back again.

"How the hell did a guy like that get with your mother?" he whispered. Peyton grinned, giving him a hell-if-I-know look, and shrugging his shoulders.

"Tyler's around here somewhere, up to no good," Hershel said, winking.

Peyton nodded, and Hershel took a swig of his beer, waving him over to meet the men. The men were wearing dress shirts that fit awkwardly over their strong arms and chests. The smell of liquor clung to their clothes and breath, like they'd been standing here drinking since early morning.

"This here is Peyton, the son I wish I had," Hershel said. The men nodded politely, apparently not caring who he really was. "Peyton, these men are my in-laws."

Peyton smiled at the men and Hershel, suddenly feeling generous. Peyton pointed to the table and Hershel nodded.

"Help yourself. When I was that age, I could drink anyone under the table."

The men laughed heartily, their heads bobbing in agreement.

Peyton grabbed a beer and popped it open. It tasted good. One of the men started a story about when he was a teenager. Peyton knew, by the way the man ran his words together, he wouldn't be drunk enough to find the story funny. He waved a friendly goodbye, excusing himself, and walked into the house through the sliding door.

The living area and kitchen formed a large, open space, and someone had furnished it tastefully in browns and burgundies. Margaret stood over the island stove, stirring something in a pot. She had aged dramatically. Deep wrinkles encased her mouth and eyes, and streaks of gray lined her hair. A toddler sat on a stool snapping the heads off green beans.

"Hi, Margaret," he said, walking into the kitchen.

She glanced up, and she stared at him, confused. Then a flash of recognition passed over her face. "Abigail's son?" she asked.

He nodded. "Who is this?" he said, looking at the little girl.

"Oh, our daughter Sarah." She wiped her forehead with the back of her hand. Peyton was absurdly resentful, as if the little girl had taken his place in the family.

"I don't know what I'll do without Greta," Margaret said. "I just don't." Her mouth twitched, as if she were about to cry.

Peyton nodded, wondering about that too. "Where is she?"

"Oh, upstairs. I just don't know.…"

She started crying, the tears dripping down her face silently, and he saw her eyes were already red. Sarah reached over to wipe her mother's tears, and Margaret leaned over so Sarah's tiny hand could cross her cheek.

"You'll be okay," he said, but even to him, his words sounded insincere. She nodded, her lip curled, her tears continuing to run. Watching Sarah wipe her mother's tears away, he was pissed off. Margaret was already expecting Sarah to take care of her.

"I'm sure Greta will still help out," Peyton said. He gave her a placating smile, and stepped back. "I'm going to say hi to Greta."

Margaret nodded, and turned back to the stove, stirring a frying pan of onions and peppers.

The staircase circled around the foyer, and upstairs, he walked down the hallway, opening doors, and admiring the rooms. Adam's room was stacked high with books, and dismantled electronic equipment.

In the last room, Greta stood in front of a mirror in her bra and underwear. She was studying her image, and her hands carefully caressed her soft belly. It had grown rounder since he'd last seen her.

She sighed and turned around. Seeing him, she smiled broadly.

"Peyton," she said warmly. "Come in. It's so good to see you."

"I'm sorry. I didn't know you were still dressing."

"That's okay. I'm sure it's nothing you haven't seen before." She laughed.

He smiled and sat down on her daybed. "This is a great house."

"I know. My new house will be much smaller." She had turned back to the mirror and stared critically at herself as she spoke, running her hands over her body. Her thighs and butt were covered with little craters and he had an urge to reach out and squeeze them, feel the consistency.

"Peyton? You've had sex?"

"Sure."

"Does it hurt?"

"It will probably hurt a little bit the first time. But it's not so bad."

Peyton didn't really know how it was for the girls. He hadn't paid that much attention. He figured it couldn't be that bad though.

She nodded and walked over to her closet and pulled out a short, white dress.

"So what does this fellow do?"

"Matthew, he's a minister."

"Huh," Peyton said, surprised, but immediately reconciled to the idea. A minister would suit her well. "Good. That's good."

"Yes. It will be nice to be a minister's wife. He's such a gentleman," she said, pulling her dress on over her head. "How do I look?"

"Beautiful," he said reflexively. The dress was of cheap fabric and hung stiffly, and the cut was off, pushing her breasts against her chest. But she seemed happy.

"It's really good to see you," he said, smiling.

"You too."

"Hey, how's Adam?"

She raised her eyebrows, and stared at a point on the wall, her face forlorn. "He's in his room all the time. But the house is so big, he avoids Pa and Tyler really well. I worry about him, though. He won't talk to me much and he doesn't have any friends."

Peyton nodded, remembering the things he didn't like about Adam—the resignation, the bitterness. That reminded him.

"I got you something."

"Oh. You didn't have to do that."

"I wanted to. Close your eyes and put your hand out."

She obliged and he reached into his pocket and laid the gold necklace in her hands. "Okay."

She opened her eyes and they lit up. She ran her fingers over it.

"Wow, it's beautiful, Peyton. I don't know how you managed this."

He grinned, pleased with himself. He rarely had the chance to give someone a gift.

"Will you put it on me?"

He nodded, taking the necklace. He put it around her neck, and when his hand brushed up against her shoulder, he remembered the day he had examined her body on the rock, and he was tempted to kiss her shoulder.

The chain closed easily. She glanced in the mirror.

"It's wonderful," she said, running her hand over it. "Is it real?"

He nodded behind her. She stared at his image in the mirror, as if she wanted to say something but didn't know how. He cupped her shoulder.

"I'll let you finish."

"Okay…" she whispered.

He squeezed her shoulder, returning her serious gaze. Then he picked up his beer, finished it off, and walked out.

"Peyton!"

"Yes?"

"Will you come visit me?"

"Of course. Whenever I'm in West Virginia."

"Good," she said, smiling to herself in the mirror.

* * *

The wedding was held right before sunset, with the storm clouds growing larger in the sky. Afterwards, those towing children left, and the rest of them drank. Peyton laughed and talked with Tyler, who rambled on about women, and claimed Greta's husband was gay. The drunker Peyton became, the more intent he became on a woman wearing a tight purple tank-top. She was pretty, but he couldn't remember if she had looked that way when he was sober. He decided it didn't matter, and he noticed the ring on her finger only as they stumbled up the stairs.

"Where's your husband?" he whispered loudly.

"He's not here," she whispered back, laughing.

Inside Greta's bedroom, they made out on the bed, and he pulled up her skirt. He was surprised at the amount of hair between her legs and he laughed. "Oh, my God, there's a whole animal down there!"

She slapped him.

"Ouch," he said, clutching his cheek and laughing even more.

91

"You're an asshole," she said. The thunder struck, as if in agreement, and the rain began to pour, whipping loudly against their window.

"Oh, yeah?" he said, cuffing her wrists and pushing her back on the bed, applying his weight on top of her, wondering if his eyes lit up with the lightening.

She smiled.

The next thing he knew, the sun was streaming in through the window and he had a pounding headache.

"Fuck," the woman was saying, riffling through the sheets. "My husband is going to kill me."

Her skin was rough in the morning sun, like wrinkled sandpaper, and her eyes were circled with dark splotches. Even her body seemed lumpy. He curled over, his head was pounding and he didn't want to see her or the sunlight.

"Fuck," she muttered, pulling on her panties. "I only have one of my shoes." She smacked him on the butt. "You're no help at all!" she screeched.

She stalked out of the room, carrying her one heel.

As soon as she was gone, he laughed, pulling the covers over his head and trying to go back to sleep.

His head hurt too much to sleep, and he reluctantly stumbled out of bed, and slid on his boxers and khaki shorts. He reached for his shoes underneath the bed and felt her other heel. He laughed and scooped it up.

Downstairs, people splayed out over the living room, blending in with bottles of beer and kitchen plates on the couches and the floor. Margaret stood at the stove, cooking up breakfast. Her face was flushed and her hair was wild and frizzy. Sarah sat on the same stool, in front of a stack of pancakes. He saw his mother outside on the porch, drinking coffee in a red sundress.

He dropped the heel on the counter, and helped himself to bacon, eggs and a big glass of milk, staying inside to avoid the harsh light of day. The greasy food alleviated his headache, but he still felt run over.

Cliff came down later, looking as bad as Peyton felt, and nodded at Peyton. After he had helped himself to a large meal, he wiped off his hands.

"We should get going. Where's your mother?"

Peyton noticed a red mark on Cliff's cheek, as if someone had slapped him hard. Peyton didn't let himself think about this, knowing it would lead to nothing good. He stared at Cliff, warning him, and pointed outside.

Cliff frowned, and Peyton followed his gaze. His mother, sipping coffee, was talking to a tall, young man whose light brown hair glistened in the morning sun. They made a handsome pair.

Peyton walked over to Margaret. "Is Hershel up?" She shook her head, and wiped her forehead.

"Give him our best. And be well, okay?"

She nodded, her face contorted in a frantic expression, and he remembered the same expression on her younger face—a wild animal trapped in a cage. He wondered if anything would ever make her happy, or if she would carry on panicking and disappearing her whole life.

Peyton turned to the deck. Cliff was hitting his mother roughly on the back. "Let's go, Abigail," he said. His tone was loud and possessive.

His mother smiled tightly at the other man, moving her shoulder as if to get out a kink. She stood up. They walked off the deck, a few feet between them.

"Bye," Peyton said to Margaret. "Be good, Sarah." Sarah grinned, waving her small hand.

Peyton caught up with his mother and Cliff near the end of the driveway. They were walking in silence. Cliff didn't open her door like he normally did. His mother pulled herself up, and peered out her window like a child, ignoring Cliff as she smiled to herself.

Peyton climbed in the back, pulling a sweater over his head. The truck rolled to a loud start. Through his aching body, he felt a sense of excitement and possibility.

They were on their way out.

Part II

CHAPTER SEVEN

Boston was a sprawling monstrosity of concrete sidewalks, paved streets, plastic siding, and glass. Smoky, industrial air hung over the city like an ever-present fog.

Their crumbling three-story building was a giant box, part concrete and part brick, with flat, little windows. It was surrounded by dozens of identical boxes. Piles of trash and broken-down cars littered the alleyways and streets, and the drugged-out and homeless wandered aimlessly.

Sometimes, Peyton choked on the smell of mold and vile, and he couldn't breathe, and he ran to the edge of the city, where dark waters lapped against its shore.

He ran to the wealthy neighborhoods, too, a mere few miles away. They had fresher air and rectangular green parks wedged between looming buildings. The polished structures lacked the freedom and wonder of the mountains, but Peyton discovered they possessed an imposing beauty of their own. The clean, sky-high lines of the financial buildings, and the massive bridges, carrying thousands of speeding cars over a wide river struck him as incredible. It was inconceivable what men had managed to build.

The whole city was overwhelming in its size and content—walking through the malls and markets, Peyton could not believe the sheer volume of things—and sometimes he found this mass of items unbearably suffocating, drowning him in useless, ugly objects; other times, he found it impressive, the abundance protecting him from any kind of need or want—how could someone go hungry or lose his fingers to frostbite in the vicinity of all these things?

His mother traipsed him around the city, carrying his teacher's glowing recommendations, determined to find a private school for him to attend. The public school he was assigned to was dirty and violent. Less than ten percent of its students went to college.

"Pardon me," his mother said. "But that school's not worth the scrapings off a hound dog's ass. We didn't come all this way for that."

He had to take a battery of tests, write personal essays and undergo awkward interviews. He was admitted to a few schools, eventually, but there was no way they could afford the tuition.

One of the schools had a leftover football scholarship, a sport Peyton had never once played. No matter, the affable admissions officer had insisted, as they needed a linebacker, a position Peyton, with his large size, could probably pick up.

At the tryout arranged specifically for him, the coach, a stout Italian, looked him over carefully, grunting ambiguously. A few players introduced themselves briefly. The coach ordered Peyton to run laps, jump over ropes, zip around cones, and only then, after he was good and tired, did the coach tell him to put on a helmet and pads and tackle the older boys as they tried to run past him with the ball.

The first few snaps, Peyton was overeager, lunging in the direction a player feinted. Realizing his mistake, on the next snap, he waited on the edge of his toes, training his eyes on the boys' centers, watching for a committed movement. The boy went, and Peyton slammed him to the ground with a heavy thud, feeling immense satisfaction as he landed on top of the boy, the fresh smell of the green grass drifting to his nose. Popping back up, they ran it again. After each play, Peyton became surer in his hits, and more enthused about throwing the boys to the ground. He liked this sport.

The coach nodded at the end of the session, not saying much, and the players smiled, waving as they left, laughing and talking, punching each other in the shoulder. Watching their tall, muscular frames, and easy strides, he felt he belonged on the team.

His mother asked the coach if he'd done well enough, and the coach grumbled he'd be in touch, immune to his mother's flirtations.

The coach walked off the field, banging his clipboard against his thigh, and his mother pouted, "What a stick in the mud."

"But you were great," she gushed, squeezing his bicep. "I'm sure you made it." Peyton nodded skeptically, thinking this was too good to be true. The coach probably saw he didn't belong here, and would relegate him to the criminal-production factory in South Boston.

They walked through the black iron-gates and toured the grounds. They found a large, private garden, ensconced inside four brick walls. Rows of vines and flowers tumbled inside, and taking a deep breath, Peyton's lungs expanded. The school, a gothic building made of brick and stone, towered into the sky.

His mother whistled. "This place is real nice, baby. What did I tell you about the city?"

Peyton nodded slightly, not wanting to fully concede how nice it was. This was his chance to attend the school on the hill, with the children of the mine owners. He could have every advantage they did.

They heard nothing from the school for weeks, and when his mother called, the admissions officer explained it was up to the coach. Peyton was furious at the coach, and as summer came to a close, he dreaded the start of school, afraid of what he would do if he was confronted by an idiot carrying a gun. His fury was only partially appeased when the admissions officer called the last day of August, telling him to report to practice on the first day of school.

His mother was happier than he'd ever seen her as she got off the phone, and this washed away his remaining ill-will. He picked her up and spun her around, laughing.

She'd been working at a beauty parlor, sweeping the floors and answering the phones, and saving up her money, letting Cliff pay the rent and buy the food. They took the bus downtown and she bought him two gray slacks and two white, button-up shirts, the school's required uniform. When he stepped out of the dressing room, she cried.

"I can't believe it," she said, wiping her tears with the backs of her hands, to avoid smudging her makeup.

He smiled, proud, even though he knew it was mostly a matter of luck. He hadn't done much to get the scholarship.

Walking to his bus stop in the morning, he passed the public school. Behind the chain-link fence, the trashy students in flannel shirts and white high-tops loitered aimlessly in front of their graffiti-covered concrete building, with its taped-up windows and cracked steps.

Peyton lingered a few moments, watching barely concealed drug-deals and loud threats shouted across the yard, students cursing at one another in rapid fire. He felt a warm relief, a sense of having avoided another place where he wouldn't belong, where he'd keep his head down until someone looked at him the wrong way or insulted his accent.

The student body of Hunter Prep had stayed largely the same since pre-school; their parents were politicians, judges, business executives and professors at elite schools. Peyton had never seen so many nice cars in one place. The parking lot was filled with late model BMWs, Mercedes, and even Jaguars, cars he had never seen before moving to the city.

A few other students were on scholarship—athletes, minorities, and children of the staff—and, for the most part, Peyton could tell, right off, which ones they were. They lacked the ease and entitlement of the others; they were quicker to defer, and slower to offer an opinion. Their clothes, like Peyton's, were of inferior quality, bought from discount stores in the bargain bins.

He had football practice every day for two hours. They ran, tried out new plays, scrimmaged and lifted weights. The cheerleaders practiced on the track surrounding the field, and between plays, the players argued over how desirable the girls were. They used a one to five scale, awarding points for hotness and lack of sexual experience.

In the hallways of the school, when a player was chatting up a girl in front of her locker, other players walking by hooted and flashed a number of fingers. Scoring a five—tapping a smoking hot girl who'd never been tapped before—netted major accolades in the locker room. Peyton was happy to play along, and quickly realized it was an easy way to fit in.

After practice, Peyton often returned to the library to study, as he preferred the soaring ceilings and musty old books to Cliff's dilapidated and cramped one-bedroom apartment. Cliff and his mother rarely cleaned, and the kitchen surfaces and the shower had a crusty layer of green mold. Roaches darted across the tile floor. Piles of take-out boxes and newspapers sprawled over the living room, where Peyton slept on the couch.

Occasionally, Peyton would scrub everything down with scalding hot water and a bar of soap, and lug the trash down to the incinerator, where he had to toss it in from a distance, or risk burning his hand. He walked through the neighborhood and the building quickly, keeping his eyes on the ground. He didn't want anyone to notice him.

Two months after they moved in, in the warm heat of summer, he had heard a gunshot and a piercing scream, and turned around and saw a strung-out young man, only a couple years older than him, splayed out and dead on the concrete steps of the neighboring building. The shooter had disappeared into the lingering crowds of people. Peyton had pounded up the steps, out of breath, disbelieving what he'd seen. The image of the boy, his limbs askance, his forehead blown off, still haunted him.

His mother was surprisingly tolerant of all this. Men smiled and whistled at her, and she waved back. She loved having a hot shower and a toilet, and locked herself in the bathroom for hours. She was saving her money and searching for other work so they could leave Cliff, and the nasty apartment. For her, this was just a way station on the road to a better life.

Peyton was occasionally steamed when he sat in his friends' expensive cars or partied in their seven-bedroom mansions, knowing that his mother would have to work for dozens of years to cover the cost of one minuscule painting nailed to the bathroom wall.

When he was drunk, he would disappear into the recesses of the houses, finding something—a scarf, towels, sheets, a man's shirt—to take. He was careful never to take anything too notable, and hid whatever it was underneath his uniform and pads in his team duffel bag. With something in his bag, he felt smug, like he had righted a wrong. Because at the end of the night, when the others cruised back to their beautiful Boston townhouses, or Cambridge mansions, he still had to run home, alone, to South Boston.

The school library was amazing—it had towering rows of books on every possible subject. Peyton stared at the hundred books on the Civil War, amazed, and read them one by one. Even though it was popular to study the Cold War and communism, Peyton preferred the Civil War, finding it more relevant to American life.

In class, Peyton sat with his football buddies near the back. They were all good students, but generally remained quiet in class, passing notes to each other. This suited Peyton well, because his mind was like a large chunk of Swiss cheese, with strange gaps of knowledge. He knew a great deal about certain subjects, but knew absolutely nothing about many subjects the other students had studied since they were young, like French or Chinese history.

He participated only when he felt strongly about a topic, or was annoyed with another student, usually one of the boys who said, with every word, nobody knew as much as them, or one of the self-labeled Frights, four "feminist communist" girls who never brushed their hair. He couldn't believe everyone else let them run on, unrealistic drivel pouring forth like vomit, and, sometimes, when they talked, he imagined stuffing their mouths with their dirty socks, telling them to shut the hell up.

All four wore square black-frame glasses and pants, protesting the dress code that dictated girls wear skirts, and one day before class, Peyton yanked a pair off one of the girls and peered through them.

"I knew it," he said victoriously, passing the glasses to his football buddies. "These are fake."

Everybody laughed, and the Frights glared at him furiously, demanding the glasses back, insisting they were a light prescription. For the rest of the year, whenever one of them walked by, someone would yell, "Hey, can I borrow your glasses?"

* * *

Leaving the library late one night, long after everyone else had gone home, Peyton noticed a light streaming out of an art studio, a pale yellow triangle covering the floor of the dark hallway.

Curious, he walked over, shifting his duffel bag so it lay across his chest.

A tall, lithe girl was painting at an easel. Her almost-white hair was piled in an overflowing bun on top oof her head, and her strokes were quick and forceful. Her white tank top and tan arms were splattered with various colors of paint. He wondered if she were a student as he was sure, if she was, he would have seen her before.

She stepped backwards and walked in a semi-circle, eying the painting from every angle. She stepped on top of the table and looked at it from above. When she put her brush down, her chest rose and fell and she rubbed her mouth, as if she were dissatisfied with what she had done.

She went over to the sink, her back to him, and washed her hands, undoing her bun. Her hair rolled down her back, ending at her waist. She scrubbed her hands and then, giving one last look to her painting, slid on a brown leather jacket.

As she walked toward him, throwing her denim bag over one shoulder, he stepped back, realizing he had been too transfixed to move. The lights went out.

She opened the door, and screamed.

Seeing who it was, she laughed, revealing straight, white teeth. She had striking green eyes, like titled almonds. Even in the dim light, her coloring was bright and healthy. He didn't imagine she was conventionally pretty. She was unusual looking—her pink mouth was a bit large for her oval face, and her nose, otherwise narrow and straight, had a slight bump in it.

"Sorry," she said, pulling the door shut. "You scared me."

She walked down the hall and he ran to catch up. "I'm Peyton."

"Oh? I'm Isabelle."

"Are you a student here? I've never seen you before."

"Yes." Her strides were quick, and even though her legs were a few inches shorter than his, he had to speed up. "Six years and running. My mother works in the admissions office."

"What grade are you in?"

"Ninth."

"Me too. I started this fall."

She nodded, as if this didn't concern her, and she pushed open the old, wood doors. Outside, it was cold. The winding tree branches were practically naked, peppered with a few orange leaves, stragglers who refused to let go.

She turned to him. "I'm going to run home."

"Where do you live?"

"Somerville. It's a mile from here."

"Okay," he said, grabbing her wrist. "Hey, would you like to go to a party this weekend?"

"I don't care for parties." She smiled at him gamely. "We could do something else."

"Okay," he said, trying to think of something to do, but finding nothing. "Saturday night?"

"Sure," she said, pulling a notebook out of her backpack and a pen. She wrote down an address and her name, Isabelle Woods. Her writing was large and sloping. She tore out the piece of paper and handed it to him. "Seven PM. We'll get dinner."

He nodded, grinning as she took off running, her plaid skirt and blonde hair whipping in the wind. He stared at the piece of paper proudly and folded it up neatly in his pocket. He didn't know why, but he was excited. The image of her in the art studio, staring intensely, pleased him.

He suddenly wanted to see what she had been painting. He opened the school door with his key, and walked down the empty hall, to the art studio. He jiggled with the handle, even trying to use his school key, but it wouldn't unlock.

Damn it, he thought.

At home, lying on the couch in his boxers, he saw Isabelle, remembering an equilateral triangle of freckles on her bicep. Even the sound of Cliff's bed creaking didn't diminish his mood. Instead, he resolved to find a way to get enough money to move out. His mother deserved better. Peyton laughed to himself when the bed stopped creaking two minutes later. In his own mind, he had nicknamed Cliff, "The Quick Draw."

He imagined Isabelle painting, her long limbs moving gracefully, and soon, he fell asleep.

* * *

At practice, the players said Isabelle was a three or a four—full points for inexperience, too skinny and unkempt to be hot. Nobody seemed to know much about her. Except that she painted—every year, her work dominated the art show.

"You going to hit her?" one of them asked.

He smiled. "We're going out Saturday night."

"We have an explorer, folks! Heading into pristine land," another linebacker said, his hands cupped in a microphone.

"The only question is: will he survive in this unknown territory? Or will he die a hungry death?"

The players laughed, and Peyton was suddenly annoyed, like he'd been insulted, and he wanted to punch them. On the next play, he slammed into the opposition, hard.

"Fuck, Peyton, slow it down," the player said.

The coach started screaming and yelling at the downed boy, telling him he was a god damn embarrassment and he shouldn't ever ask somebody to slow it down. The player scowled at Peyton as he was sent to run twenty laps. He didn't care. He kept hitting hard.

In the shower after practice, the other guys gave him shit, asking him what his problem was. He ignored them, washing up, and after everybody was clean and doused in cologne, it had been forgotten. It was Friday night, and they were headed to a house party. Peyton grabbed the passenger seat in a 911 Porsche and they took off, zooming through the Cambridge streets, arriving at the house in three minutes flat.

The house belonged to two sisters, whose father ran a pharmaceutical company. At all their parties, they served bowls of prescription pills—uppers, downers, painkillers, anxiety relievers—alongside the drinks. Peyton went straight to the bowl, taking one purple and one orange pill with a shot of whiskey, not remembering or caring which pill was which.

Immediately, he was awash in pleasure and settled down on the couch with another drink. Everything was blurry and he looked over the fireplace, at an old painting of a woman in a boat. It seemed like she was staring directly at him. Her beseeching brown eyes, large and desperate, discomfited him, and he turned away.

As the night wore on, he went back for more pills and drinks, and became increasingly blitzed. It only made him more revved up and he searched around the noisy room for a girl. Though he was still happy to tap plain girls, when his buddies were around, he wanted to take down the best-looking one he could. There was nothing better than taking the hottest girl to a bedroom while the rest of the guys watched. He didn't even care if she gave it up, as long as it looked like she had.

He zeroed in on one of the cheerleaders, a blond freshman who already had large breasts on her petite frame. She was talking to a plain girl with mousy brown hair, sipping from a coke can. Peyton poured two rum and cokes and sauntered over, handing them the drinks. He smiled at the plain girl. He chatted her up, ignoring the blond.

After he talked to the plain girl for a while, he turned to the blond, introducing himself. She seemed, as he had calculated, flustered and eager to please. He pulled them over to the bowl of pills, and convinced them to take two each. They did, and soon they started to relax, their words coming faster, running over each other. He tried to concentrate on what they were saying, forgetting how he had planned to separate them. To his delight, the plain girl said she had to go to the bathroom.

He nodded vigorously, knowing he'd have five minute to get the blond.

The plain girl asked him, shyly, to come with her.

Oops, tactical error, he thought, smiling at her, his head pounding. He quickly assessed the situation, deciding he would get way too much shit for screwing around with her. He shook his head, saying they'd be right here, waiting for her. She pouted, crossing her hands over her chest, but rolled her eyes, and mumbled, "Fine," as she departed for the bathroom alone.

He grinned at the blonde, staring at her rapturously. Her face flushed.

He grabbed her wrist, "Come on," he said. "Let's go in one of the bedrooms. Just me and you."

She smiled but lowered her head.

"Quick," he said. "Before your friend gets back."

She smiled again, still staring at the floor. He took her drink from her and put it on the table, and picked her up and threw her over his shoulder. She laughed.

He carried her up the stairs to wild hoots and hollers. "Peyton! Peyton!"

He grinned, feeling awesome. Inside the bedroom, he slammed the door closed with his foot and dropped her on the bed. He plopped down next to her. The king-sized mattress was unbelievably soft. He was immediately overcome with sleepiness.

"I'm so tired," he mumbled. He was used to hard, threadbare cushions poking into his back, and the wood arm of the couch blocking his feet from full extension.

She peered over him, her blue eyes blinking as she touched his forehead. "Do you want to take a nap?" he asked.

"Sure," she said.

He kicked off his shoes and scrambled up, putting his head on the plush pillows. "Come here," he said, patting his chest. She pulled off her shoes and crawled over to him. "Come on top." She climbed on top and he ran his hands over the back of her angora sweater. Her breasts pushed up against his chest.

"You smell good," he said, hugging her closer.

She gripped a piece of his shirt in her fist and sighed. "Thanks."

Peyton drifted asleep.

* * *

On Saturday, they played "his" public school, where they were demolished. In the locker room, the players complained about how disgusting the school was—the crumbling locker room walls, the mold and feces-streaked bathrooms, the smell of condensed sweat—and how the opposing players were illiterate.

Peyton wanted to tell them to shut up. He considered throwing Brockton, the kid running his mouth the most, up against the locker and breaking his nose. Nobody realized this was his neighborhood. He clenched his fist and went into the shower alone, ignoring their are-you-crazy looks, and turned the water hot.

When he came out in his towel, they congratulated him for hitting the freshman blond—a clear five—and he smiled, not bothering to clarify that he hadn't fucked her. He was annoyed as he dressed, throwing his uniform in his bag. After the coach lectured them about learning to play like these boys, like they had nothing to lose, Peyton left as the rest of them piled on the bus, laughing to himself.

The Hunter Prep boys had everything to lose, who was the coach kidding? Walking home, his body was sore and stiff. The offensive tackles had been bulky—over six feet tall and approaching three hundred pounds.

At home, Cliff was sitting on the couch, drinking beer and watching television. He nodded at Peyton, returning his eyes to the TV. Peyton was exhausted. He changed into his jeans and a white button-up shirt. Wearing his Varsity jacket, he headed back out, and took a nap by the river on his way to his mother's work. He needed money.

When he walked in, the bells jingled. His mother was at the receptionist desk, and her face lit up.

"Hey, baby," she said, smiling. "How'd your game go?"

"We got creamed."

"Hey, Peyton," a hair stylist called. She had long nails and a nest of curly hair. He smiled and waved, leaning over the receptionist desk.

"The players were huge," he said to his mother, throwing his arm backwards to stretch it.

She wrinkled her nose. "Are you okay? I wish you didn't have to play that game. It's barbaric really."

He nodded. She glanced back behind her and then leaned in. "Baby, we have to move. I can't take any more of Cliff or the Old Colony. It's all disgusting."

He felt a strong wave of impotence. He tried to think of a way to make money. "I could get a job at night."

She shook her head, her long, black hair shimmering. "No. You have to study, baby." She glanced to her side, with a devilish smile in her eyes. "I found a new job," she whispered. "It will be enough money for us to move out."

"That's great. What is it?" he whispered back.

"Dancing. Sharon used to do it."

"Dancing in a show?"

"Yeah, exactly, a show." She paused and glanced up at him nervously. "It's partially nude."

He immediately had an intense headache, clenching his fists. "No," he whispered furiously.

"Shhh," she said, standing up. "I'm going to take a smoke," she called to the girls, picking up her pack and lighter. She pulled Peyton outside.

She took out a cigarette and handed him the lighter. He lit it for her and she took a long puff. In her light cotton dress, printed with blue and white flowers, she shivered.

"Here," he said, his voice filled with rage, handing her his jacket. She slipped it on.

"You can't do this."

"Baby, look, I've been to the place. It's classy. It'll just be for a while."

His head pounded and he took one of her cigarettes, even though he didn't smoke. He inhaled it quickly, wishing he had a drink. He tried to think if there was a job he could get that would pay a decent amount of money.

"Ma, let me work construction on the weekends. That should be enough to move."

"No, it won't be, Peyton. What about when you have games, practices? You can't miss those. And what if you got hurt?"

"I won't. That's what we're going to do."

"Peyton, you are not in charge. I'm doing this."

She dropped her cigarette and stubbed it out with the toe of her shoe. She sighed. "Baby, there's nothing wrong with it. No touching, no big deal, okay?"

He sucked his cigarette, which only intensified his headache and made his mouth dry. He dropped it on the sidewalk. Across the street, a group of trashy teenagers walked by, talking loudly and illogically. Peyton closed his eyes.

"Okay," he said, hugging her against his chest. He kissed her forehead, which fell naturally against his mouth when she was in her heels. He tried to remember when he'd grown so much taller than her. He blew out a breath of air.

"I'm going on a date tonight," he said finally.

"Oh, yeah?" she said, smiling and poking him in the ribs. "With who?"

"A girl I met at school."

"Well, make sure she's good enough for you. And treat her nice."

He smiled and she handed him his jacket. Opening the door to the parlor, she paused.

"Do you need any money?"

He shook his head. He leaned in and kissed her on the cheek.

"Have fun. Be a good boy."

He grinned. "I will."

He watched her through the glass as she walked back to her desk and sat down. She flipped through the pages of a glossy hair magazine, examining the pictures closely. She didn't seem bothered by what she was about to do. He walked down the street, his head still pounding, remembering he needed money. He had four dollars in his wallet, which he had saved by running home instead of taking the bus.

As he walked downtown, he occasionally scanned the sidewalks, as if someone might have dropped twenty bucks.

Crossing the Charles River, he imagined jumping in and swimming in the cold, strong currents. The winds were blowing over the water. A young man walked past, and Peyton was tempted to push him over the edge, watching as he tumbled desperately through the air.

In Cambridge, the mansions protected by thick trees and expansive lawns only incensed him further. He wanted to burn the houses down. He ran away from the wide streets, to Harvard Square, flying past the shops and street performers, and into the bookstore.

He caught his breath, and glanced idly over the shelves of unblemished books. Students, with their large backpacks near their feet, studied at the second-floor café, as if nothing mattered in the world but their books.

Peyton wandered to the third floor, glancing over the foreign-language and travel books. He zeroed in on a woman sitting at the end of a row, in a wooden chair, intently reading a large architecture book, occasionally flipping the huge pages. Her purse, a crumply red leather bag, sat next to her chair. Peyton pretended to browse the cookbooks in the row behind her and stepped on the strap of her purse, hooking it over his toe and dragging it silently down the aisle. She didn't move. He leaned down, found her wallet among the pens and papers and lipstick and gum and slipped it in his pocket. Quickly, he pushed the purse back near her chair, leaving it in the aisle as he strode away.

Downstairs, he slowed his pace, heading calmly for the exit.

"Hey!" a woman called.

He turned around, thinking he was screwed, trying to figure how he could explain this one. But it was only a college girl, in a cashmere sweater. "Aren't you in my English Lit class?"

He shook his head, smiling through his intense headache, and flipped on his heels, headed for the exit. Pushing open the glass door, he was on the sidewalk and free, and he sped up, disappearing into the Saturday crowds, taking a series of turns. He walked down a cobblestone alley behind a large, brick building.

He sat on the curb and smiled.

"Come on, jackpot," he muttered as he pulled the slender, brown leather wallet out of his pocket. Thirty-five dollars. Not bad, he decided, taking it out and putting it in his pants' pocket. He flipped through the rest of her wallet—pictures, credit cards, a library card, a video card, a Harvard faculty I.D.—ha!—receipts. He tossed the contents in the green dumpster, and slipped the wallet in his pocket, deciding to give it to his mother.

He needed a drink, and he found a bar and ordered one. The bartender asked for his I.D., and when Peyton said he didn't have it with him, the bartender said, "Sorry, kid."

Peyton grumbled and left. After aimlessly wandering streets, moving farther from the nice part of town, and trying a few more bars, he finally landed in a dingy one that sold him a beer. Drinking it, watching a basketball game on TV, he calmed down.

Isabelle's neighborhood was composed of small, aging houses hunched close together. The wide streets were lined with thick, healthy trees. Peyton passed a few graduate students on the sidewalk, lugging backpacks and soft briefcases, dressed in bland, scholarly clothes—an array of tweed jackets, sweaters, button-up shirts.

Isabelle lived on the second floor of a split-level house, with blue siding. The porch fit only one chair. Ringing the bell, Peyton tried to relax.

Isabelle opened the door, smiling.

"Hey," she said.

"Hey."

She pulled on a pale jean jacket and flipped off the lights, locking the door behind her. "Do you like Indian food? There's a great place on the corner."

"Sounds good to me." He had never had Indian food. At Hunter, he devoured his free lunch, and marveled at all the new tastes—the fresh mozzarella, the pesto, the pineapples. He had yet to meet a food he didn't like.

Isabelle's long hair was in a French braid and as they walked, the braid bounced up and down on her jacket.

"Look," she said, grabbing his arm, and pointing to a house.

"What?"

"The window," she said, pointing up. In the attic, there was a stained glass window in the shape of a star. When he squinted, he saw a woman in the center, her head thrown back in agony. He laughed. It was oddly compelling.

"Don't you like it?"

He nodded. She started walking again, quickly. "Where did you move from?"

"Southern West Virginia."

"Mmm. I've never been. You should take me there."

He laughed again. "Okay."

"Have you been to the Berkshires?"

He shook his head.

"It's beautiful there. We could take the bus."

"Okay," he said, laughing yet again, finding her assumed familiarity strange, but not unwelcome.

"Where do you live now?"

"In South Boston. But we're going to move soon."

"To where?"

"I don't know. We're going to look as soon as we have enough money to move out."

She nodded. "How many of you are there?"

"Just me and my mother. She's ditching her boyfriend."

They turned the corner and she pointed to a small shop filled with people. "This is it." When they reached the door, he held it open for her.

"Thank you," she said, smiling.

Inside, it was hot and loud—foreign music played out of speakers and people crowded the lobby, talking over one another. They got in line and she wrapped her arms around his.

"What's good here?" he asked her, smelling the strawberry scent of her hair.

"Palak paneer, flatbread, and a Mango lassi," she shouted.

When they reached the front he ordered two of each, and paid the cashier. She tried to give him money, but he brushed her away.

"Don't be silly," he said, taking his change and slipping it in his pocket.

After they got their trays, they climbed three flights of stairs. The unpainted wood attic had tables and chairs haphazardly arranged in the crunched space.

"Oh, the window seat is open!" she said, rushing over with her tray. He smiled. The window was in the shape of a house, about the size of a coffee table book, and tinted green. She peered into it and laughed.

"I love this window. Look," she said. He saw the busy street, surrounded by the naked trees. Everything was shaded green. It reminded him of the black shadow his grandfather left on everything he touched. He took a big bite of his paneer.

"This is good," he said. He was starved and went to work, ripping a piece of bread off and running it through the sauce. She dove in too, and for a few minutes, they ate in silence, each focused on their plates.

"Oh," she said, putting her fork down. "This is so good." She sucked her lassie up with her straw. He glanced at her, smiling. She was cute with her eyes open-wide and her lips pursed around the straw. There was something innocent and pure about her.

She let the straw drop and smiled at him.

"So good," she said.

He nodded, feeling thrown off balance and like he could use another drink.

"Did your parents divorce?" she asked, picking up her fork and returning to her paneer.

"No," he said, debating what to tell her. No one at school had asked him about either of his parents, and he hadn't offered. "They were never married."

She raised her eyebrows, waiting.

"It's okay. I never knew him so I didn't really know what I was missing."

She twisted her mouth. "Yeah. But still."

"That's true," he agreed. "There is that. But I like having my mom to myself."

"I'd like to meet her."

He laughed.

"What?" she said, her face genuinely confused. This made him laugh even harder.

"I don't know. We just met."

"You don't want me to meet her?"

"No, it's not that," he said, suddenly wanting to hug her. "You'll meet her. Right after we get back from the Berkshires." He grinned, half-joking, drinking more of his lassi through his straw.

She nodded. "Do you want to go next weekend? We should go before it gets much colder."

"Sure, why not? After Saturday morning football practice."

"You play football?" she said, incredulous.

"Yup. Linebacker."

"I always thought football players were … shallow," she said, wrinkling her nose.

"What about the ancients: moderation in all things, healthy body, healthy mind?"

"That's true. But don't football teams have a culture of superficiality?"

He laughed. "A culture of superficiality? Yes, I suppose there is some of that. But that's not the main thing."

She nodded, peering out the little, green window. "I am usually wrong about these things. People are rarely what you think they are. Did you ever notice that?"

"I don't really think much about what people are or aren't. I just react. Who did you think I was?" he said, curious.

She tugged her braid. "Do you want the rest of this?" she asked. He nodded and she pushed over her plate. "You, I didn't think anything, except, 'That's a beautiful boy.'"

He smiled at her, finishing off her plate and putting it on the tray. He never considered what he looked like. It seemed incidental, like the length of his hand.

"I'd like to paint you."

"Sure," he said, standing up and stacking the trays. He put them in the red basket. "I'll be right back," he said, going into the unisex bathroom. After he peed, he stared at himself in the smudged mirror. He rubbed his chin and furrowed his eyebrows, smiling at himself. Okay, so maybe he was a good-looking guy. So what.

She was peering out the window, her jean jacket on, her braid running neatly down the middle on her back. He tugged her braid and she jumped.

"Ready, you?" he said. She nodded, taking his hand. Hers was long and slender, and he pulled her down the stairs and through the crowd of people. Outside, it had grown colder and the wind was blowing, whipping her braid in the air. He wished he could undo it—let it all blow free.

"Can I have a ride?" she asked.

"A ride?"

"Yeah, on your shoulders," she said, grinning. "You know, put all that football practice to good use."

"Sure," he smiled. He kneeled down and she climbed on his back. He gripped her legs, right underneath her knees and she held on gingerly to his head. She was light and he walked steadily with ease. When they passed underneath a tree, she reached up.

"I got the last orange leaf," she cried, waving a large leaf in front of his face. "It's good luck!"

"Can we split it? I could use some," he laughed.

"You got it."

113

Back at her house, Peyton leaned down and she scrambled off. Peyton's body ached. He flexed his back muscles and rolled his shoulder. He dreaded the rickety couch, longing for last night's king-size bed.

Isabelle unlocked the door and pulled him inside. The television blared from the other room, and they walked toward it.

"Hey, honey," her mother called, sticking her head out from the side of her lazy-boy recliner. Seeing Peyton, she smiled. "Who's this?"

"Peyton from school," Isabelle called from the kitchen. "We're going to my room."

"Well, alright," she said. "Hi, Peyton." She smiled and drew her head back behind the recliner. He could see a man's legs on the other recliner. Isabelle took his hand and walked down the hall. She opened the door, and they bounded up half a flight of stairs, and then went through another door.

It was a "princess room"—an octagon with windows on half of its sides. The walls were painted with a million tiny colored dots, and when he got closer, he saw each dot was a face, with a different expression.

"Did you do this?" he said, amazed, running his fingers over the wall and looking at all the different faces, with unique features and expressions. She nodded.

He laughed. "That's insane. How long did it take you?"

"Years."

He remembered her in the art studio with her quick, intense strokes. Her curtains were striped with the same rich colors as the wall—red, purple, blue, green—and she unhooked them one by one, and as they fell, they blacked out the street light. For a second, before his eyes adjusted, he couldn't see anything.

"Do you need something to wear to bed?" She was ruffling through her drawer.

"You want me to spend the night?" It was the last thing he expected.

She put clothes on the bed. "Close your eyes," she ordered. He did, and heard her changing her clothes.

"Do you not want to spend the night?"

"No, I do. I am just surprised. Do you have people over often?"

"I haven't had anyone over for…hmmm… a year. But there's something about you. I trust you."

She pulled a flashlight out of her drawer and got under the covers.

He smiled, taking off his shoes and pants and shirt, folding them neatly in a pile. He climbed into the bed in his boxers. She lit her flashlight and tented the covers.

"Let's tell ghost stories."

He laughed, and couldn't stop laughing, suddenly overcome with the sheer oddity of this girl.

"What? Do you not like ghost stories?"

"No," he said through his laughter. "No." He caught his breath in deep gulps, feeling an overwhelming warmth and giddiness. "No, it's just strange. It's strange that we just met and now we are under the covers, about to tell ghost stories."

She stared, her mouth pursed in confusion.

"Is that bad?" she finally said.

He took the flashlight from her and rested it between them. Then he pulled her hand to his chest and held it. "No, it's not bad. Now, come on. Let's tell ghost stories."

They told ghost stories back and forth, and she occasionally jumped and let out a screech. After a while, they turned off the flashlight and she put her head on his chest. At some point, in the middle of a story, Peyton drifted off.

He woke up after a long, deep sleep. Opening his eyes, he was startled to see thousands of colored dots on the ceiling. Then, he remembered where he was.

Isabelle was near the window, sketching at her easel. Her braid had strands of hair flying out, left and right, and in the light, he saw her pajamas were frilled pink cotton. She was sketching his mouth, and for a while, he watched, liking the slow appearance of his face, arising off the blank page.

After she finished his mouth and nose, she turned back to him, and jumped.

"I didn't know you were awake," she said, smiling.

"I just woke up."

"I'm drawing you."

"Yes, I like it," he said, yawning and stretching his arms in the air.

She pounced over, climbing on top of him. He hugged her tight and she giggled.

"You want breakfast?"

"Uh-huh."

They got up and he put his clothes back on. In the kitchen, her parents were at the table, reading the paper and drinking coffee. The father had reading glasses on, and he smiled at both of them.

"Morning, honey," her mother said, smiling. "Morning, Peyton."

"Good morning," Isabelle said, opening the refrigerator.

"Peyton, help yourself to some coffee if you drink it," her mother said, pointing to the pot on the counter.

"Thanks, Mrs. Woods," he said, opening cabinets until he found a coffee cup. He poured it half full with milk and then added the coffee. Isabelle was cooking eggs and bacon, humming to herself and moving her hips back and forth. Peyton smiled and sat down at the table.

He grabbed the front section of the paper and started reading.

"Peyton, I remember your application. You're from West Virginia, right?"

"Yes, ma'am. Born and raised."

"Well, that is quite unusual."

Peyton smiled, nodding. Mrs. Woods was still attractive, with the same white blond hair and green eyes as Isabelle. Her hair was layered stylishly to her shoulders.

"Why did you leave?"

"There's not a lot of opportunity where we were. My mom thought we'd do better here."

She moved her head emphatically. "Absolutely. You won't have any better opportunity than Hunter. Their graduates go on to do amazing things."

Peyton smiled knowingly—the halls of the cafeteria were plastered with pictures of famous alumni. Isabelle served him a plate with eggs, bacon and toast. He thanked her effusively and dug in.

"Mom, can we go to the Berkshires next weekend? On Saturday?"

"Have you been there before?"

"Yes, many times," Isabelle said, taking a bite of her eggs.

"Okay, then. As long as it's safe."

Isabelle grinned at Peyton, winking, and he smiled back. So they were going.

After breakfast, they went back upstairs, and Isabelle opened the blinds and windows. Peyton lay down on the bed and, borrowing Isabelle's book, did his math homework, burrowing underneath the covers, while she sketched in a thick sweater. Later, he read for English and American history.

He was oddly satiated and comfortable. He was certainly happier here than at Cliff's. After she finished his face—which looked stronger and more determined than he imagined himself—they went for a walk down by the Charles River, and held hands against the blowing winds. Young families covered the path, pushing strollers and carrying babies as they walked by. Boys played baseball in a field, loose and scattered, without uniforms.

They reached his bridge, and he didn't want to go home. He wanted to keep walking with Isabelle, hand in hand. He hugged her against him, kissing her head.

"So next week: the Berkshires?"

She nodded against his chest, and then pulled her head back with her hands still wrapped around his waist. She smiled at him coyly.

"What?" he asked.

She kept smiling coyly, her face flushing a bright pink. He tugged gently on her braid and then leaned in and kissed her softly. She kissed him back forcefully, wildly.

"Woah," he said, pulling back.

"Sorry," she said, laughing. "I couldn't help myself. Next Saturday, my house," she said, grinning and running away, her braid bouncing against her back.

He watched her quick, messy stride until she turned down a side street and he could no longer see her. Then he laughed—a euphoric laugh, thinking that Isabelle was perfectly strange and, maybe, strangely perfect.

CHAPTER EIGHT

At school, Peyton's eyes roved across people's heads, searching for Isabelle, and coming up empty. In the locker room after practice, the players asked him if he broke into new territory, he shook his head, smiling to himself.

"Ohhh," they teased. "Pussy-whipped!"

"Yeah, right," he said, snapping one with his towel, and shoving the other against the locker. They punched back and laughed.

Friday night, after he was drunk, he picked up a brunette four, taking her in one of the bedrooms. He closed his eyes, and when he did, he saw Isabelle, and he became confused, forgetting whose body was underneath his.

After he was done, he yawned, satiated, and rolled over.

"That was great," he said. She nodded and closed her eyes, her chin stiff. She pulled the comforter over her naked body.

"I'm revved up," he said, stretching and jumping out of bed. He threw his clothes back on and squeezed her ankle. "I'm going to go back out, okay?" he asked.

She shrugged her shoulders, not opening her eyes. Her luscious mouth frowned slightly. "Okay."

"Great," he said, kissing her on the cheek and slipping his shoes back on.

In the living room, the players hanging out on the couches called his name, and pumped their fists in the air. He grinned, feeling like a returning soldier.

"Man, you are good," Bryan said. The others nodded.

Peyton grabbed another drink, and joined them on the couch. He remembered, happily, he was heading to the mountains tomorrow.

In the locker room Saturday, everybody was making plans and Peyton begged off, saying he had plans with Isabelle. The pussy-whipped banter started back up and Peyton shoved them until they gave up, laughing. He stopped by his mother's work on the way out.

"She quit this week," the hairdresser said, smiling. He was annoyed at his mother for not telling him this.

"Where's Sharon?" he asked, remembering the woman who had sent his mother to the club.

The hairstylist pointed to the third station, and the woman had a purple strip down the back of her black hair. She wore a green jacket made out of fake leather. He walked over to her, furious. With her navel showing and mini-skirt, she looked like a slut.

"Are you Sharon?"

She turned to him and nodded. "Aren't you Abigail's son?" she said, smacking her gum as she held a woman's wet hair between her fingers.

"Yes. Why did you tell her to go work as a stripper?"

The woman in the chair glanced away nervously.

"I didn't tell her to. I just told her it's a good way to make money, darling," Sharon said, smacking her gum again. "She wasn't making jackshit here."

Fucking bitch, he thought, wanting to break her nose.

"Darling, it's a real nice place. No funny business," she said, cutting a piece of hair, which fell to the ground. She peered at him, one of her poorly-drawn eyebrows raised. "Check it out for yo' self. It's real nice, trust me."

He slammed his fist on her workstation, knocking a jar of green saline solution over. It spilled on the woman's lap and floor. The woman screamed, and Peyton walked away, heading outside.

He ran home, as fast as he could, and found Cliff watching television, beer in hand. Cliff nodded at him and Peyton grunted, wanting to punch him, the useless sack. Turns out he was "disabled," and lived on state money. Peyton emptied his duffel and packed it with his sweater, gloves and a blanket. In the kitchen, he stole two beers.

"Later," he called to Cliff on his way out, who didn't move. He just sat there in front of the television—a hairy lump of flesh. Peyton had no idea where his mother was. He considered bailing on this trip, as he wasn't in the mood for Isabelle.

He wanted to get blasted and find some chick to fuck. But getting out of the city with its heavy, coffin-like buildings and into the mountains where he could breathe clearly sounded so good he kept on track, knocking on her door and running with her to the bus station, their packs bouncing behind them.

On the bus, he drank both beers, leaning down in his seat. Isabelle looked at him like he'd taken off his face and revealed he was a horse.

When she said, "You drink beer?" he laughed until his stomach hurt.

"What?" she said, making him laugh even more.

"I've been drinking it since I was ten."

As they moved away from the city and into the open, unobstructed land, he lost touch with his rage, as if it were an urban rat, only able to survive in the city environment. The drink settled into his bones, relaxing him, and he smiled at Isabelle.

"Hey, you," he said affably.

"Hey you,," she said, smiling and leaning against his arm. Her white hair was loose and it fell across his lap. He wrapped it around his finger and felt a desire to protect her from everything, all at once. He squeezed her slender bicep, rubbing it gently.

At the bus station, they asked a fellow passenger, an elderly man with a bowl of silver hair, for a ride into the mountains. He said sure, and they piled into a dingy blue Volkswagen with a "Peace not War" bumper sticker.

The man flipped on a tape, and it played classical music—something Peyton had heard of, but never heard. It was striking, conjuring up a sense of running on the edge of a cliff. Isabelle was sitting in the backseat with their bags and a cardboard box full of books and newspapers, and she closed her eyes and moved her head back and forth.

The man dropped them off at the foot of a trail, wishing them well on their journey, and they climbed out. The air was crisp and cold and Peyton filled his lungs. The mountainside was stripped down, its bright fall coverage torn asunder by winter, and as they climbed, they could see far into the distance. A tiny town at the base of the next ridge, and a narrow road snaking out of it, were the only signs of man. They hiked for hours, until the sun was setting and they found a stone overhang to sleep under.

They bundled up in Isabelle's sleeping bag, their skin wet with sweat, and stared into the dark blue sky, marked by the hundreds of old trees, with their limbs stretching upwards toward the sun, or maybe, Peyton thought, God.

They ate cold steak sandwiches, and then Peyton went in the forest and collected wood for a fire. He used one of his mother's lighters to start it and they strung marshmallows and cooked them until their outsides were crisp.

They finished eating and leaned back against the boulders, feeling the heat of the fire, and watching the last of the sun's light vanish.

Isabelle looked out over the land and sky and her eyes and face were perfectly serene. It was almost as if she were a mirror, embodying the image she faced.

"Do you think men can ever make something this beautiful?" she asked.

"I don't know. Probably not."

She nodded with a slight smile. "Sometimes I wonder."

"It's not all here," he said reluctantly. "This is only one face of beauty."

"I know. It's daunting, though. This is what I am up against."

She closed her eyes and he pulled her onto his lap, smelling her strawberry shampoo, and wrapping his arms around her waist. They bundled their clothes and spare blanket into a pillow and then zipped the sleeping bag up. It was too cold to take off their pants or sweaters. She shivered against him and he held her closer. The lingering flames in the fire burned out, and the sky went black. The quarter-moon and the dense web of stars shined brightly, unhindered by clouds or men's lights, and he was startled that he had forgotten what it was like to see this.

"Do you believe in God?" he asked.

"I think so," she said, interlocking her fingers with his. "It seems likely. It makes the most sense."

"Why?"

"I don't know. It's hard to understand beauty without God."

"The Christian God?"

"No. Any God. An original creator."

"Yeah..." he said. "Maybe."

His mother had no interest in church since they left West Virginia, and he realized she had only been going because it was the thing to do. Cliff was Catholic, but he never went to church either. Peyton had gone to church by himself a few times—when the Old Colony and the entitled pricks at school made him want to scream—and the minister had droned on in a monotone, his archaic words seeming irrelevant to this life. The kneeling and standing and austere singing and praying had felt like a chore, not an act of God.

The winter quiet was complete. Occasionally, the wind blew through the weeds, creating a rustle and interrupting the sealed silence. Peyton kissed her ear, thinking of the possibility of God, and fell asleep, her warm body pressed against his.

The naked sun warming his face woke him up. Isabelle was still sleeping, her mouth open slightly. For a while, he watched her, marveling at the upward angle of her eyes, as if she had East Asian blood, the overly fullness of her slightly parted mouth, and the perfect straightness of her teeth.

He kissed her on the forehead and ran a finger lightly over the bump in her nose. He climbed carefully out of the bag, and pulled on his shoes and walked to the edge of the cliff. He unzipped his pants and peed, watching the light urine spray into the open air, dissolving somewhere he could not see. He yawned and returned to the campsite, looking through her bag. He found a bag of trail mix and took it out, eating a handful.

"Hey," she said.

"Hey," he said softly, pivoting on his heel to look at her. She sat up. Her white blond hair blew gently across her face.

"What?" she said.

"Nothing." He ate another handful of trail mix and handed her the bag. She smiled, stretching, her arms poking through her curtain of hair. She put on her white tennis shoes and stood up. She left the bag of food and ran into the woods.

"I'm going to pee," she called over her shoulder. He heard her urine hitting the fallen leaves. He stood up and looked down the side of the mountain, and saw her squatting, her jeans pulled down her thighs.

"No looking!"

"Why not?" he said, smiling, and running down the hill.

"Hey, no fair!" she called, and by the sound of it, seemed to push her urine out faster. Right when he reached her, she pulled up her jeans, laughing. He tickled her and she laughed harder, trying to get away. She was feisty and they fell to the ground, rolling, choking with laughter. He held her down, his body on top of hers, grinning.

"Okay. You win," she said, smiling.

"That's right," he said and he leaned down and kissed her. They kissed for a long time and then he gently zipped up her jeans. When they stood up, they wavered uncertainly before finding each other's hands. They made their way back up the mountainside, swinging their hands and smiling foolishly, feeling drunk.

Peyton finished the trail mix and they packed their things and headed back down the mountain. It was warmer, and after a couple hours, Peyton tied his Varsity jacket to his duffel.

As they hiked down the mountain, she would occasionally stop, grab his arm and point to something, her voice excited—a perfect right angle made by two intersecting tree branches, a complimentary set of colorful leaves strewn across the forest floor, a gutted, moldy log center.

These discrete frames, picked out from the running river of life, were beautiful. And even when they weren't—even when they seemed to him plain or unremarkable—he couldn't help but be moved by her enthusiasm and clarity of vision. He knew, in her mind, she had created beauty out of what to him seemed like nothing, and this made him smile. It must be what made her an artist.

Emerging from the woods onto the two-lane road, they started walking toward the bus station single file. He walked behind Isabelle, wanting to protect her from any cars zipping along the narrow, country road.

When he heard a car coming, he pulled her off the road, up against the rocky cliff and stuck out his thumb. The car drove by without stopping and Peyton curled his fist, and muttered, "Fucking assholes." Isabelle laughed, tugging the bottom of his sweater and giving him a hug. He grunted, only slightly placated, pissed off at the strangers who couldn't be bothered to stop.

They walked on the road for an hour, Peyton growing increasingly hungry and frustrated, before a Mercedes station wagon finally pulled over. They ran to the car, relieved. A man in his forties, his face smooth and round like a pancake, smiled. They piled in, Peyton in the passenger seat, and Isabelle in the back.

The car sped up.

"Where you headed?"

"The bus station," Peyton said.

"No problem. Where are you taking the bus?"

"To Boston," Peyton said. The man glanced at Isabelle in the rearview mirror and smiled at her. Lecherously, Peyton thought, closing his fist and banging it lightly against the siding.

"Are you students?"

"Yes," Peyton said quickly. "Do you live up here?"

"Nope. I live in New York. I was visiting my sister. She and her husband are fucking rich hippies." The man laughed heartily. Peyton smiled, trying to conceal his annoyance. He did not like this man.

"What about you two lovebirds? What are you doing?" The man smiled at Isabelle when he said this, raising his eyebrows up and down provocatively. She giggled. Fucking pay attention to the road, Peyton wanted to scream.

"We were camping," he said, his voice barely controlled.

"Yes," Isabelle said from the backseat. "It was quite beautiful. Don't you love it?" she said, smiling.

He smiled back at her, and the car swerved off the road. "Whoops," he said, jerking it back on track. Yeah, Peyton screamed to himself, watch the fucking road!

"I'm not really one for nature," he said to Isabelle, again not looking at the road.

Peyton wanted to grab the wheel from him, even though he'd only driven a few times, when his mother or grandfather had gotten drunk in town. The car swerved unsteadily, taking the curves widely and crossing over into the other lane.

"I'm a city fellow myself. What about you?" he asked Isabelle.

"Oh, I love the mountains."

"Really? You look like a nice city girl to me," he said, winking at her. Peyton curled his fist.

"You should put on your seatbelt," Peyton said to Isabelle. She looked confused.

"Okay," she said, snapping it on.

"What school do you go to?" the man asked, still staring at Isabelle in the rearview mirror.

"Harvard," Peyton said. "We go to Harvard."

The man whistled. "Wow, I picked up some smarty pants!"

Isabelle smiled nervously, as if she couldn't sustain the lie. Peyton nodded. "I'm studying to be a doctor."

"Good old pre-med, eh? What about you, sweetie?" The car rolled into the other lane. Peyton squeezed his hands into fists, cutting into his palms.

"I'm a visual artist."

"Oh, how unusual. I'd love to see some of your things."

"I don't have any showings right now."

The car made a sharp turn into the parking lot of the bus station. Peyton jumped out, slamming the door. He opened Isabelle's door and she handed him the bags.

"Here," the man said, handing her a business card. "Call me and I'll take a look at your art. I love to buy art."

Peyton rolled his eyes.

"Thank you for the ride," she said, smiling and stepping out of the car. Peyton waved as the man drove off. Good riddance.

"That man was a douchebag."

"What do you mean?"

"He was trying to get in your pants."

She laughed. "He was just being friendly."

Peyton sighed, and sat down to wait for the next bus. He was starving and annoyed. Isabelle started sketching in her book. He took out *The Lord of the Flies*, his assignment for the week, and read it. He wished he too was stranded on a deserted island. He would rule the roost, not taking disobedience from anyone. In an unrestricted state of nature, he knew he would win. He was made for that. Instead, he was stuck here, where everybody else had a leg-up and he had to make himself from nothing.

The bus finally pulled up and they got in. The seats were empty, except for a mom and her young son sitting near the front. Isabelle and Peyton took the back seats. Isabelle kept sketching and he returned to his book. When they chased a wild pig, he was distracted by images of pork and bacon. He was so hungry.

He cursed himself for not having remembered food. Not that there was anything at Cliff's to eat. At house parties, he usually made his way to the kitchen, helping himself to leftovers and granola bars. The rows of every sort of food stocked in the pantries and refrigerators amazed him. One could eat for years off that food. Once, he'd even made a bag of ice and later, when everyone was blitzed, took a juicy two pound steak and stored it in his homemade cooler.

The bus drove back into the city, and Peyton leaned over, and asked to see what she'd sketched. She shook her head.

"It's no good," she said, ripping it out of the book and crumpling it up in a ball. She threw it on the floor.

She seemed angry, and started again, on a new sheet. Her fingers were shaded black, and he noticed a red bump on her pointy finger.

He smiled, feeling a rush of affection for her, wanting to pull her close to his body, and get rid of her anger. But he knew it wasn't that kind of anger.

She kept drawing, intent, her eyebrows furrowed, and she didn't notice when the bus pulled into their stop. He touched her shoulder gently. She jumped.

"What?"

"We're back."

She flipped her book closed roughly, and shoved it in her pack. He took both the bags and they walked off the bus. Rows of buses and the oiled parking lot reminded him of the city's nastiness. Taking a breath, he choked on the industrial air.

"I'm going to school to work," she said, taking her pack and hoisting it on her shoulders. Her mood was dark and focused, as if she couldn't register anything except her sketches. He pulled her against him, cupping her head and kissing her forehead.

"Okay, I'll see you later," he said.

She nodded, hugging him lightly, distracted. She pulled away and took a pink rubber band off her wrist and tied her hair in a high ponytail. She took off running, her large pack bouncing underneath her long hair. He watched her until she turned toward the bridge into Cambridge and disappeared.

Walking by a sidewalk vendor, he pulled a bag of chips off the side of the cart. The woman at the front of the line, ordering, shot him a nasty look, as if to say, what do you think you are doing?

He shrugged and winked at her, and her face softened. He ate the chips as he debated where to get food. He went to a rundown Mexican restaurant that served chips and salsa while you waited for your food, and he ate two baskets of chips while they made his four-dollar chicken quesadilla. When a family left behind three uneaten tacos, he scooped the basket up on his way to the restroom, eating them in the stall.

After he finished his dinner, he paid his bill and, on the way out, smiled as he took a few leftover tortillas, still warm, from another table. He ate them and was finally full and sleepy, and jogged home slowly.

Cliff had apparently not moved. He was still plopped in front of the television, watching a football game and drinking a beer. His mother sat at the kitchen table, smoking a cigarette.

"Hey, baby!" she said, her eyes lighting up. "Come sit. Do you want something to drink?"

"Sure," he said, dropping his bag on the floor and sitting down. She got a beer out of the refrigerator and handed it to him.

"Abigail," Cliff said. "Those are mine." Cliff kept his eyes on the television as he said it.

She rolled her eyes as she took a puff of her cigarette. She threw the beer back in the refrigerator. "You want some water?"

"Sure."

She poured him a glass from the tap, and the brownish water came out in spurts. He thanked her, but didn't take a sip. The tap water was disgusting.

She smiled and lowered her face next to his ear. "Next weekend," she whispered. "We can look for a new place." She clapped her hands together silently. He smiled back at her. He wanted to get out of this dump. He didn't care anymore how they had to do it.

She pointed at Cliff and mouthed, "So gross." He laughed.

"What have you been up to this weekend?" she said, her normal voice breaking the quiet.

"Isabelle and I went camping in the Berkshires."

"Camping? Didn't you get enough of all that in West Virginia?"

"It's beautiful, Ma. You know I don't like the city."

"But the city is where everything happens. Whoever this girl is, she better not distract you from your studies," she said firmly, putting out her cigarette in an empty beer can.

"She's not, Ma."

"Good. Because you'll have plenty of women when you're a successful businessman. Trust me."

"I know, Ma. Don't worry."

She squeezed his hand. "You're my good boy."

He squeezed her hand back and kissed her on the cheek. "I'm exhausted," he said. "I'm going to knock off for a while, before I study."

She nodded nervously. "Okay."

He changed his clothes and spread his blanket in the corner of the living room, falling asleep to the television, his mother flipping the pages of a magazine, and Cliff's heavy breathing.

CHAPTER NINE

Their apartment search lasted for a month. Every place Peyton and his mother visited was either dilapidated or in a trashy neighborhood. Their standards lowered each weekend, like a brick wall crumbling to pieces, and they were reluctantly settling on a garden studio—whose tiny windows let in a few streaks of sunlight, and offered a world-class view of people's feet and ankles—when a dancer at his mother's club offered them her small one-bedroom in Cambridge.

The dancer was moving in with her boyfriend; otherwise, she never would have left, as the apartment was a rare find on their budget—a decent place in a clean neighborhood. They put down the deposit that day.

The apartment had hardwood floors, a decorative fireplace, a galley kitchen, and French doors separating the living space from the dining room. This meant, for the first time in his life, with the simple hanging of a cloth, Peyton would have his own bedroom.

The neighborhood was working class, but diligent. People went to work in the morning. They put out their trash, and taught their children to say please and thank you. They turned their lights out early, and went to church on Sunday morning.

This respectful quiet was a welcome relief. Cliff's neighborhood had flouted its decrepit state, like an obese person throwing his weight around. People had loitered at all hours of the day. They threw their trash in the street, shouted, sold drugs, and stumbled around aimlessly, intoxicated on one thing or another.

Their apartment windows looked over an alley directly into the windows of another apartment. The beige curtains were pulled back, and sitting on the fire escape, Peyton could see the inside clearly. It was blandly furnished. A mother cooked dinner and her two boys, both pallid with carrot colored hair, wrestled each other on the floor. A squat balding father read the newspaper at the kitchen table.

Their physical proximity made it easy for Peyton to imagine he was part of the family, as if he were the oldest brother, reading his book as the rest of the family whirled around him. He often studied on the fire escape, peeking up to see how "his" family was doing. He listened to their arguments, their apologies, the boys' schemes, and the parents' making love. He almost could believe they were his. But he knew he was really an unnoticed intruder, invasively drinking up their private moments.

His mother was at work, and the apartment was dark. A friend of his mother's, one of the hairstylists, had given them a ride over here with their quickly-assembled boxes of stuff. His mother had packed the sheets, towels, toilet paper and the rest of the beer, claiming she was entitled to half. She left Cliff a note saying they were leaving. Peyton thought she should tell him in person, but she shook her head wildly, claiming Cliff would take it poorly, and follow them here in a drunken rage.

Months later, Cliff inexplicably found the apartment, and he pounded the door with his fist late Saturday night, calling Peyton's mother a whore and saying she was a selfish bitch who tricked him.

Peyton cracked open the door and told him his mother wasn't home.

Cliff pushed past him, stumbling into the apartment. His face was bright, alcoholic red, and covered in a spotty black beard.

Cliff flung open the door to the bedroom, screaming, "I know you're here, Abigail!"

Peyton laughed. When Cliff realized she was out, he sat down at the kitchen table and started crying.

"How can I get her back? She's the most beautiful woman I have ever been with."

Peyton shook his head and handed him a beer from the refrigerator, which Cliff grasped like a baby blanket.

"Pull yourself together, Cliff. Women come and go. Get over it."

Cliff opened the beer, and started drinking. He looked terrible. He finished his beer, and rested his head in his hands. Peyton suddenly felt sorry for him. His mother had used him, and she was significantly more beautiful than any woman he would ever be with again. His mother would be a standard against which the women in his life would be measured, and they would all fall far short.

"Look, you have to find someone who loves you more…"

Cliff pulled his head up and nodded. "I know, I know I had no right being with her in the first place. But I just want her back so badly. Things just seem so ordinary now …" He rubbed his face with the base of his palm, and stood up. He stumbled to the door.

"Just tell her I stopped by. Tell her I want her back."

"Sure," Peyton said, smiling sadly. Some people don't get it, he thought.

He couldn't believe his mother had ever been with Cliff; it seemed ludicrous, an unnatural, freak event. He grabbed himself a beer and climbed out on the fire escape. The family was eating ice cream at the dinner table. The boys were digging in, barely looking up. The mother and father talked in the corner and, occasionally, the father would gently brush the hair from her face. This reminded him of Isabelle, and he was annoyed. She must have been over an hour late by now. She often didn't show up on time, consumed by her painting.

He heard a knock at the door, and despite himself, felt excitement in his chest. He took his time climbing back in the window, wanting to make her wait. He was still going to tell her off.

He slowly opened the door. The fact that it was only his neighbor Joseph simultaneously disappointed and aggravated him.

Joseph had come over the day after Peyton had moved in, nervously shuffling around the room, wondering where their furniture was, and blushing when his mother said hello from the floor, her practically bare legs stretched out. Only after Joseph mentioned it did Peyton remember why Joseph looked vaguely familiar: Joseph was in Peyton's biology class.

Peyton asked his teammates at school and found out Joseph's father had gone to prison for financial fraud three years ago. Joseph and his older sister had attended Hunter since preschool and the school decided to give them scholarships to finish their education. But the students had been less graceful. Joseph and his sister were socially dumped, unceremoniously spurned by the other students, as if they bore the contagious sins of their father.

At the library, Peyton had pulled up all the newspaper coverage on microfiche. Joseph's father, like Joseph, was a slight man, with narrow shoulders and a sloped chin. In the pictures, he glanced nervously away from the cameras, and his eyes, focused on the ground, were unreadable. Physically, he lurked behind his boss, a tall, balding man who smiled directly at the cameras, waving, a gold watch wrapped around his bulky wrist.

According to the papers, they had run a fifteen-million-dollar swindle over a twelve-year period. They had convinced small-time investors to purchase stakes in bogus partnerships, promising large annual returns. In reality, the money went to risky investments, most of which failed, and funded their lavish lifestyles, including mansions, private jets and women.

As long as they acquired enough new money to spread around, the scheme kept perpetuating itself; once they couldn't pay their initial investors, the government began investigating the complaints, and shortly thereafter, they were charged with 28 acts of criminal fraud. Though how much Joseph's father knew remained unclear, both he and his boss received a 25 year prison sentence.

Peyton was fascinated by this, by Joseph's father, who was described as having led a double life for ten years: on the one side, he was a good boss and reliable family man, and on the other, he was taking private jets to the Caribbean, gambling, and snorting coke.

This two-faced life was incredibly ballsy. It had never occurred to Peyton that he could construct another self, which he could then put on and off like a suit. There was something freeing and exciting about this.

Joseph's father's stunning duplicity lent an air of intrigue to Joseph, as Peyton eyed him with the possibility that he too might have a radically different self. Probably because he no longer had any friends, Joseph had taken to Peyton like a dog. Joseph was always there, nipping at his heels, and though he was often annoying, his absurd loyalty and his interesting father ended up justifying his presence.

Joseph was prone to ranting against capitalism and liberal society, spitting as he talked of these "twin evils." Peyton was a fan of capitalism, probably because he believed he would thrive in an unrestricted market, and so they got into long arguments on the fire escape, loudly debating the virtues and vices of various political arrangements.

"Hey," Peyton said, opening the door for him. "Isabelle was supposed to be here over an hour ago."

Regardless of the occasion, Joseph dressed formally, and he was wearing khakis, a white button-up shirt, and a blue tie. He nodded and walked into the apartment, pacing back and forth.

"I'm writing a response to Dr. Buchanan's response to my Cold War paper," he said, rubbing his slender chin. He looked like a boy playing dress up in his father's clothes and it occurred to Peyton they probably were his father's clothes. His mother couldn't afford to buy new clothes.

Peyton nodded, taking another drink of cold beer and plopping down on the tan couch they had bought at the Salvation Army. He spread out his legs.

"He's not objective. There are realities he refuses to see. I've got the original documentation."

"Nobody's objective," Peyton snorted.

"Don't fall for that one. Facts matter. He's ignoring the facts."

"Hey, do you want to hit up Nathan's party?"

"No, no. I have to finish this paper. It's imperative." He looked directly at Peyton. "I thought you said Isabelle was coming."

"She's over an hour late. I'm not waiting anymore."

"You know she's just painting, lost in her own mind," Joseph said, exasperated.

Peyton stared at him blankly. "So? Hey, when are we going to visit your father?" Joseph dismissed his father as a "worthless scumbag" and, in three years, Joseph had never visited him in Devens. Only his little sister had gone, while their mother waited outside, fuming, sitting in her luxurious BMW, the last remnant of her previous life, one she refused to give up. Joseph had allowed that Peyton could come with him when he finally went to visit.

Joseph shrugged. "There's no time for the scumbag now. Peyton," he said, pausing. "Can I work here? My mother is watching romcom drivel and the saccharine soundtrack keeps invading my thoughts through the cheap plywood doors."

"Sure," Peyton said, smiling and drinking the rest of his beer. "Just don't finish the beer," he added facetiously.

Joseph never drank, and he curled his lip indignantly. "You know I have a history of alcoholism in my family."

"Yeah, I know," Peyton said, hitting him on the shoulder. He pulled on his jacket and picked up his keys. "If Isabelle shows, tell her I went to Nathan's and will be back late."

Peyton strode quickly to the end of the hall and jogged down the stairs. This was the third or fourth time Isabelle had left him hanging. Once, he'd tracked her down and found her painting in her room, her hair a mess, her madly efficient strokes crossing the canvas. She looked startled, and then became angry he barged in. She'd forgotten their plans, and even when he reminded her, she seemed skeptical they had ever existed.

He considered going to her house, but he didn't see the point. If she was going to stand him up, then he had better things to do.

People had already started drinking when he arrived. The living room was packed out and punk music was playing on the stereo. Peyton went right to the kitchen and took two shots of vodka.

Back in the living room, cold beer in hand, he saw a group of players and joined them on the couch. The football season had ended a couple of months ago, and most of them, including Peyton, had switched to running track and lifting weights. He sorely missed the football games. Track was a poor substitute for knocking into someone full force. It was intoxicating to hit a lug without restraint, sending him straight to the ground, the packed crowd chanting his name in the stands while the cheerleaders blew kisses and clapped, their short skirts flapping in the wind. In those moments, his whole existence was free and justified. He hit as cold and hard as he wanted, and the endless, booming mass of people loved it. They called for more violence, more power, more destruction. And he gave it to them.

The players lounging on the couch offered up high-fives. "Peyton, buddy," they said. Peyton grinned and sat down, popping open his beer.

"Hey, did you hear about Veronica?" Nelson said, leaning in. Peyton shook his head.

"She was giving Vincent head while he was driving her father's car, and he crashed it into a tree."

Peyton laughed. "Nice."

"Not classy. Major loss of points."

"I'm so sorry, father," Michael said, raising his voice to a feminine pitch. "I was blowing a boy and caused a major accident."

They laughed. Three junior girls, part of the student council, sat down on the coffee table, each carrying a plastic cup.

"Hey, boys," the shortest one said. "What's so funny?"

Nelson stretched his long arms across the back of the couch and smiled. "Give us the inside scoop on school politics. What's the dirt?"

The white tank-top smiled, revealing a row of blindingly white teeth. "Well, we heard Dr. Montgomery screwed Principal Morrison so she could have more science equipment."

The boys laughed. As the banter went back and forth, Peyton spaced out, thinking of Isabelle, wondering what she thought she was doing, pissed she stood him up. He tried to focus on the people in front of him, but his head was pounding and he wanted to beat somebody up. He was enraged at Isabelle. He excused himself and went out the back door. The porch lit up when we walked outside. He put his head in his hands, rubbing his temples. He let out a sigh and finished his beer.

"Hi," a girl said.

Peyton turned around. It was the white tank-top. She sat down next to him at the table.

"I came over to talk to you and then you left," she said, fake-pouting, her hands on her hips. She was pretty—she had tan skin, and shiny, brown hair, which was cut to frame her round face. Her hips were wide and soft.

"Sorry," he said, hitting his empty beer can on the table. "I'm in a bad mood."

"Porque, senor?"

He realized then she was the junior tutor for his Spanish class. He had chosen it because it was supposedly the easiest language to learn.

He leaned back in his chair. "No lo se… ella me dejo chifanlando en la loma."

"Ahh," she said. She reached out and took his hand. "Olvídesela."

He tried to remember what that meant, but drew a blank. Maybe he never knew. "What?"

"Forget her."

He pulled her hand closer and leaned in and kissed her.

He kissed her aggressively, his rage surging up and coming out of his hands. He took her hand, and pulled her off the deck into the unlit backyard. He pushed her up against a tree, feeling the rough bark on his palm.

"You must be cold," he said. She nodded and he took off his jacket, giving it to her.

She slipped it on and put her arms back around his neck. He kissed her hard, his mouth open, his hands under her shirt, running over her full breasts.

She pulled away, taking a breath. "Woah, senor," she said. "Too much."

He took a deep breath and banged his head against the tree, over her shoulder, wanting to scream.

"Hey," she said, her face becoming sympathetic. "It's okay." She rubbed his hand with both of hers. "It's really okay."

She kissed him again and he tried to keep his hands under control, as they begged to lash out. He wanted to destroy something.

"Do you want to go upstairs?" she said, surprising him.

He nodded, gripping her hand tightly as they went back inside. They took the back stairs and opened the first door. She giggled. It was a little girl's room

135

as large as Peyton's apartment. The walls were painted pink, and a rose-covered canopy hung over a white wood bed. The cabinets and floors teemed with finely-made, plush toys.

Peyton stared at her for a moment and then stripped off her jacket and pulled down her pants, kicking the stupid toys aside. He tried to remember if this girl was easy, but he couldn't, and so he treated her like she was anyway. He knew it was perverse—fucking her in a little girl's room—but he didn't care. He couldn't stop himself. He turned her around and bent her over a cabinet.

The cabinet rattled against the wall, her hands tightly gripping the sides. Peyton moved harder and faster until he came. His body finally unclenched. He rested on top of her, feeling her back rise and fall through his t-shirt and the sweat on his forehead.

He stood up, wiping his brow. He zipped his pants and then looked around, as if he had lost something but couldn't remember what it was. She was still bent over, her hands still curled around the sides of the cabinet.

He tugged her shirt down and then lifted her upright. He realized he didn't know her name. He moved the brown hair off her forehead.

"That was nice?" she said, shyly.

"Yeah, it was," he said, sitting on the bed. She walked close to him and he laid his head against her stomach, resting his hands on her hips. Her fingers played in his hair.

"We should do it again," she whispered.

"Yeah," he agreed, squeezing her hips. He meant it too. This girl was sweet. He realized he felt better, as if his anger had been purged. He closed his eyes. The barely audible sounds of punk music and laughter drifted into the room, and her fingers circled around and around his hair, lightly touching his scalp.

"I have to get home," she said. "Curfew."

He nodded, not really caring. She picked up a pink stationary pad from the girl's dress and scribbled something.

"Here."

It said Veronica and her phone number. He folded the paper and slipped it in his pocket.

"I'll call you," he said, unsure if he was lying.

She leaned in and pecked him on the cheek, and then scurried out the door.

"I'm so late," she called over her shoulder, her tone apologetic.

"See you later."

He was in no hurry to leave. In the far corner of the room, he saw a dollhouse of mammoth proportions. He strode over, drawn by the tiny bright lights. It was a couple feet taller than him.

Inside, it had dozens of rooms, many of them with thumb-sized Tiffany lamps, and well-built oak furniture. In the upstairs bedroom, a blonde woman, with a straight nose and high cheekbones, stared primly in the mirror, wearing a silver evening gown and high-heels. Her walk-in closet had rows of clothes and hundreds of shoes. Everything was finely constructed with quality materials—the stove was silver, the countertops marble, and the faucets gold.

Peyton laughed, incredulous, finding the house perfectly outlandish: it had probably cost more than their apartment. He thought of the dirty bums in Cliff's neighborhood and the poorly fed children in West Virginia, wearing shoes too large or too tight.

He wanted to destroy the dollhouse with its extravagant, ridiculous, self-indulgence; he wanted to burn it down. That this girl could have this lavish dollhouse in a sprawling bedroom adorned with plush toys and bright paintings of ballerinas and rainbows, while other children had only a box of used clothes and half a single bed struck Peyton as violating some fundamental law of nature.

It was not possible these two children's lives could co-exist, and so he wanted to burn this life down, leaving its occupants with nothing, ending the disparity once and for all.

He seized the woman out of her bedroom, sticking her in his jacket, and he knocked over the tiny, elegant bedroom furniture, leaving it in a mess, as if the house had been ransacked.

Downstairs, a few boys were still sitting on the couches, talking and drinking. Peyton nodded but went out the back door, and climbed over the wood fence and on to the next street. He pulled the doll out of his jacket and ran home, carrying her by the waist. Her coiffed hair remained stiffly in place.

Inside the apartment, Joseph was lying on the couch, an old, musty book sprawled open on his chest. Peyton put the book on the floor and lifted Joseph's legs onto the couch. He set the blonde doll on top of the fireplace. She stood primly in her evening gown and high-heels, oblivious to her crappier surroundings.

Peyton lifted the blanket covering the clear French doors. Isabelle was sleeping on his single bed, wearing her white cotton pajamas. Her duffel bag was on the floor. Peyton stripped to his boxers and stared out the window, his arms crossed.

They did not have the heat on in the apartment, and the cold crept up on him quickly, chilling his bones. He welcomed it, wanting to push it, to prove he was tough. He'd grown out his dirty blonde hair and wore it in a half-ponytail, and as he stood, half-naked in front of the window, he imagined he was a Samurai headed into battle.

He looked down at the asphalt and the green dumpster, and then straight at the dark apartment—he could barely see the lines of their furniture, and perhaps he only imagined he could see them.

After months of watching, he knew he could conjure up the exact lines of the apartment without seeing anything at all. He spread both his hands against the cold glass, and for a second, he wanted to make a fist and shatter the window, and watch as the glass fell to the asphalt below.

He turned around, leaning against the cold window, and watched Isabelle sleep. She was curled in the fetal position, her fist gripping the blanket, her face expressionless. She was a remarkable sleeper, unmoved by bright light, stalling cars, or pointed shoves. He would crawl into the small bed, put his arm under her neck, and wrap his leg and arm around her body, and through this, she would remain tangled in her private web of slumber.

He was still angry at her, pissed she blew him off, and part of him wanted to choke her, yelling and screaming until she became incapable of standing him up again. He wanted to wake her up and tell her that he fucked Veronica.

But he wouldn't. Even now, he felt an immense, blinding affection for her, and as he watched her sleep, a specter of guilt, of real wrongdoing, quickly overrun by anger—she had made him do it—rose in the room's shadows.

He climbed into bed, wrapping himself around her, brushing her long hair out of her face.

"Don't do this to me, Isabelle," he said adamantly, squeezing her. "You can't let me down like that. Don't you get that?"

Holding her, feeling her soft skin and the jut of her ribs, smelling her neck and hair, the anger dissipated. He felt safe. As he fell asleep, he succumbed to a vague feeling of everlasting happiness.

* * *

As spring lengthened the day's hours, and the trees and flowers rose back to life, their apartment accumulated pieces of furniture and decorative objects, making it feel more like a home.

On the weekends, Peyton, his mother and Isabelle trekked all over town, searching in thrift shops for cheap, quality pieces. Isabelle seemed to have a sixth sense; within minutes of entering a store, she'd find the only beautiful object amidst the piles of broken crap.

She had found a smooth mahogany coffee table with only a few scratches on the legs, rich, crimson drapes, a small Greek statue of a woman in a robe, a print of Degas's dancers, oak dressers and cream-colored dishes.

His mother gave him new black shoes and a leather bag. She was generous with her money, and her face was proud whenever she purchased an item, no matter how mundane. Her personal tastes had become noticeably trashier: her clothes were tighter and covered less of her body, and her makeup was brighter and more dramatic.

She kept her piles of cash in an antique trunk. He often caught her standing over the trunk, her hands gripping both sides, beaming, as if she were looking over a sacred book, taking strength from its eternal power.

Peyton tried to ignore her job, forget what she was doing. When he considered it, he was disgusted and angry, and indulged in a fantasy of standing outside the club and pummeling the lawyers, bankers and spoiled college kids one by one.

His mother was friendly to Isabelle and delighted with her eye for beautiful objects, but occasionally, she would frown at Isabelle or look at her aggressively, like a dog protecting her territory. His mother encouraged him to socialize more and the few times he brought Veronica to the apartment, his mother was excessively friendly, refilling Veronica's drink, offering her cigarettes, insisting she stop by more.

Veronica was flattered by the attention, gushing later she "loved" his mother, and Peyton didn't tell her his mother's flattery had more to do with who Veronica wasn't than who she was.

Over the months, his mother's disapproval grew stronger, and one Sunday night, she came right out and told Peyton he was too young to be with one person, and, either way, he should be with someone more stable. Isabelle, she said, leaning forward, was crazy. Peyton laughed.

His mother was indignant, her chin trembling, her face taking on the frustrated pose of someone who knows they are right, but powerless to convince others of the truth.

"I'm telling you, Peyton," she said, her voice barely controllable. "You'll regret being so serious."

Peyton shrugged, not believing a word or understanding why she cared. He hugged her, and rubbed her back, wanting her to relax, and see how this was the last of their worries.

He started to conceal parts of his relationship with Isabelle. Originally, he had shared everything with his mother—his frustrations with Isabelle's artistic trances; the sheer strangeness of her. Now he was careful never to mention when Isabelle showed up hours late, or disappeared, without warning, for days.

He didn't tell his mother, either, how he and Isabelle hid in the art museum's restroom near closing time, spending the night locked in, sitting in front of paintings for hours, running their hands over cold sculptures, or how, after midnight, they jumped the fence to the community pool and swam naked, splashing and giggling in the dark.

Or how they dressed up in their finest clothes and snuck into operas and symphonies at intermission, proceeding confidently to the best open seats. Or how, every day of the summer, when he worked on the docks, Isabelle sketched or painted on the shore, her hair blowing wildly in the wind.

Nor did he tell her how uncontrollably furious he became when Isabelle went missing, drinking an obscene amount of alcohol to quell his anger, drowning it in white noise, and inevitably, seducing another girl, her yielding eyes reinvigorating his sense of control.

Or how any time a male over the age of eleven smiled at Isabelle, he wanted to punch them in the face. When they had gone to the beach, and three college boys whistled at her as they walked past, Peyton punched the closest one, breaking his nose, and initiating a nasty three-on-one-fight. He lied to his mother, telling her the bruises were from a pickup football game in the city.

At the end of the summer, Peyton and Isabelle ate picnics near the water, the warm sun beating down on their skin. They read books until it turned dark and then took long walks along the river, Isabelle always seizing his arm when she found something striking. Over time, he realized that many immediately ugly things—a squirrel's cracked skull, a homeless man surrounded by piles of trash, a slug—could be beautiful if you stared at them long enough, their human meanings stripped away until only their aesthetic form remained.

Isabelle liked to see things from different angles, and so he often hoisted her on his shoulders, and they walked around town, her fingers in his hair, her soft voice narrating the view from the sky.

The house parties were smaller in the summer as many students went abroad or had internships in a different city, but they still happened every weekend. Peyton went when he needed to blow off steam. For the first time, he had a steady supply of money, and he put most of it in his mother's box, but he kept enough to buy beer.

Down by the docks, dressed in his work clothes, the pubs rarely carded him. He liked the work—it was hard, physical labor—and he liked the men he worked with. They were strong and didn't waste words. They reminded him of his grandparents. When they finished their shift, the men wiped their brows with handkerchiefs, nodded to one another, and headed to the pub for a drink. They respected each other for a job well done and, under these rules, Peyton won their respect. He felt like a real man, not just a boy who had lied about his age to get a job.

Peyton lamented having to leave the docks. The truth was, these men felt more natural to him than his classmates. They were in his blood.

His initial return to football practice was jarring. The locker room banter seemed incredibly juvenile. At the parties he attended over the summer, he was so drunk that he soaked everything up indiscriminately. Sober, and used to the silent work on the docks, the boys' boastful conversations struck him as inane and narcissistic. It was for this reason that, in early September, when he had to pick an extracurricular club to join—a sophomore to senior year requirement—he signed up for Joseph's "Philosophy Club."

The other football players joined the "Future Business Leaders of America" or the "Sports in the Media" club, the latter, varsity-athletes-only, read magazine articles and biographies about famous sports figures. By mid-season, Peyton had forgotten his opposition to the banter, and he took a lot of flak for being in the "Philosophy Club." This was half in jest, as the club's social worth was provided for by William, its president.

William was the most well-known person in the school. People flocked to him like roaches to sugar. Even tightly-wound drones would break rules for him—he turned forms and papers in late, uptight girls dropped their pants, he convinced the school to throw lavish parties. While he could have wielded his power over people in mean ways, he didn't. He was a diligent class president, an honor roll student, a basketball starter, and, in his limited way, kind to everyone.

William came to the first meeting of the Philosophy Club, along with six or seven other students, and announced, if Joseph didn't mind, he'd like to be the president. Later, when the club had dwindled to Joseph, Peyton and Isabelle, William explained that his father had wanted him to take an active interest in "serious issues of the mind," and if he were president of the philosophy club, his father would consider it done. But at the time, he simply said he wanted the role.

Joseph glanced around indecisively, biting his fingernails, apparently flattered William had shown up, seeing this as a potential ride out of his social Siberia, but reluctant to cede control of his club. After a weighted pause, he relented, and William grinned, never expecting any other answer, and said, "Great."

Joseph smiled widely.

Immediately, William plopped down at the table and appointed Joseph vice-president and "head of each week's agenda."

Joseph beamed, realizing he now had it all—William giving his club social cache, and the ability to dictate what they discussed.

Peyton quickly discovered the source of William's charisma: a deep-rooted sense that he would obtain everything he ever wanted in this life. This unflappable confidence in the brightness of his future meant William approached everything with an effusive lightheartedness, and to most people, ensnared in their own desperation, doubts and insecurities, this lightheartedness was a drug, allowing them to feel, briefly, like they too were invincible, free from anger and fear, capable of anything.

William's objective qualities—his status as heir to a hundred-million-dollar publishing conglomerate, his intelligence and good looks—shut down any doubts a person might have had about his invincibility. If it were an illusion that William was invincible, it wasn't an illusion that would be punctured.

Over the years, it became apparent, though, that a barrier existed between William and other people. While William was fawned over by students, teachers and staff alike, he wasn't particularly close to anyone. Even after sustained interaction, William still remained at a distance, impressing on people that his social orbit was large, deflecting anybody's desire to monopolize his time, or lean on him. He floated in and out of social groups, liked by all, claimed by none.

It was for this reason that Isabelle did not like William. She thought he was irredeemably shallow, merely gliding effortlessly across the surface of life, like a person who could walk on water, as the rest of humanity was forced to swim, fighting tempestuous rapids and perilous detritus.

Though this shallowness occasionally infuriated Peyton, too, making him want to punch William's smiling face in, he usually found this quality intoxicating. William's disposition seemed justified by his circumstances; there was little doubt, in Peyton's mind, that if he had been born into such a decadent life, he too would have cruised over the surface of things. He would have bought fast cars, flown private jets, slept with hundreds of women, and dined on the finest food.

When he told Isabelle this, she punched him over and over, exclaiming urgently, "Don't say that. Don't say that."

"Why? It's true."

She refused to accept this, and he finally relented, saying it was possible he would have been different, that he would have seen the selfishness and superficiality of his ways. She latched on to this thin strand, her eying weary but determined.

He did not understand why she cared—after all, he was who he was. There was no changing that. Why did it matter who he might have been in some other world?

The philosophy club convened at William's brick, neo-Gothic mansion. They sat in large, brown leather chairs, surrounded by rows of books. More books than had existed in all of Lamar County. Renaissance paintings of voluptuous women hung on the wall, and a giant, Oriental rug covered the pale wood floor.

William and Peyton drank Scotch from the liquor cabinet. The debates were heated, and only William remained constantly aloof, stating opinions that he stuck to, but in a way that implied it didn't much matter one way or the other—as if he were making a claim on whether one should write in blue or black ink. He did, however, listen intently, quickly soaking up the content of the various philosophies, and Peyton imagined him rattling this information off to his father, proving to his father that he'd "taken ideas seriously."

Joseph, in contrast, did take ideas seriously. It was as if he believed convincing others to a proposition would somehow convert the reality, as if the actions required for worldly transformations were superfluous. He was an adamant neo-Marxist, shorn of the deterministic element, and when disputing an important point, he stuttered and flushed, wagging his fingers.

If anyone agreed with him, he tried to shore up his advantage, "Yes, that is exactly right! See? See?" he'd say to the unconvinced parties. Ironically, because of his desperation to persuade, he was inept at it. The more he clung to and pumped an idea, the more unappealing it became to everyone else.

Isabelle, who was detached from philosophy, usually pointed out flaws in other people's arguments rather than endorse any position herself. Listening to her point out logical flaws in book after book, Peyton was startled, not knowing, until then, how sharp her mind was. The sharpness in her mind did not produce a systematic philosophy—Peyton imagined her mind cutting down any structure it tried to build—and the "philosophies" she subscribed to were nebulous, marked more for their beautiful writing and imagery than for making coherent points. They invoked experiences and intuitions that one either related to, or didn't. Many times, she'd lose interest in the discussion, and stare at the naked women on the wall, leaning back in her chair, enraptured, or walk around the library, touching the old globe, peering at the glass vases and rifling through the old books. Peyton watched her, often losing the thread of dialogue, feeling jealous of those objects and paintings, wanting her to come back to him.

Peyton was drawn to the view that the primary virtues of humans were the production of greatness and loyalty. He and William essentially agreed on this. What they disagreed on, in Peyton's mind predictably, was the value of equality. Peyton thought hoarding was deeply unjust, period, a point Joseph considered fundamental. For hundreds or maybe thousands of hours, they tried to convince William of this. William believed hoarding was justified by a job well-done—shouldn't a worker keep the products of his labor?—and this, naturally, included the right of parents to pass their wealth down to their children.

To some degree, Peyton succumbed to William and Isabelle's detachment: there was no argument, no matter how logical, that would convince Peyton the self-indulgence of rich people should coexist in the same world with backbreaking poverty. It was something he felt in his bones, and he knew nobody could say anything to change his mind. He believed this even though, despite Isabelle's protestations, if he had been born to William's mother and father, and grown up in his ten-thousand square foot house, traveling the world, his pale, clean hands always touching the finest objects and people, he would have believed, to his core, exactly what William did.

Sometimes, he would see this shadowing their words as they argued, and then, he had to laugh at the futility of it, embracing William's jovial detachment and Isabelle's easy distraction—because in those moments, he saw so clearly their words didn't matter.

Other times, of course, he believed his words were without a doubt true, and then he became loud and heated, stalking around the room, furious with his interlocutor. He spouted about untreated diseases, frostbitten fingers, stunted growth and suffocating, neverending labor.

Once, he became so enraged with William's insistence that the hundred-thousand-dollar dollhouse was morally justified, he punched him in the face and stormed out of the house. He kicked a marble statue on the lawn, stubbing his toe. Isabelle told him William had moaned in pain, and then laughed loudly.

Later, William thanked him for giving him his first black eye. He had relayed the story to his father, adding on he had punched Peyton back, and his father had been delighted, pleased they were so inflamed about ideas. Apparently, William's father's hero was Ernest Hemingway, "a man of the mind who was still a man."

"But you do know," William added, grinning, "You're insane." Peyton laughed, ceding the point. By then, he'd calmed down, and picked his intellectual detachment back up.

The philosophy club convened almost every week for three years. It drifted into broader activities—they critiqued and edited each other's papers, or in Isabelle's case, her sketches and paintings; they read novels, attended movies, plays, art exhibits, and discussed them over dinner, all the expenses put on William's bottomless credit card; senior year, they wrote their college essays, and picked Isabelle's college portfolio from her hundreds of paintings and sketches.

They had become smarter—or at least they appeared smarter to others—as they were able to recognize variants of arguments and rattle off criticisms and counterpoints without reflection. But, ironically, Joseph was the only one who changed his philosophical outlook, drifting from his neo-Marxism to a social communitarianism by the end of their senior year.

Junior year, for the first time, Peyton's post-high school life seemed imminent and he studied longer hours, staying at the library until two or three in the morning, and working out harder at football practice. The relaxed disposition of the other students grated on him. He knew he alone had no room to fail. Freshman and sophomore year, they'd all bummed rides off upperclassmen, but by junior year, nearly everyone had a car.

The other scholarship and staff kids, with the exception of Joseph and Isabelle, no longer registered on Peyton's radar, and he sometimes felt a surge of annoyance at always having to bum a ride, defensively waiting for someone to needle him about it. But no one ever did.

Isabelle, too, worked a great deal. While he burrowed away in the library, reading books and writing papers, she burrowed in her art, sketching and painting longer and longer hours. Her school attendance and grades were erratic, something her parents shrugged off indifferently.

Peyton found her report card in the kitchen trash, unopened. He opened it, seeing she had 18 "excused" absences, and a 2.7 G.P.A. Her parents treated her more like a sibling than a daughter. She had her own key to the house, and came and went as she pleased. They only idly inquired where she'd been and never seemed remotely perturbed by Peyton spending the night. In fact, her mother was unflappably polite and an excellent host, offering him drinks, food, laundry service, and extra blankets.

Isabelle's house had become his second home. At the end of sophomore year, she gave Peyton a copy of her key. He used it whenever he felt like it, availing himself of their food and cable television.

When his mother started dating Ronnie, a greasy Italian she met at the club, Peyton slept at Isabelle's almost all the time. Peyton could not stand listening to his mother and Ronnie have sex. The minute they went into her bedroom, he left. If he was too tired to walk to Isabelle's, he slept on Joseph's couch.

He had once woken up on Joseph's couch in the middle of night, and found Joseph's mother sitting near him.

He stared at her, confused, his jaw tight. He did not move. It was dark; maybe he was dreaming. Her fingers lightly touched his thigh, and he jerked back.

She clumsily stood up, and the shape of her hips, surprisingly narrow, were visible through her satin teddy. "I'm sorry. I didn't mean to disturb you," she whispered.

Her narrow eyes lingered on him. He could see, underneath the rough aging of her face, she had once been pretty, maybe even very pretty.

"Okay," she said softly, suddenly seeming confused, as if she had no idea how her life had led her here. She turned slowly, and walked back to her room.

He took a deep breath, watching her go, the shadows complimenting her naked back and long legs. He considered following her, if that's what she wanted. But the image repulsed him. It was Joseph's mother, after all.

He abruptly felt despondent. He imagined her in her bed, lonely and forgotten, staring blankly at the wall. Joseph's father deserved to be beaten to a bloody pulp. Maybe he had been in prison.

After that night, he switched to sleeping on Joseph's bedroom floor, and he went out of his way to compliment his mother, telling her he liked her hair, or her dress. But in general, he went over there, feeling depressed every time he remembered how she had stood over him and touched his thigh. He didn't want to think about how her life had been ripped away from her, and how she walked around like a confused and empty shell, unsure of what to do, unable to locate a second chance.

Many times, when it was not football season and Peyton and Isabelle were both exhausted from working, they took her mother's car and drove to the Berkshires, spending the weekend hiking and camping, and if it were warm enough, swimming in the dark blue waters.

She took photographs, beautiful black and whites they hung on their bedroom walls, and in their lockers at school. Ever since Peyton's mother had started dating Ronnie, she became effusive about Isabelle, forgetting all her initial objections, and Peyton was content, like the pieces of his life had fallen together and made a solid whole.

The four of them often went to Ronnie's restaurant for dinner on the house. Peyton lamented Ronnie's refusal to let him drink, particularly when Ronnie launched into one of his painfully boring stories. He droned on about his relatives, wines, and his vacation home in Florida, which he intended to take "the little lady" to.

After a couple bottles of wine, Ronnie started talking about "big titty" women. Peyton smiled at Isabelle, his hand on her thigh underneath the table, and she smiled back. They both thought Ronnie was an ass. Peyton was frustrated with his mother but he didn't say anything because she seemed genuinely happy, only giggling at his vulgarities.

* * *

One night in the fall of junior year, he went to Isabelle's house from the library, exhausted and bleary eyed, and found her curled up in her bed, her face damp with tears. She stared at him with intense hate, a look so disgusted and damning he was immediately ill.

"Why are you looking at me like that?" he asked.

"Did you fuck some girl at a party?"

"What? When?"

"Ever."

"Yes, I've had sex, Isabelle," he said, crossing his arms in front of his chest, leaning against the bedroom wall.

She sobbed violently. "When?"

"I don't know. Six months ago."

"Six months ago?" she screeched. "You had sex with someone six months ago?"

She ran over and punched him in the face.

"Shit," he said, bending over. She punched him in the back and kicked him in the shins. He grabbed her around the waist and put her on the bed, climbing over her and holding her hands. He took a deep breath. His eye stung, and he had an intense headache.

"Isabelle, we never said we weren't seeing anybody else."

She laughed bitterly and closed her eyes. "Oh, well, okay then. My misunderstanding."

Tears ran down her face, even though her eyes were blazing angry, not sad. He let her hands go and sat at the edge of the bed, his hands holding his head.

"Isabelle, it was six months ago."

"You don't love me?"

"Yes, of course I do!" he said. Even though he had never before considered this, the affirmation came out vehemently. He didn't need to think it over. Of course he did.

"It was six months ago," he repeated. "Isabelle, you just disappear without saying anything. What do you expect me to do?"

"Fine. There's a boy in my art class. I'll fuck him."

"You don't even fuck me!"

"Turns out that's a good thing, too."

"Isabelle, I love you. Nobody else. Those other girls meant nothing to me. Isn't that enough?"

"No, it's not fair. You were supposed to wait for me. You were never supposed to be with anyone else."

"Isabelle, I was with people before we even met. And I am waiting for you. You're the only one I care about. You're my best friend."

The anger drained from her face, replaced by a distant sadness. She was almost cold. This made his stomach drop out. Anger he could take. Not this.

"Isabelle…" he said softly.

"This is too much right now. Let's just go to bed."

"Okay."

He took off his shoes and clothes, folding them on the floor. She turned out the light, and climbed back into bed, her clothes still on. She laid her head on his chest and put her leg over his thighs.

"I love you, too," she said, her voice lethargic with remorse, as if she regretted this about herself.

She fell asleep, almost instantly. He stared at the dark ceiling, trying to see the dots. The hole in his stomach remained. For him, fucking girls had become just something he did to blow off steam and make himself feel in control.

He couldn't remember most of the girls he'd fucked; they'd been that insignificant. When he fished deeper in his mind, they started appearing, slowly, in all their different shapes and sizes. Seeing them lined up, one after the other, he felt powerful. He wasn't sure he could give that up.

The next morning, he and Isabelle had breakfast, barely speaking, and walked to school, hand in hand. He steeled himself, waiting for her to do something—cry, lash out, make demands. But she didn't. He considered promising to never do it again, but he couldn't bring himself to say the words. He wasn't sure he could follow through. He didn't trust himself; when he was really pissed, he needed to drink and fuck and fight. It was all he knew.

In front of the school, she dropped his hand and leaned over, her mouth touching his ear. She whispered, "Bye, Peyton," and she ran to the art studio, her long hair flapping against her backpack. He watched her go.

During class, he was distracted. Isabelle interrupted his thoughts, and he started to feel sick, believing maybe he had lost her. The idea made him unbelievably angry but also sad. At football practice, he went all out, refusing to yield, slamming boy after boy to the ground.

"Play's over!" the coach screamed, but Peyton ignored him. He kept hitting. "Peyton, it's over!"

After practice, he took a scalding hot shower, feeling his skin burn, ignoring the dirty looks. He went looking for Isabelle, first in her art studio and then back at her house.

She didn't come home that night, and he slept in her bed, restless, and he tossed and turned and stared at the ceiling. He was pissed that he hadn't studied and was losing sleep. Her seat was empty in each one of her classes the next day.

Whenever she went missing, he was furious, and this time, it was worse because he was afraid she wasn't coming back to him. He swung radically from thinking he would promise her complete fidelity, begging for her forgiveness, to thinking he would make out with some chick in front of her, yelling at her for being unreliable and fickle. Either way, he wasn't sleeping and his head was pounding.

When she finally showed up at his apartment a week later, he was exhausted. "Where the fuck have you been?" he said harshly, barely cracking the door.

She stared at him. "Painting mostly."

She pushed inside and wrapped her arms around his chest. "I really do love you, you know?"

"Painting where?"

"By the river. By the bay. In Harvard Square."

"Where did you sleep?"

"Various places. The Y. Harvard. The library. The backyard."

He sighed, wanting to pull her hair until it hurt. He gripped it and tugged backwards, and her head went back, her face expressionless. He leaned down and kissed her, roughly. "Do you want to get dinner?" he asked, sighing again.

She nodded. As they walked through the neighborhood, hand in hand, her eyes observing everything, her full mouth in a bright smile, he felt his anger, as usual, replaced by affection. He missed her. He smiled and she smiled back. He stopped, and kissed her again.

"I love you, too," he said, looking at her sternly.

"I know."

"You have to stop running away like this. Run away from everyone but me."

"I know. So do you."

He laughed. "Fair enough."

CHAPTER TEN

When Peyton's eyes blurred from reading and his fingers were raw from writing papers, he got plastered, ready to punch someone at the slightest provocation. He started a couple bar fights near Harvard Square, and the second time, he broke his arm. He waited for ten hours at the free clinic, downing aspirin, surrounded by hacking coughs, wads of used tissues, scummy floors, babies' cries and men's shouts, in order to receive dubious medical care.

He left with a shoddy cast, and the flu. Later, he had to pick up trash near the highway in an orange vest.

Over the summer, he lined up a paid internship at a men's magazine, courtesy of William's father. Isabelle won a fellowship to an artist commune in Maine, and Peyton was immediately lonely when she departed the second week of summer, her paints and canvases and suitcase packed in the back of her mother's car. His mother's shifts started at four, while he was still at work, and so they only briefly crossed paths, her about to leave for the club, or for Ronnie's house, in her black leather jacket and red high heels.

She hugged him and gushed, "Baby, how's school? Are you doing well?" while tugging gently on his t-shirt.

He said, "Great," regardless of the truth. He was jealous of Ronnie, furious his mother saw the douchebag more than she saw him. But he kept this to himself. He could see she was still happy and, for once, not just faking it to get something from a man. She liked dating the owner of a restaurant, being at the center of their small world, and the gold jewelry, the furs, and driving around in his sports car.

The men's magazine was staffed with mostly twenty-something men and a few hot women of the same age. Peyton managed to dump most of the menial work on the other interns, convincing the staffers to let him tag along for the photo shoots, where bikini or underwear-clad B and C-list celebrities posed for the camera.

He also co-wrote filler, like, "How to Bed a Girl in One Date," and "How to Get a Girl to Dump You." The magazine was stupendously meaningless and the only features worth looking at were the soft-porn pictures and the occasional humorous column.

Every Thursday and Friday, the staff went out drinking, and the raunchy culture turned more obscene as the night wore on. He laughed at the pick-up lines of the male staffers, which more often than not, bombed. Peyton drank to forget he missed Isabelle.

Isabelle rarely called—only when she had finished one project, and before she had started another. While she worked, she lived, breathed and slept the project. Calling him would break her concentration. He kept thinking about how much better last summer was, when he was on the docks, Isabelle painting on the shore. He was like someone with phantom limb syndrome—he could see a part of him was gone, functionally useless, but at the same time, it was still there, haunting him, like a shadow, reminding him how much he needed it.

He couldn't forget unless he was blitzed. One Friday, he pulled his favorite staffer to the shady corner of the bar. She was a 24 year-old Harvard graduate with serious brown eyes, and round, black glasses. She reminded him vaguely of the communist feminists, which made him want to pummel her. She was wasted, and he took her drink and kissed her. She kissed back aggressively, pulling away five minutes later.

"Peyy-ton," she said, stretching his name out like a piece of chewed gum. "You're a kid! This is illegal."

He laughed, pulling her close to him. "I'm eighteen," he lied. She seemed puzzled, wrinkling her button nose.

"You can't be. You're still in high school," she said, uncertainly.

"Anyway, it's legal if you're over sixteen."

She smiled knowingly. "Yeah, maybe, but it's not right…"

He ignored her and kissed her. Later, after a couple more drinks, she came back to his apartment. For once, he was glad his mother wasn't home. That would have ended the night.

The next morning, he made her coffee and eggs. She was embarrassed, flushing and pushing her glasses up her nose, and made him promise not to tell anyone, ever. He laughed.

Despite her embarrassment, the next week, after she had a few drinks, she came over and smiled at him, not saying a word. He laughed, and sure enough, she ended up back at his house. They kept this up—the same pattern—until he finished his internship, leaving to start football practice in August.

On his last day, she approached him in the hall, looking like she wanted to say something, but didn't know how. He waited patiently, and she blushed, and her mouth opened, and then closed.

He hugged her playfully, telling her it had been fun.

Flustered, she nodded, pushing her glasses up her nose. "Yeah, it has," she said slowly. Indecision flickered across her face, and then she tilted her face away. She moved down the hall, glancing back at him briefly, before carrying on.

He was confused. She couldn't have wanted to date him. He shook it off. By then, he was thoroughly sick of the men's magazine, and desperate to resume his studies. He allowed himself, a week away from Isabelle's return, to think of her.

He took the bus to Watertown and visited every single artisan shop before returning to the jewelry store. For more money than he had ever spent, he purchased a silver necklace. It was composed of a hundred interlocking hands, and the hands were so tiny one couldn't see them from a foot away. He knew she would love it; it was the perfect complement to the miniature faces on her walls.

On the day she returned, he went to a gourmet grocery store and walked around, entranced by the delicious smells and shiny floors. He gorged on free samples. He bought soft cheese, bread, and salami, and put it in his pack.

The knock at the door made his heart beat rapidly, and his fingers tingle. He threw open the door. He was filled with relief, as if he had been holding his breath all summer and just now he could breathe again. She jumped on him, hugging him tightly, wrapping her legs around his waist.

He smiled, swinging her around in circles. They kissed for a long time.

They both talked at once, laughing, their faces flushed.

The rest of the night, they couldn't stop talking. It was as if they had to eliminate their separation as quickly as possible, erasing it, so in thirty years, Peyton would only vaguely remember that he had not gone to the artist commune with her, sitting by the shore, sleeping in a one-room cabin, dining with other artists.

She wanted to show him the three paintings she had completed, and they went back to her house, the silver necklace around her neck, and they stayed up all night in her bedroom, looking at each one, discussing their implications. He was blown away, thinking they were better than many he had seen hanging in the Boston art museums. He could not believe these paintings had come from her, and when he finally dozed off, he saw them vividly in his dreams.

They slept late, and Peyton reluctantly left for practice, kissing her face and fingers. Football practice exorcized him, as usual, temporarily relieving him of the testosterone that coursed steadily through his veins.

As he walked back to Isabelle's, he was more in love with her than ever. He was proud of her, still stunned by the fact that she had produced art that remarkable, the kind of art that moved people, and made them think.

This revelation, that Isabelle had some sort of greatness in her, somehow made her disappearances more bearable. He was still affronted when she went missing, but he was able to drop his rage. He recognized she needed this freedom to work. Instead of growling at her when she returned, he hugged her, whispering he missed her and stroking her hair.

The fall semester, he slept at her house almost every night. He was working all the time—talking to football coaches, filling out applications for colleges and scholarships, studying intensely to maintain his G.P.A., traveling to games. The philosophy club was devoted to working on college essays and papers, as they all had more papers than ever before.

At night, Peyton dropped in the bed, exhausted, angry at the other students, who had their parents' money to bail them out if they failed to get perfect grades. She wrapped herself around him, petted his hand, and whispered, "I love you," before falling into her deep sleep. Those moments, he felt very clearly his hard work was justified, like there was some greater purpose to it all, and he was making a life for them.

As he lay there, holding her, and falling asleep, he could see himself as a man, driving home from work in a suit, through the rolling countryside. He stops at a wood house, where Isabelle is painting on the porch in her bare feet. Their four children run through the yard, yelling, "Daddy! Daddy!" He smiles and picks up the youngest girl. He walks to the porch, the three other children bouncing around him, and Isabelle comes over, her clothes splattered with paint and her long blonde hair flapping in the wind.

"You're home," she says, kissing him, the bright blue sky radiating behind her.

It was to this hazy image he fell asleep.

* * *

Spring semester, life slowed down. College applications were done. The football season was over. The resentment Peyton felt for his classmates as he worked himself to the bone, feeling like he alone had to turn in perfect assignments, perfect performances, perfect tests, dissipated.

He went back to the weekly house parties. Life was saturated with a sense of freedom and excitement. Seniors skipped class and stared out the school windows. People were planning extravagant trips to Europe, Asia and South America. Peyton listened to this without even a flicker of jealousy. He planned to take Isabelle to West Virginia, and he wouldn't have traded that for anything.

In March, Peyton came home Sunday morning to change his clothes, and he heard his mother sobbing in her bedroom.

He stood still. He had not heard her cry in years, and the sound was all the more heartbreaking because he had stopped expecting it.

He cracked open her door and saw she was on the bed, in the fetal position. His despair deepened, and he climbed into bed with her, wrapping his body around hers. She was so tiny.

"What is it, Ma?"

"Ronnie…" she gasped.

"What happened to him? Is he okay?"

"He…left….me."

He stroked her hair, and for the first time, he noticed she had fine cracks in her skin, etched around her mouth and eyes. He stared at them for a while, scared. He knew, even though he didn't care for Ronnie, he had been counting on him to marry her, and take care of her. She could not keep dancing forever. She had already been forced to move to a trashier club.

"Ma…" he said, trying to say something reassuring. "Ma, you'll find someone better."

She sobbed louder and he wanted to kill Ronnie. Literally, kill him. Go over there and beat his greasy Italian face with a baseball bat.

"He said he loved me," she let out, gulping deep breaths, as if she were drowning. "He said he was going to marry me, and have children with me."

155

"Ma, he was never good enough for you," he said, stroking her hair. He kissed her cheek. "I'm going to make you some tea," he said, immediately realizing that it was Isabelle's house that had tea, not theirs. "Coffee," he corrected.

Peyton walked into the kitchen and filled the pot. While it dripped, he went to the living room window. He could hear his mother's sobs and he ran his fingers through his hair, blowing air out of his mouth.

In the apartment across the alley, the red-haired mother was serving her husband and her two boys breakfast, carting the scrambled eggs around the table, ruffling each one's hair. The father said something with a smile and they all laughed.

Peyton wanted to shatter the window. He imagined himself knocking the father down, leaving him all bloodied and broken, while the mother and the boys stood there, screaming and terrified.

Peyton walked back to the kitchen. He cursed loudly. He poured a cup of coffee and took it to the bedroom. Ronnie had made his mother happy. And now that was gone.

"Ma, here, sit up here," he said, patting to the wall behind the bed. She gulped, and sat up, her face red and splotchy, her round blue eyes sparkling with her salty tears.

"Here," he said, handing her the cup of coffee. She took a long sip. He sat next to her and rubbed her thigh. She rested the warm cup on her lap and it trembled lightly.

"I really thought this was it," she said, her lips pursing, her face about to break again. "He said we'd get married. That I was the one. I let him…."

"Ma, he's not worth it," he said, putting his hands on her cheeks, looking at her firmly. "You don't need him. You will find someone better."

She nodded, but her face was overflowing with despair. He put the cup of coffee on the nightstand, and sat next to her and pulled her against his chest, stroking her hair. He remembered when Mr. Ramsey left, and he envied how he felt then: torn up by her pain but oblivious to the full scope of it.

He had no sense of the future, or the frustration that comes from losing over and over. Now, he felt the full weight of her loneliness, stretching its arms deep into the past, and raising a specter over the coming decades, threatening to remain until her death. Seeing the wrinkle lines around her eyes, he had an acute sense of the clock moving forward impatiently, refusing to wait. He wanted to fight time off, but it was too much. He was tired of fighting. He was tired of cobbling everything together.

His mind went to William, and his wealthy, charmed life, but then he reprimanded himself. He was better off than most. He would go to college. He had someone he loved.

He smiled bitterly, remembering Schopenhauer's claim: humans must be miserable if they can only console themselves by the fact that others are worse off.

His mother fell asleep, her mouth hung open, saliva falling on his shirt. He carefully got up, laid her head on the pillow and took her cup of coffee to the kitchen. Watching it run down the drain, he wished he could blight Ronnie from the face of the earth. God damn Ronnie.

Like when Mr. Ramsey left, she stayed in bed for months, sleeping all the time, her only willing energy spent on crying. He and Isabelle stayed in the apartment, helping his mother to change clothes, making her eat and take showers. She let them feed, clothe and wash her, too tired to object, and sometimes, in the shower, she'd start laughing and crying, crumpling over in a ball, saying, as if by explanation, "I really thought he loved me."

When he received his college acceptance letters and scholarships, he at first showed each one to her, thinking it might lift her out of her mood. He could see her face try to be happy.

"That's so good, baby," she said. "So good." But then, as if this reminded her of a life she would never have, she started crying. "I'm going to lose you too."

He pulled her to his chest and said, "Ma, you will never lose me. Do you hear me?" and she nodded against his chest, her wet face soaking his t-shirt with tears and snot.

As he opened acceptance after acceptance, he was thrilled, as if the world had at last come to operate under just rules. The best schools in the country, probably the world, were inviting him in. His long hours of work had paid off. With a degree in his hand, he could do anything. This was his passport to his rightful future.

He and Isabelle celebrated alone in the Berkshires, reluctantly leaving his mother for the weekend, asking Joseph to look in on her. Despite her poor grades and worse attendance, Isabelle had won a full scholarship to the best art school in the country, the Rhode Island School of Design. Even though it meant he'd have to play football, work a job and take out loans, he sent in his acceptance to Harvard. He didn't want to leave his mother alone, and he wanted to stay close to Isabelle. But also, he could not resist the mystical lure of Harvard. He wanted the power that came from having the very best pedigree.

He saw no details, but he knew, somehow, a Harvard degree would propel him into wealth and success.

Even at Hunter, where half of the students went on to the Ivy League, Harvard carried a particularly strong cache. Most had applied and been rejected. For the rest of the semester, the whole school treated the seven students admitted to Harvard with a newfound respect, even Joseph, who had long been regarded as a social leper. It was as if the students and teachers believed Harvard possessed profound insight into people, and its stamp of approval superseded their previous judgments, whatever they might have been.

Isabelle's mother was impressed, too, taking them both out to dinner. Her father was mysteriously absent. Isabelle's mother joked that Peyton shouldn't forget them when he was rich and famous. Isabelle rolled her eyes, and Peyton laughed, feeling good about the praise and seeing the ridiculousness of it at the same time. Her mother ordered a bottle of wine, and Peyton drank one glass, and then another.

After Isabelle's mother had polished off a couple glasses herself, she talked more freely, idly fretting Isabelle would be a starving artist, wishing she had chosen a more conventional path.

"She's always been stubborn, Peyton," her mother said, shaking her head, her hand on her glass of wine. "When she was five, at the beach, this one time, her father and I were relaxing on the towels, and somehow, she got away at some point. We ran up and down the beach looking for her, shouting her name."

She took a sip of her wine. "Finally, some man called us over. There she was, behind a giant rock, rubbing wet sand on it. I grabbed her, hugging her and I was so relieved, you know? She just glared at me, 'I'm busy!' she said, turning back to her rock. The man, he couldn't believe it. 'Look,' he said. And I did. Isabelle had drawn her father's face with the wet sand. It was truly remarkable, I have to say."

Peyton smiled, running his fingers over Isabelle's hand. Isabelle nodded, and her face was resigned, like the story contained a truth she would only grudgingly acknowledge.

"I remember that," she said, running her finger over the edge of her plate. "I was mad at you for interrupting me."

"I'll always worry about you, you know."

This was surprising, as her parents had given her free reign, and seemed fairly occupied with their own lives. Isabelle nodded skeptically, as if she had heard this before, and still did not believe it. She wasn't close to her parents, and seemed almost indifferent to them. "I'll be okay," she said, taking a bite of her steak.

"Peyton," her mother said, smiling. "Promise me you'll watch out for her."

"Of course, Mrs. Woods," he said. He put his hand on Isabelle's thigh, squeezing it protectively. Isabelle smiled at him flirtatiously, sticking out her tongue.

* * *

Peyton and Isabelle took groceries from her house and put them in the apartment. With his mother not working, there was only enough money to pay rent. In May, the utilities were shut off, and so they used flashlights and candles at night, telling ghost stories underneath their sheets, and eating cold sandwiches and warm soda.

A couple weeks before their graduation, Peyton and Isabelle climbed out of bed early Saturday morning, and found his mother sitting in the kitchen, showered and dressed.

"Hey!" he said, happy to see her back to life.

She smiled, tucking a piece of her black hair behind her ear. She was smoking a cigarette. "I'm going to see about my job. Hopefully, it's still there," she said, laughing. He kissed her on the cheek. Isabelle half-smiled, and went into the living room.

"Baby," she said, stubbing out her cigarette in the ashtray. "What happened with college?"

"I accepted at Harvard," he said. It still sounded incredible to him.

She smiled, staring off into the distance. He wondered if she still wasn't herself until the tears began pouring down her face, and she laughed wildly.

She jumped up and hugged him.

"I can't even believe it!" she squealed. He held the back of her head against his chest, her tears soaking his t-shirt.

"We're going to be okay," he said. She leaned back and wiped her face off.

"My baby is all grown up, and going to Harvard. Okay," she said, rubbing her hands together. "When is your graduation? I'll have to buy a new dress, and get you a nice present."

"Two weeks."

She winked at him. "Plenty of time."

She went in the bathroom and came back out with her makeup reapplied. She was wearing her three inch heels and a light, clingy dress. She still looked beautiful.

"Okay," she said, straightening out her dress, and picking up her red purse. "Wish me luck."

"Good luck."

At the door, she turned around and smiled, and jumped up and down. "I still can't believe it," she giggled. "Harvard! Your grandparents would never even believe it."

He walked over and hugged her again, feeling proud. He had earned it. They had earned it.

After she left, he realized Isabelle was still sitting on the couch, staring into space, her hands wrapped around her knees. He sat down next to her.

"Hey," he said. She glanced over at him, distracted. She stood up and went into the other room, coming back with her backpack. She slid on her sandals and walked to the door.

He caught up and grabbed her arm.

"Hey," he said harshly. "What are you doing?"

"Going home."

"Why aren't you happy?"

Isabelle shrugged.

"No," he said, cuffing her wrists in front of her chest. "She's been in bed for months. How can you not be happy?"

"Leave me alone," she said, pulling away her wrists, squirming. He didn't let go. He was tempted to throw her against the wall.

"Why are you doing this?"

She glanced at the door.

"Fine," he said, disgusted, dropping her wrists.

She ran to the end of the hall, disappearing into the stairwell.

He stood there, dumbfounded and pissed. It seemed like every time one aspect of his life rose from dark and dank waters, another sunk down, displaced.

"Fuck."

The rest of the day, he waited for her to come back, restlessly trying to read Hamlet, but she didn't. Neither did his mother, who he assumed was welcomed back at the club. At night, Joseph stopped by, and they both went to a party, where Peyton got completely wasted, and belligerently argued with some kid about Footloose. He ate Chinese food leftovers out of the refrigerator, and danced in the living room, banging his head to the punk music.

He saw Joseph sitting on the couch, completely sober, talking excitedly to another boy. Now that he was de-exiled, Joseph was up for going out any night. But he still talked on and on about philosophy. Seeing him so earnest, Peyton laughed, and snuck out the back door. The party had only made him feel worse. He couldn't take this anymore. He wanted to break into William's house and steal the fireworks they had been building and blow them up. He wanted to destroy something.

He ran to Isabelle's house. He was going to yell at her. Her house was dark and he remembered it was the middle of the night. He was annoyed that her parents were sleeping and he would have to be quiet. He stumbled to the stairs, accidentally knocking over a vase, which crashed to the floor and broke. He cursed, and picked the pieces up with fingers, putting it in a small pile in the corner.

Inside Isabelle's room, he closed the door and waited for his eyes to adjust. He pounced on the bed and shook her violently.

She opened her eyes, and they were full of panic and fear. Then, in recognition, they went flat, vacant.

"What the fuck is your problem?"

"I'm sorry."

He rolled off her, holding her hand and staring at the ceiling. "Why did you do that?" he said softly.

"Because I'm afraid."

"Afraid of what?"

"Losing you. Your mom waking up reminded me things are changing. We're moving apart."

"You won't lose me," he said, emphatically.

"How do you know? You'll have a whole life at Harvard without me."

He pulled her onto his chest, holding her tight. "Isabelle, I will never let you go."

"Do you promise that? Don't lie to me. Only promise if you can."

"Yes, I do."

Her face was abruptly resolved and calm, as if his words were enough to make it true. "Okay."

He leaned over and kissed her. Feeling her soft lips and eager hands in his hair, he knew it was true. He would never let her go.

Part III

CHAPTER ELEVEN

It was not the accident itself which threw a decisive shadow over his life, as he had thought it would, but the night after. It was the last time he had seen Isabelle, and though she said it at the time—"I'm gone. Forever."—he had not believed her. Even now, he didn't believe it. Her absence from his life still seemed like a cosmic accounting error. Any day, the universe would tally the ledgers, and the error would be fixed.

Images of that night often occurred to him without provocation, willing themselves up at inopportune times. They arose when he was closing a business deal, when he was meeting a C.E.O., when he was speaking at a convention in front of two hundred people. He became an expert at separating his mind into two tracks, smiling confidently, speaking warmly, while some other part of his brain watched his eighteen-year-old self talking to Isabelle on his mother's bed.

He remembered the paleness of her tan skin, her unwashed blonde hair falling over her face, her strangely quiet despair. He avoided looking at her. When he spoke, he focused on the triangle of freckles on her slender bicep.

She, alone, wanted to turn them in. He had felt confessing wouldn't have done any good, that his life, as he was constructing it, would have ended, dropped out, and he would have fallen beneath ground, through the dirt, into an intolerable existence, living for eternity among the beetles of the earth.

The night dragged on, and it seemed, at times, like a meeting of the philosophy club; they were merely discussing a hypothetical, what's the right thing to do when you negligently start a fire? It was temporary, sweet relief, and then reality punched him in the face. This wasn't idle talk. This was real.

The night wore thin, like a moth-eaten cloth, and even William became agitated, something that, under normal circumstances, Peyton would have reveled in. But then, it scared him. Though William's calmness and seeming indifference repulsed Peyton, it also protected him from a truth he didn't want to confront. William's invincibility was a shield, blocking them from the burning light of what happened.

If he focused on William, he knew nothing bad could have happened. Bad things didn't happen to William, with his handsome, easy smile, cashmere sweaters and German sports car. William took him outside on the fire escape, and they smoked a cigarette, passing it back and forth. William told him, snubbing out the cigarette nervously, he had to "take care of" Isabelle.

And he had. He talked to her alone, in his mother's bedroom. He explained to her how he and Joseph would never survive this. He tried to make her feel selfish, telling her she was in a field where it wouldn't matter if she were convicted of a crime. They were the ones who would take the fall, not her. She could still be a famous artist. He and Joseph would never be able to go to college. He trotted out other reasons he can't remember. Anything he could think of. "It was done, what good would it do for them to know who did it?"

She listened silently, tears running down her stony face.

Isabelle wrapped herself around him, and he wrapped himself around her, and he closed his eyes. They were a compact whole; he did not begin where she ended; they were one. For a moment, which may have lasted thirty seconds or two hours, he forgot the drill grinding between them, causing them to fall apart and topple over in opposite directions. He could no longer remember, now, what that oneness felt like. The words he uses to describe it are accurate, he knows, but he can't conjure up the feeling itself. He never again was a part of another person, and he could no more remember what it felt like than a blind person, who had seen for one moment, could remember what it was like to see color.

Then, she'd whispered, "Peyton."

"Yes…"

"Let's just tell the truth. Please. It's the right thing to do."

Their oneness shattered. "I can't." He disentangled from her. "If you do this, I'll never forgive you," he said, roughly, the long night drawing on his patience, dredging up his anger.

She stared at him. "If I don't do this, I'll never forgive you."

They sat silently, at a crossroads, neither one wanting to turn, as if they could stay stopped at the intersection of a country road, indefinitely. He can't remember what he was thinking; only that he had wished he could stop time from moving forward, knowing that was no more likely than him stopping an industrial ship from leaving harbor by swimming in front of it.

"Okay," she said, putting her hands over her face.

"Look at me," she said, rising up, removing her hands. He had, and he silently pleaded, please, help me, Isabelle.

"I won't say anything," she whispered.

His chest beat in relief. He was euphoric, and he reached out to touch her. She slapped his hand away. "But then that's it. I'm gone. Forever."

His memory here fades. He remembers not believing her, sure, after enough time passed, she'd come back—what did she know about forever? But he also remembers a degree of coldness, of deciding, even if he lost her, he had to save himself.

"Okay."

That was it. "Okay." Then she was gone. She ran out the door.

The rest of the summer was a blur of anxiety. He had worried more about the police showing up at his work or his apartment than what happened to Isabelle. A few days after the accident, as he sat in his living room, watching the news on the fuzzy TV, the blond pouf-haired newscaster stiffly reporting four people had died and seven people had severe burns. He'd puked, and gone on a two-week drinking binge.

It had taken a couple years before he stopped, reflexively, clenching at the sign of a police officer. He refused to think about the accident, and whenever it occurred to him—if he saw a fireplace, or a lighter, or random things that vaguely reminded him of the night, like an empty lot, the brand of beer he'd been drinking—he would tell himself quickly, that never happened, and run, blindly, to another image or thought. If the police ever came, he did not want to betray his knowledge with a tick, or a flash of doubt. Only his dreams disobeyed his strict self-control: freshman and sophomore year of college, he often woke up in a sweat, terrified, having seen black, abstract figures burning in a building, calling for help, as he stood idly by, watching them scream and wither.

Years later, when it was clear they'd never be caught—the investigation must have long since languished and fallen into a cold case file—he let himself think, briefly, about what they had done. He tried to find information about the dead, but they were working class people, and he found only their short obituaries, listing their unremarkable jobs and the names of the loved ones they had left behind.

By that time, it seemed like something that had happened to someone else. After the night when they decided what to do, they had never spoken of it again. Joseph, who had a series of breakdowns in college, had once tried to talk to him about it, but Peyton had shook his head, and then ran away, not even letting him get the words out.

He wrote one of his senior papers on the guilt of Vietnam soldiers who committed acts of atrocity during the war. His history professor had recorded interviews of 1,048 vets ten years after they had left Vietnam, and he allowed Peyton to borrow the tapes.

To Peyton's surprise, the vets who committed war crimes, as a class, felt nothing more than those who had not. Most of them spoke of their actions as if they had occurred in their dreams, like a ghost had taken over their bodies, committed horrific acts and then departed. Veterans forced to recall their role in burning villages, or firing on women and children, described the scenes mechanically, as if they were reading from a newspaper about a faraway event that did not concern them. One soldier, after he blandly described himself shooting a family of five, stated without emotion, "I know it was wrong. But I don't feel anything. I don't feel anything. Hey, you aren't recording my name, right?"

Peyton had stopped the tape and stared at the tape player. He whispered, even though he was alone in his apartment, "I killed four people and I don't feel anything." This made him nauseous, and he ran to his bathroom, and threw up.

When he won an award for his paper and had to present it in front of the history department, he took two anxiety-relievers with a shot of whiskey. Answering questions gave him an intense headache, and even though he was comfortable speaking in public, sweat dripped from his forehead.

He had once believed the truth was as unavoidable as falling if you stepped in a well. Now, he knew better: some truths could lose their force if he simply turned his back on them. And, with the accident, he had. He got wasted every Fourth of July, and holed up in his apartment and put in earplugs. But he only obliquely acknowledged the accident, even then. It was a smudge in his rearview mirror.

It was Isabelle he remembered. It started near the end of his freshman year—it was just a vague longing that would occasionally hit him acutely, like a migraine. Most of the time, he was too consumed with work to notice. He shelved books in the library, played football, ran track and studied. With the little free time he had, he got wasted and slept with girls.

Senior year of college, after, courtesy of a teammate's father, he secured a job at a venture capital firm in Boston, he felt like his life was finally starting. On a whim, he skipped class and took the bus to Rhode Island. He was disappointed to find Isabelle wasn't listed in the student directory, and the senior painting teacher, an older, hunched-over man, peered at him skeptically and refused to tell him anything. After a few hours of asking around, he finally found a girl with tar-black hair and a pursed mouth who knew Isabelle.

Isabelle had not come back after freshman year, the girl explained, pushing her hair behind her ear. But she'd had an exhibit in Boston earlier this year.

Riding back on the bus, Peyton punched the seat in front of him, feeling as if the ground had been whipped out from underneath his feet. Even though he knew it did not make sense, he was furious she dropped out of school without telling him.

In Somerville, he knocked on her door. Her mother answered, and he was relieved: relieved she was still here; relieved she had not aged. He had the strong sense of coming home after a long journey, as if he were Odysseus. He had lived and breathed in this house for years, and it was still here, waiting for him.

"Peyton," she said, surprised. "I'm having a party…"

He could hear people talking and laughing inside. He smiled, pushing down the despair suddenly springing up in his throat. "I'm trying to find Isabelle," he said, his voice barely louder than a whisper.

She tucked a strand of her blonde hair behind one of her ears, and tilted her head, frowning. "Well, Peyton," she said finally. "I don't really know where she is."

"Oh," he said, not sure what to say. "When's the last time…?"

She sighed. "Peyton, I don't know if this is any of your business. What you did to her sent her off the rails." She glanced back over her shoulder. "I really should go."

"What do you mean—what I did?" His heart beat rapidly, and he felt constricted, like a rubber band was tied around his chest.

"Cheating on her," she said. The rubber band snapped off.

"I haven't seen her in four years," he said.

"Yes, Peyton," she said, exasperated. "But that's when she…she called us once her freshman year. Once." She blinked her eyes rapidly.

"Sorry," she said, pulling the door shut. "I can't deal with this right now." The lock clicked.

He considered banging on the door, demanding to know more. But he didn't. Instead, he got drunk, and picked a girl up at a bar, and left her apartment in the middle of the night, stumbling home.

Later, he tracked down Isabelle's art exhibit in the newspaper archives. The gallery owner only had her agent's number, and the agent refused to tell him anything, except, reluctantly, that she was still painting. He was frustrated, and furious, as if she were hiding specifically from him.

He wished he could embark on a sustained effort to locate her, but this was impossible. With forty-thousand-dollars of student loan debt and an empty bank account, he had no choice but to start working immediately. His impotence cast a subtle, but dark shadow over the commencement of his adult life. He quietly resented his friends traipsing around Europe, flush with their parents' cash. It symbolized the freedom and adventure he lacked.

He moved into a three-bedroom apartment downtown with his mother, his little sister Sicily—Ronnie had come back long enough to impregnate his mother—and Joseph. Joseph had kept on at Harvard, seeking his Ph.D. in English literature, and as far as Peyton could tell, this was largely because he was too anxious to leave the safe and predictable walls of school.

Peyton did not love the labors of a financial analyst—this was no surprise; he had majored in economics and taken no great joy in it—but he did derive immense satisfaction from finishing each project, and finally, being able to pay for his mother to stop dancing. He was always available to the firm, and month after month, he worked eighty to ninety hours every week.

Most of the time, the firm operated as a meritocracy—if he worked harder, he would get ahead—but occasionally, he would be reminded that, even here, there was no such thing. Fellow analysts obtained inside information or brought in new business courtesy of their family's friends; fathers advised their sons on the machinations of office life. When he was shown up by these covert forces, his anger was palpable, and he wanted to pummel his competitor in a dark alley.

The day he turned twenty-five, he received a large package wrapped in brown paper at his work. It lacked a return address, and for a second, he considered one of the companies he had evaluated poorly, or a coworker he had screwed over sent it to him, and inside, he would find something disgusting. Perhaps he was paranoid, but he called his secretary, a stern woman in her fifties, and asked her to help him open it.

As they tore off the thick paper, he saw the back of a wood frame. His secretary's face took on an unusually soft light. Her hand covered her mouth.

"What?" he said.

She pointed. Holding the frame up, he walked around to her side. It was a painting of him as a teenager in the Berkshire Mountains.

"It is a lovely portrait of you, sir," she said, standing up, wiping off her skirt, and returning to her desk, clicking her tongue, impressed.

The colors were rich and blurred together, almost impressionistic, but the lines and the strength of his face were clearly visible. His face was proud and angry, which contrasted to the light blue sky and flush green landscape.

He put the painting in his closet, not wanting anyone else to see it. Occasionally, when he was working late into the night, he poured himself a glass of whiskey, and took the painting out. He propped it up across from his desk, and glanced at it as he worked, feeling emboldened and enraged by it.

It was a beautiful painting, depicting him honestly, and this made him all the angrier at her for not coming back. One night, when a quasi-pro bono project he had been working on for months—investing in a private school for working-class families—fell through, he destroyed the painting in a fit of rage, cutting it into dozens of pieces with his knife.

* * *

One of the companies he analyzed, Terra Firma, made "earth friendly, all natural" homeopathic remedies and cosmetics. Their P.R. department, like many P.R. departments, was filled with comely and chipper young women. Generally, these women were annoying, with their glassy-eyed friendliness and hollow smiles.

At the company's party, drunk, he found himself talking to one that seemed less sterile. She had a sarcastic look in her eyes, and a throaty laugh. Her hair was light and wispy and it framed her heart-shaped face and clear blue eyes. She introduced herself as "Hannah from Wisconsin," as if there were another Hannah she might be confused with.

She took him home that night. The sex was plain and familiar, as if they had been doing it for years. Surprisingly, this was comforting, like throwing on his ragged Harvard sweatshirt he'd had since freshman year.

Hannah called him the next day and asked if he wanted to see a basketball game. He agreed, and even though he ended up bailing for work, he invited her to fly kites with his mother and Sicily the following weekend.

This too was easy—Hannah tickled Sicily and made her laugh with funny faces, and she gushed with his mother about the theater. The afternoon turned into dinner, and a movie on their couch, everyone lounging in their pajamas and eating cookie dough.

Soon, he was seeing her most of his time off. She never complained or acted peeved about his long hours or his canceling plans at the last minute. He appreciated her self-sufficiency. Most of his "relationships" had ended after a month, when the women had demanded more attention than he was willing to give. Hannah had grown up poor, one of five farmer's daughters, and he laid his head on her stomach and eagerly listened to her stories of country life. He felt close to her, then, like she understood where he came from.

On his twenty-sixth birthday, he received another large package, unmarked. He was annoyed, and he left the package in his work closet, unopened, for months. It still haunted him, though. He knew it was there, and sometimes, he would stare at his closet, and feel an intense longing burning his chest. He drank a double shot of whiskey, quelling the anxiety and the anger coursing through him.

A warm summer night, he took Hannah to her favorite restaurant for dinner. She had plain tastes in food, hating spices and foreign dishes, and it was a bland, American restaurant, a midlevel chain, where she ordered steak and potatoes. She was talking about the P.R. girls at her office—silly things they said and did to get the product marketed—and, as she talked her words ran together, and he realized he was bored. He interrupted her, restless.

"Hannah, do you want to go skinny dipping?"

She looked at him oddly. "Where?"

"In a community pool. We'll climb the fence. I used to do it when I was a kid."

"No," she said, cutting a piece of her steak. "We could get arrested for that."

He rubbed his forehead. "Okay, well, let's go to a club, then, go dancing."

She shrugged. "If you want to." She returned to her steak, cutting up thick bites, her cheek bulging as she chewed. As she ate silently, he felt trapped, like he was ever-so-slowly suffocating. He flagged the waitress over and asked for the check. Hannah stared at him quizzically.

"I have to get out of here. You can stay."

She ate another piece of her steak. "That's okay," she said, taking a large drink of water, and some of it spilled on her chin. She was like a teenage boy.

Inside the club, she scrunched up her face. "It's so loud in here!" she shouted over the techno music.

He smiled. Lights were flashing and the floor was packed, smelling like sweat, cologne and alcohol. He ordered two drinks. She demurred and he chugged them both.

On the floor, she danced tightly next to him, barely moving. The trolling light flashed over her face. Her slightly dour expression made him want to slap her. He grabbed her wrist and pulled her outside.

"What's wrong, honey?" She looked at him sweetly, and he felt, for a second, guilty.

"You're not having fun. You should go home."

"But I want to be with you," she said, squeezing his wrist, smiling.

"I know." He kissed her cheek. He flagged down a cab and opened the door for her. She glanced at it uncertainly.

"Go on, I'll call you tomorrow." He kissed her on the lips and she nodded, her face still confused.

"Okay," she said, stepping into the cab.

He gave the cab driver twenty dollars and shut the door. He watched it drive away, relieved.

He did not go back inside the club. He walked the two miles to his office. A few office lights were on, but everything else was dark. The ambient street light came in through his window and he retrieved the package out of his closet. He poured himself a shot of whiskey, and swallowed it. The brown paper came off easily.

The painting had the same background as the last one, but this time it was Isabelle's face. It was stunning, and in his memory, the foggy lines of her face sharpened. It relieved him her face was in calm repose, open and peaceful, reflecting the mountains. He wanted, desperately, to reach into the painting and pull her out. He wanted to hold her again.

He slammed it on his desk.

"Why are you doing this?" he shouted.

He took his pocket knife and cut down the center of her face. Then he slashed it haphazardly, until he could no longer tell who it had been.

He tossed it in the dumpster behind the building.

* * *

At home, he opened the door to Sicily's room and watched her sleep soundly, clinging to her brown stuffed bear with the red bowtie. Sicily was round and dark, with her father's brown eyes. When she was younger, she had

173

thrown terrifying tantrums whenever his mother left, screaming and pounding her own chest; the neighbors had called social services, fearing she was being abused. Now, in third grade, she was the ring-leader of her Catholic school friends, getting them in trouble with the nuns and turning them against one another. She cajoled and lied to get her way. Peyton figured that was Ronnie's genetic contribution.

He kissed her on the forehead, and she turned her face away, mumbling.

Joseph's light was on, and Peyton, hearing the sound of his fingers furiously tapping away on his computer, chuckled. He imagined Joseph's girlfriend, a Ph.D. student in cultural studies, was reading on the bed, her nose wrinkled critically. She was pudgy, wore pantsuits, and had plain brown hair cut sharply in a bowl cut. Her hair moved rigidly up and down when she spoke in her know-it-all voice. She curled her lips smugly as she spoke of patriarchy, narratives of oppression, scripts of the body and embedded, dialogical normativity.

Peyton tried not to laugh or, if he were overworked and exhausted, tell her to shut the fuck up. She, of course, argued Peyton was a typical example of a privileged oppressor. When Joseph told him she had grown up in a San Francisco five-bedroom mansion, and lived in a two-bedroom Cambridge apartment paid for by her father, Peyton laughed so hard he started crying.

His mother's light, in the converted living room, was off, and he went to his bedroom, the smallest one, and unbuttoned his shirt and hung it in his closet. He took another shot of whiskey and lay down on his bed.

As he fell asleep, Isabelle came into his field of vision, standing in the mountains, her face clear now. She was lovely, and he longed to touch her.

Stop, he told himself, thinking of Hannah, with her sweet, rosebud smile, and the homemade cookies she dropped off at his office in a heart-shaped tin. He promised himself he would send her flowers.

* * *

The next year he worked even longer hours as on his horizon stood the prize of becoming the youngest partner in his history of the firm. The money piled up in his bank account. After he paid off his student loans, his rent, and Sicily's tuition, there was still an obscene amount of money left over. It was his natural instinct to hoard it, and he didn't have time to spend it anyway. His mother never asked him for more. She was working as a hairstylist, and since he paid for their living expenses, she made enough to buy herself things she wanted.

174

On his twenty-seventh birthday, he was so exhausted that, when the unmarked package came, he threw it straight in the dumpster. It seemed so childish, sending him unmarked packages. In the middle of his four hours of sleep, he woke up, panicked, feeling like he had made a terrible mistake, as if there might have been something incredibly important in the package.

He walked back to work, quickly covering the deserted streets, his hands stuffed in his pockets. He was relieved when he saw the package sticking up out of the dumpster right where he had left it.

He opened it there, in the cold, dark alley, illuminated by a street lamp.

The painting had the same background as the others—bright blue sky, flush green mountains. Isabelle was leaning on his teenage chest, her eyes closed, and his arms were wrapped around her, protectively. His eyes were closed, too, and his face was content.

From where he stood—on two hours of sleep, having worked every single day for the last year, staring at data until his eyes bled, chatting up companies and partners with energy he didn't have, carefully screwing over the right people—the image seemed like a gateway to a better time.

He wanted to start over, return to the Berkshire Mountains, before the accident, and choose another path, making sure not to lose hold of what he had then. Because they were fundamentally happy, a feeling he could not remember having. Now, his emotions flared wildly—he was thrilled to close a project, devastated to fail, and quick to blow up, shouting and waving his arms at his secretary when he lost, simply because she was there.

What was he doing?

He sighed heavily. "God, Isabelle," he cried. "Where the fuck are you?"

He took the painting up to his office and put it in his closet. He went to the break room and locked the door, drinking from a bottle of whiskey like it was a baby bottle. He slept fitfully, vacillating between the dream of having her and the nightmare of losing her.

* * *

He and Hannah never fought, but eventually she came to seem like a burden, an obligation he dreaded and fabricated excuses to avoid. In the beginning, he had listened for hours about her past: growing up on a mid-western farm, riding with her four sisters in a rickety bus to the schoolhouse two hours away.

He had imagined little Hannah rising with the sun, milking the cows, and sitting with her father on the tractor. Her whole life had seemed endearing. He could see them together as two hardy people, working side by side, on parallel tracks.

But this had imperceptibly transformed. Her stories had become predictable, and listening to them was like rereading a mediocre book. He did not care about her farm life, the fights in the P.R. department, and the travails of her cat, or her aerobics class.

Friday night in August, he and Hannah were walking, hand in hand, by the river. She was wearing a green summer dress, sleeveless, and carrying a large picnic basket. The dress and the swing of her arm drew attention to her bicep, and he noticed, unkindly, it was flabby and undefined.

They had not seen each other in two or three weeks, and as they sat down on the blanket he had unfurled, he remembered himself as a teenager, standing in the spot right across the bridge, watching Isabelle run away in her plaid skirt and sheet of blond hair. Then, an image of himself talking to her in his mother's bedroom appeared. "I'm gone. Forever." He felt brushed by desperation, and he wondered where she was, silently wishing for her to come home, telling her this had gone on long enough.

"Peyton," Hannah said.

He glanced over. She had neatly arranged the food on the blanket, her rosebud mouth in a small smile, and she offered him a cracker with soft cheese.

He shook his head, and rubbed his chin indecisively. Looking at the still waters of the Charles River, he suddenly longed for West Virginia. Three years ago, he had gone back for his grandparents' funerals. She had died first, and, because they were one, he had died two weeks later.

Hershel had tracked their phone number down. His mother had stayed in Boston, mumbling she could not step foot in West Virginia again. "Sicily can't miss school," she said loudly. This was a ridiculous explanation, and she never told him the real reason. He had heard her sobbing for weeks and so he forgave her, letting her mourn them in her own way.

"What's wrong?" Hannah asked, smiling at him gently. He stared into her glowing blue eyes, and for a moment, their vivid beauty made him want to stay. It had happened before—her open, honest eyes, reminiscent of turquoise, the brightest blue, had stopped him from leaving. In retrospect, it seemed foolish. It was a silly reason to stay.

"Hannah," he said.

Seeing his teenage self across the river, watching Isabelle run, he knew he had to leave. He did not love Hannah. He admired her independence, but he was impatient. Every time she talked, he wished for her to move on or be quiet. But she never did move on.

"Hannah," he repeated. Her face went hard, but he plowed forward. "This isn't working anymore."

She did not say anything, looking at the soft white cheese on the plate, next to three olives. She poked it with a toothpick.

"Wow, okay," she said finally. She stood up and dusted off her dress. "Well, goodbye, then, Peyton," she said. She turned and walked up the grass swiftly. She had flat, practical sandals.

Seeing her walk calmly across the street, he laughed. He was relieved, like he had taken off a belt that had grown too tight. He was shocked at her reaction. He had expected her to cry or argue, telling him he had used her. Part of the reason he had kept seeing her, he suspected, was it had been easier than dealing with her outrage. But there was no outrage.

He ate the picnic leisurely, and then, abruptly, packed up his stuff and walked to Isabelle's house. He was euphoric, and only then, was it clear how right he'd been. When he knocked on the door, a man shouted, "Coming!" and a dog barked. Heavy footsteps approached.

The door swung open and a tall, black man appeared, smiling.

Fuck, Peyton thought.

"Hey," the man said, blocking off a golden retriever.

"Hey, do the Woods still live here?"

The man shook his head. "We bought it from them three years ago."

"Oh. Do you know where they went?"

"No idea."

Peyton nodded, wondering if her millions of dots had been painted over. He didn't want to know. He didn't want to see the house changed, with new furniture, and new paint, erasing their existence.

"Thanks," he said abruptly, and walked down the steps.

"Hey!"

Peyton turned back, hoping for something.

"What I do know is they were going through a divorce."

"Really?"

"It was a deal for us. They were trying to sell fast."

Peyton nodded, at first surprised, but then seeing a certain amount of sense in it. Isabelle's father had lurked in the background, only half-there, often nodding absent-mindedly at his wife and Isabelle. She must have left him. He stopped at the nearest phone booth, and found her mother's listing.

It rang seven times, and then he hung up.

* * *

A few weeks after his twenty-eighth birthday, he realized, when he was working late in the office one night, Isabelle had not sent him a package. This caused flickers of disappointment and anger. He wondered if something had happened to her. He tried to shrug it off—who knew where she was?—and returned to his work. He couldn't worry about her now, he reprimanded himself. He had to keep going, stay focused on the prize.

Two months later, he won: he was promoted to partnership. Ma, Sicily and Joseph celebrated with him, although Joseph was the only one who really understood what it meant, and his congratulations were laced with bitterness and jealousy, and after dinner, he returned to his cave, as Peyton had labeled it, closing the door, to work on his dissertation.

The firm took Peyton out for an expensive dinner. As he drank fine whiskey and ate a fifty-dollar entree, the partners, all men, laughed and bantered, flirting with the beautiful waitresses, congratulating and toasting Peyton on his astounding success. He smiled, ordered more whiskey, and wondered why he didn't feel better.

For the last eighteen months, he had been putting in ninety hours a week. He'd analyzed data until three in the morning, cajoled people for inside information on companies and mergers, lied to colleagues and potential clients, schmoozed with bombastic assholes, and got by on four or five hours of sleep. He was wealthy now, he reminded himself, as he took another drink.

But all he felt was tired.

* * *

Five months after he had broken up with her, Hannah called the house, leaving a nice, friendly message. He planned to call her back, but he never did.

One night, as he was leaving the office, she jumped in front of him on the street.

"Hey!" she gushed.

"Hey, Hannah," he said, smiling. He was surprised she was twenty-odd-pounds heavier, and her face was puffy.

"What a coincidence running into you," she said.

"How have you been?"

"Good, good. Everything's good. Do you want to get a drink?"

He glanced at his watch. He had a date in an hour.

"Sure, but I'm meeting somebody in an hour."

"Okay."

They walked into the nearest bar, a place he hated. It had pink walls and black, geometrically shaped tables. He grabbed two ridiculously overpriced drinks from the bar and they sat down. She took a long drink. He told her he'd made partner and she was thrilled, and kept saying she was so proud of him, gushing and fawning over him. He realized she was drunk.

To get her on another topic, he asked her how she'd been. She talked about her sisters' kids, which she'd gone to visit in Wisconsin.

He finished his drink, and smiled at her softly, patting her forearm.

"I should head out. It was good running into you." He squeezed her shoulder. She seemed angry, and pulled his hand.

"I was wondering," she said. "If you'd like to…" She leaned her head in and put her hand on his thigh. It was large, almost like a man's hand, and he tried to remember if it had been that way before.

"Hannah, we broke up."

"I just mean sex. Nothing else." She forced out a laugh.

He was embarrassed for her. "Hannah," he said, speaking gently. "I really don't think that's a good idea."

"It's perfect. We already know each other. It'll be safe."

"If that's what you want, you should do it with someone you don't have a history with." He remembered, of all things, Joseph's mother touching his thigh when he was a teenager.

She breathed in through her nose. "Please, Peyton," she said loudly. The idea of having sex with her, overweight and needy, did not appeal to him.

"You should move on," he whispered.

"You said you loved me," she said, crying this out louder. He glanced over his shoulder. People were staring.

"Alright," he said harshly. "You want to have casual sex? Then, come on."

He grabbed her arm and dragged her outside. "Okay. Where do you want to do this?"

Her chest heaved. He flagged down a cab and opened the door. Hannah stepped in, and he climbed in after her. She pushed herself close to him.

"Hannah, where to?"

She gave the cab driver her address and wiped her face with the back of her hand. She leaned on his shoulder. At her house, they sat on the stoop. He felt so sorry for her, he tried one more time. He gave her a series of platitudes, encouraging her to move on, find someone else.

She nodded, as if she understood, but after he stopped talking, she still tried to pull him inside. He was sick of fighting her and went in. She tried to stop him from wearing a condom but he insisted. When he was younger, he had never worn one, but now he was paranoid about pregnancy and diseases. He was fascinated by how much heavier she was, how different her body looked from before.

When he was done and stood to leave, she seemed satisfied, nodding at him from her bed. She was on top of the sheets, still naked, her expansive, pale flesh spreading out.

They repeated this same interaction a few times—him resisting, her wearing him down, him doing it for some mix of annoyance and pity.

Then he let go of his resistence, and for a few months, their arrangement worked flawlessly: they had sex in her apartment whenever he felt like it. He sensed she was not in it the way he was—in bed, she had become increasingly desperate, willing to do anything he asked—but he ignored this, and told himself they were seeing it the same way.

Back at his house, after his shower, it occurred to him that he liked her desperation, her willingness to humiliate herself. But he brushed this thought away, too.

Eventually, though, she started calling him more, trying to do other things, and he knew he had to end it. Reluctantly, he went over to her apartment and told her he couldn't do this anymore. She clocked him on the shoulder, and threatened to kill him, and then herself. He panicked and called her sister in Wisconsin, handing the phone to Hannah.

She wouldn't let go, though. She was often waiting for him after work, sitting on a bench across the street, watching. She left angry messages at his house and office. He figured she would get bored with it soon, and this was his comeuppance for taking advantage of her desperate state, of once saying he loved her.

But after a few weeks, he was fed up and he accosted her on the bench, yanking her wrist and telling her if she didn't leave him alone he would call the police. She asked him why he wouldn't come back.

"I need you," she explained.

When this had no effect on him, other than a slight flash of pity, she scrunched up her face in fury and told him he'd used her and lied to her.

He could not believe this was the same woman he had dated. She had always been so self-reliant. It was one of the reasons he had related to her.

"Get a hold of yourself, Hannah. We were never married. People break up," he whispered fiercely, tossing her hand down and walking away.

When she called his house, he slammed down the phone. Once, he came back from a woman's place in the middle of the night and she was standing there in front of his house, waiting. He looked at his watch. It was 2:30 A.M. He wanted to punch her. If she'd been a man, he would have beaten her until she was unrecognizable. He walked past her and she grabbed his arm.

"Peyton, please. I just want to know why you left me."

He pushed past her and went inside, locking the door. She pounded on it, "Please," she shouted. "Please, please, please."

He walked in the kitchen and opened a beer. He could still hear her. She had lost her mind. Sicily appeared in the doorway, half of her face imprinted with her blanket. The words "Hot Stuff" were scrawled all over her pajamas.

"Somebody's at the door," she said, yawning.

"It's a crazy person. Go back to bed, baby."

She nodded and gave him a hug before shuffling back to bed.

He finished his beer, and laughed when he remembered how pleased he had been Hannah had taken the breakup so well.

CHAPTER TWELVE

After he made partner, the pressure to work slacked off, like the slight lifting of a thumb pressed into his jugular notch, and Peyton slid back to a seventy-five hour work week. He often contemplated his new business cards, pinning one to the refrigerator to remind himself who he was.

He moved into a new, more extravagant office—it had a mahogany desk, two stiff couches, a liquor cabinet, and a sprawling oriental rug—and he brought his mother and Sicily to see it. His mother stood in the doorway for a long time, and then circled the room slowly, running her fingers over the furniture. She settled in front of the window, her eyes on the bustling street below.

Sicily ran around, jumping on the couches, peering out the expansive windows, and opening books, flipping through the pages.

"Wow! This place is awesome. Wait till I tell Margaret! Her dad doesn't even have an office."

Peyton stared at her hard. "Don't you ever do that, Sicily," he said sharply.

Sicily shrugged, picking up a paperweight in her hand.

His mother tilted around, and smiled at him. She had a rare look of real satisfaction on her face. A black leather dress hugged her body tightly, holding her breasts up like a gift.

He had taken pleasure in introducing her around the office as his mother. People had been friendly, but skeptical, as if they were waiting for him to explain the joke. When he didn't, they glanced away, and smiled at Sicily warmly, patting her on the head. Sicily stuck out her tongue. She peered over people's shoulders, demanding to know what they were doing.

An older partner, a professorial man in his sixties, frowned, like he thought they were a spectacle, and went into his office, shutting the door.

Peyton was tempted to run in there and tell him to go fuck himself, but he didn't.

* * *

On the Fourth of July, Peyton reluctantly joined a C.E.O. of an internet startup on his yacht. He mustered up the courage to go because the account was crucial, something that could make the firm a large sum of money, and increase their credibility in a new industry. He downed a great deal of whiskey as they bantered, and the fireworks exploded over the Charles River.

He had not seen fireworks in ten years, and he had an intense headache, and he kept seeing their fireworks, the one exploding perfectly, and the other… the building on fire, the woman… driving home, across the bridge… Isabelle.

He went into the bathroom and splashed warm water on his face, telling himself to focus, keep his eye on the business. He kept the water running until it was scalding hot. He put his fingers in the stream, letting them burn.

He couldn't do this.

Back upstairs, he smiled stiffly and took another drink. The C.E.O. was drunk, too, and he grabbed his much younger girlfriend's ass, laughing hysterically. "Peyton, buddy, isn't this a great ass?"

The lily-white girl smiled nervously, giving Peyton an apologetic look.

"Yes, sir," he said, grinning.

The C.E.O. excused himself to the bathroom, and stumbled down the stairs. The girl stared at the fireworks intently, her mouth slightly ajar, and Peyton wondered if she was dopey. He imagined her life, probably a shopaholic with expensive tastes, giggling with her similarly minded girlfriends. When the show finally ended, and the night was quiet, the girl sighed. Peyton was relieved. Maybe now it would feel like a normal night.

The girl said she was going to check on the C.E.O., and she came back out a few minutes later, palms up.

"He passed out."

Peyton chuckled, taking another drink. The girl sat down in the chair across from him, her long legs hanging over the chair, her face relaxed. She was wearing a pink polo shirt and white capris, and gold sandals dangled from her feet.

"That's how he is when he drinks," she said, laughing, and sipping her glass of wine.

Peyton nodded knowingly. "What do you do?" he asked.

"For work? I'm a lawyer."

He was surprised and raised an eyebrow.

"Yes, I know," she smiled, "I don't have to be with someone as old as my dad."

Peyton had estimated a 25-year age difference, but the C.E.O. was portly and balding so it was hard to tell.

"My parents think it's my way of rebelling."

She ran her finger around the top of her drink. She had high-cheekbones, perfect skin, and round, brown eyes. She was very attractive in an upper class kind of way. He had no idea why she was with this guy.

"And what do you do?" she asked.

"I work at a private equity firm," he said, leaning closer to her. It was a horrible idea, but he was drunk. He wanted to touch her.

She stood up and walked up the second set of stairs. He followed her, noticing she did have a great butt.

She had her hands on the railing, looking out over the black river. He walked up behind her and ran his fingers over her bare neck and shoulders. Her skin was soft, and her long, brown hair shimmered.

He knew he was being stupid. This account was important. He would lose a lot of money. Touching this girl was not worth a million dollars, he chided himself. He turned her around and cupped her face.

"You're very striking."

She smiled. "I know." She tilted her head to the water. "What would you risk for a beautiful woman?" she teased.

He stiffened. He knew she was right. This was pathetic—hackneyed and feeble-minded.

"I should go," he said, annoyed with her for saying the truth aloud.

But even as he said it, her large brown eyes and her smooth skin softened him, and he wished he could run his fingers over her face, and kiss her small, round mouth. He wished she would revert back to the illusion that this made any sense.

"Oh," she said, mock frowning, her hands on her hips. "But what about me?"

She took off her shirt, and this startled him, it was so ajar with the scorn in her words.

Then he saw, in the boat lamp's weak light, a silver, jagged scar running down her chest, over her left breast and past her stomach. It was a giant centipede attached to her body.

He couldn't help but gawk.

"Still beautiful?" she asked, her eyes challenging him.

The scar wasn't. Maybe because he was completely wasted, she seemed like a character in a horror movie, a poorly sewn-up zombie. But there was also something subservice about it, about her and how quick she was to show it.

He reached out and ran his finger slowly over her scar. She shook lightly as he did it, taking a depp breath.

It reminded him of Isabelle, of how she had found beauty in the most unlikely things. He leaned down and kissed her breast, grazing the scar, feeling its crimpled texture against his mouth.

She stepped back, as if the game had gone on longer than she had wanted. She turned completely around, facing the water as she tugged her shirt back on.

He studied her back. Something about her was sad. He suddenly didn't care about the account anymore.

"I should go," he said. She didn't respond, just kept staring out at the water, her hands on the rail.

He flipped on his heels and flew down the stairs and leapt off the boat. He ran up the ramp and onto the dock. He kept running for miles, and as he moved farther and farther away from the dead river and the fireworks and the disturbing girl, the fog in his head dispersed particle by particle, diffusing into the night air.

Back at his apartment and out of breath, his head was clear, and he cursed himself for being reckless. Who knew what the girl would tell the C.E.O.

Oh, well, he thought, as he struggled to unlock the door.

He heard a rustle on the sidewalk, and turned toward it, furious. "That's it, fucking Hannah," he muttered. He didn't care how wronged or depressed she was, he was going to kill her. Enough was enough. Fuck the law.

She came out from behind a tree.

He was confused. It was not Hannah.

"Peyton."

He couldn't breathe and closed his eyes and opened them again. It was still her. Was he experiencing a hallucination? Had the girl or the C.E.O. drugged him?

She was altered—her cheek bones had come in high, her hips were rounder, her waist more noticeable. But she was the same—her long white hair hung past her waist, her full lips, her straight nose with a slight bump, her green, cat-eyes staring at him veraciously.

"Where have you been?" he said, angry, as if she had merely shown up an hour late.

She walked over and wrapped her arms around him, resting her face against his chest.

He was cold.

"Where have you been?" he repeated, furious. "I didn't even know if you were alive."

She held onto him tighter. "Peyton?" She said this as if she wasn't sure it was him inside his body.

He had a desire to take the life out of her, and cause her to fall limp in his arms, and leave her on a shelf in his room. His coldness was cracking. The sound of her voice and her fruity smell and the warmth of her body was a pick drilling into his ice.

"Isabelle," he said, his voice filled with reproach but also longing.

He sighed and hugged her, pushing her body against his.

The liquor he had been drinking all night suddenly took a violent toll on him, wearing out his bones, and absconding with the last of his energy. "I'm really beat. Do you want to come in? I need to go to bed."

She nodded her face against his chest.

They went straight to his room. He pulled his sleeping bag out of his closet and gave her his bed.

"Night, Isabelle," he said, reaching up and grabbing her hand.

She squeezed it. He was exhausted, and pulled his hand back, curling up in his bag. Waves of contentment washed over him as he fell asleep.

When he woke up, on the floor, he stretched uncomfortably. His body was stiff and he had a pounding headache. He rolled back over, pulling the pillow over his head to block out the light.

The hardwood on his back reminded him he was on the floor, and why he was on the floor, and he popped up. His bed was empty, and unmade. Had he only dreamt it? He rubbed his head and took two aspirins out of his nightstand, swallowing them dry.

He paced into the kitchen.

There she was, sitting at the breakfast table with his mother, Sicily braiding her long hair.

His mother looked at him askance, shaking her head. "I about had a heart attack this morning. Why didn't you tell me Isabelle was coming?"

"I'm sorry." Out of old habit, he did not explain Isabelle had shown up unexpectedly. He opened the refrigerator and pulled out the orange juice.

"Peyton, I haven't seen her in ages. What a trip."

Peyton nodded, drinking the juice from the carton. Isabelle smiled at him, and he smiled back, wiping his mouth with the back of his hand. Sicily's braid was a mess, only catching half of her hair.

"I'm going to grow my hair this long," Sicily announced. Her dark hair was layered to her chin.

"Okay," his mother said, finishing her coffee, and standing up. "Sicily, it's time to go to Abby's."

Sicily ran away. "Just a sec!" she shouted from the other room.

"Isabelle, it was good to see you."

Isabelle smiled brightly. Her teeth were slightly yellowed, and Peyton wondered if she smoked. His mother and Sicily left out the front door, kissing him on the cheek, and Peyton sat down at the table. He was dumbfounded and reached out for her hand, to make sure she was real. She clung to it, stroking his fingers.

"Where have you been?" he asked gently.

"In the mountains, mostly," she said. He stared at her lustfully, searching for a further explanation.

"Painting," she added, as if this accounted for everything. He remembered the paintings she had sent and felt, for a moment, guilty for destroying them.

He nodded slightly, but did not say anything. Her refusal to elaborate sat fatly between them.

She fidgeted uncomfortably. He wanted to break the silence, but he did not know how. The task seemed overwhelming.

"I see you are a partner," she said, withdrawing her hand and pointing to the business card on the refrigerator. He tried to discern if there was judgment in her voice. Was she really saying, 'That's what you did this for?'

"Congratulations," she said. She sounded sincere, but nearly apathetic, like she saw it as a minor accomplishment, on the order of graduating from college.

"Thank you," he said, standing up and walking over to the small kitchen window. It stared into the back of another building. Red brick was all you could see. He had considered moving, but he was hesitant to buy what he considered an indulgence.

"Your sister is great."

"Yeah." His headache returned swiftly, and he rubbed his temple. "Her dad's a prick, though."

"Is he around?"

"Not really. He stops by on her birthday. That's about it." Peyton laughed bitterly. If it wouldn't have made Sicily unhappy, he would have beaten Ronnie to death.

He turned around and stared at Isabelle. She stared back at him, her eyes open and searching. He thought about telling her he had missed her, or saying he was sorry, that he could not say he would have chosen differently, but he wished more than anything there had been no choice. He thought about saying he had to go to work, but he was afraid, if he left, he would never see her again.

"Isabelle…" he said, his voice choking on itself.

She stood up, wrapping her messy braid in a bun and tying it with a rubber band on top of her head. She put her hands on his biceps. "You probably have to get to work."

He nodded.

"I don't have a phone," she said. She wrote an address down on the refrigerator notepad. She handed it to him. "I'm staying here."

He put it in his pocket. "Will you be there tonight?"

She nodded. He grazed her cheek with his lips, and let himself, briefly, feel her warmth, his intense desire to have her, and own her.

In his bedroom, he quickly pulled on gray slacks and a blue dress shirt, and ran a comb through his hair. She smiled when he came out, her hand flying over her mouth.

"You're a man now."

He smiled. "And you're a woman."

"No," she said, shaking her head. "At least not like you in a suit and an office."

It struck him, then, as absurd—that he was here, wearing adult clothes, and she was there, with a woman's body—and he laughed loudly.

Soon they were hunched over and crying, both seeing themselves from the eyes of their eighteen-year-old selves.

They walked to his work, and she hooked her arm through his. Next to her, not having to look at her or say anything, he lost his anxiety, his desperate need to overcome the dark mass standing between them. He felt exceedingly light.

It crossed his mind, briefly, the dream he used to have: driving home from work to Isabelle, painting on the porch in her bare feet.

When he stopped at his building, she looked up at it, her neck arched back, and smiled.

She kissed him on the cheek, her lips soft and full, and then sprinted down the street, her gait inefficient and quick, her army green cotton skirt whipping around her long thighs.

Once he walked in the building, seeing the offices, he remembered last night, on the boat. Normally, this would have put him in a funk, but today it was irrelevant. He didn't care about the account.

The C.E.O. called later that day, and laughing hysterically, he apologized for blacking out. They talked like college buddies for a while, reminiscing about drunken escapades and women they had slept with, and then they drifted into the logistics of doing business.

When the call ended, Peyton felt happy the girl had not tanked the deal. It was quite possible she simply did not have that power—the C.E.O did not seem like someone who would let a girl get in the way of a business deal. Peyton liked to think, though, that she had not even tried, that she had forgiven him his clumsiness.

The work day dragged on unproductively. He was distracted by Isabelle's address in his pocket. He tried not to think about her, but she persistently came into his mind, and he would shake his head, still not believing it.

She had been a figment of his imagination for so long he considered the possibility she would not be how he remembered, or she would have changed in some fundamental way. What if in her returning, he lost her for good?

At six, he ran out the door, no longer able to tolerate waiting. He was confused when he arrived at a storage facility, and he double checked the address. It was right. Maybe, he thought, anger thick in his throat, she had given him a bogus address, and she had already left town, traveling back to wherever it was she came from.

Jumping the black fence, he wandered aimlessly down the aisles. Light poured out from one of the lockers, and he sped to it. It was a space big enough for two sedans, and he peered under. She was there, with a couple duffel bags, paintings, canvases, water and paint. It was dank, and she had unfurled a sleeping bag and pillow.

She pointed her flashlight at him. He was not ready to see her paintings, and after they talked for a bit in the half-light, he pulled her out.

They went to dinner at a small, noisy Chinese restaurant, where the servers were brisk and the food was cheap and greasy. Talking and laughing with her, he felt eighteen again, full of energy and open road. He told her about his clients and coworkers, and his depiction, accompanied by her quick giggles, made them seem foolish. He had forgotten that, how it was not normal, and was in fact ludicrous, to care immensely about how many millions you could make in one year, the prestige of your child's preschool, or the youth of your wife and the social breeding of her family.

After mocking all of it, he suddenly needed her to know what he did that was good. He explained the firm's activities, the companies they had invested in, enabling important products to come to market, including a pill to alleviate arthritis, and a medical alarm system for seniors. She did not discount this, and her eyes lit up while he talked.

She was still vague about where she had been, explaining her agent had put on an exhibit nearly every year, and her paintings had sold well enough for her to keep working. He bristled against her obscurity, annoyed, but let it go, deciding instinctually not to push her.

At work, he used the media databases to find the reviews of her exhibits, something he had avoided in the past out of a desperate need not to think of her. His eyes glided over the description of the paintings. He gathered from his skimming she had drawn abstract paintings of fire, and realistic mountain scenes with herself and a "ruggedly handsome" young man. He did not want to know the details of any of this.

The reviews were glowing and some of them bordered on cultish. *The New Yorker* labeled her "an art world mystery." Some of her paintings had sold for hundreds of thousands of dollars—this shocked him, since she was living in a storage locker—but "the beautiful, young artist" had dropped out of the prestigious Rhode Island Institute of Design after only one year, and refused to give any interviews. Only her agent knew where she lived, and how she worked. Reading this, he was vindicated. He wasn't the only one that believed her work was astounding. It was everyone.

Closing the documents, he poured himself a drink, and stared out his window, over the other tall buildings. Sipping his whiskey, he decided he wouldn't lose her again. He wouldn't let her go. It wasn't clear how she would stay in his life, simply that she would.

* * *

He ended up working longer hours than before she had shown up. He was always distracted by her presence—his mind would roll over to her, painting in her storage locker, her triangle of freckles, her blond hair covering her slender back—and he indulged this, letting himself think of her, smiling. Every project took twice as long this way, and he ended up staying well past midnight to finish.

He had dinner with her every night, indulgently taking a cab back to the office afterwards. He felt guilty doing this, but he didn't have time to walk or wait for the subway.

He often slept at work, and after a month, he remembered to call his mother and explain where he was.

She was silent, and he could hear her breathing sharply. Finally, she told him to be careful with Isabelle.

He was annoyed, and hung up the phone.

He stared at the phone for a second, letting his anger seep into the air, before calling back and apologizing. He told her he would be careful.

She said, "Uh-huh," as if his angry response had only proved her point.

One night, as he was leaving Isabelle in front of the storage locker, he kissed her forcefully, and it was as natural as moving his hand off a hot stove. He ran his fingers through her hair, pushing her against the wall, and he was consumed with desire, wanting to have her, and jealousy flickered in his mind, as he wondered who she had been with. He couldn't imagine she was still a virgin. Their clothes flew off, and they were naked on the sleeping bag, their bodies pressed tightly together, each trying to eliminate any space between them.

Suddenly, she stopped him, gasping for air, as if she were drowning.

"Not yet. Not yet," she called out. Her face was flushed, and she pushed back her sweaty hair. He wanted to take her without her consent. He was barely able to constrain himself, closing his eyes, feeling the intense ache of full throttled desire.

"Isabelle," he said, burying his face in her stomach, letting her pull his hair roughly as he clenched his fists. "Isabelle."

"Not yet."

She could still be endearingly childish, and this made him feel alive again. She was playful, demanding at times to ride on his shoulders, and grabbing his arm to look at certain scenes, and laughing and running in circles around him, tugging at his shirt.

Late one night, they walked under an overpass, barely lit by the ambient streetlight, and she grabbed his arm and demanded a dance. She sang clearly, a gospel hymn, putting one of her arms around his neck and stretching the other out, intertwining it with his. He let her lead, and her movements were quick, outpacing her song.

The collage of graffiti—a red FUCK OMAR, a white figure eight, colorful tags and random lines—the wide, empty street, and the sleeping homeless man buried in a pile of trash, provided a surreal ambiance, and he laughed, kissing her on the nose.

But there was a more serious, almost vacant side to her, too. She would abruptly shut down, like her battery had run out, and reemerge morose. She was goofy and alive, her face bright, and then, with the drop of a window shade or the ring of the phone—quick, meaningless events—she would be miserable. In those times, she would barely move, her eyes closed and her body still for hours, even though she was not sleeping. It was jarring to be lost in laughter, truly happy, and have it, without warning, run out.

He tried different tactics to lure her back. He put his arm around her protectively, as if this might shield her from her sadness; he reprimanded her, gently, telling her to snap out of it; he walked away, not capable of handling it. None of this worked. He was losing her to a vague force he could not see, feeling like he was, in some nebulous way, to blame.

Those moments, reality bottomed out, and he stood on solid ground as she sat in a deep, grimy pit, her hands wrapped around her knees. He coaxed, shouted, dropped down a rope, and she remained still, ignoring his pleas, wrapped up and held down by her own misery.

On the weekends, they traipsed through art museums and art galleries; they took in plays and films, and listened to live music in smoky bars. This lit a dark part of him back up; he realized his life since college had been a sprawling cultural wasteland. He had been so occupied with work and taking care of his mother and sister, he had done little but drink and eat and fuck.

She sang softly when she was in his shower, and when they cooked dinner at his house. Her voice was high and clear, praising the Lord, and she said all the songs she knew came from her church in the mountains. This image—of her sitting on a wood bench, singing with a gleeful choir, the priest blessing her with a cross—comforted him, giving all those missing years a safe, harmless face.

He could no longer bear her sleeping in the storage locker, alone, and insisted she move in with them. She did, reluctantly, leaving her paints and canvases in the locker, and, when he was at work, she listened to Joseph for hours, as he explained his dissertation on the "hermeneutics of power structures in the text and in society."

She confessed, as they lay in bed, it didn't make any sense. He laughed, having felt the same way, remembering drowsing at the kitchen table as Joseph had talked. "But what's the relevance?" he had finally asked, jerked awake by Joseph's pacing. Joseph stared at him blankly. "The power structures underlie all of society," he said stridently, as if he were speaking to a petulant child. "Experience is only understood by the text we impose upon it." Peyton nodded. "Okay, Joseph, if you say so," he said, patting Joseph on the back, heading to bed, unimpressed.

Joseph had built some kind of wall of words between himself and reality. Peyton wished he could knock the wall down with a sledge hammer, forcing Joseph to trudge out of the rubble. But he didn't know how, and he figured Joseph would stay behind the wall the rest of his life, eventually turning it into an impenetrable fortress. After he finished his Ph.D., he would immediately become a professor, and ensconced permanently in the academy, he would have no incentive to temper his useless and abstract thoughts.

With much prodding, Joseph joined them for outings, and the three of them developed an easy rapport. Joseph seemed almost comfortable in the normal world, forgetting, for an afternoon, his need to deconstruct society.

One Saturday, they took the train to an arts and crafts fair in the country, and wandered from stand to stand. Isabelle bought a hand-painted wood box for her brushes and as they walked, they made fun of the mostly ridiculous items—knitted sweaters for cats and dogs, the life size Jesus figures, the gold plated golf bags and bizarre paintings of clowns in thinly veiled sexual positions.

They sat down for lunch in the center square when Peyton saw Randy Hamilton, another partner, strolling with his wife and children. Peyton went over to say hello. His wife was small and petite, completely manicured, and two blond children sat patiently in the stroller, while a third, a girl with poker straight brown hair, held her mother's hand.

Peyton was surprised he was immediately envious of this, of him having a whole family.

Randy greeted him warmly, and his wife seemed peeved, eager to move on to the next stand, until Randy explained he was a fellow partner, and her disposition changed. She smiled at him warmly, her eyes lit up with interest.

This social-status-driven worldview annoyed Peyton, and he smiled at her tightly, thinking, 'fucking bitch.' The children, even the youngest one, politely said hello.

After he said goodbye, he watched them walk down the aisle. His wife's blond hair bounced back and forth in a high ponytail. He was ripped—who did she think she was being so fucking snooty? He hated people like her.

He walked back to the table, and as he moved closer, he stopped.

Joseph was crying. His face was splotchy, and he was wiping tears from his face with one hand, his mouth moving quickly as he talked. Isabelle held his other hand in the middle of the table.

Peyton circled around the tables, staying a good distance away, so he could see her face. She was sobbing too, her free hand on her cheek.

People glanced at their table furtively. Peyton's instinct was for flight, to flee to the station and jump on the first train. He remembered junior year of college. Joseph had come over, and pushed out through his tears, "Don't you ever feel guilty—" and Peyton had shouted, "Shut up!" and run out of his own apartment, forgetting his keys or his wallet.

He couldn't deal with it now either. He backed away and then started running toward the train station. He ran as fast as he could out of the market, dodging people and their children, hoping Randy didn't see him. The train was on the track, the doors open and he jumped up the steps, taking a seat in the back of the car. As it took off a moment later, he let out a breath. He stared out the window, watching the houses fly by.

He went to his office, poured himself a drink, and analyzed data for a small pharmaceutical company working on an improved anxiety reliever. It crossed his mind that, eventually, there would be a pill for everything. Then, people could feel good and empty all the time.

Fucking great, he thought. A world of fucking zombies. He finished reviewing the studies, and decided, if the science was right, the pill would sell to the middle and upper class like white bread sold to the poor.

Fucking Approved.

He slept in the office, and came home late the next night. The apartment was dark, and he sat in the kitchen, drinking orange juice. A picture Isabelle had sketched of Sicily was on the refrigerator. When Sicily first saw it, she put her hands over her heart, and exclaimed, "I love it." She kissed Isabelle on the cheek, and took the picture, running out of the room. "I have to show Margaret," she cried. "She'll be so jealous!"

Peyton left the glass in the sink, and opened his bedroom door. He was relieved to see Isabelle, asleep, her long blond hair spread over most of the single bed. He hung up his clothes and climbed in. He put his arms around her, and she squeezed his arms but did not wake up.

He had a theory that what a woman did in her sleep said a lot about her and her feelings toward him. He had been with women who screamed at him for waking them up, or rolled away, or pushed or kicked him. He'd been with women who woke up, groggy, and then smiled, burrowing into him or mumbling a few sweet words.

Isabelle was the only woman who kept sleeping and wrapped herself up with him. He felt like this must mean her love for him transcended consciousness—and, when she reached out for him, clinging tightly, still sound asleep, it always filled him with a contentment he couldn't even articulate.

* * *

When they were walking home from dinner late at night, hand in hand, the cold autumn air blowing on their necks, Peyton saw a woman sitting on their stoop, her hands resting on her knees. As the woman's shape formed into Hannah, he was pissed.

What the fuck was she doing here, he wondered, remembering her months of calls and her sitting on the bench outside his work, waiting. Which had somehow just stopped.

"Are you okay?" Isabelle asked. His hand had clenched around hers. He nodded, loosening his hand. He wanted to shove Hannah away.

"Peyton," Hannah said.

He instinctively stepped in front of Isabelle.

"Is this your girlfriend?" Hannah said.

196

Peyton laughed, finding the question ludicrous. "What are you doing here, Hannah?" Her name came out lined with disgust, even though he hadn't intended it to.

"I need to talk to you," she said, picking at her loose skirt.

"That's okay," Isabelle said, dropping his hand and kissing his cheek. "I'll be inside," she whispered.

He watched her go, grudgingly. At the door she smiled at him sympathetically, and he longed to be inside with her, curled up on the couch.

He sat down on the steps, next to Hannah, and stared into the empty street.

"So," she said, rubbing her hands together. "I wanted to let you know that I'm going back to Wisconsin next week."

He nodded, relieved. He was relieved she was leaving; relieved he hadn't come to yell at him. "That's good." He rubbed his right palm with his thumb. The calluses were still there.

"I just wanted to know … why you left me," she said. Her voice was hollowed out, like she had been screaming for months, and only its skeleton remained.

He leaned his chin against the base of his palm, blowing out a long breath of air. He really wanted to go inside. "Hannah, I don't know what to tell you."

"We were together for over two years," she said. "We always talked about the future, like it was a shared thing. And then you were just gone."

He looked at her with interest. The fat had shrunken her blue eyes, embedding them further in her face. "We were together for over two years?"

"Yes. How can you not know that?"

He shrugged, truly surprised. "I was working a lot, trying to make partner. Everything else was kind of a blur."

She rubbed her chin, which was softer, more rounded out.

Peyton saw Isabelle, with her long, slender limbs, and childlike smile. "Hannah," he said, shaking his head. "The truth is I don't think I loved you. I liked you, but I didn't love you."

"But you said you loved me."

"Yeah," he said, finding it strange. He didn't have an explanation. The time when he'd found her endearing enough to say that seemed like a hallucination, a misapprehension of reality he could no longer remember the details of. But love was just a word they had used. It had never felt the way it did with Isabelle.

"I'm really sorry, Hannah. I didn't mean for our wires to get so crossed."

197

She stared miserably into the street. Her face seemed flattened from the side. In her silence, he pitied her, forgetting, for a moment, his long-standing sense of her as being a nuisance who lost her mind.

He put his arm around her, and she leaned against him, sighing heavily.

"Oh, Hannah…" he said, rubbing her shoulder. "You'll be okay. You'll find your person. Or you won't, and you'll be happy on your own."

Looking at her so downtrodden, so much fragiler than when they met, he was angry with himself, regretting their months of casual sex, where he had let her degrade herself. He'd been overworked, relentlessly performing around the clock—staring at spreadsheets and running models until his head ached and his eyes blurred, smiling, cajoling, scheming, and yakking it up with arrogant pricks—it had been such a release to stroll into her apartment and order her around. He'd taken pleasure in it, controlling her completely without having to apologize.

As she sat on his steps, a bloated version of her former self, his behavior seemed horribly misdirected. He remembered her crawling around on all fours as his sperm rained down on her head, matting her hair, and streaming over her pale back.

He shook his head, and focused on her here, underneath his arm, her body buried in a cotton tunic.

"Hannah, I really am sorry …" he said, trying to reach her in some way, to make some kind of amends.

She crumpled forward like a crushed soda can, sobbing, as if she had seen herself crawl on the bedroom floor. He rubbed her back gently, struck by how soft it was. It made her seem matronly.

Her blond, wispy hair fell over her shoulder, and he touched it, remembering when he'd first seen her at the company party in a shiny green V-neck and tight, black pants, standing among the stick-thin P.R. girls, smiling at him, as if to say, 'This is complete bullshit, huh?' How clearly he remembered that night, before he had touched her.

She raised her head up, and looked at him. He wanted to say something helpful and grabbed her fingers, shaking them. "Will you be okay in Wisconsin?"

She nodded, her face composed. For a moment, she almost looked like her old self. She took one of her hands and rubbed her nose. "You shouldn't have—"

"I know, Hannah. I'm sorry."

She sighed and patted her lap. "Okay," she said. "I think that's all I wanted to hear, really. I'll be okay. I should go." She stood up and walked slowly down the path. At the gate, she turned back and smiled at him ruefully, or perhaps disdainfully, it was hard to tell.

He waved.

After she left, he put his head in his hands and closed his eyes. When he'd been with her, the first time, she had been so completely independent. She made it clear she didn't really need anyone, including him. He took pleasure, later, in subverting that. He subjugated her because he kept seeing her as fundamentally indifferent.

And, really, there was part of her that had never stopped being indifferent. He remembered, once, seeing her face in her bedroom mirror. He was doing something to her, but her face was composed and distant, like she had just evaluated a pair of Italian leather shoes and found them severely lacking. That look had pissed him off, and he had gone at her harder, trying to break the expression, but he hadn't broken it.

Even when she sat on that bench outside his work, for hours, waiting and knitting, she managed to look like she was in perfect control, prim and undisturbed by the passing traffic or the fact that she was waiting for someone who had no desire to see her. It was this quality of independence from what surrounded her, like a man walking calmly through a tornado, that had attracted him in the first place—she could be a P.R. girl and still know that the P.R. girls were chattering dolls—but ultimately this quality had come between them.

He never got close to her, never felt like they were intimate, and her aloofness for life outside of herself had grown boring. Even when she became fat, she had displayed no self-consciousness; she let her breasts flop wildy over her round belly. It was as if she was above even her body.

He was afraid he was too much like her. Sometimes, when he throttled her, choking her, he had seen, in a flash of self-awareness, it was not her he was trying to tear open, but himself.

"Peyton?"

He turned around. Isabelle, dear Isabelle, was standing at the door in her white cotton pajamas. He stood up and walked over to her. He hugged her, smelling the apricots in her hair.

"Are you okay?" she asked.

He nodded against the top of her head, pushing her head against his chest, feeling like he was drowning.

Promise me you'll never leave, he wanted to say.

She tugged his arm and pulled him inside, smiling gently. She jumped back in bed, watching him as he took off his clothes.

"Who was that?"

"A girl I used to date."

"Oh," she said. Her face crumpled. "Did you love her?"

"No," he said adamantly, climbing into bed, and holding her face in his hand. "Only you. Always only you."

She smiled, looking down at her hands.

"Have you?" he asked, remembering the long expanse of time between them. He saw her with a tall, dark man in the mountains.

"Have I what?"

"Loved someone else?"

She shook her head and licked her lips. "Not love, no."

He felt a surge of jealousy, and wanted to put his hand on her face and see everywhere that she had been. He flopped down on the pillow and pulled her up against him. He wanted to know each and every man she had been with.

He kissed her, feeling the long curves of her body, pressing up against her. She was voracious, pulling him on top of her, thrashing, drilling into him, kissing desperately, until she pulled away, mumbling, "Not yet, not yet."

She fell asleep clasping his hand. He lay awake for twenty minutes, waiting for his painful desire to pass.

The desire was with him all the time. He did not ask for an explanation, but he was constantly longing for her. He could barely listen to her without wanting to press up against her. He was always touching her, pulling her on his lap, holding her back, stroking her hair, and every night, when she breathed, "not yet, not yet," he waited for his longing to disappear. He stared at every woman lustfully. Even his middle aged secretary, with her grandmother's body, came to seem sexual, her curves suggestive. He slept at the office more frequently, finding the incitement of his desire, night after night, too much to bear.

A few weeks later, when the first real snow was falling outside the window, instead of saying, "Not yet, not yet," she let him go forward, and they made love on his single bed, underneath his down comforter. He felt so connected with her, so close, that he couldn't bear to come. He lasted for hours, longer than he ever had.

When they weren't kissing, she was moaning intensely, and when she came, she shook and convulsed, shaking her head. But he stayed inside of her, not wanting to leave. He wanted to be closer to her.

When he finally came, they collapsed on the bed, sweaty and laughing. The comforter was on the floor.

"We should have done that earlier," he said, pulling her to him, stroking her hair, feeling wonderful. Her head was on his chest and her long leg stretched over his stomach and down his thigh.

"I know we should have," she said, staring dreamily out the window, watching the heavy white blanket fall over the city.

"Isabelle?" he asked.

She was breathing steadily. She had already fallen asleep. He felt protective of her, and he wondered, idly, who she'd slept with. She wasn't a virgin. He imagined stealthy, burly men, and he wanted to hold her so tightly he could erase them from existence, make it so no other man had ever touched her.

* * *

Once they had done it, Isabelle wanted to make love to him all the time. She was always touching him, trying to get closer. Her hands clawed at his back and her legs squeezing him tightly. His hand had bite marks on it from quieting her at night.

On Fridays and Saturdays, they went to the storage locker, where they could make noise, and they made love on the sleeping bag, growing high on paint fumes. He grew more possessive of her, and one night, lying on the floor, sweaty and light-headed, he couldn't take it anymore, and asked, "Who did you sleep with?"

She didn't say anything and he tugged her hair. "Hey," he said.

"A painter at school," she said, running her finger in a circle on his chest. Fucking pansy, he thought.

"Who else?"

"A forest guide. A singer. A complete stranger…"

"Is that it?"

She didn't say anything. He tugged her hair.

"William."

"Our William?" he bellowed, sitting up.

"Yes," she said, staring at him openly, her head on the pillow, her hair sprawled out around her. She looked so innocent, he wanted to kiss her gently, but he was furious.

"It was a dumb mistake," she added.

"When? Why?"

"I was 25, living in the Berkshire mountains. I rarely saw anyone at all those days. One evening, I came across a bunch of guys camping. I immediately ran away, but somebody followed me. I kept running, panicked, and then I heard, 'Isabelle, it's me!' and I turned around and it was William."

Peyton nodded, remembering the dozen or so times he'd run into William. He was friendly and charming as ever, and he had only grown more attractive: taller, stronger, and sharper features. He was furious William had not told him he had seen—fucked—Isabelle. The bastard.

"He came inside, saying his friends would be fine without him, and he looked at my paintings, and then we started talking about the accident. We cried, and—"

"William cried?"

She titled her head, thinking back. "You know, probably not. I cried and he held me. In retrospect, I was the one talking, saying how horrible I felt, how I couldn't move on. At the time, I'd felt like we were both saying that, though. And after talking and crying for hours, I felt close to him. So he kissed me, gently, and one thing led to another …"

"That fucking shit," Peyton said, standing up. He punched the wall. "God, how low can he go?"

"Who knows? Maybe he does feel guilty."

"I don't think so, Isabelle. I've seen him. He's as carefree as ever." Peyton hit his fists against the wall, groaning. If he saw William, he was going to beat the shit out of him.

"Peyton," she whispered.

He lay back down next to her, and she put her head on his chest. His knuckles hurt. She flipped off the flashlight.

"Peyton?"

"Isabelle," he said, his voice filled with warning. He didn't want to talk about it. "I can't believe you had sex with William before me."

She giggled. He started laughing, despite himself. It was absurd. He looked at her, laughing, and they both laughed harder, until they couldn't breathe.

When it ran its course, she sighed. "I never really liked William," she said.

He hugged her close, trying not to think about the content of their conversation. He could see William clearly, dressed in his two hundred dollar, non-functional tennis shoes, khakis and a button-up shirt, smiling at her in a wood cabin, pretending to understand what she was feeling. Peyton didn't want to think about how she felt, though. He'd rather think about how William was a douchebag.

"Hey, let's look at your paintings."

"Okay," she said, knocking over the flashlight. She picked it back up and turned it on. She slipped on his t-shirt.

"Sit over there," she said, pointing to the wall.

He moved the pillow over and leaned against the wall. She rummaged through her paintings, hesitating for a moment, and then put a canvas across from him.

The red and orange and blue flames flickered and danced, eating the painting-within-the-painting, a little girl with brown braids playing with jacks on the sidewalk.

"Isabelle…"

"This is the only one I kept from this series."

She was sitting next to the canvas, facing him, her hands on her knees, and she started crying. He wanted to run. He was angry with her for sleeping with William, with other men, and he didn't want to see this. He stood up and pulled his pants on.

"Peyton," she sobbed.

He put on his shoes, and she latched on to his leg.

"Stop," she cried. "Please talk to me."

"Isabelle," he said, leaning down and kissing her head. She peered up at him, her green eyes violently lit with her tears.

"I need you! I need you to talk to me."

He sighed and sat down, holding her against his chest. She sobbed, her slender body shaking.

"I feel so guilty. Don't you understand that?"

He hugged her tighter. "Isabelle, it was an accident. We were kids. We never meant to hurt anyone."

"We were careless!" she screamed. "A child lost her mother, do you know that? A child! How can we go on keeping this a secret?"

He was taken aback, and afraid. He considered bolting, running as fast as he could through the cold winter winds.

"Isabelle," he said, feeling somehow if he said her name enough, he could call her back to him. "Isabelle."

He pushed her back so he could see her face. It was filled with a rumbling and inchoate despair, and he lurched backwards.

"Isabelle," he repeated, staring at his hands. "What's the point of this? It won't undo what's been done."

She collapsed forward and sobbed harder, her body now shaking like a willow in the wind. He picked up the flashlight and turned it off, not wanting to see this.

He sighed and pulled her shaking body up against his on the sleeping bag. He wondered, briefly, if she was having a seizure. Her screams were feral and he covered her mouth with his hand, and it was soon soaked with her saliva.

He tried to imagine what she felt like. To him, the fire seemed accidental and locked in another era, like a random act of God in the time of the Corinthians. He considered his mother and Sicily and Isabelle dying in a fire because some dipshit kids had made their own fireworks. Fucking punks. He'd want to kill them. But he couldn't convert that to guilt. Maybe he would have felt guilty if he had fully considered what he had done years ago, but now it was too late. He was hardened to it. His benign intentions exonerated him.

"Isabelle," he said, holding her tighter. He wanted to tell her something that would make her forget, or forgive, but he couldn't find the right words. He had not come to where he was by argument. It had simply been his instinctual reaction. The world had given him jack shit, and that is what he owed it.

She had fallen limp in his arms and was breathing deeply. His hand was wet with his blood and her saliva, and he wiped it on his jeans. He decided he would try to get her to see a priest. He didn't believe anymore, but she did.

CHAPTER THIRTEEN

In February, the two-bedroom apartment above theirs opened, and he and Isabelle moved in. The apartment had vaulted ceilings and a spacious living room with hardwood floors. They slid across the floor in their socks, laughing and falling over.

She set up her canvases in the second bedroom and in the living room near the street-facing window. When he came home from work in the winter, the air was dense with paint, as if billions of tiny particles had drifted from her brush and settled into the atmosphere. In the spring, they opened all the windows, and the breeze collected the particles as it passed through.

They ordered a beautiful maple bed, carved with flowers and vines, and long arms which reached up in wooden waves. It had the vague appearance of a ship, and they referred to it nautically.

"Hey, you ready to set sail, my fair maiden?"

"The ship is taking voyage to Sleepsville, sailor," she would shout as she slid across the wood floor to the bedroom, her hands in the air.

Their continual amusement with this trope made them think they were either deliriously happy or high on paint fumes. Maybe both.

Other than a folding table with two chairs and a single bed in the living room, "the ship" was the only furniture they owned. Their clothes were hung up in the closets, or balled up on the bedroom floor. Her paintings covered the walls, and they often felt like they were living in an under-construction art gallery. The apartment had a dishwasher, and they stuffed it past capacity, and it groaned loudly, occasionally sending water and soap all over the tiled kitchen floor, soaking the pile of trash around the garbage bin.

The chaos didn't bother him, though. He loved their life. He left the office eager to get home and see Isabelle, covered in paint, at her easel, or sitting on the single bed, reading. Immersed in a project, she would keep working, and he would watch her, sipping whiskey and smiling to himself. Her new paintings were of modern women in the Renaissance-style. The soft, rich colors depicted, instead of voluptuous, naked beauties posed in eternal innocence, an anorexic in front of a mirror, her face anguished, or a woman in a sharp business suit, sitting at her desk, staring at a picture of her children.

He never grew bored seeing the images arise from the clean, white canvas. It still amazed him, how such striking beauty could arise from her slender, quick hand, with the bitten down fingernails and chaffed knuckles and calloused fingers, and he could barely control his desire to lift her long, blond hair and kiss her neck, and run his fingers over her arm, tracing her triangle of freckles.

Her library books stacked up in the corner. She read widely—biology, religion, history, ecology, literature—as if she were looking for a particular piece of information but had no idea of its source. At dinner, she would share what she'd read with enthusiasm, her hands gesticulating wildly and her eyes bright. He was always taken in, hanging on her every word as she explained string theory or the breeding patterns of penguins.

Sometimes, they had dinner downstairs. These dinners tasted far better than their usual fare, as his mother had dated a chef and though he was long gone, she had kept some of his cooking skills. Peyton and Isabelle were hapless in the kitchen, and when they ate by themselves, they usually stuck to foolproof entrees, plain slabs of meat with white rice.

His mother and Sicily gabbed non stop, competing for everyone's attention, and he and Isabelle smiled affectionately, holding hands under the table. His mother gossiped about the beauty salon. She was shocked by most people's lack of class, and she complained about her customers and co-workers. She was particularly aggrieved at what young women wore—stressed blue jeans, shapeless sweaters, and worst of all, flannels.

She glanced pointedly at Sicily when she said this, as if Sicily were scheming to wear such clothes. Normally, Joseph would have interrupted this nervously, and gone off on a rant about how fashion standards oppressed women. With Peyton's mother, though, he just nodded and laughed gleefully.

His mother was still beautiful, in a trashy sort of way, and men continued to go out of their way to lend her a hand. Her bathroom was covered with exotic bottles of anti-aging lotions and creams. The tightness of her skin made Peyton think she had gotten work done at some point, but he never asked, not really wanting to know. He imagined being that beautiful all your life, it was hard to let go.

After dinner, Sicily went to bed, and they sat on the porch drinking bottles of cheap wine. His mother told stories from West Virginia. In the past few years, when his mother was drunk, she romanticized Lamar County. She was suddenly the Norman Rockwell for rural life. Peyton was engrossed—she was a good storyteller—and amused, remembering how much she hated living there.

One night, he came home and found Isabelle reading in the chair, her long legs sprawled in front of her. She was dressed like someone in Vogue magazine.

Her eyes were circled in black; her lips were painted red; her cheeks were brushed with color; and her hair rolled in shiny curls.

She rose to her feet, and a green slinky dress clung to her body, its long, lithe shape pronounced by her high heels. She could have been a model, and he gaped at her for a second, stunned.

He had never realized.

He didn't like it. He wanted her to take it off.

She saw him staring, laughed, and he was relieved. It was only a joke, of course. When she walked over to him, though, she moved carefully and elegantly. Her loping was gone.

He grabbed her up by the waist, and spun her in the air. She squealed and shrieked.

"Your mother and Sicily insisted on doing it," she laughed. "I wanted to show you. Now, I'm going to wash it off. Uck, this stuff is sticky."

Good, he thought, putting her down. She kicked off her heels and ran to the bathroom.

She came back out in her gray sweats, her face pale and scrubbed clean, and jumped on him, smiling.

After a quick dinner, they went downstairs. The apartment was empty, and they found Joseph on the stoop, smoking a cigarette. They sat down next to him, and Peyton sipped at his whiskey.

Joseph told them about the latest developments in his dissertation, which was, finally, near its end. His defense date was in a few weeks. Peyton and Isabelle smiled at each other knowingly as he talked. Most of the time, he didn't make any sense. Even when he did, his positions were so outrageous it was difficult to argue with him. He no longer believed in morality. He believed society was purely a construction, yet it was a construction that needed to be deconstructed and analyzed ad nauseam.

This time, though, he went too far down this line. He was too adamant there was no morality, no truth, and Isabelle exploded, yelling at him and hitting him on the shoulder.

Joseph held up his hands, crying out. His face was startled, but also pleased, as if her reactions proved the truth of what he was saying.

Peyton scrambled over to hold Isabelle back. She let him pick her up and take her upstairs.

He told her not to take Joseph seriously—Joseph didn't really mean what he said—but she shook her head, crying.

"It's not true. It's not true."

"I know. Of course, it's not true. It's bullshit," he said.

She nodded, still crying.

* * *

For years, Peyton had honed in on becoming a partner, his life speeding past like a finely aimed arrow. He had never considered what being a partner entailed. He had vaguely assumed, once he was a partner, his job would be better in some fundamental way.

As it turned out, he had more authority, more money, more of a stake in the firm, but he was basically doing the same shit as before. It was anticlimactic, and without an unquestionable goal to chase, he was disoriented.

It was the same with women. Before he slept with a woman, he barely registered her as a whole person. Everything was observed with the goal of getting her in bed. Only when he was no longer jacked up on seducing her, did he notice her illiterate habit of saying "like" five times in one sentence, or the annoying way she talked about her job all the time.

After he was no longer singularly chasing his goal of becoming partner, he started, similarly, seeing the people in the firm more clearly. He was no longer out to win them over. Most of the partners, he realized, were entitled pricks, and as the company had expanded with the flush economy, their egos had ballooned with their bank accounts.

He still thrived on the competition, taking pleasure in showing them up, bringing in bigger and better accounts, but he wanted more autonomy. He didn't want to be restrained by their decisions. He was sick of pretending to give a shit about Robert's gold-plated faucets, Michael's French villa, Evan nailing an account on the 9th hole of Pebble Beach, or Reynolds fucking two "models" in the VIP room at a club. He developed a constant headache from grinning through his annoyance.

He was flailing about for an exit strategy, when he came across a rejected proposal from a corporate-team-building company, one that offered in-office stunts and dopey games. The idea was trash but the business proposal convinced him there was a flush market for corporate team-building. That gave him an idea for intense, survival style, corporate team-building. He could lead the teams into the mountains, and force them to provide for themselves—kill a deer, start a fire, make a shelter.

He smiled, imagining some of the white-teethed, pot-bellied partners hiking through the woods, backpacks strapped on. Isabelle loved the idea, and they talked, breathlessly, about moving to the mountains, where she could paint and he could start the company.

As he researched the logistics of the business, he and Isabelle came up with a name—Great Expeditions—and she designed the logo and marketing materials. He slacked off at work, spending less of his time on his accounts, and more of his time on his business plan. He was thrilled for a viable way out, a chance to be in charge and do his own thing.

He went to bed excited, thinking about running the company with no assholes to report to and coming home to Isabelle through the rolling mountains and tumbling green woods. He had never stopped dreaming of West Virginia, swimming in the water, running through the thick forest, shooting a deer, and with his plan in motion, these dreams became more vivid. Sometimes, he would see Isabelle, standing at the top of a waterfall, her blond hair covering her breasts, as she smiled down at him in the water below.

He had not thought of returning to the mountains, except tangentially, for years. The city, with its industrial air, had long ago come to seem like his natural environment. His youth had slipped into a different era, one as irrelevant to his life as rural India.

But now that he saw himself moving back to the mountains, it roared in his blood, and the city, whose blocks he had run for a decade without consideration, came to seem, again, suffocating and overbearing. Isabelle, too, was overflowing with excitement. She had always hated the city, feeling like it boxed her in, clouded her vision with ugly people, consumer crap and industrial sludge. She had only returned for one thing: him.

One night, he came home from work late, well past midnight, and heard Isabelle sobbing when he opened the door.

She was on the living room floor, crumpled up like a pile of dirty laundry. Seeing her, his chest caved in.

Her jaunts of misery had come less frequently, but when they came, his whole life felt like it was under threat. Everything he loved and looked forward to was wrapped up in her, and here she was, on the floor, suffocated by forces he didn't understand and couldn't control.

"Don't give into this, honey," he said to her, touching her back, which only made her sob harder. "Isabelle, why are you crying? Tell me why you are crying."

She shook her head, still sobbing, and when he pulled up her body, there was a large kitchen knife, its blade shiny and red, laying in an expanding pool of blood. He looked over her, frantically. Her wrist was cut.

"Why the fuck did you do that?" he said jumping up, and running to the kitchen. "What the fuck is the matter with you?"

He ran a kitchen towel under the faucet, wanting to scream, and whipped it through the air to dry it. He pushed her back gently and cleaned off her wrist, and tied the towel around it.

"Isabelle," he said, shaking her. "Why did you do this?"

Her eyes were vacant and pained, and he laid her down. He got one of his t-shirts and scrubbed her blood off the floor. In the kitchen, he poured himself three shots, drinking them down as fast as he could, puckering his lips in disgust. The alcohol rushed to his head, making him slightly dizzy.

He went downstairs and into his mother's bathroom. She was sitting on her bed, applying lotions to her hands.

"What is it, baby?" she said. He grabbed a few Band-Aids, which were plastered with pink bunnies, and shook his head. He didn't want her to think Isabelle was crazy.

"Isabelle accidently cut herself with the kitchen knife," he said calmly.

She nodded. "You better take the alcohol, too. To clean it up."

He grabbed the bottle, catching a glimpse of himself in the mirror. He looked miserable, his brows furrowed, his mouth twisted.

He kissed his mother on the cheek. "Thanks, Ma."

She stared at him questioningly in the mirror, but she didn't say anything. As she had gotten older or as he had gotten more successful, she had stopped worrying so much.

Upstairs, Isabelle was sobbing, and he picked her up and put her on the single bed, laying her down. He pushed her back when she tried to curl up in a ball.

"Stay there, damn it," he said, cleaning her wrist. The cut was deep, probably half an inch. But it was not in the "right" spot. He stuck the bunny Band-Aids on it and tied a t-shirt around it. He climbed on top of her, holding himself up on his forearms.

She smelled like sweat and blood, and he waited for her to fall asleep, seething. What is the matter with you, he wondered. When her eyes closed and her breathing settled, he rolled off her, and took the bottle of whiskey and climbed out on the fire escape. His fingers were cold but he didn't go back inside until he finished the bottle. He slept in the bedroom, locking the door. He didn't want to see her.

* * *

When he left for work, she was sleeping on the single bed, curled into a perfect yellow ball, and when he came home thirteen hours later, she was in the same position. He moved the hair from her face, and her eyes were shut, her body barely moving, like she was in hibernation. He put his hand on her wrist to feel her pulse. Dried blood had leaked from the bandages, and he pulled them off, cleaned her wrist and applied new ones. He gently shook her, but she did not wake up.

He poured himself a drink, and pan fried chicken and beans. He ate it next to her, staring at her self-portrait on the wall—her eyes were down, and her long hair partially obscured her damp face. She seemed vulnerable and sad, and he squeezed her warm calf, wanting to save her, to take her back.

This continued for days, and then a week, and then two weeks. The loaf of white bread on the counter lost slices, and he imagined her walking over in the middle of the day, eating bread, and then returning to sleep. He moved her into the bedroom, but by morning or night, he would find her in the single bed, her face turned to the wall.

He vacillated between anger, frustration and sadness, and he got drunk every single night, staring at her paintings, and pacing. He told his mother she had the flu. Saturday night, he threw his glass at the painting of them together in the mountains, and it bounced off, shattering on the floor.

He shook her violently, calling her name, and she woke up, weakly pushing him away. Her lips were cracked, and dark blue engulfed her eyes. She blinked at him.

"Peyton," she said, out of breath, as if she had just run an incredible length to get here, to this bed. "Can we move to the mountains?"

"Will that make you better? Yes. Yes, we'll go."

"We will?"

"Yes."

She sat up, and jerked unsteadily, as if she were drunk. "I'm thirsty," she croaked.

He went to the kitchen and brought her back a glass of water, and she consumed it in one gulp, the water trailing down the sides of her mouth.

"Isabelle, are you sick?"

"No," she said, dropping the glass, which broke on the floor. Her hair was plastered to her head with grease. "I can't stand the city," she said. "Especially this city. I hate the way people look at me. It's as if they know what I did."

"Isabelle, if anybody is looking at you, it's because you're pretty. Trust me."

"No."

He sighed. "Isabelle, God! Do you know how scary it is to have you like this for weeks?"

"I'm sorry," she said, as if it were out of her control.

"Then why do you do it? Why can't you buck up like the rest of us? Everybody has shit to deal with!"

"I know they do. I can't help that I feel things so strongly. It destroys me. I know it's not like that for most people.." She scratched her head. "I have to take a shower."

She stood up, wavering, and then made her way to the bathroom. The sheet fell to the ground and fallow skin clung tightly to her ribs. She had lost weight she couldn't afford to lose.

He went into the kitchen and put dinner on, adding extra butter to everything. Even though it was late, he had forgotten to eat. He was too angry.

She came into the kitchen, a white towel around her head and tied at her chest. She was scrubbed clean. She sat down at the table and traced her finger over the cracks.

He glanced out the window at the brick wall. The steak was still bloody, and he served it up, rare. He grabbed two of the cleaner dirty plates. He hadn't washed a dish in weeks, and the crusty pots and pans littered the counter.

She cut her steak into big pieces, chewing quickly and smiling at him.

"Isabelle."

"I need to leave the city," she said softly. "I just do."

"Okay. We'll go. Give me two weeks. Okay?"

She nodded. He stared at her gently. "Promise me you won't do that again."

She squinted at him like he was thirty feet away and she was trying to discern his features. "I love you."

"I love you, too. Promise me you won't do that again."

She smiled, finishing her steak. "That was delicious." She stood up and opened the freezer, pulling out the ice cream and grabbing a spoon from the drawer. She sat back across from him, digging into the ice cream.

"I can't promise that," she said.

He dropped his plate in the sink, and it clattered against the other plates. He wanted to destroy the bricks, open the space, so he could see the sky. He tried to slow down his body. He felt as if his blood were racing through, causing him to overheat.

She wrapped her hands around his chest. Her fingers were cold.

"I will never let you go," she whispered, holding him tightly.

He sighed, and turned around, pressing her head against his chest. "I know," he said into her clean, white towel. "I've missed you so damn much."

* * *

His mother was furious when he told her they were leaving. He asked her to come with them, knowing full well there was no chance in hell she would take Sicily to West Virginia. She shook her head, and her pink curlers rattled.

"Peyton, why would you want to go back there? You're so successful here. Your little sister is here. She needs you."

"Ma, she doesn't need me. She's happy and you know it."

"She still needs a male role model. You want her to end up dating a bunch of losers! I just can't believe this. West Virginia is filled with trash! Don't you remember that? Poor, drunk good-for-nothings."

"Ma, I know what it is. I grew up there. Isabelle wants—"

"Peyton," she said, shaking her head. "Do not give up your life for a woman." She leaned in and whispered fiercely, "Isabelle is no good for you, Peyton. She's a sweet girl, but she's always been off her rocker. You think she could take care of children? You're old enough now to find a good wife, someone who would make a good mother."

"Ma, Isabelle is right for me."

"Oh, yeah? Then why were you separated for ten years?"

"Ma, we were young. I love her, and you should support me. I've supported you no matter what I thought about your choices."

"What is that supposed to mean?"

"It means I always thought Ronnie was a dick, but I didn't say anything because I wanted you to be happy," he shouted.

She flinched, staring at her painted red fingernails. She shook her head.

"Alright, Peyton." She wiped her eyes with the back of her hand. He sat next to her on the bed, and put his arm around her.

"Ma, it's not that far. I'll visit."

"I know," she sniffled, wiping her eyes again. "I'll just miss you, baby. You're the best thing I've ever done."

He smiled and hugged her, feeling a brush of sadness. He had lived with her his whole life. "Thanks, Ma."

She laughed and patted his thigh. "Good," she said, standing up. "Now, I have to get ready for my date."

* * *

Peyton had a hard time leaving the firm. The process took months, and Isabelle fell in and out of her moods, asking him, "Are we leaving soon?" like a child, her eyes hopeful and dependant. By the time he disentangled from the firm on good terms, he was ready to go, but as he cleaned out his office, it still felt like a defeat, like he hadn't been able to hack it.

After it was clear he was leaving, some of the partners grew distant and dismissive, looking past him, as if he no longer mattered. This infuriated him, and gave him ludicrous fantasies of crushing them with the immense success of his new company.

"You're being an asshole," he said to one, who was staring over his head. The partner looked at him, startled, and then smiled snidely.

"Fuck you," Peyton said, walking away.

He was surprised to discover he would miss some of the partners, not realizing, until he was on the way out, how much mutual respect had grown up between them.

Beside his slightly wistful regrets, he had a tremendous sense of freedom. He had been cuffed to his job since he graduated from college, and he felt like a freed prisoner, his days no longer structured by the specific demands of the institution. His time was his own again. The world seemed full of possibility, and he envisioned running his company, hiking in the woods, swimming, and having Isabelle and a small brood of children at his heels.

They bought a sturdy, new van and packed their clothes and her canvases and paints. They managed to tie the "ship" to the top with bungee cords. His

214

mother cried like a baby as they left, and Joseph seemed to fight back tears, rubbing his nose and hugging Isabelle intensely.

"Hey, buddy, you're moving soon too for your big professor job," Peyton said, patting him on the back.

Sicily moped, refusing to say goodbye, crossing her arms over her chest. He picked her up in the air and hugged her, kissing her belly. She laughed and screamed.

As they drove out of the city, Peyton patted Isabelle's thigh and smiled at her. She clapped her hands and screamed, leaning over and kissing him on the cheek. "Here we go!"

He grinned. "Here we go."

CHAPTER FOURTEEN

The cabin was musty, and an empty Vodka bottle sat on the dresser near the bed. The sheets were crumpled. Peyton stepped on an old, dried out condom. He assumed it was Hershel's, as he was the one who had been checking in on the property, even though it still belonged to Peyton's mother.

Still a lazy dog, Peyton thought, picking up the trash and removing the sheets.

They put Isabelle's paints in the office he rented in town above the grocery store. To his surprise, the town seemed to be doing well. It had expanded and become a Disney-fied version of its old self. There was now a gift and souvenir shop, a storefront offering tours, a hotel, an outdoor supply store, four restaurants, and a pub. It occurred to him this wouldn't be bad for his business. He could partner with the shops and hotel to take even more money from those enrolled in his courses.

They went on one of the tours and at least half of what the guide said about the land's history was bunk. He invented Civil War battles and bloody labor strikes that never occurred. The two middle-age women, taking the tour with them, nodded with interest as the guide talked.

One said, "Did you hear that, May?" and the other said, "Isn't that something!" after every tidbit. Peyton whispered in Isabelle's ear, "Not true," and she laughed, pushing the guide for details. They smiled at each other as the guide stuttered uncomfortably.

A lot of the old company housing was vacated, with boarded up doors and windows, and the rest of it was filled with poor people, many of them sitting on their porches, staring, waiting for something impossible to discern.

217

It took months to install plumbing in the cabin and fix the air conditioner, and Isabelle's paints warped with the heat. She sketched instead, carrying her pad around, her fingers turning black.

The property was pretty much the same. He could see Hershel had taken down some trees, but it was still flush and full of life. They hiked and camped for weeks at a time, surveying the land. Peyton was scouting out where to take the corporate groups on the expeditions. A few more vacation homes had sprouted up, miles away, but outside of the two-street town, the land was still, to his relief, barely touched by the human footprint. Peyton wished he had the money to buy the rest of the land up, as far as he could see, and sell it back with a conservation provision attached, so it would remain this way, wild and undeveloped.

His body transformed quickly, growing strong on the hikes, swims and hunts, and fed by the fresh mountain air and abundance of sleep, it recovered more quickly. He had forgotten how good it felt to be truly strong. It gave him a constant feeling of power and possibility.

He had also forgotten how beautiful the mountains were—the endless ridges bumping up against the pale blue sky, the pink sunsets, the green life crawling over everything, competing to get closer to the sun, and at night, the web of stars thrown over the dark blackness of night.

The silence, at first, was eerie. The voices in his head, of people he had known, of strangers on the street, buzzed, afraid of the quiet. Quickly, though, he sunk into it, becoming attuned to the gentler noises—the rustling of the leaves, the hoot of an owl, or the buzzing of a wasp.

He and Isabelle would hike for days and the time would melt by with only ten words passing between them. They smiled and held hands, and slept intertwined, making love in the coldest part of the night, without ever feeling the need to speak. Words, which had occupied almost every minute of his waking life in Boston, faded away.

It seemed strange and foolish that he had ever left the mountains. One night, after they had swam naked in the swimming hole, and lay drying on the grassy shore, looking up at the orange moon, fingers loosely intertwined, a light breeze washing over their skin, he felt, then, a person could have a million different lives, but there was an inexplicable force pulling you toward the right one. And there was an intense feeling of belonging and oneness when you arrived where you were supposed to be.

That was how he had ended up back here in the mountains, with Isabelle; this was his destiny. He could feel his business being a success and their unborn children running through the woods. He knew it did not quite make sense, but he felt it anyway: this is where the universe, some kind of a God, wanted him to be.

In the summer, after two trial runs and endless paperwork and permits and registrations, he led his first corporate expedition, for a finance company he had worked with in Boston. After the training, Isabelle came along to help carry and cook. It was mostly men, and they bantered and goaded one another, fighting to shoot the gun.

At night, they cooked the deer one of them had killed, and talked trash over the campfire. Men flirted with Isabelle, offering to carry her pack and fetch her water. This distracted Peyton, and he vacillated between pride and jealousy. By the end of the week, the group was sore, dirty and hungry, spotting nascent beards and blistered heels. When one of the men complained, the others teased him for not keeping up with one of the women, a marathon runner who loped easily over the long distances.

They walked into the town, where they went to the restaurant, and ate and drank with abandon until the van showed up to drive them to the airport.

He and Isabelle waved them off.

He was beat and stumbled as they put the equipment into the office. Isabelle laughed at him in a loving way. They jogged home, both exhausted from the week of constant chatter, and they slept in their soft boat of a bed until noon the next day.

The air conditioning was finally installed, and Isabelle filled the spare room he built for her with paints and canvases. She stayed in the room for days at a time. He watched her paint from outside the window, her hair piled on top of her head, her long, tan arms moving intently across the page. If he was home, he left her meals right inside the door.

She slept and ate in a seemingly haphazard way, as if she painted until her body just gave out. He might glance in at 3 or 7 P.M. and see her curled up at the foot of her easel, sound asleep, or eating her dinner, staring at her painting as the food absentmindedly went in her mouth. Her paintings were beautiful, striking something inside him, pushing him into a better world. It was nothing like the trendy pieces of postmodern and conceptual "art" they had seen in some of the Boston art galleries—chunks of wood, toilets with feces, unmoving artists naked and staring at the wall.

But, occasionally, after she had been painting for days, he would watch her and feel lost, and jealous. He could not see her loving him or their unborn children completely. There would always be this: her art, her self, tied together, with him on the outside, looking in. This hit him hard, every time, because he always forgot there was this, too, when she was running with him, laughing, climbing on his back, whispering, "I love you" in his ear, her breath warm.

There were still moments when she was forlorn, staring at the stove, looking as if she were about to cry, but her moods, for the most part, were cheery, and he thought, until they started up again in the peak of summer, that the city, with its haunted streets, had caused her malaise.

She was wary of other people getting close to her, and she liked the expeditions because she could talk to people without having to see them again. Except for her calls to her agent and her holiday calls to her mother, she had no regular contact with anyone but him and the clerk in the general store. They visited his relatives every few months, but they didn't have much to say to each other, and mostly sat around drinking, as Hershel rattled on.

Hershel had put Margaret in an institution years ago, and was living with an illiterate girl in her early twenties. He relentlessly mocked the girl, calling her stupid and smacking her ass, and Greta, whose husband had left her and fled to New York City, declaring he was gay, was listless, trying to raise four children by herself in Hershel's shadow.

Peyton had offered her money to move out, but she simply smiled and shook her head, saying it wouldn't make a difference. Tyler was a world-class drunk, with a frazzled wife and three small children of his own. Sarah and Adam had apparently fled town years ago—fifteen-year-old Sarah in cutoff jean shorts, hitchhiking along the Interstate, and Adam to West Virginia University, where he taught chemistry. Adam getting out of here made Peyton happy.

When Isabelle's days of comatose sleep started up again, he was flooded with an immense despair, asking her to see somebody. Though he wasn't, generally, a believer in therapy or psychiatric pills, finding the modern tendency for people to talk about their predictable, uninteresting lives for hours a week self-indulgent, he was desperate.

He had tried every approach on his own, and nothing had gotten her out of bed any earlier than she was ready. In Boston, she had gone to a priest, but came back shaking her head, saying he had been of no help, only dispensing prayers. She had prayed all she could. She only stared at him with a perplexed expression on her face, though, when he suggested therapy.

As he expanded the company, he was gone more, training college kids to run the expeditions, sending out promotional materials, calling companies he had worked with in the past. When she was not in a state of malaise, Isabelle ordered books through the general store, and soon the cabin was stacked full of them. She drove the van over the ridges and bought walnut bookshelves, lamps and flowery curtains and blue and white china. The cabin looked more like a home than it ever had before.

At night, they ate dinner on the rocking chairs, listening to folk music, watching the trees shimmer in the wind and the sun fall below the horizon. When it was dark, they wandered into the woods. They went into the nearby vacation homes, which often had unlocked windows or back doors, and ruffled through their rooms, looking for signs of life. Isabelle liked looking at people's photos and folded letters, imagining who the people were, what they did. They made up stories, pretending they knew the arc of their lives.

He liked to have sex on their beds, as it felt mildly illicit. She thought it was wrong, but she always gave in, laughing, and glancing at the door, as if the people might appear out of nowhere. They dipped in the hot tubs, Peyton drinking their liquor, convincing Isabelle they would never know it was gone, and then, when they were both sweating and flushed, they would run through the woods to the swimming hole, scratching their arms and stubbing their toes, jumping into the dark, unmoving pit and splashing each other by the light of the moon.

One night, in the thick of autumn, when the tree leaves were shining violently in oranges and reds, they returned from camping, and found an open backdoor on an empty house eight or nine miles away from the cabin.

"Let's just sleep here," he said, flicking on the lights and dumping his pack. She smiled, putting her backpack on the floor.

"Ok," she said, stretching. She jumped up, wrapping her arms and legs around him. He laughed, staggering backward. He steadied himself and spun her around, her hair flying wildly in a circle.

"Peyton." she said, laughing.

"Yeah?" he said, putting her down.

"I love you."

"I love you, too," he said, opening the cabinets, looking for liquor. He found a bottle of whiskey and poured two shots. "Here, drink this."

She shook her head.

"Drink it."

She took it and swallowed it down, puckering her lips. "That tastes like poison. I don't know how you can drink so much."

He took his shot down and poured them both another. "One more." She shrugged and took it, only finishing half the glass. She shook her head, grimacing, and he laughed. She drank the rest of it.

"Mmm…that was intense."

They walked into the living room, and studied the framed pictures sitting on the mantle.

"Look at this guy," she said, pointing to a picture of a thin man with a narrow face and chin, wearing glasses for the legally blind. "Looks like a character in an arthouse film."

Peyton nodded. Isabelle grabbed a different frame and held it to her chest.

"So cute," she said, peering at it adoringly. He leaned over her shoulder. It was a plump baby in blue jeans and a cotton t-shirt, holding a rattle.

He smiled, and watching her, staring lovingly at the baby, he saw them clearly with a baby of their own, on a red sling while she painted, or in his backpack as he hiked. He saw her round belly as she walked through the woods, her hands around it protectively.

"Isabelle."

"Let's have a baby," she said, her eyes wide open.

"Yes," he replied simply.

She put the photo down and hugged him, her arm hitting him in the face. "Oops."

He touched her neck. "Do you really want to have a baby?"

"Yes. Don't you?"

"Yes," he said, rubbing her flat stomach. He went back in the kitchen and poured two more glasses. "Here, let's celebrate. To our beautiful baby."

She clicked her glass against his and took it down. She ran through the living room, opening the door.

"Let's check out the other rooms."

Her motions were clumsy, and he heard something crash against the floor. She laughed. The house was small—one floor and two bedrooms—and after they looked through it, they settled on the living room couch, and ate a bag of chips they had found in the kitchen. Isabelle turned on the television and flipped through the channels, looking for anything interesting. She stopped it on the all-music channel. She leaned her head against the couch.

"I feel so wasted," she said, laughing.

He squeezed her thigh, watching women gyrate in the music video.

Isabelle started crying, and he felt himself harden. Not now.

"Peyton…"

"Why?" he said, turning to her, seeing, in her drunken state, a chance to get the truth.

"Because we did it. We still did it. And then you left me because I wanted to do the right thing."

He slammed his fist down on the coffee table. "It wasn't the right thing, damn it. Why would things have been better? We would have gone to prison and they would still be dead!"

She shook her head, crying. "Because it would have been done! We could have been forgiven."

"By who? They're dead!"

She jumped up. "By everybody! We could have paid up, served our time."

"God damn it, Isabelle," he said, standing up and waving his hands at her. "It wouldn't have made any difference. Don't you understand that? The moment we set those fireworks off, it was done. There was nothing we could have done to change it! God, turn off this stupid music."

He picked up the remote and shut off the television. "God damn it, Isabelle," he cried, stalking into the other room and slamming the door.

He locked it. The anger coursed through his veins. He was so mad. He wanted to scream. He picked up an angel figurine and threw it against the wall, watching it shatter. He imagined the people coming home and finding random items inexplicably broken. He fell down on the bed, and waited for his anger to go away, clearing his mind of any thoughts.

* * *

When he woke up the next morning, the sun streaming in through the window, he could hear her singing in the kitchen. He opened the door, and she was at the stove, flipping a pancake. A stack of pancakes and the opened pancake mix sat on the counter.

She turned to him and smiled. Her nose was covered with white dust.

He grinned.

"I made us pancakes." She hummed softly, moving her hips, as she threw another on the pile. It was burnt. He kissed her on the neck, and hugged her body against his. He felt the roundness of her hip, and he remembered their words last night, their promise to have a baby. He reluctantly pulled away, pouring himself a glass of water and sitting down at the table.

After she finished the pancakes, she brought two plates over to the table.

"Isn't this great?" she asked, covering her pancakes in maple syrup.

He nodded.

They talked about the next expedition, which started in two days, and he grinned because she still had the flour on her nose. He leaned over and wiped it off.

"Thanks," she said, smiling softly. He leaned over and kissed her, and her lips, or his, tasted like maple syrup.

"I love you, Peyton," she said.

"I love you, too."

* * *

Peyton drove to visit his mother and Sicily, and his first night back, he told his mother he was going to propose to Isabelle.

She smiled, shaking her head. "Does she seem better?"

He nodded, wanting her to love Isabelle, wanting his life to be one seamless whole. "Ma, she's brilliant."

"Of course she is. That's not the question."

"Ma, I know. I've always loved Isabelle."

She nodded, sighing. She hugged him hard. "I know."

She ran her fingers through her hair, and took a deep breath, her slender chest rising. "Okay. Congratulations, baby."

They went shopping for rings, and his mother kept pushing him to buy a large diamond—"what every woman deserves"—but he knew Isabelle would hate it. He bought a simple silver band, etched with their initials and the word "eternity" on the inside of the band. His mother shook her head, clicking her tongue.

"Ma, I promise this is better," he said, rubbing her arm. He kissed her on the top of the head. "Trust me."

* * *

He convinced Isabelle to go camping with him in northern West Virginia. It was a more mountainous and beautiful terrain, filled with stone ledges and age-old pines. He wanted to ask her in a distinct place, one she could remember. The snow started falling once they entered the woods, and it fell slowly, partially obstructed by the pines. Their faces grew cold, and the rest of their bodies grew warm, hidden under thick knits and revved up by their internal furnaces. The dark tree trunks, a few feet apart from one another, and the gently falling snow occupied the landscape as far as they could see.

When they broke the ridge, they could see for miles, the ups and downs of the land, blanketed with the fresh, white snow. They stared out for a while, stunned, warmed with the beauty of everything in their view. He cleared off a spot underneath a ledge, and set up the tent, leaving her to look. The ring was in his pocket, and his hands shook as he set up the tent.

He walked to the edge of the ridge, and reached out for her thickly gloved hand. The snow was falling, and her face was red and sticky. She smiled at him, a half-smile, and he fell to his knee. He took off his glove, and his fingers froze as he pulled out the box, opening it.

"Isabelle, you're the only woman I have ever loved. The only one I will ever love. Will you be my wife?" he said, his heart on fire. She reached out for the ring, stunned, and took off her own glove.

"Yes, of course, I will," she whispered, her teeth chattering.

He felt free.

She read the inscription and she smiled, staring at him like he had done exactly the right thing, like in that one gesture, he revealed he knew exactly who she was. He slipped it on her finger, and he believed everything was, finally, as it should be.

They made love in the sleeping bag with their sweater still on. He had not bothered to bring a condom, and when he came inside her, he felt closer than he ever had, and he thought, maybe, they were bringing their child into this world.

* * *

They agreed, easily, to have a small ceremony in Boston in February, with Sicily, Ma, Joseph, and Isabelle's mother. Neither of them had any interest in a large gathering, finding people they barely knew an invasive distraction. Isabelle ordered materials and set about making her own dress. Peyton bought a camera and started taking pictures of everything, feeling like it was important to show their children what it was like before they were born.

He had always wished his mother had told him more about her life before he was born, and thinking about his wedding, he had a flicker of desire for his father to be there. But he let this pass, like a rowboat in the night. He did not want to upset his mother, or himself, with unwanted intruders, lost to the darkness. He had made it this far without a father.

He worked longer hours on Great Expedition. He hired a manager and trained more guides. In the winter, they switched over, mostly, to taking individual groups on "survival vacations." The corporate trips were better suited to fairer weather. He was pleased the fees had already covered the initial outlay on equipment and training, and now they were well into denting the first few months' operating costs.

Isabelle wore her ring all the time, even when she was painting, and though she washed it, it remained crusted over with paint. Whenever he noticed it on her slender yet strong hand, he smiled.

They had sex, and it was closer than before, as he felt the gravity of the act, knowing they might be creating a child, a wonderful, beautiful child, uniting himself and Isabelle permanently, in one flesh.

"Isabelle," he said, resting his head on her belly.

"Yes?" she asked, petting his hair absentmindedly.

"I love you."

"I love you, too…forever."

He laughed and rolled over. "Forever, huh?"

She smiled, but her eyes were serious. "I mean it. You know that, don't you?"

"Of course, I do," he said, leaning into her body. "I love you forever, too."

He kissed her on the lips, and she kissed back, pulling his body violently against her own.

Her cheek was wet, and he raised his head, opening his eyes. Tears ran down her face. "What is it?"

She shook her head, smiling. "I'm just happy, that's all."

He rolled over, not quite believing it, and she snuggled her head against his chest. He stroked her long hair, and held her back firmly, and soon her breathing steadied.

She was asleep.

CHAPTER FIFTEEN

In early January, he returned from an expedition, exhausted, and he ran home from town, and stumbled into bed and fell asleep. He woke up in the afternoon to snow falling outside, fogging up their windows.

He yawned and put the kettle on, flipping through one of Isabelle's books, *On the Fall of the Roman Empire*. He drank his coffee, and then piled on layers of clothes, and walked down the path to the road.

The snow drifted in the air, back and forth, as it lazily made its way to the ground, as if they were inside a just-shaken snow globe. He reached the end of the path, and their van was gone, its tracks covered by the snow.

He tried to remember if Isabelle had said she was going anywhere. Perhaps she had simply gone to buy more groceries. He was uneasy, because it was unlike her to leave without saying so, and jogged back up to the house.

There was no note on the table or in the kitchen or near the bed. It occurred to him that someone might have stolen the car. He walked quickly to the spare room, his sense of unease more pointed now, and opened the door and flipped on the light.

He stared for an indeterminate amount of time, trying to process what he saw: a few half-empty paint tubes, a couple brushes, an easel knocked over.

Okay, he thought, maybe she took all of her paintings somewhere. Or maybe someone assaulted her.

He raced back into the bedroom. He flung open her drawers, each faster than the next, throwing the last one to the ground. They were all empty. He went into the bathroom. Her toothbrush, her shampoo, her conditioner: all gone. He threw the toothpaste on the floor. He considered calling the police, but then realized there was nothing they could do.

The rest of the afternoon was a blur. He was drinking, crying, and breaking plates. Reality had been pulled inside out and turned over on its head. He felt like it must be a sick joke.

When she came back, he decided, he would tell her this was unforgivable.

* * *

The next few days, he did not leave the house. He waited for her to come back, and he was thinking of how he would punish her, ignore her, yell at her, chain her to the bed, make her beg for forgiveness.

When he heard a noise outside, he felt an intense, dizzy rush of relief, and then fury, as he prepared to tell her how much of a scared bitch she was.

But, then, the noise stopped.

And he was still alone.

He ran to town when the snow cleared, and he developed his pictures. He hoped they might provide some sort of explanation, a clearer view of reality. He brought them back to the cabin, and after drinking half a bottle of whiskey, thumbed through them.

There was nothing.

It was just Isabelle, smiling, sticking out her tongue, painting, sleeping, staring into space. Them together, kissing, posing for the camera. He wanted to tear them apart, but he couldn't bear to.

After a few weeks, he nearly lost his nose to frostbite from wandering through the woods, aimlessly, drunk. He was empty. He had screamed how and why so many times his voice had gone hoarse. The words had echoed endlessly inside of him, reverberating up against themselves, without answer.

He managed to pack his clothes and call an insanely expensive cab. He didn't care. He was rich, wasn't he? He laughed bitterly.

His mother opened the door with a smile, and when she saw his face, she looked horrified, and held out her arms.

Part IV

CHAPTER SIXTEEN

When Peyton first saw Laurie—dancing across the stage, her strong legs propelling her gracefully through the air—his face was bruised, his left wrist was fractured and his right leg was in a full-length cast.

He'd driven his motorcycle, drunk, right off the edge of a cliff. He flew, madly, freely, into the open air, before he slammed into a rock and rolled over and over, finally landing on a stone ledge, passed out and broken.

If a car, filled with a suburban family of five, had not been driving in the opposite direction, right at that moment, and seen him disappear into darkness, their mouths dropping in surprise, Peyton would have bled to death on that ledge.

When he woke up in the hospital, his body ached in places he had never before felt—joints, muscles, organs, veins.

Though his body was shot, he left the hospital feeling better than he had in a long time, as if when he had flown off the cliff, shooting aimlessly through the air, his soul vomited. For years after Isabelle left, he had been consumed with a self-igniting rage, and he had drunk, fought, fucked, and built up his company without regard for any person standing in his way. He had been a human cyclone.

But lying in the hospital bed, barely able to move, he was tired. Flying through the air, losing contact with the pavement and then his motorcycle, he idly observed he was going to die. There had been no part of him that screamed, 'No, wait, I don't want to die.'

It was only, so here it is, the end of my life. When he woke up, he did not feel grateful for his survival. He had not been given, as they say, 'a new lease on life.' He only felt free from his rage, and willing to live.

He pled guilty to a DUI, and he turned in his license, and trashed his broken motorcycle. He cut back on his drinking, and saw his mother and her husband Phillip more, and Sicily, when she was willing to part from her dozens of friends.

At work, he noticed, with some compassion, his employees were nervously obsequious. The company's turnover rate was exceptionally high. He stopped exploding at people, made an effort to acknowledge good work, and, gradually, the palpable tension loosened.

He had been living alone in a small, one-bedroom apartment near his company's headquarters, with only a single bed and a folding table and chair. He and his mother went on a shopping spree, making the place livable, rather than a bachelor crash pad, and he brought a friendly, brown mutt home from the pound.

He chucked his greasy diet of take-out and liquor, and started walking to the organic grocery store every week, tying Thomas up outside, and stocking up on fresh vegetables and meats, putting them in his backpack as he hobbled home on his crutches.

It was Saturday night, and he had gone to the ballet with his mother and Phillip. Phillip dozed in his seat. His mother watched intensely, clapping even when no one else did, and afterwards, she lamented the fact that she had never had a chance to "do ballet."

"Crackers don't do ballet," she said. Phillip, thoroughly smitten with his mother, smiled empathetically.

Laurie came out in the second number. She was not the principal, and she floated across the stage with three other dancers, performing the same motions. But Peyton could see only her, transfixed by her perfect control over her body.

Her round face was the color of golden ivory, and her strong cheekbones led to a small, straight nose and voluptuous red lips. Her dark eyes, slanted and titled, appeared to him half-closed. Her dark black hair was pinned in a bun, and her face was still and unmoving. Her ribcage did not discernibly rise and fall, as if the weight of her breathing, too, was under her control.

After the show, he charmed his way backstage, and found her, sitting in front of a mirror, removing her makeup. She sat erect, as if she had a pile of imaginary books on top of her head, and the movement of her arm, wiping a cotton ball across her face, was elegant.

People-filled pictures lined her mirror. He complimented her performance, and she smiled politely, moving her chin a few millimeters. He asked her to dinner, and she looked at him very carefully before accepting with a simple "Yes," and another polite smile, agreeing to meet him at an Italian restaurant in the Back Bay.

She came to the date wearing a lilac wrap-around dress, high heels, finely applied makeup, and a pearl necklace. She smelled lightly of an intoxicating perfume. He could tell everything on her was expensive, of only the best quality. As she talked, her voice was even, her disposition was gentle and self-possessed. He found her refreshingly unobtrusive, and feminine. More than wanting to sleep with her, he wanted to protect her.

He discovered, quickly, the rest of her life was like her dancing—gentle, clean, organized, and under her complete control. She lived in a spotless Victorian townhouse her parents had purchased for her in the Back Bay, furnished with solid wood, ancient scrolls, colorful rugs, and abstract paintings.

It contained a beautiful stream of Chinese and Western influences. Her days were planned out months in advance, and her life was full with scheduled events. She practiced for hours every day before teaching children ballet, and, on Saturdays, she tutored at a Chinese school for immigrant children.

She scheduled a massage and acupuncture session one night a week, and her nails and hair every two weeks. She had three close girlfriends, two Chinese-American and one of European descent, who she had gone to college with at Columbia, and she met up with them every Friday. Her two sisters, one a surgeon, the other running an immigration non-profit, both still lived in Manhattan near their parents, and she made regular trips to see them.

Peyton liked the tidy completeness of her life. Their courtship moved slowly, as she gradually opened her life to make space for him. Peyton was secure in her steadiness. He never felt like she might enrage him. She made decisions over time, taking life line by line, accumulating pieces of sand one by one in front of her, rather than reaching out, abruptly, for a handful. There was no chance he would wake up one morning and find her gone.

She fit seamlessly in his new, healthier life. He walked Thomas to her house in the evening, bringing groceries and wine, and they listened to classical music and cooked dinner. She was excellent in the kitchen, and he happily took on the position of sous chef, cutting and chopping according to her instructions. After dinner, they watched the news or an artsy film on DVD,

233

and read magazines. A year or so into the relationship, he began spending the night, sleeping next to her in her soft, king-size bed. He accumulated slacks and button-up shirts that he wore to work in her walk-in closet.

They never fought, and when they had disagreements, they ignored them as long as possible, and then one of them would relent wholesale, without discussion. Their life together was easy because their incongruities were never mentioned. It was if they had made a silent pact to conceal the differing parts of themselves.

A small part of him was repulsed by her unreflective life of luxury. She had grown up with money and she never hesitated before buying a designer dress or making a reservation at a four star restaurant. Their vacations involved expensive hotels, guided tours and front row seats to world-class shows. Her father paid her credit cards, and she did not concern herself with how the money arrived, or whether she should spend it so freely.

He kept this feeling to himself, seeing it as something she would never change; she had lived this way since she was a child. She and her family and friends saw her as a good person—she was kind, volunteered with immigrant children, and donated money to charity and redistributive political groups— what more could she possibly owe?

The palatable nature of the experiences, and the widespread social approbation of their lifestyle, made it easy for him to ignore his unease, most of the time. He would lose himself in the hot baths, soft sheets, succulent food, beautiful clothes and the poignant plays. Only occasionally would he catch himself and wonder what the hell he was doing: how could he be living this life?

He knew that she too avoided parts of him. She ignored the events in his life he knew she must find repulsive: he had almost killed himself driving drunk; he had two misdemeanor assaults, and settled a sexual harassment suit that arose because he had slept with an employee at the same time he was bedding her prettier friend. He had mentioned these things to Laurie to be fair, rattling them off quickly, and she, briefly, gaped at him in shock and disgust. Then, she carefully shut down her face, settling into an inscrutable stare. She said quickly, "Well, you're not like that anymore." And neither of them had spoken of it again.

They threw dinner parties for her friends and family, and Peyton's clients; they attended Sicily's college graduation, her cousin's wedding, her sister's baby shower, her grandmother's funeral. They met up with other couples. Peyton missed her when he was out of town for work, wishing for her gentle smile and bright face at the end of his long day.

But, then, he had searing moments of doubt. He would stare at her over his magazine or across the dinner table, and feel he was making a mistake: he did not feel the same passion he had felt for Isabelle. Isabelle had understood him; their life together had been more than the sum of all its arrangements and activities.

Laurie was objectively extraordinary—she was beautiful and kind, elegant and cultured—but she was also irredeemably ordinary, a person who had never questioned her lot in life, and simply embraced the lifestyle and views of her social class. This can't be it, he'd think. This can't be my life. He should leave, and find a woman he would love and who would love him in the raw heart of a cold winter, when other people and other things had disappeared.

He knew Laurie would never sleep beside him in a single bed, in a room smaller than her closet, or live with him in a cabin in the woods. She needed her comfortable life even more than she needed him.

These moments passed as quickly as they had come, and he was still there, with Laurie, their life happy and secure, intertwined with dozens of other people and objects, a comforting and warm web too strong to break.

In her last year of dancing professionally, they decided to get married. He could not remember who brought it up, but there was no proposal. It was a decision they made together. They were already living together in her house. She wanted to open a ballet studio, and while her parents were willing to pay for it, Peyton did not feel right accepting their money, and so it seemed sensible to make their relationship formal.

Her parents threw a lavish wedding in Manhattan, with three hundred guests. Peyton fought his repulsion at the cost, getting a headache at every flower and dinner plate he saw. There was one moment, where he looked out at the hundreds of people in the extravagant ballroom and he felt like running. This wasn't who he was.

Then Laurie's dad shot him a big grin, his white teeth glistening. Peyton smiled back, reflexively. Her father was a kind man, with a philosophical temperament. He had always treated Peyton like a son. Peyton turned away, touching Laurie's bare shoulder, the gentle, elegant curve, and when she smiled, her dark eyes lit up in pleasure, the feeling of being in the wrong place was forgotten.

A few months later, she was pregnant. Peyton was thrilled. As her stomach grew, he put his hand over the hard, round bump to feel the kicks of his child.

She was sick in the beginning, but she never complained, and she managed to keep working on her studio until the day she gave birth to their son, Nathan.

Peyton's company was expanding, but he came home at seven every night, making sure she and the baby had everything they needed. Nathan was a quiet and peaceful baby, and Laurie managed to sleep well, rising and falling briefly a few times a night. Peyton adored his son, the warm weight of him in his lap, his little fingers grasping his thumb. He watched him sleep, endeared with his fragile lashes and how they fell on his smooth cheek.

Every once in a while, though, he would be accosted by his son's golden skin, tuft of dark hair, and narrow eyes, and lament he could not see more of himself there. When Laurie spoke or sung to him in Mandarin, wagging his little finger back and forth, he felt he was outside, peering in. He wanted to tell her to speak English. But this was important to her, and her family, and so he stayed silent, watching.

They hired a bilingual college girl to watch Nathan when Laurie needed space, or at night, when they were going out. On Saturdays, Laurie brought Nathan, in his designer clothes and carriage, to her girlfriends' house to play with their Mandarin-speaking children.

When Nathan started speaking, he used both languages, moving back and forth between them with ease, as if he did not recognize the difference between the two. Peyton picked up a few phrases, but he was not around enough to pick up more, even if he had been trying, which he wasn't. He tended to space out when they spoke to one another in Mandarin, feeling excluded and distant. For some reason, it was a bridge he could not make the effort to cross.

As Nathan grew older, Peyton loved him even more, seeing his son as a distinct person. When he got home from work, the house smelled like Chinese spices and freshly cooked vegetables, and Nathan toddled over to him, hands out, crying, "Da-da! Da-da!" as Thomas wagged his tail wildly.

Peyton scooped Nathan up and Laurie smiled at him from the kitchen island, stir-frying a spicy meal. He walked over and kissed her cheek, and he felt, then, happy. He lifted up his son's shirt, kissed him on the belly, making him squirm and laugh and yank down his shirt with his small hands.

He and Laurie had their first real fight over his mother and Phillip. They asked to take Nathan away for the weekend, and Laurie refused. Peyton pushed her for an explanation, and she said, calmly, she was worried about the influence they would have on him.

"What do you mean?" he demanded.

"What if they curse in front of Nathan?" she said, her voice soft and leveled. "Or leave him in the hotel room? Or let him watch television? Your mother has very different standards than I do."

Peyton exploded, grabbing his cup of water and throwing it against the refrigerator. "Are you fucking kidding me? He's my son, too. They're taking him. And that's the end of it."

She stared at him stonily.

He grabbed his keys from the hook and walked out the door, slamming it behind him. He went to a hotel bar, steamed. He ordered whiskey after whiskey. He had not been drunk in a long time, but he felt desperate to dull his anger, and the liquor hit him hard. He was angry at Laurie, and angry at himself. This was his comeuppance.

A woman in a soft gray business suit smiled at him from across the bar. He nodded.

She came and sat next to him. "I'm Michelle," she said. "I'm here for the night from New York. Seeing a big client."

He stared at her. She was a slender blond, in her early thirties, but she seemed large compared to Laurie, who was so petite, with delicate bones and lean muscles. Thinking of Laurie, he remembered what she said about his mom and he was annoyed.

He leaned over and whispered in the woman's ear, "I'd like to fuck you."

She flushed, peering at the floor with a smile on her face. She cocked her head to the door, and he put down a few twenties and followed her out.

In the elevator, he noticed she had a ring on her finger, too. A large diamond, just like Laurie's. The last time he had cheated on Laurie had been years ago, soon after they had married when he had been drunk at a party, consumed by one of his moments, thinking he had made a mistake, and feeling washed out with despair.

In the woman's room, her briefcase was open on her bed, papers strewn across the ruffled comforter. She put the papers away and took off her jacket, hanging it neatly over a chair. He pushed her to the bed, and she laughed.

He was rough, pounding her hard, and her face changed from fickle to serious, as if she were trying to match his rage. Her nails scraped up and down his back, and he pulled her blond hair backwards, making her scream.

When he was done, he collapsed on top of her, sweaty and exhausted. The liquor had gone to his head.

"Wow," she said.

He laughed, closed his eyes, and curled up to the door, feeling disgusted with himself, with his life.

* * *

He woke up, and the room was dark, almost black. The clock blinked 9:30. He had a headache, and stumbled to the bathroom, and flipped on the light. Her toiletries were gone, and a note lay on the sink. "Last night was amazing. Had to get to work. I'll be back here in three weeks, same time, same place, G."

He crumpled this in a ball, and threw it on the floor. He ripped open the sample packet of aspirin, taking both down. He ran the hot water in the large tub, and climbed in, half-sleeping as he stretched his arms and legs out.

By the time he left work, his annoyance had simmered down, and he was ready to talk to Laurie. The events of the night before seemed like a strange hallucination. He walked in, and Laurie smiled at him from the kitchen. Peyton scratched Thomas on the head.

"I told Nathan he is going on vacation this weekend with his grandparents," she said gently, her tone conciliatory.

"Vacation!" Nathan cried, sitting on the stool, reaching out for Peyton.

"Good," he said to Laurie, kissing her on the cheek, and picking up his son, patting him on the back. He wanted her to apologize for what she had said, but he knew she couldn't, honestly, and so he poured himself a glass of wine.

* * *

Shortly after Nathan's third birthday, Laurie asked if they could start trying to have another child. Peyton had always wanted a large family, but now he was ambivalent. He could not identify why, grasping for reasons like tiny fish darting in murky water, his hands coming up empty.

Perhaps it was because Nathan was a reserved and intelligent boy, and he fit effortlessly into the life they had constructed. Perhaps it was because he still, after all this time, had doubts about her and the life they were leading.

Laurie was persistent—she was almost thirty-five—and Peyton, seeing no legitimate reason to say no, consented. She did not get pregnant easily this time. After seven months, she read fertility books, and changed their diets, and orchestrated their sex life, demanding specific times and positions.

Their sex life had always been constrained. She was a skilled and careful lover, with a beautiful and flexible body, but like everything she did, her passion was under her strict control. Laurie's methodological instructions, the added orchestration, made him feel acutely aware of her body and his own, seeing them both medically, as bodies capable of reproduction, like Mendel working carefully with his pea plants.

He was distant, and while he obliged her, he found himself thinking about what he needed to do at work, or fantasizing about women he had been with during his wildest years. Everything about those women were sloppy—their clothes were trashy, the way they blabbed on about nothing, and stumbled about the bars.

They had never gone to college, and didn't have much of interest to say. He had gotten wasted with them and sped around the city on his motorcycle, the woman screaming on the back, one of her hands thrown in the air. When they had fucked, they had both turned themselves entirely over to their bodies, and he had felt free, free of himself, free of everything. It was pure, intense pleasure, like swallowing ecstasy.

It took them over a year, and Laurie's anxiety ballooned. She complained about the problem nonstop, to him, to her friends and family on the phone. Her disposition changed, too; she was quick to find fault with him and Nathan, and she sulked by herself, spending more money on clothes and shoes, coming back to the house with large bags of stuff.

He had no patience for this, and he said nothing, but came home from work later and later, his disgust with her so intense, he felt guilty, and he ordered her flowers and jewelry to feel like a better husband.

When she finally became pregnant, he knew the moment he walked in the door, tired from work, because her face was bright with genuine, unbridled joy. He was grateful the trying was finally over, and his excitement at getting his wife back outweighed any excitement for another child. He took her to New York to celebrate, dropping Nathan off with her parents, wanting to avoid another fight about his mother.

She was euphoric, laughing at everything. Anxiety was not a natural emotion for her, and she had worn it poorly. They went dancing at a club in the East Village, and her body moved perfectly in tune with the music, its subtle curves underneath his hands. People gawked at her, the most beautiful woman in the club, and he was overcome with affection.

He pushed her up against the wall, out of the light, pressing his body against hers. He reached his hand under her dress, and her eyes went hard and she shook her head.

He slowly withdrew his hand, and her appeasing smile erased his annoyance. She couldn't help it. He wrapped his hands around her, pulling her closer, and stroking her hair. He would protect her. She led him back to the center of the dance floor, and lowered her body against his, rubbing against his legs.

The club announced last call, and they walked into the street. She shook her head, exclaiming, "I've never been to a club that loud. My ears are ringing."

He smiled at her innocence. He kissed her, feeling her joy and contentment that had been gone for so long.

She was much sicker during this pregnancy than the last, her face taking on a pale whitish tint as she lost five pounds during the first three months. Even so, she never complained, and when she stayed home from work, Nathan took pleasure in bringing her water, crackers and wet towels, and sitting on her bed, reading her his books.

It pleased Peyton his son's nature was kind. There were times, though, when he turned on his son, frustrated, wishing his son was more strong-willed. He condemned this instinct inside of himself, remembering Hershel's treatment of Adam, how it had been cruel and done no good.

Laurie's stomach expanded more than it had last time, and it monopolized her tiny frame, like an overgrown watermelon. On the sonogram, they saw the boy's sizable body, and in the later months, she had to pause after walking a few blocks, stopping to catch her breath, smiling and rubbing her belly.

She watched her classes at the studio from a chair, Nathan quietly reading at her feet. Peyton was excited for the baby, knowing, already, the boy would be strong. He would take them both hunting in the woods. Nathan probably wouldn't want to go, but he'd make him go anyway. Nathan was his son, too.

CHAPTER SEVENTEEN

Peyton had run into William at a party, years ago, before he had met Laurie. William took him aside, and whispered, "Did you see Isabelle is painting burning buildings?" and Peyton shook his head no.

"She's never had any common sense."

Peyton laughed hard, violently, muttering, "No, shit."

He stared at William, who had of course aged well, and cuffed his bicep harshly, remembering, briefly, that William had fucked her in the woods.

Much later, after his motorcycle accident, and after he lost his encompassing rage, he wondered what had become of her. He did not want to see her, but he wanted to know where she was, what her life was like. He hiked up to the attic and pulled out his old pictures of them in West Virginia, which he had buried in a box of winter clothes.

As he went through them, he cried, deeply saddened by what might have been. His head leaning against the wood, a ray of light falling across the boxes, he thought he could have changed everything that one night, on his mother's bed. He knew his life now was full. But seeing Isabelle's strange, genuine smile, he felt as if he had given up more than he would ever have again.

He searched for information about her, and he found art reviews for exhibits offered every couple years, and two cultish fan sites. Nobody knew where she was.

The fan sites were filled with idle speculation and rabid cries of devotion. He wondered if she read these sites, if she took any pleasure from knowing "ArtSlave5" was willing to "pay 10000 dollars to lick her tit!!!" He wondered if she knew what he had done, if she knew he had married someone else, and had a child.

These thoughts were more obtrusive when Laurie was desperately trying to get pregnant, when doubts about his own life were rising, carrying with them his sunken desires and regrets. He almost hired a private investigator, but his guilt and uncertainty over his own motivations made him hang up the phone, the man's number not dialed. His wanting faded with the long-awaited pregnancy, and his mind had not fallen on Isabelle in quite some time when he received a message from her lawyer.

It was Laurie's seventh month of pregnancy, and he had come back to work from the OBGYN's. His third message read, "Adam Green, Esq. called regarding Isabelle Woods. Urgent."

Peyton stared at the message, as if it might be a joke. He felt like his past had popped out of a locked box and grabbed him by throat.

He felt an odd sort of hope, considering, briefly, what he would do if she came back, asking him to leave his wife, begging for his forgiveness. He knew it would be insane, and unforgivable, but part of him, he realized, still missed her. Part of him would shout yes, let's go, damn the consequences, damn everyone else. But maybe he simply missed his youth and freedom, his wildness, the sense that anything was possible. He wasn't sure.

Before he called the number, he searched for information on her. Her last art show, as far as he could tell, was over a year ago, and her fan sites had gone relatively dormant. Perhaps she had ceased painting, married a corporate lawyer, and had children. He could not picture this. The idea of her domesticated, with somebody else's child, infuriated him.

Still, why would her lawyer contact him? They had never married. He put off calling back, and when the lawyer called again in the afternoon, he told his secretary he couldn't take it.

She walked in his office, and said, "He says it's urgent." Peyton waved her away.

That night, having dinner, reading to Nathan, watching a movie with Laurie, he was excited, and he couldn't sleep for hours, staring at the ceiling, remembering, in West Virginia, when he and Isabelle had been hiking for days, and they stopped at the top of a ridge, looking over the vast, thick forest, full of life, and she said, "Did I ever tell you I was an accident? The result of a broken condom?" He shook his head. "My mother told me a few years ago," she said, smiling, putting her hands on the straps of her backpack. "Isn't that strange? If it hadn't broken just then, I never would have come to exist. They never wanted a child."

He'd been surprised, at the time, her mother had told her this, and surprised it had happened, and he wasn't sure why he was remembering it. Perhaps only because, to him, Isabelle had always seemed like a force of nature, and it made sense to him half of her would punch through the latex, against all odds.

The following afternoon, when the lawyer called again, Peyton hesitated. Part of him wanted to linger here, in the dark, hoping for the best. But he knew that was ridiculous and childish, and he picked up the phone.

"Thank you for taking my call," the lawyer said, his words stated nervously, on edge. "Uh…my name is Adam Green. I'm a tax attorney in Kansas. I was appointed by the court. You know Isabelle Woods, correct?"

"Yes," Peyton said, finding this strange, drawing a blank on why a court would appoint her an attorney.

"Okay, great." The lawyer paused, and Peyton could hear a pen hitting a table, over and over.

"Is she okay?"

"Yes. I mean, no, no, she isn't. Something happened to her. I don't know how to say this."

Peyton reluctantly plowed on, wondering if he was jumping over a cliff. "Just say it."

"Well, I'm sorry about this, but she's dead."

"She's dead?"

"Yes, that's correct."

Peyton hung up the phone, staring at it, like it was a pile of feces on his desk. "She's dead?" he repeated, confused. The phone rang and he heard his secretary answer it.

"A Mr. Green for you, sir, on line three."

"I'll get it," he shouted, though there was no reason to shout. She could hear him clearly over the intercom. The line blinked red. He picked up the phone and pushed it.

"Sorry. This is a shock."

"I understand. The reason I am calling—"

"How did she die?"

"Um, it says here, 3rd degree burns, suicide. I am sorry I don't know… ummm… any of the…details."

"Oh," Peyton said mechanically.

"Well, you see, she left you as executor of her estate. She also left you legal custody of her daughter, which according to the birth certificate is also your daughter?"

"No. That's impossible. I haven't seen her in…over ten years."

"Well, the child, Abel, is ten. It says here she was born July 2, 1997. Is that right?"

"I see. That could be right. But she never told me she was pregnant."

The rest of the conversation occurred without him there. He saw his hand write down the address, what he was supposed to do. Abel was staying with a neighbor. His hands were trembling when he hung up the phone, and he made his way to the liquor cabinet and poured himself a double shot of whiskey.

He took it down.

"Mr. Wilson's on line two for you, sir."

"Sir?"

She hung up. Peyton stared at the phone, as if it had the power to spew out more insane realities. He sat back at his desk, and looked at his picture of Laurie, smiling kindly on the park green, in a pink blouse. Laurie, he thought, sweet, lovely Laurie. He crossed his arms on the desk, and hung his head as he had in first grade, when his teacher had said, "Put your heads down everyone. Down."

* * *

When he walked home, he was drunk. He had left work and gone from bar to bar, drinking, staring blankly at the bartender who said, "You look like you could use this," sliding him an extra whiskey, no charge. He gave them money anyway. He was rich, wasn't he? A lot of good that did.

At home, Laurie was cooking, smiling, listening to music, her large stomach making her reach out to the stove, and Nathan, who had grown out of running to the door, sat on his stool, reading a book behind his newly acquired glasses. Thomas wagged his tail, circling Peyton. Laurie glanced up at him, and she dropped the spatula in the pan.

"What is it?" she said, her face alert. "What happened?"

"Isabelle's dead," he said, sitting on a stool, laughing. "She's dead. She killed herself."

Laurie looked at him askance. "Who is Isabelle, honey?"

He laughed harder, making his way over to the liquor cabinet, stumbling. "Who IS Isabelle? What a good question. Who IS she really?"

244

He opened the cabinet and brought out the whiskey, nearly dropping it on the floor.

"Haven't you had enough?" she asked, standing near him.

"Have I?" he said, pouring a full glass of it, watching it splash over the sides. "Well, maybe you should join me," he said, sitting down on the couch, taking a sip. "Good stuff."

"Who is Isabelle, Peyton?"

"As you might recall," he said, waving his hand in the air, taking another drink, spilling some on his shirt. "I was engaged to Isabelle. That's who Isabelle is."

"Oh. I'm sorry. That's terrible."

"Isn't it?" he said, standing up, feeling the blood rush to his head. "But what do you know about terrible?"

Her face was blank, apathetic even, which only enraged him more.

"Yes, this doesn't bother you, does it?"

He took another drink, and stumbled through the kitchen. Nathan frowned at him, his eyes furrowed. Peyton laughed. "Even my son condemns me!" he shouted.

Nathan started crying.

Peyton opened the backdoor and stumbled onto the deck. The yard was exceedingly small. He plopped down on one of the teak chairs. Why did he have teak chairs? He stood up and threw one onto the patch lawn, laughing. He sat back down and took another drink, watching a squirrel run across a low branch.

"Yes, run, run, run!" he shouted. "Run away!"

Laurie came out and sat across from him. "I put Nathan in his room," she said, softly. She put her hand on his arm, her delicate, golden hand, which covered only half his forearm. It looked like a child's. Except it wasn't.

"Laurie," he said, looking at her desperately. "She killed herself."

Laurie's eyes went down demurely. "I'm so sorry, honey," she said, gripping his arm reassuringly. "It must be hard."

He pulled his arm away, cupping it around his glass, taking a long drink.

"I know, Laurie. But you don't understand, do you? Because this would never happen to you. Charmed life Laurie."

She turned away, to the neighbor's yard, obscured by dense trees. "I don't know why you have to insult me."

"I don't know why you have to insult me," he said snidely. "Blah blah blah. Don't you understand? She killed herself. I didn't do anything. Now, it's too late."

"What were you supposed to do? You said she left you."

"I could have found her."

"How?"

"Hired someone! Money! The whole point of this was money, and I didn't even use it. There's always a way with money. Don't you understand? Now, it's too late! It's too fucking late!" He took down the rest of the drink, and his eyes were watering, or crying, he couldn't tell.

"Peyton," she said, wrapping her arms around his neck, pressing her cheek up against his. "It's okay. It wasn't your job to go after her."

"Laurie…" he slurred, stroking her arm. "My sweet, steady Laurie. You would never do this, would you? Not in a million years. Not in a million lives. Oh, I love you, Laurie. Don't worry. I love you."

She held him tighter and he sighed, relaxing against her. "I haven't even told you the rest."

"It's okay. You don't have to tell me everything right now."

He turned around in his chair, pulling her in front of him, rubbing his hands against her belly. "Our second son is coming soon."

She smiled at him cautiously.

"Yes, he is," she said, putting her own hands on top of his.

"Here's the thing. Here's the thing….I am drunk…very drunk…"

"I see that. It's okay. You'll sleep it off. You'll take aspirin."

"Sweet Laurie… but here's the thing… I have to catch a plane tomorrow. Remember that time Isabelle left me? Ten years ago?"

"Yes."

"Here's the thing," he repeated, taking his hands back and standing up. He stumbled over to the railing. Everything was fuzzy. He needed to lie down. "Um, yes. She left, no note, no nothing. She never called, never wrote, never offered an explanation." He glanced at her over his shoulder. She had her hands on her belly, rubbing it, and she nodded.

"Yes."

"Well, the funniest thing," he said, laughing, turning back to the tree. He leaned over the railing. "Turns out, when she left, she was pregnant. I guess she never thought, 'Hey, maybe I should let Peyton know I gave birth to his daughter!' Just a thought, you know."

He laughed, sitting down, slumping against the railing. He fell backwards, and his head slammed against the deck. He could barely see the black sky through the neighbor's lights.

"She had your daughter?"

"Yes."

She ran away, inside the house, slamming the door. He should chase after her, he knew, but he was so tired. He couldn't deal with it.

He closed his eyes.

* * *

He woke up in the middle of the night, cold. His body was soaked in sweat, and he felt like he'd been run over by a monster truck, his body crushed. He sat up, wrapping the quilt he didn't remember having around himself. A glass of water and two aspirin in a cup sat next to him. He took them and stumbled inside, crashing on the couch.

* * *

The sun was streaming in from outside and his head pounded. He ran to the bathroom, past Laurie in the kitchen, reading a magazine, and vomited.

He washed his mouth out in the sink. He looked like he felt: beat.

A glass of orange juice and two aspirin sat on the counter, and Laurie was buttering a pan for eggs. Peyton sat on the stool, swallowing the aspirin with the sweet juice.

"Morning," she said curtly, cracking the second egg, tossing it in the trash. "When do you have to leave?"

He had scrawled the information on his palm. "My flight's at one."

"Good. You can eat this. I'll take you to the airport."

"Okay," he said, rubbing his forehead. "Did I tell you … everything?"

"I assume so," she said, serving the eggs onto a plate and sliding it over to him. "You told me about your … daughter."

The toast popped up and she walked over to it, spreading it with butter. From the back, one could barely tell she was pregnant. She was so small.

"Laurie."

She set the toast on his plate and got the cream out of the refrigerator, filling a mug with coffee. She handed it to him, and he took a long drink, the heat warming his mouth and throat. It made him feel better, like a straight shot of testosterone.

"Laurie."

She sat on the stool catty-corner to him, and he put his hand on hers. She looked at him, her eyes firm.

"We'll handle it," she said, her voice tired. Her eyes were puffy. "You didn't know. It's not your fault."

He was overwhelmed with gratitude. "Laurie," he said, sweetly. He squeezed her hand, and took it back, eating his eggs, and downing more coffee. "I …"

"It's okay," she said, standing up, rubbing his shoulder. "It's okay." She kissed him on the cheek. And her face implored him not to speak of it again. "What do you want to take? I'll pack."

"Khakis, jeans, two polo shirts," he said. She nodded, and walked gingerly to the stairs.

"Laurie!"

"Yes?" she said, her hand on the railing.

"I love you."

She stared at him sadly. "I love you, too."

* * *

He slept on the plane, still hung over and exhausted. When he arrived in Dodge City, he rented a car, and drove the two hours to where she lived. The land was flat and brown. He thought this is what Hell must be like, a void, with nothing in every direction. Moving endlessly to nowhere. At least Sisyphus had his rock and his hill. Here, there was nothing, no sweat, no air, no rise from the earth.

He saw a few buildings stacked together on the horizon. It was dark, and he was tired. He pulled over, outside of "town," and camped out, underneath the stars.

At least, now, there was something: the naked night sky. He remembered his younger self and Isabelle, lying on top of the ridge, their long limbs intertwined in a warm sleeping bag, falling asleep. The universe had remained untouched, brilliant and sprawling as ever, an immense web dwarfing earth and its inhabitants. Only their small, insignificant lives had shattered. He saw her smile, her full lips, and he wished life could rewind to that moment, when they were lying underneath the same sky. Somehow he would change things. Somehow he would never let her go.

But no. There was no going back. There was only going forward—the whole universe always shuttling unapologetically forward. He was still here. And she was still erased.

* * *

In the morning, after a restless night of sleep, he performed functions without awareness, driving, eating, calling the lawyer. He met Mr. Green, a timid man with spectacles, who acted ashamed, as if he in some way bore responsibility for what had happened. Isabelle's parents were also there, and they seemed surprisingly old.

"This is my fault," her mother bawled. "This is my fault. I never should have left her alone."

Her father was silent, and he said he knew of Abel, he had seen her a few Christmases; her mother attacked him, pounding her fists against his chest.

"Why didn't you tell me?" she screeched. "Why didn't you tell me?"

"I assumed you knew," he said quietly, staring out the window.

Peyton was furious at her father for keeping Isabelle and Abel to himself, and he didn't step in to pull back her mother's fists. Mr. Green cautiously forced them apart.

They were shocked to hear Isabelle had seventeen-million dollars. The names in the will, other than Abel's, were unrecognizable. She had left her parents a self-portrait—six year old Isabelle on the beach, smiling.

As Mr. Green talked, it suddenly occurred to Peyton: Margaret Ann Henry had died in the fire. Sophie Henry was probably her daughter. He didn't recognize any of the others, but he knew when he went home, he would find the names listed in her will matched up with the injured and the descendants of the dead. He laughed bitterly. It was the accident to the very end.

Outside the lawyer's office, Peyton stood with Isabelle's mother in front of their cars. Her father walked past them in his black leather jacket and blue jeans. He had lost most of his hair, and had combed the remaining wispy strands over. He stopped in front of his car.

"Isabelle wasn't really part of my life," he called, as if this absolved him of responsibility. He stepped in his rental car and drove away.

They watched him go, back into the middle of nowhere. Still facing the road, her mother said, "Had you talked to her?"

"No, not in ten years."

"She called me a few years ago," she said. "I should have pushed it. I should have pushed it. I never should have left her alone. I never thought…" She stared at the ground. "She was so damn hard to relate to."

"It wasn't your fault," he said, though he only partially believed this. She still looked vaguely like Isabelle, and it occurred to him Isabelle would never grow wrinkled and gray; her body would never slow down, falling apart piece by piece. She would stay forever young.

Her mother wiped her nose with her handkerchief. He noticed a ring on her wedding finger, and wondered what sort of life she led.

"Okay. You'll bring Abel by?"

"Yes, of course."

"Okay." She turned away, stared at him with a half-smile, and opened her car door. She took a deep breath, wiping off her tears, before turning the key. She lurched over the curb.

It was strange, he thought, how ordinary her parents were, how they had birthed such a wondrous person, a person barely of this earth. He stepped in his car, and riffled through the papers. He was surprised to find an envelope with his name, addressed in Isabelle's sloping handwriting. He flipped it over. There was a single sheet inside. He put it on the passenger seat and drove toward her house.

When he was at a crossroads, alone, in the middle of the flat, brown fields, he pulled over. He opened it, his fingers shaking.

Dear Peyton,

If you are reading this it is because I am dead. If Abel is alive, I know you will take better care of her than I ever could. What remains of me is in her and my paintings.

Isabelle

He crumpled it up, furious. Why did she even bother? He threw it out the window, and gunned the car, putting the gas pedal all the way down, straight to hell. The car shook under its own weight. He slammed the brakes as he approached a crossroads. He took a hard right, and the car drifted off the road, into the field, running over crops. He accelerated back on, blasting it.

He fiddled with the radio. It was all static.

He took another hard right, down her dirt driveway, seeing a one-story ranch house in the distance. He sped up, screeching to a stop a couple feet from the door.

He got out and walked around the property. There was a small barn in the back. All he could see, no matter which way he looked, was flat, faded brown fields. He didn't understand why she had come here.

In the barn, he found dozens of mounted canvases, of all sizes, plastered with thick, black paint.

"Isabelle," he cursed, reprimanding her.

He stared at the black canvases, and imagined her painting them, her hands thrashing violently.

He lay down in the dirt and stared at the high, steep ceiling. It was almost like a church. He closed his eyes. He couldn't move.

He remembered when he was five or six, sitting on the porch, his mother had run off, and his grandfather, rocking in his chair, had said to him, "Dun ever ferget, boy, life is damn hard."

Peyton opened his eyes and stared into the empty rafters. "Life is fucking hard!" he shouted, his voice echoing back to him.

After a while, he stood up, wishing he had a drink, and wandered into the house. It smelled like mold. It had old, worn-out furniture, torn and scratched with decades of use. There was an army green couch. There was no television or computer. Books were piled up everywhere, and the kitchen was covered with dirty dishes and trash.

He was pissed, imagining his daughter living here.

He picked up a white plate and threw it against the wall, shattering it. He threw another.

"How could you do this ?" he shouted, sitting down at the kitchen table, knocking the dishes to the floor, pulling at his hair.

He opened and closed all the cabinets. Above the refrigerator, to his relief, was a bottle of red wine.

"Thank God," he said, screwing off the top, and taking a long drink.

He carried the bottle with him as he went into one of the bedrooms. It was tidy, with a single bed and rows of books stacked neatly against the wall. In the closet, he found a pair of girls' tennis shoes and sandals, arranged in line, next to one another. Her jeans were narrow and straight, but long. She was probably as tall as Laurie, five and a half feet.

Underneath her bed, he found a shoebox filled with bunches of hair, tagged with people's names.

"What the fuck," he muttered. This couldn't be good. He searched the tags and found Isabelle and Abel. They circled identical long, blond strands.

He sat on her bed, staring at her white tennis shoes, drinking the wine. The shoes seemed so clean and innocent, and he let himself imagine her happy, running through the fields, her blond hair whipping in the wind, and he smiled.

He jumped off the bed.

Isabelle's room looked like she had thrown books, dishes, canvases and paints randomly across the floor.

He kicked his way into the room, and picked up a white t-shirt. It smelled like her. He inhaled it, finding it hard to believe she had worn this a few days before, when she was still here, alive, in this bed. He crashed on the bed. Her pillow smelled like her. A pair of red cowboy boots stood in the closet, caked in mud.

He turned over. The afternoon light streamed in the window, and fell on a leather book with blank pages, underneath a pile of clothes. He picked it up, and opened it, taking another drink. He flipped through it, finding only one page with writing, near the end of the book, in Isabelle's sloping letters.

i am breaking

The final G fell wildly off the page, as if she had had a stroke. He closed the book and hugged it against his chest, drinking more wine, wondering where things had gone so wrong, how Isabelle had ended up dead, how he had ended up in her bed in the middle of a flat, lifeless hell, surrounded by the smell of her sweat.

He remembered the two of them, on his mother's bed, so young, their long limbs intertwined together. She asked him to stay, and he had walked away, chosen to save himself instead.

What would have become of them? Would they have moved on together, as one? Would they now be living modestly in the cabin, with their four blond children running through the woods, as he led expeditions through the mountains, and she painted madly at her easel? Or would he have been unable to find work, trapped by a criminal record?

Would she have killed herself still, him coming home one night, the children sitting in dirt, crying, as she lay burned to death on the ground?

He would never know. The bottle slid from his hand, landing softly in a pile of clothes, and the rest of the wine ran to the floor.

He pulled the sheets around his body tightly, inhaling her scent, trying to remember what it was like when they were one. He closed his eyes and pretended she was still here with him.

* * *

He dreamt of Isabelle in the mountains. She stood at the edge of a cliff, her long blond hair dancing on the wind, reaching out to him. She looked over her shoulder, and smiled, weakly.

"Do you believe in God?" she asked.

He shook his head, walking toward her, and she frowned slightly.

"I didn't think you did."

She turned away, facing the open mountains, and when he was almost there, she swan dived into the air, her lean body following a perfect arc.

He ran to the edge, and watched her body disappear into a black hole.

"Isabelle! Isabelle!"

His own words came back to him, echoing in the endless canyon. Isabelle, Isabelle. He crouched over, rubbing his temples. Isabelle, Isabelle.

He heard light footsteps and saw Laurie's legs out of the corner of his eye. He glanced up. She stood there, smiling, in designer hiking gear, her hands on her large belly.

"We'll be okay," she said.

He wasn't so sure, and he turned back to the canyon. Isabelle.

* * *

In the morning, he packed Abel's clothes, one of Isabelle's t-shirts, and her box of hair in a duffel bag and put it in the car. He drove to the neighbor's house, twenty miles away. A large woman, her face like a bulldog's, answered the door, waving him in. Her face was splotchy and her eyes bloodshot.

"She's upstairs," she said, listlessly, blowing her nose. "She's doing well. Considering."

Peyton nodded, staring at the large crucifix nailed to the living room wall, as the woman slowly made her way up the stairs. A picture of Mary hung in the hall.

Abel walked down the stairs, a backpack on her shoulders, wearing the same red cowboy boots he had seen in Isabelle's closet, and her chin was down, obscuring her face.

He lost his breath, choking.

He was seeing Isabelle as he had first encountered her, decades ago. Her white-blond hair fell to her waist, and her limbs were long and tan. She raised her face up, and he was startled to see her eyes were his pale blue and Isabelle's tilted-almond shape. Her jaw was square and her nose was straight, like his. Her full mouth was her mother's.

She stared at him.

"You look like me," she said, her tone accusatory.

He nodded.

"Sandra said you're my father. Is that true?"

"Yes."

"Isabelle said you might come back some day."

He winced. "I didn't know where you were."

"Why?" She looked at him straight.

"I don't know, she never told me where she was. I guess I was lost."

She nodded. "That's what Isabelle said. She said one day you might find us." She glanced at the giant crucifix on the wall.

He tried to conceal his tears, wiping them quickly with his hand. "Ready to go?"

She nodded, and they walked outside, the neighbor following. The neighbor grabbed his wrist.

"Dear," she whispered. "I don't know if anyone told you. Abel is the one who found her mother. God bless her heart."

Peyton nodded. "Thank you," he whispered, his head pounding, an image of Abel seeing Isabelle burning in the field, flailing.

"God bless," she said. "God bless, Abel," she said loudly, wiping her eyes with the back of her hands.

Abel nodded, and opened the passenger door, sliding in. Peyton kissed the woman on the cheek, and jogged to the car and got in, checking her seatbelt, and turning the key.

As he drove down the long driveway, he glanced over at her. Her cheek was on the window, her eyes staring out, her long hair covering half her face.

He fiddled with the radio, but it was all static.

"There's no radio here," she said, her eyes on the fields.

"Oh," he said, shutting it off. "Abel…" he said, not sure what he wanted to say. He wanted to know what her life had been like. He wanted to know what Isabelle had been like.

"Were you in school?" he said, finally.

"Yes. The Rambler School. Didn't you get my records?" she said, turning to him. "We'll need my records."

"Okay. I'll get them."

"Good. We'll need them. The records."

"Where was your school?"

"In Rambler. An hour and a half away."

"How did you get there?"

"I ran to the main road and got on the school bus. We didn't have a car." She tapped the window with her index finger. "We had a horse, but it died."

"Oh. Your new school will be close by. Laurie, my wife, will drive you."

"You shouldn't have done that," she said, shaking her head, tucking her hair behind her ears so he could see her profile.

"Done what?"

"Gotten married. Isabelle was really sad."

"She knew?"

"Oh, yes. I was sad, too. I knew you wouldn't be coming for us anymore."

"How?"

"How what?"

"Did she know?"

She shrugged. "You should have come earlier," she said, closing her eyes. She seemed to fall asleep.

Near the airport, he got out of the car and called Laurie on his cell. Abel was still sleeping, her head against the window.

"Hey," she said. "How's it going?"

"It's okay."

"How is Abel?"

"She seems okay." He looked at the airport terminals, boxy, concrete buildings and sighed. "This place is depressing. Flat and brown." He drummed his fist against the car. "The neighbor told me Abel was the one who found Isabelle."

"Oh."

"Yeah." He stared at Abel, a girl who looked like him, soundly sleeping, her long blond lashes barely visible on her tan face. "Okay. I'll call you when I know when we'll get it."

"Okay," she said. "Peyton?"

"Yeah?"

"Everything will be okay."

"Yeah, I know. I love you."

255

"I love you, too."

After he checked the rental car in, he woke Abel up, and they walked inside.

As they waited in the ticket line, he saw Abel, out of the corner of his eye, step forward and snip a piece of hair off the head of the woman in front of them. She slipped the hair and scissors in her pocket, and tapped the woman's shoulder.

"Yes?" the woman said.

"What's your name?" Abel asked.

The woman peered at her curiously. "Madeline Stevenson, dear."

"Oh, thanks. You look like my mother's friend."

The woman nodded, smiling, and turned around. A two-by-one inch piece was missing from her poker straight, brown hair. Peyton found it ludicrous.

"You can't take those scissors on the plane," he whispered in Abel's ear. Her hair smelled lemony. "Let's put them in the bag."

She took the scissors out of her jean pocket, offering them up on her open palm. He smiled, and took them, unzipping the duffle and slipping them in. They moved to the front of the line, and she stood in front of him, facing forward, her backpack on her shoulders. He wanted to wrap his arms around her.

She slept most of the day. He drank on the plane, watching her, like she might shatter, a glass doll falling to the ground, breaking into small, nonsensical pieces. When they started descending to Boston, he gently nudged her bare shoulder, saying her name softly. Her eyes stayed close. He shook her harder.

Her eyes blinked open.

"What happened?" she asked, twisting around in her seat, opening the window.

"We're almost there."

"Where?"

"Boston."

"Oh. Is that where you live?"

"Yes."

She leaned back against her seat, looking forward. "I've never been on a plane before."

"No?"

"Once we drove to my grandfather's. I didn't like him."

Peyton laughed. "Your mother didn't either."

"I know."

"Did you know you have a brother?" he asked, softly.

"No," she said, looking at him abruptly. "Where is he?"

"He's at home. He's five."

"Isabelle was his mother?" she asked, confused.

Peyton shook his head, picking at the frayed seat in front of him. "Laurie is. There's about to be another brother. Laurie's very pregnant."

"Oh," she said, pensively, staring forward, letting her hair fall over her face, like a dropped curtain. "A half-brother, then."

He reached over and laid his hand on top of hers, squeezing it.

After they picked up their luggage, they walked out to the curb, where Laurie was already waiting in their dark green BMW station wagon.

"There it is," he said, pointing.

"That's a pretty nice car.'

"Yeah, Laurie likes nice things." He winked at her, and she grinned. Her teeth were white. He felt, for a moment, like they had known each other their whole lives.

Laurie stepped out and walked over, graceful, even with her large belly. She looked up at him, expectantly.

"Hey," he said.

"Hey."

Abel peered at the ground, her head lowered, her hair over her face. Peyton waved Laurie back in the car, and put the bags in the trunk. He opened the backdoor and put his hand on Abel's shoulder.

"Ready to go?" he said, softly. She climbed in the backseat, scrambling, and he shut the door behind her. He jumped in the front.

"Hi," Nathan said to Abel. "I'm Nathan."

"Hi. I'm Abel."

Laurie started driving, glancing at Abel in her rearview mirror.

"How was your flight?"

"It was fine. No problems," he said, feeling exhausted.

"Good," she said, patting his thigh.

They drove home silently, listening to Brahms piano concertos. Peyton stared out the window, watching the cars and buildings pass by. Though he'd seen these streets thousands of times, they appeared surreal and foreign.

At home, he saw Abel had fallen asleep. He woke her back up. She startled, and grabbed his hand violently, squeezing it.

"I'll show Abel her room," he said to Laurie, who was standing, waiting, her hands on her stomach. She nodded, her eyes tired.

He took Abel up the stairs, to the third floor, and showed her the guest room, which had pale yellow wallpaper, and a queen-sized bed with a flowered comforter. White lace curtains fell over the street-facing windows.

"This is your room," he said, putting her bags on top of the bureau. She let go of his hand and sat down on the bed, facing him.

"It's pretty."

He smiled, nodding. "Do you need anything? A glass of water?"

"Where's my brother?"

"Nathan, he's in that last room over there. The bathroom is in the middle. You two will share it."

"Okay." She leaned over and took off her cowboy boots. She put them neatly in the closet. "Can I call you Dad?"

"Of course," he said, smiling. "Our bedroom is on the second floor. Come down if you need me, okay?"

"Okay," she said, pausing. "Dad."

He watched as she took off her jeans and folded them, square after square, and put them in the drawer, and he was caught by the strangeness of it, of how she looked so much like him, and Isabelle. It seemed impossible she had lived in the world for ten years, and he had never known, or even sensed, she existed.

"Abel."

She peered up at him, her pale blue eyes half-open, as if she were about to cry.

"Will you be okay up here?"

She nodded, slightly, her chin barely moving. She took off her tank top and folded it three times. Her chest was tan and flat as a boy's. "You don't have to worry. I'm used to taking care of myself."

"It's okay to be sad," he said.

"Maybe."

"Well, goodnight," he said, closing her door. He leaned up against it, closing his eyes.

* * *

Downstairs, Laurie was in bed, reading a novel. She smiled at him, softly.

He grimaced. After he hung up his clothes and brushed his teeth, he climbed in the bed and closed his eyes. She turned off the light and shifted her body down the bed. He felt her proficient hands on him, rubbing, and then her wet mouth. He stared at the ceiling, trying to relax, trying to forget. He

258

imagined himself with a woman in an apartment he had long forgotten, but it kept being interrupted by Isabelle, her looking at him plaintively.

"I'm sorry, honey," he said, tugging her arm. "I'm just too distracted."

She stiffened and then lifted her head, wiping the sides of her mouth. She rested her head on his chest, and he put his arm around her, rubbing her belly, feeling their son. Laurie put her hand on top of his. He imagined Abel in her room, her white hair spread around her, her mind lost in a nightmare, and Nathan in his plaid pajamas, his glasses on his nightstand, his shallow eyes closed, in an easy sleep. How strange, he thought, all of them living in this one house, together.

* * *

He woke up, startled. Abel was staring at him, her white hair reflecting the street light, covering her nipples, her fingers on his bicep, pulling, the soft pads of her fingers pushing into his skin.

Laurie was sleeping soundly, her hands on her tummy, protectively. Peyton stumbled out of bed, and Abel pulled him upstairs, back to her bedroom. She shut the door behind them.

She pulled his arms around her chest in bed, and he wondered, briefly, if he should talk to her, but then he fell back asleep, one of his hands on her narrow, strong stomach.

CHAPTER EIGHTEEN

Peyton took off from work, keeping tabs with his cell phone and laptop. He considered hiring someone to deliver the money in Isabelle's will, or sending a letter, but he was compelled to do it himself. His own bank account had grown to astronomical proportions, but he hadn't given any of it to the victims of the fire, and though his own death seemed impossible, he had written a will, leaving half of his property to his mother, ten percent to Sicily, and forty percent to Laurie. It had never occurred to him to leave it to anyone else.

A few days after he returned from Kansas, reporters called and congregated outside the house. Laurie had walked outside Tuesday morning, on the way to drop Nathan at school, and dozens of reporters had blocked her path, hurling questions at her like stones.

She had come back inside, her face startled. Peyton had walked her to the car, shielding her with his arm, and carrying Nathan, who stared curiously at the hovering reporters like they were tigers at the zoo, his glasses on the tip of his nose, a small smile on his face.

"No comment," Peyton had said firmly. When Laurie had driven away, he had told them to get off his property or he would call the police, and walked back inside, the cameras flashing furiously, wiping out his peripheral vision.

He called William, and found out a *New York Times* magazine reporter was writing an extensive article on Isabelle, her life, her work and her connection to the Boston fire. The reporter believed Isabelle might have started the fire, and, William warned, it would only be a matter of time before the reporter considered the three of them might have been involved.

They had always known there were four people in the field. As long as they didn't say anything, though, the evidence was flimsy, and William would have any implication of their involvement squashed. Peyton, distracted, thanked William, insincerely agreeing to have dinner with him and his wife.

It annoyed him that William had this ability to quiet the reporter's suspicion about their role, leaving Isabelle to be their lightning rod, taking the blame for all of them. It was unfair.

But he told himself she was dead, gone from this earth, and no good would come from throwing himself under the carping gaze of the public. He avoided the news coverage of her death and her obituaries. He did not want to know what they were doing to her.

* * *

The descendants of the dead and the surviving victims of the fire were, for the most part, grateful for Isabelle's money, as for them, it was an unexpected windfall. They had never heard of Isabelle and they seemed thoroughly ordinary, fully recovered from whatever harm the fire had burned into their lives.

Peyton lied without hesitation in the face of their curiosity, pleading befuddled ignorance at why Isabelle had left them money. If it weren't for two of the victims, the whole exercise would have wrapped itself up neatly, verifying his sense that the fire had long ago ceased to have meaning in this world.

A woman who had lost her husband in the fire was a pink-faced, middle-aged drunk, living in a filthy apartment with cats. Her saggy breasts hung partially out of her stained nightgown.

She showed Peyton photos of her and her husband, and in the old photos, stained with greasy fingerprints, she appeared normal enough—wearing flower print dresses, sitting at the kitchen table, smiling, on the beach in her bathing suit, drinking a pint of beer next to a Christmas tree, opening a present. It was a stark contrast to who she was now.

She was largely vacant and offered no explanation for her condition; she seemed disinterested in the fire or the money, and it took her months to cash the check. Still, Peyton cleaned her apartment, and checked in on her, bringing her crème-filled donuts so she would eat.

Her life reeked of resignation—she was always wearing the same dirty nightgown, drinking cheap vodka—and she nodded at Peyton indifferently, her pulse only rising above a flatline when she explained the plots of her soap operas, pointing eagerly to the screen.

Peyton left her apartment frustrated, wanting to punch somebody and buy back his motorcycle so he could tool through the city at rubber-burning speeds. But still, he felt no sense of responsibility, or guilt. He didn't feel like he had put her here. It was simply the fate of most human lives: hard as nails, drilling those who wouldn't fight into the ground.

* * *

Sophie was a woman a few years younger than him, and the only victim who was visibly scarred. Half of her face and chest had melted in the fire. The skin was grayish and plastic, mounded with tiny hills and crevices. She was an accountant, and when he saw her in profile, from her untouched side, pretty. She had silky brown hair, creamy white skin, and round blue eyes. Her mother, who had died in the fire, she explained, had been an actress, a life she had planned to take up herself, before the fire.

"I was good, too," she said, staring at the check he had given her. "Isn't that funny?" she asked, glancing up, smiling softly, tilting her head away. "How a few people's stupidity completely changed the course of my life?"

He nodded. "Aren't you glad you're an accountant, though?"

She seemed surprised. "Oh, yeah, it's a dream job," she said, laughing. "Maybe this isn't politically correct anymore, but honestly, I would rather have been a beautiful actress, or even just beautiful."

"You're not ugly," he said adamantly, wanting this to be true.

"Do you know how easy life is when you're attractive?" she mused, tilting her head to a full profile, so he could not see her burned skin, and he was struck again by how lovely she was.

"When I got out of the hospital, I moved to Iowa to live with my mother's parents. Boys called me 'scarface.' Strangers glanced at me with disgust, and pity. Before, people had bent over backward for me."

"I'm sure it sounds shallow to you," she said, turning to face him, so he could see her scars. "But it's different for a woman. Before the fire, I just thought the world was so damn nice. I didn't realize it was only so nice because I was pretty."

She clicked her pen against her desk.

He wanted to touch the burnt side of her face tenderly.

"Sophie," he said quietly. "You're still beautiful." He said this even though it wasn't true.

She laughed skeptically. Her hair fell over her face. "You know it's funny, I bought one of Isabelle's burning building paintings five years ago. When I saw it, I was struck. How did she know exactly what it was like?"

"She was an amazing artist," he said, playing with his wedding ring, pulling it up and down on his finger.

"It's over my bed." She stared at him sharply, tucking the hair behind her ears. "Do you think she started the fire? Why else give us so much money?"

A hundred thoughts flew through his head, like arrows in a battle; he discarded all of them. She was the only victim who seemed to really knew Isabelle's work, and he, perhaps foolishly, had not considered what he would say to this.

"Do you?" she repeated, her eyes hard as she tied her hair in a ponytail.

He couldn't bring himself to lie, or to tell the truth. He glanced out her office window, at the clear blue sky, and he wanted a drink. He stood up and walked over to the window. He looked down. The trees were in full bloom and people milled around outside in shorts and t-shirts.

"I don't know what happened or why she left you the money," he said, finally. This was both true and false.

He put his hand on the cold window, leaning over, looking at the grass. He took a breath, feeling like he was drowning, and he shifted his eyes to the full treetops. "Man, I need a drink."

She tapped her pen against the desk again, a definitive bang, and he walked back to her, standing in front of her chair. She stared up at him.

"You know, don't you," she said.

She was suddenly crying, and he pulled her up and pressed her body against his, holding her as tight as he could. He felt the crumpled nature of her skin through his dress shirt. He held her harder, as if this could undo the damage, as if he could consume her into him, making her whole by the strength of his will.

"I don't, but I'm sorry," he whispered.

She pulled back, and stared at him with disgust. He closed his eyes, blacking out her image. He shook his head.

"No," he said, and he reached out and touched her broken face with his fingers, feeling its papery texture, running his fingers over he cheek and down her neck, following the scars to the top of her shirt, where he left them.

His chest felt heavy and hot, and his heart was beating rapidly. This is what he had done. He lifted his fingers and ran out of the office, shutting the door, and walking quickly down the hall, to the stairwell.

Outside, he burst into the warm afternoon, running as fast as he could through the city streets, knowing she was probably watching him from her window.

He went to the middle-aged woman's apartment and scrubbed it clean, removing all the trash and dirt, working for hours, as she glanced at him idly during the commercials.

* * *

He and Laurie commiserated about the reporters, who kept vigil for weeks, but they didn't talk about why they were there. He came into their bedroom one Sunday afternoon, and heard her crying softly, talking on the phone. He listened for a few minutes, her fragile voice spilling out words in Mandarin.

He walked quietly away, trying to forget he had heard her cry.

Laurie was subdued, slower to smile, but in good humor, trying her best to keep their lives under control. Abel ignored Laurie, looking down when Laurie spoke to her, but Laurie remained patient, telling Peyton she understood Abel did not want her to replace her mother.

Abel latched on to Peyton and Nathan, who she hugged aggressively, telling him she loved him, and pulling his hand to her room or his. Nathan was a sweet boy and he obliged, but occasionally, he would burst out crying, calling for his mother in Mandarin and ordering Abel to let him go. Once, Abel slapped him for saying this, leaving a bright red mark on his face, and Laurie had called Peyton in a panic.

"I can't take this anymore. I can't take this!" she had screamed in the phone, dropping it, and Peyton had rushed home from work, leaving in the middle of a meeting. Laurie was sitting in the kitchen, still holding the phone.

"I can't do this," she said. "This is not the life I planned on."

Peyton held her until she was calm.

Abel was laying on her bed, rocking in the fetal position and sucking her thumb; Nathan was in his room, reading a book, looking tired, and he nodded seriously when Peyton asked him to apologize.

"I'm sorry," he said to Abel, putting his hand on her arm. She'd turned around quickly, and hugged him intensely, wrapping her long limbs around his small body.

"It's okay, brother," she said, picking him up and smiling.

"Okay," Peyton said, pulling them apart, thanking Nathan, and asking Abel if she wanted to go for a run.

He had bought running shoes for Abel so they could run along the Charles River, feeling like it would be good for her to get outside and diffuse some of her energy. When they ran, her long hair whipping in the wind, he imagined Isabelle on the shore, smiling, her long legs moving wildly, and he told Abel this, how he used to run this same path with Isabelle, when they were younger.

They ran into Cambridge, and he showed her Isabelle's old house, and his, pointing out all the places he and Isabelle had gone together, and then, the city seemed haunted by their ghosts. Abel's eyes lit up at each new memory. Once he started looking, he saw Isabelle and himself, their past selves, everywhere.

Abel was a serious, responsible child, and yet she had Isabelle's wildness inside of her, and she seemed to be struggling to contain it, afraid it would destroy her like her mother, carry her to the fields and burn her down too.

She kept everything around her neat and ordered, and she liked to make plans, to know exactly what would happen, when. She didn't paint, but she wrote, carrying a book of blank pages with her wherever she went. When she filled it up, she put it in the garbage and started a new one. Peyton wanted to read it, see what she was feeling, what she remembered, but he didn't, letting the sanitation workers come and haul it away.

In school, she got into fights, punching a girl who knocked over the papers on her desk and, later, a boy who said something nasty about Isabelle. The teachers, knowing of her mother's death, were patient, and called Peyton regularly to let him know she was okay. She latched on to a sweet, brown-haired girl named Molly, and talked to no one else, except to tell them to move, or to leave her alone. She was bossy, and liked to do everything her own way.

When Laurie and Nathan spoke in Mandarin, Abel made two fists and glared at Laurie, shouting, "Stop it! Stop it!"

Peyton scooped her up, taking her in the other room, trying to explain that Laurie was Chinese, and it was important to her to teach Nathan Chinese. Abel refused to hear, silently moping, and he took her outside, and they threw stones in the river, her anger following the waves of water rushing out from the fallen stones.

Then, he longed to take Abel to the mountains, remembering Isabelle in the mountains, running to him on the trail, surrounded by the violent green leaves, shimmering in the wind, her white dress rising, as she grinned, and jumped into his arms.

Sunday morning, two months after they had returned, they were eating breakfast in the kitchen, reading the paper, listening to NPR, Thomas sitting on the floor, eating a bone, when Peyton saw Isabelle's face on the cover of the magazine.

Her face was tilted slightly to the side, her eyebrows furrowed, like she was in the process of turning away from the camera, telling the person not to take her picture. She was still striking.

Across the bottom of the page, in block letters, it said, "Solving Two Mysteries at Once: A Reclusive Art Prodigy Kills Herself and the Boston Fire of 84." He looked up. Nobody had seen it but him. He took the magazine and went to the bathroom upstairs.

He locked the door and sat on the toilet, flipping to the story. It had two more pictures of her. The first was from a junior-high yearbook. She seemed so innocent, her cheeks still filled with baby fat. More innocent than he'd ever known her. In the second photo, she was far away, riding her horse, her hair in a French braid, her face focused and intent. She was wearing the red cowboy boots. Her whole body was arched forward and tight, like she was desperately trying to outride someone.

He went through the pages—prints of her paintings populated the edges of the story. Seeing them laid out, he was taken aback. Over the years, she had tumbled from style to style, as if she were looking for the right philosophy and could never find it, marching on, picking up one way after the next.

He recognized the tropical green abstractions and the realistic winter landscapes she'd painted in West Virginia, her early paintings of them in the Berkshires, the abstract fires, and the burning buildings with their wriggling black figures. The others he had never seen—voluptuous flowers birthing bees, the empty, dull landscape of Kansas, a lone man on its horizon, and, most disturbing, happy, healthy children, playing in a schoolyard, whose faces, on closer inspection, were in agony, their bodies bit by a thousand tiny wasps.

Peyton closed the magazine and put his hands through his hair.

He needed a drink. He blew out a breath of air, and stood up, staring out the window. The street was lined with nice cars and flush trees. A woman walked her tiny dog on a pink leash.

He sat back down and turned to the words. As he read, he grew angry. This was not Isabelle. It was a purified, idolized version of her, all the grains and dirt wiped away. It seemed like the reporter was blinded by infatuation, unable to see the flaws that were so obvious to anyone who knew her.

The reporter did not see her life as foolish or wasted; he saw her as a brilliant, beautiful artist with an irreproachable conscience, a woman who made one mistake and was so pure of heart she ended up "paying the ultimate price" for that single mistake. Her "self-imposed solitude" culminated in her "brutal self-execution."

True to William's word, the reporter wrote that despite a police investigation and his extensive digging, the identities of the three people with her the night of the explosion were "completely unknown." Even Isabelle's own involvement was "likely" or "alleged."

The reporter had hounded Peyton at home and at work, calling, waiting outside his door long after the other reporters had left, trying different tactics, mentioning the philosophy club, Abel, Peyton's love for Isabelle. The reporter knew who they were. But William's invincibility had worked again. Peyton resented this, even though he had done nothing to stop it.

In detailing Isabelle's "self-imposed life of solitude" the article quoted her neighbor saying Isabelle hardly ever left her house, and Isabelle's mother sobbing, saying Isabelle had vanished after high school, and refused almost all contact.

The article had a picture of Isabelle's house in the middle of nowhere, the flatlands stretching out in every direction. It mentioned Peyton as the main relationship in her life, and quoted him saying, "She lived as a hermit," something he had forgotten he had shouted at the reporter after the reporter had yelled, "Can you explain why Isabelle killed herself if not for the fire?" The article went on, "The extent and nature of the relationship between Mr. Ryder and Isabelle remains a mystery. Mr. Ryder probably knows more about her than anyone else. Unfortunately, he is extremely hostile to reporters, refusing to comment on their relationship."

Peyton remembered how the reporter had stood on the sidewalk, his Blackberry in hand, day after day, like a dumb cow. Peyton had threatened him repeatedly, telling him to get lost, almost punching him in the face.

The article surveyed the entirety of her work. She'd painted more than most people did in a full lifetime. Her whole body of work defied classification, as it cut across styles and moods, changing with the years, stopping a couple years before her death. The reporter quoted various art critics assessing the quality of the work. One said she was an artistic dilettante, each stage of her work was shallow and underdeveloped; another said it would stand the test of time, that she was a true artistic genius. In any event, the article went on, the price of her paintings have skyrocketed since her death, a few pieces from the burning building series fetching well over three-million dollars a piece.

The reporter concluded by quoting a few clichés on tragedy, art and guilt, and wondering what would have happened if Isabelle had confessed to starting the fire in 1984—would she still have committed suicide? Would her art have been less grand? The answers to these questions, he concluded, like the identity of her conspirators, and how they have dealt with their guilt, remain elusive.

Peyton was grateful the article did not mention Abel except to say, in passing, that Isabelle had one daughter. But he knew this was not to spare Abel, but for self-serving reasons. The image the reporter had painted of Isabelle, as a beautiful woman riddled with guilt, driven to correct her one wrong at all costs, would be, at the very least, complicated by the fact that she had raised her daughter in oblivion, abandoning her daughter in both life and death.

Peyton threw the magazine against the tiled wall, putting his head in his hands.

When his pulse slowed and he felt clear-headed, he picked up the magazine, and walked back downstairs. Abel and Nathan were on the couch, reading books; Abel had her hand on Nathan's leg, protectively. Laurie was reading the paper, sipping tea.

"Hey," she said when he sat back down. He smiled and squeezed her hand.

"I want you to read this," he said, sliding the magazine across the table. She glanced at it.

"She's interesting looking," she said, her tone observational. He nodded, pretending to read the arts section of the paper. Laurie flipped to the article quickly, her face lowering to the page, examining the paintings.

"I didn't know she was such a good artist. I thought all the reporters were just here because of the suspicion about the fire. You never told me she was so famous."

"I knew she was talented but I didn't realize how coveted her paintings were."

She lingered on a painting of him and Isabelle in the mountains, pointing at it with her finger.

He had one like it in the basement, covered. She read the article, her eyes moving across the page. Her mouth turned a bit, in surprise, and when she finished, she looked at him, expectantly.

"Is this true? Do you think she started the fire?"

"I don't think so," he said quickly. "I think she was just moved by it because it happened when we lived here."

With those words uttered, he knew he would never tell her the truth. Something between them would break. Like a leak in the roof of a house, it could let in a pool of doubt and suspicion, which could stagnate, and mold and vermin could multiply, until the structure became inhabitable. Or maybe it would just slowly drip after bad storms.

"I really don't know what happened to her," he said softly.

She closed the magazine, nodding. She put her thumb on the top of his hand and smiled. "You should keep this for Abel. She could read it when she's older. Isabelle was a really good artist."

Peyton nodded. "Laurie."

She stood up abruptly, putting the plates in the dishwasher, shaking her head. "I'm going to take Nathan to Jennifer's, okay?"

"Of course," he said, picking up his plate and Abel's, walking over to the dishwasher. He put his hands on Laurie's belly, rubbing it, hoping to feel Daniel kick.

"I love you," he said.

She smiled, putting her hands on top of his.

He turned away. Abel was scowling at them, her nostrils flaring. Peyton walked over to the couch, kissing both Abel and Nathan on the cheek.

"Abel, time for a run," he said. She glanced at her watch, nodding. She kissed Nathan on the cheek, and jumped off the couch.

"Bye, brother," she said, running up the stairs. Nathan peered up at him, morosely, as if to say, she is too much. Peyton smiled at him.

"What are you reading?"

"Matthew and the Three Foot Dog," he said, handing the book over to Peyton, and pushing the glasses up his nose. It was a thick book for a five-year-old.

"Looks good, buddy," Peyton said, handing it back. Laurie called something out in Mandarin and Nathan responded, sliding off the couch. He walked to the kitchen. They spoke rapidly to one another; her hand was on his back, pushing him to the stairs. Peyton couldn't understand a word. Nathan trudged up the stairs.

Abel bounded down in her running shorts, nearly knocking Nathan over, and stopped when she saw Peyton kissing Laurie.

"No."

Peyton stared at her, thinking for a second of Isabelle, and feeling guilty, like he was betraying her.

"Abel," he said. "Do not order us. Okay?"

She scowled, her eyes falling to the floor, her long hair covering her face. He kissed Laurie on the cheek.

"See you later?"

She nodded. Her face was tired and puffy. She tied her black hair in a ponytail.

He picked Abel up, and threw her over his shoulder. She laughed and kicked her legs and arms in the air.

Outside, he put her down. They started walking to the river. He wanted to tell Abel to stop treating Laurie like she was an interloper, to embrace Laurie as part of her family. But he didn't. Maybe he wasn't ready to share Abel, or let go of Isabelle.

As they ran along the river, he let her run a few steps ahead, and he watched her long, tan limbs and flying white hair. He was suddenly immensely grateful she was here. He imagined Isabelle peering down on them from the clear blue sky, and he willed her to know he would take care of Abel; he would take care of Abel like he should have taken care of her.

CHAPTER NINETEEN

After the baby was born, Laurie's patience frayed under the weight of their second son. Daniel was an ornery baby, and though he had golden skin and narrow eyes, his strong chin and large frame lent him a mild resemblance to Peyton.

Laurie tiptoed around, Daniel in her arms, bags under her eyes and an expression of resignation plastered to her face. When Abel shouted at her or told her to speak English, Laurie snapped and told her to be quiet.

Most nights, they managed to have dinner without interruption, the five of them together, eating, and talking about their days, items they had read. Peyton stayed on edge, trying to block any fights off at the pass.

Abel rose, now and then, to play with Daniel or hold him in her arms, rocking him back and forth like a doll, smiling, and Laurie watched this warely, as if Abel might drop him to the floor.

Laurie was unusually quiet, as it took most of her energy to feed herself and Daniel. Peyton was unjustifiably annoyed with her wanness, wanting her, now more than ever, to be connected to him, to be close to him.

Isabelle's death and Abel's presence had brought Isabelle back to the front of his life, and he thought and dreamt about her, seeing her everywhere, remembering her eyes and the intensity of her painting. He wanted Laurie to compel him back to her. He wanted to love only his wife.

He asked Laurie if she wanted a night nanny to help with Daniel. She shook her head, and said she would ask her mother to visit instead. Her mother came the next weekend, with two suitcases, parking herself in the guest room. She tended to the baby throughout the night.

273

With eight hours of sleep, Laurie quickly returned to her resilient, competent self, her skin glowing more by the day, her smile quicker to appear. She and her mother talked in Mandarin and Peyton felt like an outsider in his own house, their chirpy voices carrying nonsensically over his head.

It had always seemed like too much of a task to learn the language, but now, with Laurie, her mother and Nathan speaking rapidly in their foreign tongue, he was annoyed with himself, wishing he had bothered. He rolled his eyes at Abel, smiling, and she grinned, sticking her tongue out, climbing up into his lap.

At night, in bed, Peyton reached over and held Laurie's hand, and she intertwined her fingers in his. They fell asleep that way, and when Abel didn't come for him in the middle of the night, he woke up and saw Laurie, still sound asleep, her head on the white pillow, her shiny black hair spread around her like a Chinese fan.

She seemed peaceful and sweet, and he felt grateful for her, grateful she had so easily accepted Abel into their home.

He wanted the feeling to stay, but it ebbed and flowed, like a rain-fed river, crowded out by memories of Isabelle's strange smile. He told himself he was simply lusting after his youth, and maybe he was, but it didn't matter. He kept seeing her everywhere, whenever Abel smiled a particular way, or whenever her hair fell across her face the same way it had for Isabell.

In his mind, Isabell morphed seamlessly from seventeen to twenty-eight; she was hitchhiking, her slender arm extended, the strong curve of her neck tan and exposed, she was naked on his bed, her hair covering her breasts, her long legs spread out, a devious smile on her face, she was swimming in the water, laughing, splashing him; she was painting, her face and clothes streaked with color, as she stroked madly across the canvas; she was jumping into his arms, her head thrown back in wild laughter.

He realized part of him had still expected that after his children had grown and his marriage had run its course, that he would find Isabelle again, painting in a cabin in the woods, waiting for him.

"Where have you been?" she would have said, smiling, her hair long and silver. They would both laugh, too old for guilt and pain and secrets.

And now, nothing. That was over. That ending was erased. He was stuck here on this earth, alone.

At night, he would often find himself in the attic, drinking whiskey. He flipped through their old photographs and stared at the painting of them, together, in the Berkshires. He would look out the small, circular window at the Charles River, dark and unmoving, and wonder how he had ended up here, in this beautiful house, with his beautiful wife, drunk in his attic.

He would stumble down the cramped attic stairs and into Abel's room. He would sit in the white wooden chair. Her knees were folded to her chest and her long, white hair covered her naked body like a blanket. Her face was calm. He would watch for hours, drinking.

Sometimes, she fidgeted, her face contorting in fear. She shook her head back and forth, trying to dissolve an image in her head. He put down his whiskey and crawled into her bed, holding her sweaty body tightly, whispering, "Abel, Abel, Abel."

She took a deep breath, as if breaking the water's surface, and clutched his hands, crying, in one croak, "Dad."

He rocked her until she fell back to sleep. Sometimes, he fell asleep too, their limbs intertwined. Other times, he stumbled loudly down the stairs, crashing into bed with Laurie.

One night, he came off the stairs, banging into the wall, and Laurie's mother was suddenly in front of him, grabbing his wrist.

"Jesus," he said. "You startled me."

Her fingers tightened, pushing into his skin.

"Peyton," she said sharply. Her wide face was still smooth, her eyes firm. "Life is filled with loss. Not just you." Her fingers pinched his skin.

He stared at her blankly, thinking, what did she know about loss?

"You have an obligation to your family," she whispered, her eyes unblinking. "You have three children now. You have to be present."

He was pissed, wanting to yell at her, 'Don't tell me what I have. I know what I have, damn you.'

He closed his eyes, seeing white light, feeling his head pound. He took a deep breath, and gripped her hand.

"I know," he said thickly, suppressing his annoyance. He dropped her hand and hugged her, for Laurie's sake, feeling her bony back underneath his hands, the whiskey bottle pointing awkwardly in the air.

She patted his back with her fingers and nodded at him, with slightly castigating eyes.

He went to bed, and he found Laurie curled up, asleep, her breasts full with milk. "Your mother's so nosey," he whispered, falling on the mattress, feeling estranged from both of them.

Staring at the chandelier dangling from the ceiling, he saw Sophie, the woman with half a face. He turned his head and studied Laurie's profile, her soft skin, her straight, wide nose and small, full lips.

He imagined waking Laurie up and showing her a picture of Sophie, saying, "Look what I did. I did this.," Laurie would run away in fear, carrying Daniel and holding Nathan's hand, leaving him behind, her face mournful and confused. Her parents would welcome her in their home, using their money to keep him away from their daughter and grandchildren. The truth was her parents loved him until they didn't.

He rolled on his back and closed his eyes. He wanted to fall asleep, but he kept seeing Sophie and her mounded, plastic skin.

He put his head on Laurie's stomach, holding the soft curve of her hip, and she mumbled his name softly, her competent fingers stroking his hair gently, tugging at it lightly.

"It's okay, baby," she whispered softly, her voice hoarse.

He rubbed his face against her stomach, gripping her. Her choked up voice, repeating the words, 'it's okay, it's okay,' and her elegant fingers tugging at his hair, lulled him asleep.

* * *

Under Laurie's mother's stern care, Daniel calmed down, his tantrums evaporating under her quick old hands and scolding eyes. Peyton appreciated her help, but he resented her constant presence, feeling like she was standing in the shadows of the house, judging him and his ambivalence, whispering to Laurie.

Peyton was annoyed with his own mother, who was living in her and Phillip's Fort Lauderdale condo, drinking and playing cards in her flower-print sundresses, deflecting his requests for her to come visit with invitations of her own, insisting they would all have more fun on the beach, staying in the nearby hotel, which had an outdoor pool, cable and a free buffet breakfast.

Finally having an adoring husband she could rely on, his mother had mellowed and grown absent-minded, failing to check in for weeks at a time. Even though she had never cared for Laurie, finding her "snooty," she still thought everyone should get along merrily, like the Brady Brunch.

She tried to speak to Abel on the phone, bubbly and eager to share her Florida adventures, and Abel nodded, repeating, "Okay...okay...okay," expressionless, before losing interest and handing Peyton the phone.

A couple months after Laurie's mother arrived, she announced Laurie's father needed her to come home. Her last night, Laurie slept with her in the guest room, and Peyton could hear them chirping like birds, laughing and talking well into the early morning.

When they dropped her off at the airport, she kissed Nathan and Daniel on the cheek, speaking to them in Mandarin, pinching their cheeks. The sounds ran over each other in Peyton's ear, like clanging bells coming from different directions.

"Goodbye, dear," Laurie's mother said to Abel, reaching over the seat and squeezing Abel's shoulder. Abel, who sat in the backseat by herself, next to the luggage, shrugged off her touch, rolling her shoulder into herself. "Bye," she said.

Peyton opened the backdoor. She stepped out on the curb, her back stooped over, and he unloaded her luggage from the trunk.

He leaned in and kissed Abel on the belly. Abel grinned, ruffling his hair, and scrambled over the seat, pushing Nathan to the side, sitting herself in the middle.

Laurie hugged her mother on the curb. Her mother spoke firmly in Mandarin, glancing pointedly at Peyton. Can you be any more obvious, he thought. Laurie nodded her head, her black hair shimmering around her shoulders like oil on the ocean.

Laurie's mother walked over to Peyton, and he flexed his fist. He leaned down and hugged her, feeling her ribcage.

"Please respect your family. Be the good man we know you can be," she whispered, so quickly and quietly he couldn't be sure, a second later, if she had said it. She jerked his earlobe with her thumb and finger.

She rolled her suitcases inside, her silver-streaked hair in a French twist, her posture leaning forward. Peyton was glad she was gone.

Laurie wiped her eyes with her fingers, smiling at him. Her breasts were still full with milk, and they poured out of the top of her bra.

"It was so nice to have her here," she said, opening the passenger door.

Peyton kissed Laurie on the lips. Her mouth tasted like spearmint. He put one hand possessively on her hip, feeling relieved and unobstructed, like a thick snake wrapped around Laurie's body, its beady black eyes watching him, had slithered away, into the airport terminal. Then he felt bad for thinking this. He knew her mother had helped with Daniel, and that she meant well. Heck, she probably even cared for him and Abel.

He jogged to the other side of the car, and once he was seated, glanced in the rearview mirror. Abel had her arm over Nathan's shoulder, petting his bicep, and Nathan stared out the window. In the seat mirror, he could see Daniel sleeping, his long, black lashes visible on his light skin. They were all there, accounted for.

They merged into traffic, and he opened the window for the warm summer air, his hand on Laurie's thigh. They talked about finding a babysitter and enrolling the older kids in summer camps. She stroked his hand, smiling. He smiled back.

A silver necklace ran over her delicate collarbone, holding a triangular piece of jade over her round breasts. Her shiny hair didn't have a hair out of place.

"Hey," he said, patting her thigh. "How about we go to the beach?"

Laurie smiled, nodding, turning her head to the backseat. "What do you say to the beach?"

Abel stiffened, tightening her grip on Nathan, frowning at Laurie. Nathan shrugged.

"Okay," he said.

"Good," Laurie said, turning forward. She squeezed Peyton's hand.

At home, they changed their clothes, packed lunch, a giant umbrella, towels, and Daniel's baby bag. Abel came to their bedroom while he was changing his clothes.

"I don't have a bathing suit," she said, standing in the doorway, crossing her arms.

"That's okay. Just bring an extra pair of shorts and a t-shirt."

"Alright," she said, turning on her heel, pounding up the stairs.

They drove to the Wingaersheek Beach, their windows open, and parked the car. Abel pushed past Nathan and ran over the dunes, to the water. Peyton took the beach bag and umbrella and ran after her, smiling at Laurie apologetically. Laurie waved him on, her face sympathetic.

Abel ran over the dunes, straight to the water. She kicked off her sandals and threw off her shirt in a single, swift gesture, and hit the water, hard, tripping, falling face first, breaking the water's surface.

She stood up, pushing her hair behind her ears, and dove forward, kicking and throwing her arms and legs. It didn't look like she knew how to swim. He put the bag and umbrella down, and threw off his shirt.

The water was cold, and he inhaled sharply as it surrounded him with an icy embrace. She was floundering when he reached her, gasping for air and throwing her arms through the water. He put his arm around her waist. She knocked him in the chin and he swam to the shore, pulling her body, his face angled in the other direction.

When he could stand, he did. He held her out from him, his hands around her naked chest. Her hair was plastered to her head, until it hit the water and pooled like blonde algae. She gasped for air, and her chest rose and fell underneath his hands. Goose bumps appeared on her tan skin.

"Abel," he said firmly. Her eyes flashed with wildness and fear. His fingers fell from her skin.

"Abel," he repeated. She beat the water with her hands, and her foot kicked his knee. Her head rolled to the open water.

"Let me go!" she cried. "Let me go!"

"I'm not touching you."

"Abel," he said softly, reaching out for her. She slapped his hand.

"Leave me alone," she burbled, her chin falling under the water. She sunk under the surface.

He reached under the water and picked her up by the waist. She punched him in the nose and kicked him in the shin. He threw her over his shoulder, pinning her arms to his chest. Her calves beat against his back and she screamed, "Let me go! Let me go!"

He dunked her head under the water.

He pulled her out, and she screamed, kicking his back.

He dunked her back under.

He kept doing this, again and again, until she stopped screaming and kicking. Saliva ran over her chin. He swung her around, holding her like a baby. Her wet hair dripped to the ground.

People glanced at him judgmentally, in faux shock, whispering to one another.

"Mind your own fucking business," he said loudly.

Able reached up and put her arms around his neck, choking him. "Don't leave me. Please don't leave me."

He paused, staring at her pleading face, covered in tears.

"Abel, look at me. I will never leave you. Do you understand?"

She curled her lips in, and her eyes were scrunched in fear.

"Abel. Do you understand that?"

She nodded, pushing her face against his chest.

He hugged her closer. On the beach, he searched the crowds of people, relieved to see Laurie and Daniel sitting on a towel, underneath the striped umbrella. Nathan was playing nearby, building a sand house with his bucket and shovel. They looked so normal. Peyton wove through the crowds, holding Abel close to his chest, relieved.

He stopped at the edge of the towel, smiling down at Laurie, feeling gratitude for her, for her stability.

"It's cold in there," he said.

"It usually is this time of year," Laurie said, tilting her face up. She had large sunglasses on. She patted the towel. "Sit."

He sat down, keeping Abel in his arms. Abel curled herself in his lap, sucking her thumb, something she occasionally did. He wrapped a towel around her, drying her off. He felt an urgent need to protect her, make her whole.

The clear-blue water lapped gently against the sandy shore. Kids played near the beach, splashing and diving under the surface. The water stretched to the horizon, cornered by dark ridges underneath the pale blue sky.

"Would you ever want to buy a house closer to the water?" he asked. His eyes were on the lighthouse in the distance.

Laurie laughed. "No," she said, pushing her sunglasses back on her face.

"But isn't it so beautiful out here? Don't you feel freer?"

"Yes," she said, shifting Daniel to her other side. "It is beautiful. But our lives are in the city. Their school, our house, our work…"

He nodded. "I know. You're right."

She set Daniel on the towel between them, and took off her sundress. She had on an emerald and gold bikini. She shifted over, out of the umbrella's shelter. She laid down, her hands underneath her head.

"This feels so good," she said, yawning.

He took in her full breasts and slender stomach, and he felt a strong pull of desire. Seeing her nearly naked, in the full glare of sunlight, reminded him how beautiful her body was. Fathers stared openly as they walked by.

He tried to remember the last time they'd had sex. Two weeks ago, quietly, Laurie stiff and unmoving, terrified her mother might hear.

He shifted himself, uncomfortable. Abel had fallen asleep and he put her carefully on the towel, next to Daniel. He kissed her forehead, moving her wet hair off her face.

He got up and walked over to Nathan. He helped him build a garage for his three story house. He poked his small, round stomach and threw sand at him, laughing. Nathan wiped away the sand, smiling, pushing up his glasses.

* * *

That night, he tucked Abel in bed, telling her again, "Abel, I will never leave you. Do you understand?"

She reached for his hand. "I know, Dad. You're not like her. You're more stable."

He nodded, though this made him sad, too. "I'll always have you back," he said, kissing her on the forehead.

"Good," she said.

He sat on her bed for a few minutes, letting her fall asleep.

Downstairs, Laurie was in the bathroom, staring at herself in the mirror as she rubbed her hands with cream. Her satin teddy clung to the curve of her hip and he remembered her lying on the beach, her full breasts overflowing her bikini, the other men staring at her.

He turned out the light and shoved her up against the bathroom wall, running his hand between her legs. He squeezed her breast, and then lifted her body onto the counter, facing him. He lifted up her nightgown, bunching it at her neck, almost, but not quite choking her with it.

Her chest rose and fell. In the street light, he could see a flicker of discomfort in her eyes. He looked away, pulling down his zipper and pushing himself up against her. He made love to her violently, his jeans chafing against her skin, and the harder he pushed against her, the freer he felt, forgetting everything.

Afterwards, they collapsed against the mirror, sweaty and out of breath. She reached for his hand.

"Peyton…" Her voice was pregnant with confusion.

He kissed her chastely on the mouth and then backed up. "I'm going to take a shower."

He dropped his clothes and hopped in. He closed the door and turned the water on full blast. He heard her walk out of the room. He let the hot water scald his skin, not wanting to think.

He took his time, and when he came back out, she was curled up in bed, her eyes closed. He got into bed next to her, and pressed his chest against her back, feeling the steady rise of her breathing. Soon, he fell asleep.

With Laurie's mother gone, Abel and Nathan attended a local summer camp, dropped off by Laurie and picked up by Sarah, their new babysitter. Laurie took Daniel with her to her ballet studio, and came home around four.

Laurie told him that when she got home, Abel always clung to Sarah, a petite college student, crying, "Don't go! Don't go!" Sarah apologetically disentangled herself from Abel, promising she would be back tomorrow. Sometimes, when Sarah left, Abel would run to her room and slam the door.

Peyton always tried to get home by 6.30pm, so they could have dinner together. He was expanding the company to wilderness vacations, and this was mostly because he knew he had to stay busy. It was only when he went semi-idle that Isabelle, or Sophie, the woman with the burnt face, jumped to the forefront of his mind, inciting a brief sensation of vertigo. In response, he sped up, checked his email on his Blackberry, scrubbed a dish, or tickled Nathan, flicking thoughts of them away with his thumb.

The first Sunday in July, they were sitting at the kitchen table, reading the paper. In the arts section, by chance, Peyton's eyes crossed over a listing for an exhibit of Isabelle's lifetime works at the Boston Museum of Fine Arts. No shit, he thought. He finished his breakfast and passed the listing to Laurie.

"You should go with Abel," she said.

"I will," he said softly. He had shown Abel the photographs of him and Isabelle in West Virginia, and she was pleased, at first. Then, halfway through, she started sobbing, hitting his chest with her fists, asking him, "Why didn't you keep her? Why didn't you keep her?"

He had closed his eyes, and held her down against the wood floor. "I don't know, Abel. I don't know."

Laurie nodded, taking a sip of her green tea. "That's a good idea."

He stood up, leaned over and kissed her on the cheek. She was a good wife. Abel was on the couch, rocking Daniel in her arms, humming.

"Abel," he called. "You and I are going to the museum."

"What kind of museum?"

"Art. We're going to see your mother's paintings."

She dropped Daniel down on the couch and ran to the kitchen. Daniel started crying, his fists waving in the air. Laurie rushed to scoop him up.

Abel put on her tennis shoes. Nathan looked at them from the table.

"My mother has an art exhibit!" Abel said to Nathan, sticking out her tongue. Nathan peered at Abel skeptically, glancing to Peyton for confirmation.

"Yep. Alright, Abel," Peyton said, nodding at Nathan. Peyton slipped on his loafers. "Let's go."

Abel was wearing dark blue jeans and a white tank top, and Peyton picked up her cashmere sweater from the floor. Laurie had taken her shopping, and Abel had reluctantly allowed this. He patted Nathan on the head.

282

"See you later, buddy."

Outside, it was warm and noisy. The trees on their street were in full bloom.

"Dad, can I have a ride?" Abel asked, taking her sweater and wrapping it around her waist.

"Sure," he said, leaning down so she could climb up on his shoulders. He held her shins and she put one of her hands in his hair. She reached out with her other hand to touch the tree branches, picking off a twig with a bunch of leaves. When they turned, she scraped it against the brick wall. The sidewalks were packed with tourists and families, and he weaved in and out, grateful Abel couldn't reach anyone's hair. He'd had to pay off "victims" of her scissors more than once.

"Dad?"

"Yes?"

"Was Isabelle a good artist?"

"Yes. She was very good."

"She painted for days in the barn. She didn't eat. Or shower."

He laughed. "That sounds like Isabelle."

"That's why our horse died. She didn't get to the vet. She just kept painting. I was so mad."

He squeezed her leg.

"But I could never stay mad at her for long. Dad?"

"Yes?"

"Do you promise you'll never leave me?"

"I promise, baby. No matter what."

He swung her down, over his head, and blew on her tummy. She laughed.

"Stop, stop," she called, pushing away his face.

Inside the museum, they were greeted with a rush of cold air. He paid for the tickets while she milled around a Greek sculpture of a young man. He held his hand out to her and she ran over and grabbed it. He guided her past the pamphlets, which were in poor taste, topped with purple cursive, "Isabelle Woods: A Life of Burning Mystery." At the front of the exhibit was a poster-size photograph of Isabelle on her horse, riding toward the camera.

"Hey, look," Abel said, pulling him to the photo. "It's Jewel!"

"It's a nice looking horse," he said. He skimmed the text. At the end it referenced the Boston fire, speculating she might have accidentally started it. He pulled Abel past.

"No," she said, tugging. "I want to read this."

283

He sighed, letting go of her hand. People reading the post whispered. "Such a beautiful woman…how sad…what an interesting life…"

He was annoyed, wanting to tell them to shut the hell up. Abel turned to him.

"It doesn't even mention us."

He shook his head.

"Strange," she said, pulling his hand into the exhibit. "They like her, though," she said, smiling. She didn't mention the Boston fire. She stopped in front of a painting from the Berkshires.

"Hey, Dad, look," she said loudly. "This is you."

People glanced over at him, looking back and forth between him and the painting, raising their eyebrows questioningly. Abel pushed herself next to the painting, and was looking at him over her shoulder, expectantly. He nodded. She turned back to the painting, reaching out to touch it.

A security guard barked, "You can't touch that!"

Abel nodded and walked to the next painting, pushing her way through the crowd.

There were too many people. Peyton stayed back, watching Abel wiggle through the throngs of people to stand in front of each painting. He couldn't hear her but he wouldn't have been surprised if she'd been saying, "Move, please, this is my mother's work."

They wandered through the exhibit, which had about 25 paintings, Abel frequently calling to him, "Oh, I remember this." When the crowds parted he read a couple of the descriptions of the paintings. The descriptions were alternatively obscure ("reminiscent of Barnett Newman's 1940 work") and obvious ("This painting invokes struggle and pain.") He saw paintings she had done in Boston and West Virginia, and he smiled, remembering everything: the storage locker, the chaotic apartment, the mountains.

The burning buildings were the most popular. While Abel shoved her way to the front, he stood behind, looking at the dense crowd of people, elbowing past one another. It struck him as strange, these ordinary people with their balding heads and fleshy arms, in their unremarkable clothes, out on a Sunday afternoon, jostling to see Isabelle's paintings, born to a rickety barn in dead, brown fields. Paintings arising from the hand of a woman whose wildness flowed, like mad, rushing waters, over the infinite lengths of those endless, hellish horizons.

In the middle of ill-proportioned people, he saw a beautiful, still woman. She stood on the outskirts of the crowd, her face drawn, as if she too were disturbed by the incongruence between the viewers and the viewed, as if she longed to erase the misshapen people with their loud voices and Velcro shoes.

It was Sophie.

He could not see her burned side, and from this angle, she was almost breathtaking. Her hand fluttered to her chest and she looked down at the floor. He saw, out of the corner of his eye, people glancing at her twice, expressions of sadness and repulsion instinctively and quickly running over their faces.

An older woman stared at Sophie as she ambled past, mouthing to herself, "Oh, the poor dear." That—the pity from an old, ugly woman—made him furious. What did she, an old hag, know about Sophie?

He wanted, desperately, to heal Sophie's crumpled skin. He wanted to tumble backwards through time, through himself, through Laurie, Abel, Isabelle, his sons, his work, and take it back: chicken out, and throw the fireworks in the river. Start over again.

She titled her head, her eyes roving over the crowd, and he panicked, feeling a need to escape as her eyes followed the path of a half-circle, leading to him.

Her eyes settled.

It was too late. He could see, even from here, her eyes were wet, and her face half-flushed. The crumpled skin remained, eternally, grayish blue. She stared at him, pleading clearly, and her plea was louder than if she had shouted, "Tell me who did this."

He saw he had a choice. He remembered Isabelle's oval face, her skin flawless, but her features contorted in the same pose, filled with desperation and a booming plea, talk to me, talk to me. He had turned away then. He could stay now. The noise of the crowd had shifted in his mind to a distant echo, and he and Sophie were alone: her beseeching, "Tell me, tell me," and him, standing still, trying to breathe.

And then, his chest hardened, like a wild, rolling river frozen into ice. It was too late to change course. He had chosen this life.

He turned away.

The noise of the crowd returned, and he watched its pieces and boundaries shift and reassemble. He sat down on a dark wood bench, next to a teenage boy. The boy was hunched over his cell phone, rapidly texting messages, oblivious to his surroundings. He looked heartbreakingly young. He wasn't old enough to choose the course of his life.

"Dad," Abel said, rushing against him, standing between his legs. He tugged her hair sadly.

"You ready?" he asked.

She nodded.

The sun was bright, and he shielded his eyes as they walked down the museum's stairs. In the park, he bought two cokes. They sat in the shade, under a tree.

"Did you like it?" he asked. A man rode a unicycle through the park, carrying one red balloon in each hand.

"I love her paintings," she said, picking a long strand of grass. "Don't you?"

"Yes," he said. "I always have."

"Can we buy some?"

He didn't want to have her paintings in the house, or even in Abel's room. He didn't want Isabelle in his life.

"Of course," he said, taking a long drink of his watery coke. Staring at Abel, her tilted-almond eyes and long, white hair covering her back, he knew he would always see Isabelle. Here she was, in the flesh of his daughter.

"What's wrong?"

"Nothing, baby. Nothing at all. I love you."

She grinned, watching the man on his unicycle, his face painted with an exaggerated red smile. Her face became cloudy, as if she had seen a great darkness on the clown's white face.

"Dad," she said. She dug a hole in the dirt with her thumb. "Do you think Isabelle loved me?"

"Yes, baby," he said, reflexively. There was no other answer. "She loved you more than anybody."

"I don't think she did," she said. "I don't think she liked me at all."

He felt an immense, sharp hatred for Isabelle. He pulled Abel into his lap, rocking her. She sobbed loudly.

"Baby," he said softly, not knowing what else to say. He closed his eyes. He was so filled with rage, he knew, if Isabelle were here, he would have punched her, hard. He hadn't thought much about what she had done. His sadness at her leaving this earth had blindsided his anger. But now, with Abel sobbing in his arms, he was enraged. Enraged she had run off with their unborn daughter, raising her in squalor and neglect; enraged she had left them both, alone.

Abel stood up and ran through the park. He followed a few steps behind her, letting her run. She pushed over the man on his unicycle, his real mouth opening in surprise, his drawn mouth fixed in a smile.

Abel kept running. Peyton didn't bother to stop. She ran down the sidewalk, toward their house. She passed it, crossing the street. An oncoming car swerved and honked.

She ran down the embankment and plunged into the river.

He went after her, pulling her out. She kicked and screamed, and a sharp pain hit his stomach. He held her against his chest and her screech caused him to stumble, the high-pitched noise hurting the insides of his ears.

"Stop," he shouted, putting her down on the ground, and holding her still. She took deep breaths, her blue eyes swinging like a pendulum between sadness, fear and anger, fogged up by a plea, a plea for a love, a plea for an explanation of why she was so alone.

"Abel," he said, out of breath himself, leaning his body over hers, applying his weight. "Abel, everything will be okay. We'll be okay. You, me, your brothers, Laurie. We'll be okay. Do you hear me?"

She nodded her face against his chest, clutching his neck. He stood up, and she clung to him. They smelled like dirt.

"Don't leave me," she said into his neck. "Don't leave me. I'll be good. Please don't leave me. I promise I'll be good."

"I will never leave you, Abel," he said, hugging her as hard as he could.

She loosened her grip, mumbling, "I'll be good. I'll be good."

"You are good, baby. You are."

He opened the door to the house and stood in the entryway, staring at his beautiful house, dumbfounded.

"Hey," Laurie said softly.

She stood in the doorway, wearing jeans and a white cotton t-shirt. "Are you two okay?"

He nodded. Abel was limp in his arms. "She went in the river. She needs a bath."

They went upstairs. Laurie turned the water on in their master bath, pouring soap in it. Abel let them strip off her clothes and put her in. Peyton jumped in the shower. Laurie sang softly near the tub, her voice clear and even. He removed the dirt from his hair and his ears, and he turned off the water and stepped out. He dried himself with a fresh towel.

Laurie was lathering Abel's pounds of hair with shampoo and Laurie smiled at him, her face full of pleasure. Abel's pale blue almond eyes followed Laurie's face, and they were sleepy and content, shielded by a pointed wariness, a fence he knew might never come down.

Peyton was thankful. Laurie's graceful, elegant hands gently cleaned Abel's hair, scrubbing away the dirt, letting it fall into the clean water.

He left them alone, his daughter and his wife. In the bedroom, his eyes roamed over the antique wood bed and bureaus, the scrolls, the vases, the settee and the chair. He walked to the window. The neat, clipped rows of green trees lined the street, stopping short of the dark river's grassy shore.

He could see his eighteen-year-old self standing on the sidewalk, his arms crossed, his body bruised. He would condemn this life.

But the boy did not understand. The boy made the choice.

And here it was.

Book Club Questions

1. How did Peyton growing up in poverty impact his choice to cover up the fatal accident?

2. Did Peyton and Isabelle experience true love for one another or did they need to be together longer to know how special it was? Does true love mean you never leave each other voluntarily?

3. Does Peyton treat women better as he gets older? Does he treat women worse than he treats men?

4. Does Peyton view Isabelle and his mother differently than he views all other women?

5. Did Peyton not having a father impact his character and choices?

6. What factors lead to Peyton being so angry and aggressive?

7. Will Peyton ever get over Isabelle? How does having Abel change his ability to get over her?

8. Should Peyton have tried to find Isabelle after she left the second time?

9. If there had been no fatal accident, would Isabelle have been able to settle down with Peyton?

10. What role does American capitalism and the American dream play in the story?

11. Will Peyton and Laurie's marriage last? Will their family of five be a happy one?

12. If Peyton had been born fifty years later and had grown up with access to the Internet, how might the story have changed?

13. What role does the settings of the mountains and the city play in the story?

14. Is Peyton's mother selfish? Was she a good mother to Peyton?

15. Does Peyton feel enough guilt for the fatal accident? Should he have confessed when he was younger? Should he have made more amends as a successful adult?

Made in the USA
Coppell, TX
20 January 2023

11441070R00171